LYRA

PRAISE FOR
REPLICA

"A searing pair of intertwined stories about the line
between science and humanity, told with
Oliver's signature grace, uniqueness, and precision.
It's a new story every way you turn it—
but always gorgeous, always haunting."
—MARIE LU,
#1 *New York Times* bestselling author
of the Young Elites series and *Legend*

For Katy —

Happy reading,
now + ever —

LYRA

LAUREN OLIVER

REPLICA

LYRA

HARPER
An Imprint of HarperCollinsPublishers

LAUREN
OLIVER

REPLICA

To my sister, Lizzie

AUTHOR'S NOTE

Although in many cases you will find identical portions of dialogue occurring from both Gemma's and Lyra's perspectives in their respective narratives, you may also notice minor variations in tone and tempo. This was done deliberately to reflect their individual perspectives. Gemma and Lyra have unique conceptual frameworks that actively interact with and thus define their experiences, just as the act of observing a thing immediately alters the behavior of the thing itself.

The minor variations in the novel reflect the belief that there is no single objective experience of the world. No one sees or hears the same thing in exactly the same way, as anyone who has ever been in an argument with a loved one can attest. In that way we truly are inventors of our own experience. The truth, it turns out, looks a lot like making fiction.

ONE

ON VERY STILL NIGHTS SOMETIMES we can hear them chanting, calling for us to die. We can see them, too, or at least make out the halo of light cast up from the shores of Barrel Key, where they must be gathered, staring back across the black expanse of water toward the fence and the angular white face of the Haven Institute. From that distance it must look like a long green jaw set with miniature teeth.

Monsters, they call us. Demons.

Sometimes, on sleepless nights, we wonder if they're right.

Lyra woke up in the middle of the night with the feeling that someone was sitting on her chest. Then she realized it was just the heat—swampy and thick, like the pressure of somebody's hand. The power had gone down.

Something was wrong. People were shouting. Doors slammed. Footsteps echoed in the halls. Through the windows, she saw the zigzag pattern of flashlights cutting across the courtyard, illuminating silvery specks of rain and the stark-white statue of a man, reaching down toward the ground, as though to pluck something from the earth. The other replicas came awake simultaneously. The dorm was suddenly full of voices, thick with sleep. At night it was easier to speak. There were fewer nurses to shush them.

"What's wrong?"

"What's happened?"

"Be quiet." That was Cassiopeia. "I'm listening."

The door from the hall swung open, so hard it cracked against the wall. Lyra was dazzled by a sudden sweep of light.

"They all here?" It sounded like Dr. Coffee Breath.

"I think so." Nurse Don't-Even-Think-About-It's voice was high and terrified. Her face was invisible behind the flashlight beam. Lyra could make out just the long hem of her nightgown and her bare feet.

"Well, count them."

"We're all here," Cassiopeia responded. One of them gasped. But Cassiopeia was never afraid to speak up. "What's going on?"

"It must be one of the males," Dr. Coffee Breath said

to Nurse Don't-Even-Think-About-It, who was really named Maxine. "Who's checking the males?"

"What's wrong?" Cassiopeia repeated. Lyra found herself touching the windowsill, the pillow, the headboard of bed number 24. Her things. Her world.

At that moment, the answer came to them: voices, shrill, calling to one another. *Code Black. Code Black. Code Black.*

Almost at the same time, the backup generator kicked on. The lights came up, and with them, the alarms. Sirens wailed. Lights flashed in every room. Everyone squinted in the sudden brightness. Nurse Don't-Even-Think-About-It stumbled backward, raising an arm as though to shield herself from view.

"Stay here," Dr. Coffee Breath said. Lyra wasn't sure whether he was speaking to Nurse Don't-Even-Think-About-It or to the replicas. Either way, there wasn't much choice. Dr. Coffee Breath had to let himself into the hall with a code. Nurse Don't-Even-Think-About-It stayed for only a moment, shivering, her back to the door, as if she expected that at any second the girls might make a rush at her. Her flashlight, now subsumed by the overheads, cast a milk-white ring on the tile floor.

"Ungrateful," she said, before she, too, let herself out. Even then they could see her through the windows overlooking the hall, moving back and forth, occasionally touching her cross.

"What's Code Black?" Rose asked, hugging her knees to her chest. They'd run out of stars ever since Dr. O'Donnell, the only staff member Lyra had never nicknamed, had stopped giving them lessons. Instead the replicas selected names for themselves from the collection of words they knew, words that struck them as pretty or interesting. There was Rose, Palmolive, and Private. Lilac Springs and Tide. There was even a Fork.

As usual, only Cassiopeia—number 6, one of the oldest replicas besides Lyra—knew.

"Code Black means security's down," she said. "Code Black means someone's escaped."

TWO

H-U-M-A-N. THE FIRST WORD WAS *hu-man*.

There were two kinds of humans: natural-born humans, people, women and men, girls and boys, like the doctors and staff, the researchers, the guards, and the Suits who came sometimes to survey the island and its inhabitants.

Then there were human models, males and females, made in the laboratory and transferred to the surrogate birthers, who lived in the barracks and never spoke English. The *clones*, people occasionally still called them, though Lyra knew this was a bad word, a hurtful word, even though she didn't know why. At Haven they were called replicas.

The second word was *M-O-D-E-L*. She spelled it, breathing the sounds lightly between her teeth, the way that Dr. O'Donnell had taught her. Then: the number 24.

So the report *was* about her.

"How are you feeling today?" Nurse Swineherd asked. Lyra had named her only last month. She didn't know what a swineherd was but had heard Nurse Rachel say, *Some days I'd rather be a swineherd*, and had liked the sound of it. "Lots of excitement last night, huh?" As always, she didn't wait for a response, and instead forced Lyra down onto the examination table, so she no longer had a view of the file.

Lyra felt a quick flash of anger, like a temporary burst in her brain. It wasn't that she was curious about the report. She had no desire in particular to know about herself, to find out why she was sick and whether she could be cured. She understood, in general terms, from things insinuated or overheard, that there were still glitches in the process. The replicas were born genetically identical to the source material but soon presented with various medical problems, organs that didn't function properly, blood cells that didn't regenerate, lungs that collapsed. As they got older, they lost their balance, forgot words and place names, became easily confused, and cried more. Or they simply *failed to thrive* in the first place. They stayed skinny and stunted. They smashed their heads on the floor, and when the Suits came, screamed to be picked up. (In the past few years God had mandated that the newest generational crops be picked up, bounced, or engaged in play for at least two hours every day. Research suggested that human contact would keep them healthier for longer. Lyra and the other older replicas took turns with them, tickling their fat little feet, trying to make them smile.)

Lyra had fallen in love with reading during the brief, ecstatic period of time when Dr. O'Donnell had been at Haven, which she now thought of as the best months of her life. When Lyra read, it was as if a series of small windows opened in the back of her mind, flooding her with light and fresh air and visions of other places, other lives, *other*, period. The only books at Haven were books about science and the body, and these were difficult and full of words she couldn't sound out. But she read charts when they were left unattended on countertops. She read the magazines the nurses left behind in their break room.

Nurse Swineherd kept talking while she took Lyra's blood pressure with Squeezeme and stuck Thermoscan under her tongue. Lyra liked Squeezeme and Thermoscan. She liked the way Squeezeme tightened around her upper arm, like a hand holding on to lead her somewhere. She liked Thermoscan's reassuring beeps, and afterward when Nurse Swineherd said, "Perfectly normal."

She added, "Don't know what it was thinking, running that way. Breathe deeply, okay? Good. Now exhale. Good. It'll drown before it gets past the breaks. Did you hear the surf last night? Like thunder! I'm surprised the body hasn't turned up already, actually."

Lyra knew she wasn't expected to reply. The one time she had, in response to Nurse Swineherd's cheerful question, "How are we today?" Nurse Swineherd had startled, dropping one of the syringes—Lyra hated the syringes, refused to name them—and had to start over. But she wondered what it would be like to come across the dead body on the beach. She wasn't afraid of dead bodies. She had seen hundreds of replicas get sick and die. All the Yellows had died, none of them older than twelve months. *A fluke*, the doctors said: *a fever.* Lyra had seen the bodies wrapped and prepared for shipping.

A Purple from the seventh crop, number 333, had simply stopped eating. By the time they put her on a tube, it was too late. Number 501 swallowed twenty-four small white Sleepers after Nurse Em, who used to help shave her head and was always gentlest with the razor, went away. Number 421 had gone suddenly, in her sleep. It was Lyra who'd touched her arm to wake her and known, from the strange plastic coldness of her body, that she was dead. Strange that in an instant all the life just evaporated, went away, leaving only the skin and bones, a pile of flesh.

But that's what they were: bodies. Human and yet not people. She hadn't so far been able to figure out why. She looked, she thought, like a normal person. So did the other female replicas. They'd been *made* from normal people, and even birthed from them.

But the making of them marked them. That's what everybody said. Except for Dr. O'Donnell.

She wouldn't mind seeing a male up close—the male and female replicas were kept separate, even the dead ones that went off the island in tarps. She was curious about the males, had studied the anatomical charts in the medical textbooks she couldn't otherwise read. She had looked especially closely at diagrams of the female and male reproductive organs, which seemed, she thought, to mark the primary difference between them, but she couldn't imagine what a male's would look like in real life. The only men she saw were doctors, nurses, security, and other members of the staff.

"All right. Almost done. Come here and stand on the scale now, okay?"

Lyra stood up, hoping to catch a glimpse once again of the chart, and its beautiful, symmetrical lettering, which marched like soldiers across the page. But Nurse Swineherd had snatched the clipboard and was writing in Lyra's newest results. Without releasing her grip on the clipboard, she adjusted the scale expertly with one hand, waiting until it balanced correctly.

"Hmmm." She frowned, so that the lines between her eyebrows deepened and converged. Once, when Lyra was really little, she had announced that she had found out the difference between people and replicas: people were old, replicas were young. The nurse who was bathing her at the time, a nurse who hadn't stayed long, and whose name Lyra could no longer remember, had burst out laughing. The story had quickly made the rounds among the nurses and doctors.

"You've lost weight," Nurse Swineherd said, still frowning. "How's your appetite?"

Several seconds went by before Lyra realized this was a question she was meant to answer. "Fine."

"No nausea? Cramping? Vomiting?"

Lyra shook her head.

"Vision problems? Confusion?"

Lyra shook her head because she wasn't very practiced at lying. Two weeks ago she'd vomited so intensely her ribs had ached the following day. Yesterday she'd thrown up in a pillowcase, hoping it would help muffle the sound. Fortunately she'd been able to sneak it in with the rest of the trash, which went off on boats on Sundays, to be burned or dumped into the sea or otherwise disposed of. Given the storm, and the security breach, and the now-probably-dead male, she was confident no one would notice the missing pillowcase.

But the worst thing was that she had gotten lost yesterday, on her way back to the dorms. It didn't make any sense. She knew every inch of D-Wing, from Natal

Intensive to Neural Observation, to the cavernous dorms that housed one hundred female replicas each, to the bathrooms with dozens of showerheads tacked to a wall, a trench-like sink, and ten toilets. But she must have turned right instead of left coming out of the bathroom and had somehow ended up at the locked door that led into C-Wing, blinking confusedly, until a guard had called out to her and startled her into awareness.

But she wouldn't say so. She couldn't go to the Box. That's what everyone called G-Wing. The Box, or the Funeral Home, because half the replicas that went in never came out.

"All right, off you go," Nurse Swineherd said. "You let me know if you start feeling sick, okay?"

This time, she knew she wasn't expected to answer. She wouldn't have to tell anyone she kept throwing up. That was what the Glass Eyes mounted in the ceiling were for. (She wasn't sure whether she liked the Glass Eyes or not. Sometimes she did, when the chanting from Barrel Key was especially loud and she thought the cameras were keeping her safe. Sometimes, when she wanted to hide that she felt sick, she hated them, those lashless lenses recording her every move. That was the problem: she never knew which side the Glass Eyes were on.)

But she nodded anyway. Lyra had a plan, and the plan required her to be good, at least for a little while.

THREE

THREE DAYS LATER, THE BODY of male number 72 has still not washed up on the beach, as everyone had predicted. At breakfast the day after trash day, Lyra heard the nurses discussing it. Don't-Even-Think-About-It shook her head and said she was sure the gators had gotten him. If he did make it onto the mainland, she said, he'd likely be shot on sight—nothing but crazies and criminals living out here for miles. *And now those men are coming,* she added, shaking her head. That was what all the nurses called the Suits: *those men.*

Lyra had seen their boat in the distance on her way into breakfast: a sleek, motorized schooner, so unlike the battered barge that carted supplies in and trash out and looked as if it was one teaspoon of water away from sinking. She didn't know exactly what the Suits did, who they were, or why they visited Haven. Over the years she'd heard several references to the military, although they didn't look like soldiers, at least not the ones she occasionally saw on the nurses' TV. These men didn't wear matching outfits, or pants covered in camouflage. They didn't carry weapons, like the guards did.

When she was younger, the Suits had made Lyra nervous, particularly when all the replicas were forced to line up in front of them to be inspected. The Suits had opened her mouth to look at her teeth. They had asked her to smile or turn around or clap on command, to show she wasn't an idiot, wasn't *failing to thrive*, to wiggle her fingers or move her eyes from left to right.

The inspections had stopped a long time ago, however. Now the Suits came, walked through all the wings, from Admin to the Box, spoke to God, and then returned to the mainland on their boat, and Lyra found that she'd grown less and less interested in them. They belonged to another world. They might as well have been flies touching down, only to take flight again. They didn't matter to her, not like Thermoscan did, not like her little bed and her windowsill and the meaning embedded deep in a hieroglyph of words.

Today, in particular, she couldn't think about the Suits, or the mysterious disappearance of number 72. The day after trash day was Monday, which meant Cog Testing, and Lazy Ass, and her last opportunity for a week.

Lyra couldn't remember when the idea of stealing from Admin had first come to her. It had started, in a way, with Dr. O'Donnell. Dr. O'Donnell had come to Haven six or seven years ago; it was before Lyra had her monthly bleeding. ("Your period," Don't-Even-Think-About-It had said gruffly, and, in a rare moment of generosity, shown Lyra how to scrub out her underwear with cold water. "Bleeding makes it sound like a gunshot wound.") Dr. O'Donnell was—apart from Cassiopeia and numbers 7–10, her four genotypes, all of them genetically and physically identical—the prettiest person at Haven.

Unlike the other nurses and doctors, Dr. O'Donnell didn't seem to dislike the replicas. She hung around in the dorms even when she wasn't assigned to monitor. She asked questions. She was the first person who'd ever asked Lyra a question and actually expected a reply—other than "Does it hurt when I touch you there?" or "How's your appetite?"—and laughed easily, especially over the things the replicas believed, like that the rest of the world must be the size of five or six Havens or that in natural-born humans fathers served no purpose. She taught the replicas clapping games and sang to them in a high, clear voice.

Dr. O'Donnell was shocked when she found out that Haven had no library—only medical textbooks occasionally used for reference moldering in an awkwardly shaped room no one quite knew the use for, and the Bible that

Don't-Even-Think-About-It carted around with her, and occasionally used to take a swipe at replicas that disobeyed her, or to whack the ones too idiotic and brain-scrambled to follow instructions at all.

Whenever Dr. O'Donnell left the island, she returned with a few books in her bag. On Sunday afternoons, she sat in the dorms and read out loud. First it was only books with lots of pictures. Then longer books, with small type running across every page, so many letters it made Lyra dizzy to look. A few dozen replicas always gathered around to hear the stories, and afterward, after lights-out, repeated them in whispers for the other replicas, often making up or mixing up details, Jack and the Beanstalk that grew to Oz; the Lion, the Witch, and the Big Friendly Giant. It was a relief from the boredom, from the smallness of the world. Five wings, six counting the Box. Half the doors locked. All the world circumscribed by water. Half the replicas too dumb to talk, another quarter of them too sick, and still more too angry and violent.

No escape. Never escape.

But for Lyra, something deeper happened. She fell in love, although she didn't know it and would never have thought in those terms, since she didn't understand what love was and had only rarely heard the word. Under the influence of Dr. O'Donnell's voice, and her long fingers (some of them scattered with tiny freckles) turning the pages, a long-buried part of her consciousness woke, stirred, and opened.

Dr. O'Donnell was the one who had taught them the names for the various constellations—Hercules and Lyra, Cassiopeia and Venus, Ursa Major and Minor—and explained that stars were masses made of white-hot gas, hundreds upon hundreds upon hundreds of miles, farther than they could imagine.

Lyra remembered sitting on her cot one Sunday afternoon, while Dr. O'Donnell read to them from one of Lyra's favorite books, *Goodnight Moon*, and suddenly Cassiopeia—who was known only as 6 then—spoke up.

"I want a name," she'd said. "I want a name like the stars have."

And Lyra had felt profoundly embarrassed: she'd thought 6 was Cassiopeia's name, just as 24 was hers.

Dr. O'Donnell had gone around the room, assigning names. "Cassiopeia," she said. "Ursa. Venus. Calliope." Calliope, formerly 7 and the meanest of Cassiopeia's genotypes, giggled. Dr. O'Donnell's eyes clicked to Lyra's. "Lyra," she said, and Lyra felt a little electrical jolt, as if she'd just touched something too hot.

Afterward she went through Haven naming things, marking them as familiar, as hers. Everyone called G-Wing the Box, but she named other places too, named the mess hall Stew Pot, and C-Wing, where the male replicas were kept, the Hidden Valley. The security cameras that tracked her everywhere were Glass Eyes, the blood pressure monitor wrapped around her upper arm Squeezeme. All the nurses got names, and the doctors too, at least the ones she saw regularly. She couldn't name the researchers or the birthers because she hardly ever saw them, but the barracks where the birthers slept she named the Factory, since that's where all the new human models came out, before they were transferred to Postnatal and then, if they survived, to the dorms, to be bounced and tickled and engaged at least two hours a day.

She named Dr. Saperstein God, because he controlled everything.

Lyra was always careful to sit next to Dr. O'Donnell when she read, with her head practically in Dr. O'Donnell's lap, to try to make sense of the dizzying swarm of brushstroke symbols as Dr. O'Donnell read, to try to tack the sounds down to the letters. She concentrated so hard, it made the space behind her eyeballs ache.

One day, it seemed to her that Dr. O'Donnell began reading more slowly—not so slowly that the others would notice, but just enough that Lyra could make better sense of the edges of the words and how they snagged on the edges of certain letters, before leaping over the little white spaces of the page. At first she thought it was her imagination. Then, when Dr. O'Donnell placed a finger on the page, and began tracing individual lines of text, tapping occasionally the mysterious dots and dashes, or pausing underneath a particularly entangled word, Lyra knew that it wasn't.

Dr. O'Donnell was trying to help Lyra to read.

And slowly, slowly—like a microscope adjusted by degrees and degrees, ticking toward clearer resolution—words began to free themselves from the mysterious inky puddles on the page, to throw themselves suddenly at Lyra's understanding. *I. And. Went. Now.*

It couldn't last. Lyra should have known, but of course she didn't.

She had just gotten a name. She'd been born, really, for the second time. She hardly knew anything.

One Sunday afternoon, Dr. O'Donnell didn't come. The girls waited for nearly an hour before Cassiopeia, growing bored, announced she was going to walk down to the beach behind A-Wing and try to collect seashells. Although it wasn't strictly forbidden, Cassiopeia was one of the few replicas that ever ventured down to the water. Lyra had sometimes followed her, but was too scared to go on her own—frightened of the stories the nurses told, of man-eating sharks in Wahlee Sound, of alligators and poisonous snakes in the marshes.

It was a pretty day, not too hot, and great big clouds puffed up with importance. But Lyra didn't want to go outside. She didn't want to do anything but sit on the floor next to Dr. O'Donnell, so close she could smell the mix of antiseptic and lemon lotion on her skin, and the fibers of the paper puffing into the air whenever Dr. O'Donnell turned the page.

She had a terrible thought: Dr. O'Donnell must be sick. It was the only explanation. She had never missed a Sunday since the readings had begun, and Lyra refused to believe that Dr. O'Donnell had simply grown tired of their Sunday afternoons together. That *she* was tiring. That she was too damaged, too slow for Dr. O'Donnell.

Forgetting that she hated the Box, that she held her breath whenever she came within fifty feet of its red-barred doors, Lyra began to run in that direction. She couldn't explain the sudden terror that gripped her, a feeling like waking in the middle of the night, surrounded by darkness, and having no idea where she was.

She'd nearly reached C-Wing when she heard the sudden rise of angry voices—one of them Dr. O'Donnell's. She drew back, quickly, into an alcove. She could just make out Dr. O'Donnell and God, facing off in one of the empty testing rooms. The door was partially open, and their voices floated out into the hall.

"I hired you," God said, "to do your job, not to play at Mother goddamn Teresa." He raised his hand, and Lyra thought he might hit her. Then she saw that he was holding the old, weathered copy of *The Little Prince* Dr. O'Donnell had been reading.

"Don't you see?" Dr. O'Donnell's face was flushed. Her freckles had disappeared. "What we're doing . . . Christ. They deserve a little happiness, don't they? Besides, you said yourself they do better when they get some affection."

"Stimulation and touch. Not weekly story time." God slammed the book down on a table, and Lyra jumped. Then he sighed. "We're not humanitarians. We're *scientists*, Cat. And they're subjects. End of story."

Dr. O'Donnell raised her chin. Her hair was starting to come loose from her ponytail. If Lyra had known the word *love*, if she'd really understood it, she would have known she loved Dr. O'Donnell in that moment.

"That doesn't mean we can't treat them like regular people," she said.

God had already started for the door. Lyra caught a glimpse of his heavy black eyebrows, his close-trimmed beard, his eyes so sunken it looked like someone had pressed them back into his head. Now he stiffened and spun around. "Actually, it does," he said. His voice was very cold, like the touch of the Steel Ear when it slipped beneath her shirt to listen to her heartbeat. "What's next? Are you going to start teaching the rats to play chess?"

Before she left Haven, Dr. O'Donnell gave Lyra her copy of *The Little Prince*. Then Lyra was pretty sure Dr. O'Donnell had been crying.

"Be sure and keep it hidden," she whispered, and briefly touched Lyra's face.

Afterward, Lyra lay down. And for the afternoon, Lyra's pillow smelled like antiseptic and lemon lotion, like Dr. O'Donnell's fingers.

FOUR

COG TESTING TOOK PLACE IN a large, drafty room of D-Wing that had once been used to house cages full of rabbits and still smelled faintly of pellet food and animal urine. Lyra didn't know what had happened to the rabbits. Haven was large, and many of its rooms were off-limits, so she assumed they had been moved. Or maybe they had *failed to thrive,* too, like so many of the replicas.

Every week Cog Testing varied: the replicas might be asked to pick up small and slippery pins as quickly as possible, or attempt to assemble a three-dimensional puzzle, or to pick out visual patterns on a piece of paper. The female replicas, all nine hundred and sixty of them, were admitted by color in groups of forty over the course of the day. Lilac Springs was out of the Box and took the seat next to Lyra's. Lilac Springs had named herself after a product she'd seen advertised on the nurses' TV. Even after the nurses had laughed hysterically and explained to her—and everyone—what a feminine douche was and what it was for, she had refused to change her name, saying she liked the sound of it.

"You don't look so good" was the first thing Lilac Springs said to Lyra. Lilac Springs hardly ever said anything. She was one of the slower replicas. She still needed help getting dressed, and she had never learned her alphabet. "Are you sick?"

Lyra shook her head, keeping her eyes on the table. She'd thrown up again in the middle of the night and was so dizzy afterward that she had to stay there, holding onto the toilet, for a good twenty minutes. Cassiopeia had caught her when she came in to pee. But she didn't think Cassiopeia would tell. Cassiopeia was always getting in trouble—for not eating her dinner, for talking, for openly staring at the males and even for trying to talk to them, on the few occasions they wound up in the halls or the Box or the Stew Pot together.

"*I'm* sick," Lilac Springs said. She was speaking so loudly, Lyra instinctively looked up at the Glass Eyes, even though she knew they didn't register sound. "They put me in the Box."

Lyra didn't have friends at Haven. She didn't know what a friend was. But she thought she would be unhappy if Lilac Springs died. Lyra had been five years old when

Lilac Springs was made, and could still remember how after Lilac Springs had been birthed and transferred to Postnatal for observation she had kicked her small pink feet and waved her fists as if she was dancing.

But it wasn't looking good. Something was going around the Browns, and the doctors in the Box couldn't stop it. In the past four months, five of them had died—four females, and number 312 from the males' side. Two of them had died the same night. The nurses had suited up in heavy gloves and masks and bundled the bodies in a single plastic tarp before hauling them out for collection. And Lilac Springs's skin was still shiny red and raw-looking, like the skin on top of a blister. Her hair, which was buzzed short like all the other replicas', was patchy. Some of her scalp showed through.

"It's not so bad," Lilac Springs said, even though Lyra still hadn't responded. "Palmolive came."

Palmolive was also a Brown. She had started throwing up a few weeks ago and was found wandering the halls in the middle of the night. She had been transferred to the Box when she could hardly choke down a few sips of water without bringing it up again.

"Do you think I'll be dead soon?" Lilac Springs asked.

Fortunately, the nurses came in before Lyra had to answer. Lazy Ass and Go Figure were administering. They almost always did. But earlier, Lyra had been afraid that it might be somebody else.

Today there were three tests. Whenever Lyra's heart beat faster, she imagined its four valves opening and closing like shutters, the flow of blood in one direction, an endless loop like all the interlocking wings of Haven. She had learned about hearts like she'd learned about the rest of the human body: because there was nothing else *to* learn, no truth at Haven except for the physical, nothing besides pain and response, symptom and treatment, breathe in and breathe out and skin stretched over muscle over bone.

First, Nurse Go Figure called out a series of five letters and asked that the replicas memorize them. Then they had to rearrange colored slips of paper until they formed a progression, from green to yellow. Then they had to fit small wooden pieces in similarly shaped holes, a ridiculously easy test, although Lilac Springs seemed to be struggling with it—trying to fit the diamond shape into the triangular hole, and periodically dropping pieces so they landed, clatteringly, to the floor.

For the last test, Go Figure distributed papers and pens—Lyra held the pen up to her tongue surreptitiously, enjoying the taste of the ink; she wanted another pen badly for her collection—and asked that the replicas write down the five letters they'd memorized, in order. Most of the replicas had learned their numbers to one hundred

and the alphabet *A* through *Z*, both so they could identify their individual beds and for use in testing, and Lyra
took great pleasure in drawing the curves and angles of
each number in turn, imagining that numbers, too, were
like a language. When she looked up, she saw that Lilac
Springs's paper was still completely blank. Lilac Springs
was holding her pen clumsily, staring at it as though she'd
never seen one. She hadn't even remembered a single letter, although Lyra knew she knew her numbers and was
very proud of it.

Then Lazy Ass called time, and Nurse Go Figure collected the papers, and they sat in silence as the results
were collected, tabulated, and marked in their files. Lyra's
palms began to sweat. Now.

"I forgot the letters," Lilac Springs said. "I couldn't
remember the letters."

"All right, that's it." Lazy Ass hauled herself out of her
chair, wincing, as she always did after testing. The replicas stood, too. Only Lyra remained sitting, her heart
clenching and unclenching in her chest.

As always, as soon as Lazy Ass was on her feet, she started
complaining: "Goddamn shoes. Goddamn weather. And
now my lazy ass gotta go all the way to Admin. Take me
twenty minutes just to get there and back. And those men
coming today." Lazy Ass normally worked the security
desk and subbed in to help with testing when she had

to. She was at least one hundred pounds overweight, and her ankles swelled in the heat until they were thick and round as the trunks of the palms that lined the garden courtyard.

"Go figure," said Go Figure, like she always did. She had burnished brown skin that always looked as if it had been recently oiled.

Now. Most of the other replicas had left. Only Lilac Springs remained, still seated, staring at the table.

"I'll do it," Lyra said. She felt breathless even though she hadn't moved, and she wondered whether Lazy Ass would notice. But no. Of course she wouldn't. Many of the nurses couldn't even tell the replicas apart. When she was a kid, Lyra remembered staring at the nurses, willing them to stare back at her, to *see* her, to take her hand or pick her up or tell her she was pretty. She had once been moved to solitary for two days after she stole Nurse Em's security badge, thinking that the nurse wouldn't be able to leave at the end of the day, that she would *have* to stay. But Nurse Em had found a way to leave, of course, and soon afterward she had left Haven forever.

Lyra had gotten used to it: to all the leaving, to being left. Now she was glad to be invisible. They were invisible to her, too, in a way. That was why she'd given them nicknames.

Nurse Go Figure and Lazy Ass turned, staring. Lyra's

face was hot. *Rosacea*. She knew it all from a lifetime of listening to the doctors.

"What'd it say?" Lazy Ass said, very slowly. She wasn't talking to Lyra, but Lyra answered anyway.

"It can do it," Lyra said, forcing herself to stay very still. When she was little, she'd been confused about the difference between *I* and *it* and could never keep them straight. Sometimes when she was nervous, she still slipped up. She tried again. "I can bring the files to Admin for you."

Go Figure snorted. "Jesus, Mary, and Joseph," she said.

But Lazy Ass kept staring, as though seeing Lyra for the first time. "You know how to get to Admin?"

Lyra nodded. She had always lived at Haven. She would always live at Haven. There were many rooms locked, forbidden, accessible only by key cards and codes—many places she couldn't enter, many closed doors behind which people moved, helmeted, suited up in white. But she knew all the lengths of the hallways and the time it took in seconds to get from the toilet to the Stew Pot and back; knew the desks and break rooms, stairways and back ways, like she knew the knobs of her own hips or the feel of the bed, number 24, that had always been hers. Like she knew Omiron and latex, Invacare Snake Tubing and Red Caps and the Glass Eyes.

Her friends, her enemies, her *world*.

"What's Admin, Lyra?" Lilac Springs asked. She was

going to ruin everything—and she knew where Admin was. Everybody did. Even Lilac Springs wasn't that dumb.

"I'll be quick," Lyra said, ignoring Lilac Springs.

"Dr. Sappo won't like it," Go Figure said. Dr. Sappo was what the staff called God, but only when he couldn't hear them. Otherwise they called him Dr. Saperstein or Director Saperstein. "They ain't supposed to get their hands on nothing important."

Lazy Ass snorted. "I don't care if he do or don't like it," she said. "He ain't got blisters the size of Mount St. Helens on both feet. Besides, he won't know one way or the other."

"What if it messes up?" Go Figure said. "Then you'll be in trouble."

"I won't," Lyra protested, and then cleared her throat when her voice came out as a croak. "Mess it up, I mean. I know what to do. I go down to Sub-One in A-Wing."

Lilac Springs began to whine. "I want to go to Admin."

"Uh-uh," Nurse Go Figure said, turning to Lilac Springs. "This one's coming with me." And then, in a low voice, but not so low both Lilac Springs and Lyra couldn't hear: "The Browns are going like flies. It's funny how it hits them all differently."

"That's because they ain't got it right yet." Lazy Ass shook her head. "All's I know is they better be for real about how it doesn't catch." She was still watching Lyra through half-narrowed eyes, evaluating, drumming the stack of test results as if an answer might come through her fingertips.

"I've told you, it isn't contagious. Not like that, anyway. I've been here since the start. Do I look dead to you?"

Lilac Springs began to cry—loudly, a high, blubbering wail, like the cry of one of the infant replicas in the observation units. Go Figure had to practically drag her to her feet and out into the hall. Only when Lyra could no longer hear Lilac Springs's voice did she realize she'd been holding her breath.

Lazy Ass slid the papers a half inch toward her. Lyra stood up so quickly the chair jumped across the tile floor.

"Straight through and no stopping," Lazy Ass said. "And if anyone asks you where you're going, keep walking and mind your own business. Should be Werner down at the desk. Tell him I sent you."

Lyra could feel the muscles around her lips twitching. But Lazy Ass would be suspicious if she looked too happy. She took the papers—even the *sound* of paper was delicious—and held them carefully to her chest.

"Go on," Lazy Ass said.

Lyra didn't want to wait, fearing Lazy Ass would change her mind. Even after she'd turned into the hall, she kept waiting for the nurse to shout, to call her back, to decide it was a bad idea. The linoleum was cold on her bare feet.

Haven consisted of six wings, A–G. There was no E-Wing, for reasons no one understood, although rumor among the staff was that the first God, Richard Haven, had an ex-wife named Ellen. Except for the Box, officially called G-Wing, all the buildings were interconnected, arranged in a pentagon formation around a four-acre courtyard fitted with gardens and statues, benches, and even a paddleball court for staff use. Electronic double doors divided the wings at each juncture, like a series of mechanized elbows. Only the Box was larger—four stories at least, and as many as three more, supposedly, underground, although given that they were at sea level, that seemed unlikely. It was detached, situated a solid hundred yards away from Haven proper and built of gray cement.

The fastest way to A-Wing from the testing rooms was through F-Wing. She'd already decided that if anyone asked, she'd say she was on her way to the Stew Pot for lunch.

But no one asked. She passed several nurses sitting in the dayroom, laughing about two women on TV—replicas, Lyra thought, with a quick spark of excitement, until she recognized from small differences between them that they were just twins. Then came the dorms: smaller rooms for the lower staff, where nurses and researchers might sleep as many as four to a room, bunk-style; then the doctors' quarters, which were more spacious. Finally, the Stew Pot. The smell of cooked meat immediately made her stomach turn.

She hurried on, keeping her head down. When she buzzed into A-Wing, the guard on duty barely glanced up. She passed through the marble lobby with its stone bust of Richard Haven, the first God, which someone had draped in a red-and-blue cape and outfitted with a funny-looking hat: it was some game, Lyra understood, something to do with a place called U Penn, where both the first and second Gods had come from. A plastic Christmas tree, originally purchased for Haven's annual party, had for three years stood just inside the main entryway, though during the off-season it was unplugged. Photographs of strangers smiled down from the walls, and in one of them Richard Haven and Dr. Saperstein were much younger and dressed in red and blue. They even had their faces painted.

Today, however, she didn't stop to look. She pushed through the doors that led into the stairwell. It smelled faintly of cigarettes.

The closer she got to Admin, the greater the pressure on her chest, as if there were Invacare Snake Tubing threaded down her throat, pumping liquid into her lungs. Sub-One was always quieter than the ground floor of Haven. Most of the doors down here were fitted with control pads and marked with big red circles divided in two on the diagonal, signs that they were restricted-access only. Plus, the walls seemed to vacuum up noise, absorbing the sound of Lyra's footsteps as soon as she moved.

Administration was restricted-access, too. Lazy Ass had said Werner would be behind the desk, and Lyra's whole plan depended on it. Twin windows in the door looked into a space filled with individual office cubicles: flyers pinned to corkboard, keyboards buried under piles of manila files, phones and computers cabled to overloaded power strips. All of Haven's paperwork came here, from mail to medical reports, before being routed and redirected to its ultimate destination.

Lyra ducked into an alcove twenty feet beyond the entrance to Admin. If she peeked into the hall, she had a clear view of the doors. She prayed she had arrived on time and hadn't missed her chance. Several times, she inched into the hall to check. But the doors were firmly shut.

Finally, when Lyra had nearly given up hope, she heard a faint click as the locks released. The doors squeaked open. A second later, footsteps headed for the stairs. As soon as she heard the door to the stairwell open, Lyra slipped into the hall.

Lyra had been occasionally sneaking down to Admin ever since Dr. O'Donnell had vanished abruptly. She knew that every day, when most of the other administrative staff was still eating in the Stew Pot, Werner snuck away from his desk, propped the doors of Admin open, and smoked a cigarette—sometimes two—in the stairwell.

Today he had wedged an empty accordion file into the double doors to keep them from closing. Lyra slipped inside, making sure the accordion file stayed in place, and closed the door gently behind her.

For a few seconds, she stood very still, allowing the silence to enfold her. Administration was actually several interconnected rooms. This, the first of them, brightly modern, was fitted with long ceiling lights similar to the ones used in the labs upstairs. Lyra moved deeper, into the forest of file cabinets and old plastic storage bins, into mountains of paperwork no one had touched for years. A few rooms were dark, or only partly illuminated. And she could hear, in the quiet, the whisper of millions of words, words trapped behind every drawer, words beating their fingernails against the inside of the file cabinets.

All the words she could ever want: words to stuff herself on until she was full, until her eyes burst.

She moved to the farthest corner of the dimmest room and picked a file cabinet at random. She didn't care about the actual reports, about what they might say or mean.

All she cared about was the opportunity to practice. Dr. O'Donnell had explained to her once what a *real* library was, and the function it served in the outside world, and Lyra knew Admin was the closest she would ever get.

She selected a file from the very back—one she was sure hadn't been touched in a long time, slender enough to conceal easily. She closed the cabinet and went carefully back the way she had come, through rooms that grew ever lighter and less dusty.

Then she was in the hall. She slipped into the alcove and waited. Sure enough, less than a minute later, the door to the stairwell squeaked open and clanged shut, and footsteps came down the hall. Werner was back.

She had yet to fulfill her official errand. That meant concealing the hard-won file somewhere, if only for a little while. There weren't many options. She chose a metal bin mounted on the wall marked with a sign she recognized as meaning *hazardous*. Normally the nurses and doctors used them for discarding used gloves, caps, and even syringes, but this one was empty.

Werner didn't even let her in. He came to the door, frowning, when she tapped a finger to the glass.

"What is it?" he said. His voice was muffled through the glass, but he spoke very slowly, as if he wasn't sure Lyra could understand. He wasn't used to dealing with replicas. That was obvious.

"Shannon from security sent me," she said, stopping herself at the last second from saying *Lazy Ass*.

Werner disappeared. When he returned to open the door, she saw that he had suited up in gloves and a face mask. It wasn't unusual for members of the staff to refuse to interact with the replicas unless they were protected, which Lyra thought was stupid. The diseases that killed the replicas, the conditions that made them small and slow and stupid, were directly related to the cloning process and to being raised at Haven.

He looked at the file in her hand as if it was something dead. "Go on. Give it. And tell *Shannon from security* to do her own work next time." He snatched the file from her and quickly withdrew, scowling at her from behind the glass. She barely noticed. Already, in her head, she was curling up inside all those letters—new pages, new words to decipher and trip over and decode.

She retrieved the file from the metal bin after checking to see that she was still alone. This was the only part of the plan she hadn't entirely thought out. She had to get the file up to her bed, but if she carried it openly, someone *might* wonder where it had come from. She could say a nurse had given it to her to deliver—but what if someone checked? She wasn't even sure whether she could lie convincingly. She hadn't spoken to the staff so much in years, and she was already exhausted.

Instead she opted to slip it under the waistband of her standard-issue pants, pouching her shirt out over it. The only way to keep it from slipping was to wrap both arms around her stomach, as if she had a bad stomachache. Even then, she had to take small steps, and she imagined that the sound of crinkling paper accompanied her. But she had no choice. Hopefully, she would make it back to D-Wing without having to speak to anyone.

But no sooner had she passed through the doors into the stairwell than she heard the sound of echoing voices. Before she could retreat, God came down the stairs with one of the Suits. Lyra ducked her head and stepped aside, squeezing her arms close around the file, praying they would move past her without stopping.

They stopped.

"Hey." It was the stranger who spoke. "Hey. You." His eyes were practically black. He turned to God. "Which one is this?"

"Not sure. Some of the nurses can tell them apart on sight." God looked at Lyra. "Which one are you?" he asked.

Maybe it was the stolen file pressed to her stomach, but Lyra had the momentary impulse to introduce herself by name. Instead she said, "Number twenty-four."

"And you just let them wander around like this?" The man was still staring at Lyra, but obviously addressing himself to God. "Even after what happened?" Lyra knew he must be talking about the Code Black.

"We're following protocols," God said. God's voice reminded Lyra of the bite of the syringes. "When Haven started, it was important to the private sector that they be treated humanely."

"There is no private sector. We're the ones holding the purse strings now," the man said. "What about contagion?"

Lyra was only half listening. Sweat was gathering in the space between the folder and her stomach. She imagined it seeping through the folder, dampening the pages. The folder had shifted fractionally and she was worried a page might escape, but she didn't dare adjust her grip.

"There's no risk except through direct ingestion—as you would know, if you actually read the reports. All right, twenty-four," God said. "You can go."

Lyra was so relieved she could have shouted. Instead she lowered her head and, keeping her arms wrapped tightly around her waist, started to move past them.

"Wait."

The Suit called out to her. Lyra stiffened and turned around to face him on the stairs. They were now nearly eye to eye. She felt the same way she did during examinations, shivering in her paper gown, staring up at the high unblinking lights set in the ceiling: cold and exposed.

"What's the matter with its stomach?" he asked.

Lyra tightened her hands around her waist. *Please,* she thought. *Please.* She couldn't complete the thought. If she were forced to move her arms, the file would drop. She imagined papers spilling from her pants legs, tumbling down the stairs.

God indicated the plastic wristband Lyra always wore. "Green," he said. "One of the first variants. Slower-acting than your typical vCJD. Most of the Greens are still alive, although we've seen a few signs of neurodegenerative activity recently."

"So what's that mean in English?"

Unlike the man in the suit, God never made eye contact. He looked at her shoulders, her arms, her kneecaps, her forehead: everywhere but her eyes.

"Side effects," he said, with a thin smile. Then Lyra was free to go.

Lyra wasn't the only replica that collected things. Rose kept used toothbrushes under her pillow. Palmolive scanned the hallways for dropped coins and stored them in a box that had once contained antibacterial swabs. Cassiopeia had lined up dozens of seashells on the windowsill next to her bed, and additionally had convinced Nurse Dolly to sneak her some Scotch tape so she could hang several drawings she'd created on napkins stolen from the mess hall. She drew Dumpsters and red-barred circles and stethoscopes and the bust of the first God in his red-and-blue cape and scalpels gleaming in folds of clean cloth. She was very good. Calliope had once taken a cell phone from one of the nurses, and all her genotypes had been punished for it.

But Lyra was careful with her things. She was *private* about them. The file folder she hid carefully under her thin mattress, next to her other prized possessions: several pens, including her favorite, a green one with a retractable tip that said *Fine & Ives* in block white lettering; an empty tin that read *Altoids*; a half-dozen coins she'd found behind the soda machine; her worn and battered copy of *The Little Prince*, which she'd handled so often that many of the pages had come loose from their binding.

"There's a message in this book," Dr. O'Donnell had told Lyra, before leaving Haven. "In the love of the Little Prince for his rose, there's wisdom we could all learn from." And Lyra had nodded, trying to pretend she understood, even though she didn't understand. Not about love. Not about hope. Dr. O'Donnell was going away, and once again, Lyra was left behind.

FIVE

"YOU'VE BEEN LYING TO ME, twenty-four."

Lyra was on her knees, blinking back tears, swallowing the taste of vomit, when the closet door opened. She couldn't get to her feet fast enough. She spun around, accidentally knocking over a broom with her elbow.

Nurse Curly was staring not at Lyra but at the bucket behind her, now splattered with vomit. Strangely, she didn't seem angry. "I knew it," she said, shaking her head.

It was early afternoon, and Curly must have just arrived from the launch for the shift change. She wasn't yet wearing her scrubs, but a blue tank top with beading at the shoulders, jeans, and leather sandals. Usually, Lyra was mesmerized by evidence of life outside Haven—the occasional magazine, water-warped, abandoned on the sink in the nurses' toilets; used-up lip balm in the trash; or a

broken flip-flop sitting on a bench in the courtyard—
split-second fissures through which a whole other world
was revealed.

Today, however, she didn't care.

She'd been so sure that here, in a rarely used janitorial
closet in D-Wing Sub-One, she'd be safe. She'd woken
up sweating, with her heart going hard and her stomach
like something heavy and raw that needed to come out.
But the waking bell sounded only a minute later, and she
knew that the bathrooms would soon be full of replicas showering, brushing their teeth, whispering beneath
the thunderous sound of the water about the Suits and
what they could possibly want and whether number 72
had been torn apart by alligators by now—lungs, kidneys,
spleen scattered across the marshes.

But the staff bathrooms were just as risky. They were
off-limits, first of all, and often crowded—the nurses
were always hiding out in stalls trying to make calls or
send text messages.

"I'm not sick," Lyra said quickly, reaching out to grab
hold of a shelf. She was still dizzy.

"Come on, now." As usual Nurse Curly acted as if she
hadn't heard. Maybe she hadn't. Lyra had the strangest
sense of being invisible, as if she existed behind a curtain
and the nurses and doctors could only vaguely see her.
"We'll go to Dr. Levy."

"No. Please." Dr. Levy worked in the Box. She hated him, and that big, thunderous machine, Mr. I. She hated the grinning lights like blank indifferent faces. She hated Catheter Fingers and Invacare Snake Tubing, Dribble Bags and Sad Sacks, syringe after syringe after syringe. She hated the weird dreams that visited her there, of lions marching around a cylindrical cup, of old voices she was sure she'd never heard but that felt real to her. Even a spinal tap with the Vampire—the long needle inserted into the base of her spinal column between two vertebrae so that her fluids could be extracted for testing—was almost preferable. "I feel fine."

"Don't be silly," Curly said. "It's for your own good. Come on out of there."

Lyra edged into the hall, keeping her hands on the walls, which were studded with nails from which brooms and mops and dustpans were hanging. She couldn't remember what day it was. The knowledge seemed to have dropped through a hole in her awareness. She couldn't remember what day yesterday had been, either, or what had happened.

"Follow me." The nurse put her hand on Lyra's arm, and Lyra was overwhelmed. It was rare that the nurses touched them unless they had to, in order to take their measurements. Lyra's knowledge of the nurse's name had evaporated, too, though she was sure she had known it just a second earlier. What was happening to her? It was as if vomiting had shaken up all the information in her brain, muddled it.

Lyra's eyes were burning and her throat felt raw. When she reached up to wipe her mouth, she was embarrassed to realize she was crying.

"It's normal," the nurse said. Lyra wasn't sure what she meant.

It was quicker from here to go through C-Wing, where the male replicas were kept. Nurse Cheryl—the name came back to Lyra suddenly, loosed from the murky place it had been stuck—Nurse Cheryl, nicknamed Curly for her hair, which corkscrewed around her face, buzzed them in. Lyra hung back. In all her years at Haven, she'd only been through C-Wing a few times. She hadn't forgotten Pepper, and what had happened. She remembered how Pepper had cried when she'd first been told what was happening to her, that she would be a *birther*, like all those dark-skinned women who came and left on boats and were never seen outside the barracks. Pepper had left fingernail scratches across the skin of her belly and begged for the doctors to get it out.

But two months later, by the time the doctors determined she couldn't keep it, she was already talking names: Ocean, Sunday, Valium. After Pepper, all the knives in the mess hall were replaced with plastic versions, and the male and female replicas were kept even more strictly apart.

"It's okay." Curly gave her a nudge. "Go on. You're with me."

It was hotter in C-Wing. Or maybe Lyra was just hot. In the first room they passed she saw a male replica, lying on an examination table with probes attached to his bare chest. She looked away quickly. It smelled different in C-Wing—the same mixture of antiseptic and bleach and human sweat, but deeper somehow.

They took the stairs up to ground level and moved past a series of dorms, lined with cots just like on the girls' side and mercifully empty. The males who weren't sick or in testing were likely getting fed in Stew Pot. Despite the standard-issue white sheets and gray blankets, and the plastic under-bed bins, the rooms managed to give an impression of messiness.

They passed into B-Wing, and Curly showed her credentials to two guards on duty. B-Wing was for research and had restricted access. Passed laboratories, dazzling white, illuminated by rows and rows of fluorescent light, where more researchers were working, moving slowly in their gloves and lab coats, hair concealed beneath translucent gray caps, eyes magnified, insect-like, by their goggles. Banks of computers, screens filled with swirling colors, hard metal equipment, words Lyra had heard her whole life without ever knowing what they meant—spectrometry, biometrics, liquid chromatography—beautiful words, words to trip over and fall into.

One time, she had worked up the courage to ask Dr. O'Donnell what they did all day in the research rooms. It didn't seem possible that all those men and women were there just to perfect the replication process, to keep the birthers from miscarrying so often after the embryo transfer, to keep the replicas from dying so young.

Dr. O'Donnell had hesitated. "They're studying what makes you sick," she said at last, speaking slowly, as if she had to carefully handle the words or they would cut her. "They're studying how it works, and how long it takes, and why."

"And how to fix it?" Lyra had asked.

Dr. O'Donnell had barely hesitated. "Of course."

The Box was made of concrete slab, sat several hundred yards away from the main complex, and was enclosed by its own fence. Unlike the rest of Haven, the G-Wing had no windows, and extra security required Nurse Curly to identify herself twice and show her badge to various armed guards who patrolled the perimeter.

Curly left Lyra in the entrance foyer, in front of the elevator that gave access to Sub-One and, supposedly, the concealed subterranean levels. Lyra tried not to look at the doors that led to the ER, where so many replicas died or *failed to thrive* in the first place. Even the nurses called the G-Wing the Funeral Home or the Graveyard. Lyra wondered whether Lilac Springs was there even now, and how long she had left.

Soon enough, the elevator doors opened and a technician wearing a heavy white lab coat, her hair concealed beneath a cap, arrived to escort Lyra down to see Mr. I. It was, as far as Lyra could tell, the same tech she'd seen the half-dozen or so times she'd been here in the past month. Then again, she had trouble telling them apart, since their faces were so often concealed behind goggles and a mask, and since they never spoke directly to her.

In Sub-One, they walked down a long, windowless hallway filled with doors marked *Restricted*. But when a researcher slipped out into the hall, Lyra had a brief view of a sanitation room and, beyond it, a long, galley-shaped laboratory in which dozens of researchers were bent over gleaming equipment, dressed in head-to-toe protective clothing and massive headgear that made them look like the pictures of astronauts Lyra had occasionally seen on the nurses' TV.

Mr. I sat by itself in a cool bright room humming with recirculated air. To Lyra, Mr. I looked like an open mouth, and the table on which she was supposed to lie down a long pale tongue. The hair stood up on her arms and legs.

"Remember to stay very still," the tech said, her voice

muffled by a paper mask. "Otherwise we'll just have to start over. And nobody wants that, do we?"

Afterward she was transferred to a smaller room and told to lie down. Sometimes lying this way, with doctors buzzing above her, she lost track of whether she was a human at all or some other thing, a slab of meat or a glass overturned on a countertop. A thing.

"I don't believe Texas is any further than we are. It's bullshit. They're bluffing. Two years ago, they were still infecting bovine tissue—"

"It doesn't matter if they're bluffing if our funding gets cut. Everyone *thinks* they're closer. Fine and Ives loses the contract. Then we're shit outta luck."

High bright lights, cool sensors moving over her body, gloved hands pinching and squeezing. "Sappo thinks the latest variant will do it. I'm talking full progression within a *week*. Can you imagine the impact?"

"He better be right. What the hell will we do with all of them if we get shut down? Ever think of that?"

Lyra closed her eyes, suddenly exhausted.

"Open your eyes, please. Follow my finger, left to right. Good."

"Reflexes still look okay." One of the doctors, the woman, parted her paper gown and squeezed her nipple, hard. Lyra cried out. "And pain response. Do me a favor—check this one's file, will you? What variant is this?"

"This is similar to the vCJD, just slower-acting. That's why the pulvinar sign is detectable on the MRI. Very rare in nature, nearly always inherited."

They worked in silence for a bit. Lyra thought about *The Little Prince*, and Dr. O'Donnell, and distant stars where beautiful things lived and died in freedom. She couldn't stop crying.

"How do they choose which ones end up in control, and which ones get the different variants?" the male doctor asked after a while.

"Oh, it's all automated," the woman said. Now she held Lyra's eyes open with two fingers, ensuring she couldn't blink. "Okay, come see this. See the way her left eye is spasming? Myoclonus. That's another indicator."

"Mm-hmm. So it's random?"

"Totally random. The computer does it by algorithm. That way, you know, no one feels bad. Pass me the stethoscope, will you? I bet its heart rate is through the roof."

That night was very still, and the sound of chanting voices and drumbeats—louder, always, on the days the Suits had visited the island—carried easily over the water. Lyra lay awake for a long time, fighting the constant pull of nausea, listening to the distant rhythm, which didn't sound so distant after all. At times, she imagined it was coming closer, that suddenly Haven would be overrun with strangers. She imagined all of them made of darkness and shadow instead of blood and muscle and bones. She wondered, for the first time, whether number 72 was maybe not dead after all. She remembered hearing once that the marshes were submerged islands, miles of land that had over time been swallowed up by the water.

She wondered whether 72 had been swallowed up too, or whether he was out there somewhere, listening to the voices.

She took comfort in the presence of the new addition to her collection, buried directly beneath her lower back. She imagined that the file pushed up heat, like a heart, like the warmth of Dr. O'Donnell's touch. *98.6 degrees Fahrenheit*. She imagined the smell of lemon and antiseptic, as if Dr. O'Donnell were still there, floating between the beds.

"Don't worry," Dr. O'Donnell had once said to her on a night like this one, when the voices were louder than usual. "They can't get to you," she'd said more quietly. "They can't get in."

But about this, Dr. O'Donnell was wrong.

SIX

LYRA DID NOT SLEEP WELL. She woke up with a tight, airless feeling in her chest, like the time years ago when Nurse Don't-Even-Think-About-It had held Lyra's head in the sink to punish her for stealing some chocolate from the nurses' break room.

Side effects. They would pass. Medicines sometimes made you sick before they made you better. In the dim morning light, with the sound of so many replicas inhaling and exhaling beside her, she closed her eyes. She had a brief memory of a birther rocking her years ago, singing to her, the tickle of hair on her forehead. She opened her eyes again. The birthers didn't sing. They howled and screamed. Or they wept. They spoke in other languages. But they didn't sing.

She was nauseous again.

This time she wouldn't risk throwing up inside. She

would have to find someplace more remote—along the beach, maybe behind the tin drums of hazardous waste Haven lined up for collection, somewhere the guards couldn't see her.

She chose to pass through the courtyard, which was mostly empty. Many of the night nurses would be preparing to take the launch back to Cedar Key. She passed the statue of the first God, Richard Haven. It dominated the center of the yard, where all four walking paths intersected. Here she rested, leaning against the cool marble base, next to a plaque commemorating his work and achievements. He'd had a kind face, Lyra thought. At least, the artist had given him one.

She didn't remember the flesh-and-blood man. He'd died before she was made. The sculptor had depicted him kneeling, with one arm raised. Lyra guessed he was supposed to be calling out to invisible crowds to *come*, to *look here*, but to her it had always looked as if he was stretching one arm toward the clouds, toward the other God, the ones the nurses believed in. Their God, too, hated the replicas.

She squatted next to twin drums marked with a biohazard symbol and threw up into the high grasses that grew between them. She felt slightly better when she stood up, but still weak. She stopped a half-dozen times during the walk back to the main building, earning a disapproving glance from one of the patrolling guards. Normally, she was grateful for the sheer size of Haven, for the tracts of open space and the walkways shaded by hickory trees and high palmettos, for the bright bursts of heliotrope in the flower beds, and the wild taro pushing between the cement paving stones, although she had names for none of them and knew the growth only in general terms: flowers, trees, plants. But today she was exhausted and wished simply to get back to bed 24.

She heard shouting as she entered D-Wing. As Lyra got closer to the dorm, she recognized one of the voices: Dr. Saperstein. She nearly stopped and turned around. God had never come to the bunks, ever.

But then she heard Cassiopeia shout, "Don't touch them. It's not *fair*," and she kept going.

Up ahead, a nurse hurried out into the hall, skidding a little on the tile, and shot Lyra a strange look before scurrying in the opposite direction, leaving the dorm room door swinging open. Lyra barely caught it before it closed.

Then she stopped, her breath catching. Cassiopeia was on her hands and knees in front of Dr. Saperstein, trying to sweep up her collection of shells, which had been knocked off the windowsill and shattered. All of the individual drawings pasted to the wall behind her bed had been torn down, as if a hard wind had come ripping through the bunk, though it hadn't disturbed anything else. Then Lyra saw he was holding them, crumpled together in his fist.

"Unbelievable." He was shouting, but not at the girls. Instead he was yelling at the assembled nursing staff, including Nurse Dolly, who'd found Cassiopeia Scotch tape so they could hang the napkins in the first place. "Do you know how close we are to getting defunded? Do you want to be out of a job? We have a quota, we have protocols—"

"It was my fault," Nurse Dolly said. "I didn't see any harm in it."

God took a step toward her, nearly tripping over Cassiopeia, who was still on the floor, crying softly. Lyra wanted to go to her but found she couldn't move. God's shoes crunched quietly on the carpet of shattered seashells.

"No harm in it?" he repeated, and Nurse Dolly quickly looked away. Now he was speaking softly, but strangely, and Lyra was more frightened of him than ever. "I've worked my whole career to see this project succeed. We're doing some of the most important medical work of the past two decades, and yet—" He broke off, shaking his head. "*Results*. That's what we need. *Results*. This is a research facility, not a playpen. Is that clear to everyone?"

No one spoke. In the silence, Lyra could hear her heart. *Boom-boom-boom.* Like the rhythm of the chanting that carried all the way to Spruce Island from Barrel Key.

Monsters, monsters. Burn Haven down.

God sighed. He took off his glasses and rubbed his eyes. "We're doing important work," he said. "Good work. Never forget that." He started to turn away and then stopped. "It's better this way—for everyone."

But Lyra knew, from the tone of his voice, that he didn't mean the replicas.

God had to step around Cassiopeia again to move to the door. He barely glanced at her. Instead he kicked at a seashell, sending it skittering across the floor. "Someone clean up this mess, please," he announced, to no one in particular. Lyra stepped quickly out of the doorway to avoid him.

For a long moment after he was gone, no one moved. Just Cassiopeia, still sorting through the remains of her collection, now reduced to shards and dust. Finally Nurse Dolly went to her.

"All right," she said, crouching down and grabbing Cassiopeia's wrist to stop her from reaching for another broken shell. "That's enough now."

It happened so quickly: Cassiopeia turned and *shoved* Nurse Dolly. "Get off me," she said, and several people cried out, and Lyra took a step forward, saying, *"Don't."*

Maybe she hadn't meant to push Nurse Dolly hard, or maybe she had. Either way, Nurse Dolly lost her balance and went backward. In an instant, Nurse

Don't-Even-Think-About-It had crossed to Cassiopeia and wrenched her to her feet.

"Wicked thing," Don't-Even-Think-About-It spat at her, keeping hold of her wrists. "How dare you touch her—how dare you, when we've fed and clothed and kept you all these years? The judgment of God will come for you, don't you forget it."

"You don't own me." Cassiopeia's eyes were very bright and she was shaking. Lyra stared at her, filled with a sudden sense of dread. She didn't understand what Cassiopeia meant—she didn't understand where she'd found these words, this anger, and for a second she felt as if the room was splitting apart, revealing a dark gulf, a hidden fault line. "You can't tell me what to do. I don't belong to you. I'm real. I am."

"You're not anything," Don't-Even-Think-About-It said. Her face was mottled with anger, like the veined slabs of beef shelved in the kitchen freezers. "You belong to the institute, and to Dr. Saperstein. You can stay here, or you can leave and be killed."

"I'll be killed anyway." Cassiopeia looked almost happy, as if she'd successfully passed her Cog Testing, and Lyra didn't know why, knew that couldn't be right. Goosedown, one of Cassiopeia's other genotypes, stood hugging herself, as if she were the one getting yelled at. They were identical except for the vacancy of Goosedown's expression. She'd had a habit, when she was little, of smacking her own head against the ground when she was frustrated, and she still had to wear diapers to sleep. "Isn't that right? We'll all die here eventually. What's the difference?"

"Let it go, Maxine." Nurse Dolly was climbing to her feet, wincing, holding on to her lower back. Lyra was unaccountably angry at Cassiopeia. Nurse Dolly was one of the nicest ones. "It doesn't understand."

Nurse Don't-Even-Think-About-It stood for a moment, still gripping Cassiopeia's wrists. Then, abruptly, she released her and turned away. "Unnatural," she muttered. "Devil's work, all of it."

"Enough." Nurse Curly spoke up this time, addressing everyone. "You two"—she pointed at Goosedown and Bounty, still watching, frozen—"help number six clean up."

But Cassiopeia bolted for the door instead, pushing past Nurse Don't-Even-Think-About-It and shaking Lyra off when Lyra went to touch her arm.

"Grab it!" Don't-Even-Think-About-It shouted, but Nurse Dolly shook her head.

"She'll be back." She sighed. She looked exhausted. There were dark circles under her eyes, and Lyra found herself wondering briefly about the nurse's other life, the one off the island. What would it be like to have a secret world, a private place away from Haven, away from the replicas and the nurses and the Glass Eyes? She couldn't fathom it.

Nurse Dolly met Lyra's eyes, and Lyra looked quickly away.

"There's nowhere for her to run, anyway," Nurse Dolly added, but gently, as if in apology.

Cassiopeia wasn't at lunch. The replicas didn't speak about her. They didn't speak at all. It was difficult to feel comfortable surrounded by half the nursing staff and several guards, all of them posted around the perimeter of the room, silent, expressionless, watching the girls eat, many of them wearing masks or full hazmat suits that made them resemble inflated balloons.

Lyra had no appetite. She was still nauseous, and the smell of the Stew Pot made her stomach clench, as if it wanted to bring something up. But she didn't risk skipping lunch. She didn't want to go into the Funeral Home. So she lined up with the other replicas and filled her plate with mashed potatoes and chicken floating in a vivid red sauce the electric color of inner organs and pushed her food around, cut it into small pieces, hid some in her napkin.

Lyra needed to find a new hiding place. The dorm was no longer safe. She was responsible for changing her own linens—but what if one day she forgot, and the book and the file, her pen and her Altoids tin, were discovered? They'd be taken away and destroyed, and Lyra would never get over it. The book especially—that was her last piece of Dr. O'Donnell, and the only thing that Lyra had ever been given, except for standard-issue clothing and a scratchy blanket for cool nights.

Lyra headed straight to the bunks after lunch. The dorm was mostly empty: after lunch, the female replicas had a half an hour of free time before afternoon physicals. Only a half-dozen replicas had preceded her back, and there was a single nurse on patrol, Nurse Stink, an older woman who chewed special candies made of ginger and garlic for indigestion, and who always smelled like them as a result.

Lyra went straight to bed 24 and, keeping her back angled to the nurse, began stripping the sheets from the bed. At a certain point, she slid a hand between the mattress and the frame and drew out the book, and then the file, at the same time stuffing them down into a pillowcase so they were invisible. Then she headed for the door, pressing the linens tight to her chest, as if they might help muffle the sound of her heart.

"Where are you going?" the nurse asked. She was sitting in a folding chair by the door, fumbling to unwrap one of her candies.

"The laundry," Lyra answered, surprised that her voice sounded so steady.

"Laundry day was yesterday," Nurse Stink said.

"I know," Lyra said, and lowered her voice. "But it's my monthly bleeding."

The nurse waved a hand as if to say, *Go on.*

Lyra turned left to get to the end of D-Wing. But instead of going downstairs to the laundry, she ducked out of the first exit, a fire door that led to the southeastern side of the institute, where the land sloped very gently toward the fence and the vast marshland beyond it. Birds were wheeling against a pale-blue sky, and the stink of wild taro and dead fish was strong. From here, the marshes were so covered in water lettuce they looked almost like solid ground. But Lyra knew better. She'd been told again and again about the tidal marshes, about fishermen and curiosity seekers and adventurers from Barrel Key who'd lost their way among the tumorous growth and had been found drowned.

Lyra hid the bundle of sheets behind a trimmed hedge. She tucked the pillowcase with her belongings in it under her shirt and kept going, circling the main building. She spotted Cassiopeia, sitting motionless by the fence, staring out over the marshes, hugging her knees to her chest. Lyra thought of going to her but wasn't sure what she would say. And Cassiopeia had caused trouble. She'd pushed Nurse Dolly. She'd be put in solitary or restrained to her bed, kept like that for a day or two. Besides, Lyra was still weak, and even the idea of trying to comfort Cassiopeia exhausted her.

She'd need to find a place not too remote; a place she could sneak off to easily without arousing suspicion, but a place unused for other purposes, where no one else would think to look.

She kept going, toward a portion of the island she'd rarely explored, praying nobody would stop her. She wasn't sure whether she was breaking any rules, and if anyone asked what she was doing or where she was going, she'd have no answer.

The northern half of the island remained undeveloped and largely untouched, since it had, decades earlier, belonged to a timber company. Now it was a repository of old equipment, sealed chemical drums, and trailers mounted on cinder blocks and padlocked off, for the most part, with heavy chains. Lyra paused at a rusted gate hung with a large sign warning of biohazardous material. But the gate was unlocked, and she decided to risk it. Half of Haven contained biohazardous material anyway.

Here there were no neatly trimmed hedges or stone walkways. This area was cooler, shaded by coast oak and mature pines with old, sweeping branches, although to Lyra it all looked the same. As she walked, she thought about animals concealed in dark hiding places, gators crawling up beneath the fence, snakes nesting in the trees. Two years earlier, a wild hog had come bursting out of the undergrowth and run circles around the guards in front of the Box. It was one of the few times Lyra could remember seeing any of the doctors laughing.

Old tractors; rusted, coiled-up chains; plastic garbage bins; Dumpsters; even an old crane, arm raised as if reaching for the sky: Lyra moved down the long alley of broken-down equipment, her feet squelching in mud that became thicker and deeper as she approached the tidal flats. The insects were thicker here, and louder, too. She knew she was still within the limits of Haven—she could see the fence through the trees, and the flashing of the late sun on the vivid green marshes, and knew that the nearest guards were only a few hundred feet away—but she felt almost as if she had entered another world. As if she could keep walking forever, moving deeper and deeper into the trees, and never be found. She didn't know whether the idea excited or scared her.

She spotted an old motorboat, propped up on cinder blocks and covered with a blue plastic tarp slicked with mold and moisture. A perfect hiding place. She felt a rush of sudden relief. She was so tired. For a second, when she stopped walking, she thought she heard footsteps behind her. But when she turned around, she didn't see anyone.

She peeled back a portion of the tarp and froze, confused. The bottom of the boat was spotted with rust but relatively dry—and someone, she saw, was already using it for a hiding place. There was a folded brown blanket, standard Haven issue, as well as two neatly folded changes of pants, two shirts, and two folded pairs of male's underwear. There was, additionally, a flashlight and several cardboard containers of powdered milk, a can opener marked *Property of Haven Kitchens*, and half a dozen cans of soup.

Something stirred in her mind—an association, a *connection*—but before she could bring the idea into focus, someone spoke.

"That's mine," a voice said behind her. "Don't touch it."

She turned and her breath caught in her chest.

Her first thought was that the boy was an outsider and had somehow made his way in. He looked so wild, so *fierce*, she felt he must be a different species. Her second thought was that he was hungry. His cheeks stood out sharply from his face, as if they'd been whittled with a knife. His forearms were marked with little diagonal scars, like a tiny staircase cut into his flesh.

Then she noticed the Haven bracelet—a White—and the idea she'd been reaching for earlier arrived, neat and obvious and undeniable: this was 72. The Code Black. The runaway.

Except he hadn't run away, or at least he hadn't run far. He'd been here, on the north side of the island, the whole time.

"I know you," she said. "You're seventy-two."

He didn't deny it. "How did you find me?" He took a step toward her, and Lyra could smell him then—a sharp animal smell, not completely unpleasant. "Which of them sent you?"

"Nobody sent me," she said. She didn't like being so close to him. She'd never been this close to one of the males, and she couldn't help but think of Pepper, and a diagram she'd seen once of a pregnant woman, who seemed to be digesting her baby. But there was nowhere to go. The side of the boat was digging into her back. "I wasn't looking for you at all."

"Then what are you doing here?" he asked.

She hesitated. She was still holding the pillowcase with all her belongings, and she squeezed it to her chest. "I didn't mean anything by it," she said.

He shook his head. "I can't let you go," he said. He reached out, taking hold of her wrist.

And at that exact moment, the world exploded.

SEVEN

LATER THE RESIDENTS OF BARREL Key would tell stories about seeing the explosion. Several fishermen, bringing in their boats, were nearly thrown overboard by a freak wave that came racing over the sound—caused, it later turned out, by a portion of A-Wing crashing through the fence and collapsing into the shallows. Missy Gallagher saw a finger of flame shoot up in the distance and thought of Revelation and the end of days. Bill Collops thought of terrorists and ran into the basement, screaming for his wife to help him with the boxes of ammo.

The first bomb, detonated in the entry hall, directly next to the bust of Richard Haven, made shrapnel of the walls and beams and caved in the roof. It killed twenty-seven staff members, all of them buried under the rubble. The woman who was carrying the explosives strapped by means of a cookie sheet to her chest was blown into so many pieces that even her dental records were useless, and they were able to establish her identity only because she had left a bag explaining her motivations and affiliation with the Angels of the First Savior on the mainland, which would subsequently be discovered by soldiers. Her WordPress account, which referenced at length a website known as the Haven Files, suggested she was acting on directives from Jesus Christ to destroy the unnatural perversions at Haven and purge the sinners playing God. The blog had a brief three-hour surge of notoriety and readership before it was permanently and mysteriously erased.

The second and third bombs created a fireball that roared through the halls, reaching temperatures hot enough to sear metal and leave the plastic dinner trays as molten, shapeless messes. Things would not have been so bad were it not for the close proximity of a large shipment of amyl nitrate, which one of the staff members had signed for and thoughtlessly left still packaged in the entry hall, not entirely sure where it was meant to go.

Later, rumors would circulate: that the bomber believed Haven Institute was actually *manufacturing humans* to use in some kind of devil's army, and that both the creations and their creators should be punished by fire; that she had every single page of the Haven Files, all seventy-six of them, printed out, underlined, annotated, and laminated in her bag next to a copy of the Bible, a small image of

Jesus on the cross, and a half-eaten ham and cheese sandwich; that she must have been onto something, because of the military crackdown, and the men in hazmat suits who spent weeks sweeping the island, carting off debris, leaving Spruce Island bare and ruined and silent. And why didn't the story make it onto the news, or any of the major newspapers? *Conspiracy,* Bill Collops said, polishing his guns. *What a world,* Missy Gallagher said, shaking her head.

The official story—the one that made it onto the news—stated that chemicals had been mishandled by a new laboratory technician, sparking a huge chemical fire that engulfed the laboratory. But even this story, once established, was quickly suppressed, and Spruce Island, and what may or may not have happened there, was rapidly forgotten.

Of course Lyra didn't and couldn't know any of this at the time. At the time, she thought the sky had split apart. At the time, she thought the world was ending.

EIGHT

THE FORCE OF THE FIRST blast threw her off her feet. She landed palms-down in the mud, with 72 beside her. Her eyes stung from the sudden vapor of dust, which seemed to rise all at once and everywhere, like a soft exhalation. People were screaming. An alarm kept hitting the same high note of panic, over and over, without end.

It was the sound that paralyzed her: shock waves of sound, a screaming in her ears and the back of her teeth, the sound of atoms splitting in two. It took her a second to realize that 72 was no longer beside her. He was on his feet, running.

But after only a few feet he stopped, and, turning around, saw her still frozen, still belly down in the mud like a salamander. He came back. He had to yell to be heard over the fire and the screaming.

"Move," he said, but even his words sounded distant, as

if the ringing in her ears had transformed them to vague music. She couldn't move. She was cold and suddenly tired. She wanted to sleep. Even her mouth wouldn't work to say *no.* "Move now." She wasn't very good at judging feelings, but she thought he sounded angry.

She was focusing on very small details: the motion of a rock crab scuttling sideways in the churned-up mud, the hiss of wind through the trees that carried the smell of smoke, the male's bare feet an inch from her elbow, his toenails ringed with dirt.

Then 72 had her elbow and she was shocked back into awareness of her body. She felt blood pumping through her heart, valves opening and closing like eyelids inside of her.

"Now," 72 said again. "Now, now." She wondered whether his mind had become stuck on the word, whether like Lilac Springs and Goosedown and so many others his brain had never formed right. She grabbed the pillowcase from the ground where it had fallen. It had gone a dull, gray color, from all the shimmering dust. The Altoids tin landed in the dirt but she had no time to stop and retrieve it. He was still holding on to her elbow, and she wasn't thinking well.

A drumbeat pop-pop-popping sound made her heart lurch, because she knew what it was: every so often the guards, bored, fired at alligators that swam too close to the island. She thought there must be alligators—but the alligators would burn—she wondered whether their hides would protect them. . . .

They went back through the broken machinery, moving not toward the marshes but toward the sound of roaring fire and screams. Ash caught in Lyra's throat and made breathing painful. She didn't think it strange that they were heading back toward the fire—she could see a shimmering haze of smoke in the distance, beyond the trees, smoke that seemed to have taken on the silhouette of a building—because she knew they needed to find a nurse, they needed to line up, they needed to be told what to do. The nurses would tell them. They would make things better. She longed in that moment for Squeezeme and Thermoscan, longed to feel the familiar squeeze of pressure on her arm and suck down the taste of plastic, longed to be back in bed number 24, touching her windowsill, her headboard, her sheets. They moved past the chemical drums and squeezed through the fence through which Lyra had come looking for a hiding place. She was still holding the pillowcase to her chest with one arm and felt a little better, a little more clearheaded.

But as they came into view of the institute, she stopped. For a second she felt one of the bullets must have gone through her, punched a hole directly in her stomach. She could no longer feel her legs. She couldn't understand what she was seeing. It was like someone had smashed up reality and then tried to put it together all wrong. A-Wing was gone and B-Wing was on fire. Flames punched through windows and roared across the tar roof. Guards sprinted across the yard, shouting in voices too distorted to make out.

There were bodies in the grass, human bodies, bodies wearing the sensible flat shoes of the nurses and doctor uniforms stained with blood, arms flung out as if they'd done belly flops to the ground. From a distance, it was impossible to distinguish the people from the replicas except by their clothing.

One body appeared to have been lifted off its feet and carried down toward the beach—Lyra could just see, in the distance, waves breaking against a pair of legs—or maybe someone had been down on the beach when the explosion had come. Lyra thought of Cassiopeia and her seashell collection and, although she had seen replicas die and die and die, felt vomit rise in her throat. *The vomiting center is located in the rear part of the brain.* She had heard that once, from one of the nurses. She didn't remember when.

But now 72 was headed not back to safety, not to the nurses and doctors and gentle Glass Eyes, good Glass Eyes, watchful Glass Eyes, but directly toward one of the guard towers. Now people were pouring from the other wings, nurses and doctors dazed or crying, covered with soot so they looked as if they'd been cast in stone. For the first time, Lyra realized that they, too, were afraid. That none of this was planned. That no one was coming to tell them what to do.

She stumbled on something in her path: a long pale arm, wrist tagged with a green plastic bracelet. The fingers twitched. A female, Lyra thought, because of the shape of the hands. She was buried beneath a heavy sheet of tin siding that had been hurled across the yard by the first explosion. Lyra saw the fingers curl up in a fist: she was alive, whoever she was.

"Wait," she said, pulling away from 72 and crouching down to try and free the girl. "Help," she said, when 72 just stood there, squinting into the distance, looking agitated. He frowned but moved next to her, and together they managed to shift the metal.

Beneath it, Cassiopeia was lying on her back, her face screwed up in pain. Her left leg was twisted at the knee and a gash on her thigh had soaked her pants through with blood. But she was alive. Lyra knelt and touched Cassiopeia's face. Cassiopeia opened her eyes.

"Lyra," she said, or appeared to say. Her voice was so faint Lyra couldn't hear it.

"Leave it," 72 said.

"She needs a doctor," Lyra said, bringing a hand to Cassiopeia's back and helping her sit up. Her hand came away wet and dark with blood. It wasn't just her leg that was injured.

"There are no more doctors. There's no more Haven. It's done," 72 said. Lyra felt a liquid panic, as if her lungs were slowly filling with water, like in dreams where she was in the ocean and couldn't find her way to the surface.

There was no world without Haven. Haven *was* the world.

And now the world was burning: the flames had spread to C-Wing and waves of heat reached them even from a distance. The guards were still shouting—doctors were crawling on their hands and knees in the dirt—there were replicas in a line, kneeling, hands behind their heads, pinned in place by the guards with their guns—Lyra couldn't understand any of it.

She helped Cassiopeia to her feet. Cassiopeia was sweating and smelled terrible. She had to lean on Lyra heavily and go half shuffling, half hopping across the yard. In the middle of it all Lyra thought how strange it was to be so physically close to someone. She and Cassiopeia had never touched except by accident, when they were washing up at the same sink, and even when they played with the newest crops, to touch and tickle them, it was because they had to. Nurse Em had put an arm around Lyra once, but Lyra couldn't remember why, only that for days afterward she had touched her own shoulder, trying to make it tingle. Even Dr. O'Donnell had never done more than touch Lyra's forehead when she had a fever. This felt like being with Squeezeme, but more, bigger. She wanted to cry.

The guard tower was empty, the post abandoned. The smell of rotten fish and sea kelp was almost overwhelming, as if the smoke had underscored and sharpened it. Lyra at last saw where they were heading: almost directly below the guard tower was an area where the fence had been damaged, yanked out of the ground by winds or by one of the wild hogs that still roamed the island at night.

Seeing that 72 meant to go beneath it, she stopped again, dizzy with the heat and the noise and the harsh animal sounds of screaming. Cassiopeia's breath sounded as if it was being sucked in and out of an air pump, and Lyra could feel Cassiopeia's heart beating hard through her back and ribs, blood racing around to all those fragile veins. But there was a hole somewhere, a puncture. Her shirt was heavy and warm with blood.

Help. She thought the word to no one and to everyone. She knew that people believed in a God who would help them, but God hated the replicas and didn't care whether they lived or died because he hadn't made them. Dr. Saperstein had made them. He was their God. *Help.* She wanted nothing but to return to D-Wing, to lie down in the coolness of the dormitory and pretend nothing had happened.

"If you stay here, you'll die," 72 said, as if he knew what she was thinking. But he'd released her and no longer seemed to care whether she followed him or not. He went first, sliding on his back feetfirst underneath the gap.

A smell reached her—something sweet and hot she recognized from the Funeral Home as the smell of blood. She looked back at the institute, steadying Cassiopeia on her feet. The dormitories were gone. The peaked roof of A-Wing, normally visible, was gone. In its place were nothing but rolling storm clouds of smoke, and spitting angry fire.

It took forever to get Cassiopeia beneath the gap. Her eyes were closed and even though her skin was hot, she was shivering so badly Lyra could barely keep ahold of her. Lyra had to repeat her name several times, and then her number, before she responded. She was passing in and out of sleep. Finally 72 had to bend down and take her by the arms, dragging her roughly free of the fence, her damaged leg twisted awkwardly behind her. She cried out in pain. This, at least, woke her up.

"What's happening?" she kept repeating, shaking. "What's happening?"

Lyra was next. But before she could get through the fence, she heard a shout behind her. She'd been spotted. One of the guards, face invisible behind his helmet, was sprinting toward her, and she was temporarily mesmerized by the look of his gun, the enormity of it, all levers and scopes. She'd only seen the guns from a distance and didn't know why this one should be aimed at her, but for a split second she imagined the bullets screaming almost instantaneously across the distance that separated them, imagined bullets passing through layers of skin.

"Stop!" Now she could hear him. "Stop where you are."

Instead she dropped to her stomach and slid beneath the gap, shimmying her hips free when for a moment the bottom of the fence snagged on her pants. The guard was still shouting at her to stop but she was out, out and free and once again helping Cassiopeia to her feet. She didn't know why she was so afraid, but she was. At any second she expected to hear the chitter of bullets on the fence, feel her heart explode sideways, cleaved in two by a bullet.

But the shots didn't come, although the guard was still shouting, still coming toward them. At that second there was another rocketing blast (the fire had found its way to the storerooms in the basement of B-Wing, stocked with old chemical samples, medications, solutions marked *flammable* and *dangerous*), a final explosion that shot a plume of green flame fifty feet into the air and made the ground shudder. Cassiopeia slipped and fell backward in the mud. Lyra stumbled, and 72 caught her. For a few seconds they were inches apart, and she could smell him again, and see the fine dark line around his irises, light contracting his pupils, narrowing them to pinpoints.

From above came hailstones of granite and cement, several of them lobbing over the fence and thudding only a few feet from where they were standing. The guard had dropped to his knees and covered his head, and Lyra saw their chance. Together, she and 72 hauled Cassiopeia to her feet and went with her into the marsh. Lyra wasn't sure what they were going to do about Cassiopeia. Already she regretted taking her along. But Cassiopeia was number 6. Like Lyra, she was Gen-3, the first successful crop. Lyra had known her for as long as she could remember.

The water was warmer than she had expected, and cloudy with dirt. Banks of waist-high grass grew between stretches of thick mud and tidal pools scummy with dead insects, all of it new and strange to her, words and feelings she didn't know, sensations that tasted like blood in her mouth and panic reaching up to throttle her. Several years ago, the replicas had been woken by screaming: a man a half-mile from Spruce Island had his leg ripped off at the hip by an alligator before the guards scared it by firing into the air. He was airlifted to a nearby hospital. The nurses had for once allowed them out of their beds to watch the helicopter land with a noise like the giant whirring of insect wings, white grasses flattened by the artificial wind. Once, when she was a child, she'd even seen an alligator sunning itself on the rocky beach on the southernmost tip of the island, not four feet from the fences. She had been amazed by its knobby hide, its elongated snout, the teeth protruding jaggedly from its mouth, and she remembered standing there flooded with sudden shame: God had made that creature, that monster with a taste for blood, and loved it. But he had not made her.

She felt as if they were walking through endless tunnels bound entirely by mud and grass, and couldn't imagine that 72 knew where he was going, or where he was leading them. Cassiopeia was crying, and only the smoke still lodged in Lyra's chest, still turning the sun to a dull red ember and smudging away the sky, kept Lyra from crying, too. Haven, gone. They were outside the fence. They were in thin, unbound air, in a world of alligators and humans who hated and despised them. They were running away from safety and Lyra didn't know why. Only that the guard had come at her with a gun, looking as if he wanted to shoot.

Why had he drawn his gun? The guards were there for their own protection. To keep the outside world *out*. To keep the replicas safe.

The mosquitoes, at least, had been chased off by the smoke, although no-see-ums were still hovering in swarms over the water, and Lyra got some in her nose and mouth and even beneath her eyelids. From here, the sound of the fire was strangely musical and sounded like the steady roar of a heavy rain. But the sky was green-tinged and terrible, and the ash floated down on them.

Her arms were shaking from trying to keep Cassiopeia on her feet. Even the pillowcase felt impossibly heavy. Cassiopeia was clinging so tightly to her neck, Lyra could hardly breathe. Cassiopeia was passing in and out of consciousness, and Lyra imagined her mind like a series of ever-branching tunnels, like the marshland crisscrossed by fine veins of water, going dark and then light again.

"How much farther?" Speaking hurt.

72 just shook his head. She knew that human men were in general stronger than women and wondered whether the same thing was true of replicas. He looked strong—the muscles of his back and shoulders stood out—though he couldn't have been eating well since he escaped. She wondered where he'd gotten his food. She wondered why he'd been so desperate to get out, and whether he knew something she didn't. Or maybe he was just crazy—plenty of replicas had lost their minds before, like how Lilac Springs had lost her mind during her examinations, had forgotten all the numbers she was supposed to remember. There was Pepper, who'd used a knife to open her wrists, and number 220, who'd simply stopped eating,

and number 35, who'd started believing she was one of the rats and would only crawl on all fours. Maybe 72 was like that. Maybe he believed he was an animal and should roam free.

She couldn't go on anymore. Cassiopeia was too heavy. Every breath felt like it was hitching on a giant hook in her chest. She tried to call out to 72 but realized she didn't have the energy even for that. Instead she struggled with Cassiopeia into the reeds, finding footing on the muddy banks that stretched like fingers through the water, until the ground solidified and she could sit. 72 had to double back when he realized she was no longer behind him.

"We aren't safe here," 72 said. He didn't sound like he'd lost his mind. She noticed how dark his eyes were, so they appeared to absorb light instead of reflecting it. "I should leave you," he said after a minute.

"So leave," she said.

But he didn't. He began forcing his way through the reeds, snapping them in half with his hands when they resisted too strongly. The grass was so high and thick here it cut the sky into pieces. "Lie down," he instructed her, and she did. Cassiopeia was already stretched out in the mud, lips blue, eyes closed, and that sick animal smell coming off her, like the smell in the Funeral Home that no amount of detergent and bleach could conceal. Lyra could see now the glint of something metal wedged in her back, lodged deep. The muscle was visible, raw and pulsing with blood. Instinctively she brought a hand to the wound, but Cassiopeia cried out as if she'd been scalded and Lyra pulled away, her hand wet with Cassiopeia's blood. She didn't know how to make the bleeding stop. She realized she didn't know how to do anything here, in this unbound outside world. She'd never eaten except in the mess hall. She'd never slept without a nurse ordering *lights out*. She would never survive—why had she followed the male? But someone would come for her. Someone must. One of the doctors would find her and they would be saved. This was all a mistake, a terrible mistake.

Lyra squeezed her eyes shut and saw tiny explosions, silhouettes of flame drifting above Haven. She opened her eyes again. Cassiopeia moaned, and Lyra touched her forehead, as Dr. O'Donnell had once done for her. Thinking of Dr. O'Donnell made her breath hitch in her chest. There was no explanation for that feeling either— none that she knew of, anyway.

Cassiopeia moaned again.

"Shhh," Lyra said. "It's all right."

"It's going to die," 72 said flatly. Luckily, Cassiopeia didn't hear, or if she did, she was too sick to react.

"It's a she," Lyra said.

"She's going to die, then."

"Someone will come for us."

"She'll die that way, too. But slower."

"Stop," she told him, and he shrugged and turned away. She moved a little closer to Cassiopeia. "Want to hear a story?" she whispered. Cassiopeia didn't answer, but Lyra charged on anyway. "Once upon a time, there was a girl named Matilda. She was really smart. Smarter than either of her parents, who were awful." *Matilda* was one of the first long books that Dr. O'Donnell had ever read to her. She closed her eyes again and made herself focus. Once again she saw fire, but she forced the smoke into the shape of different letters, into words floating in the sky. *Extraordinary.* In the distance she heard a mechanical whirring, the sound of the air being threshed into waves: helicopters. "Her dad was a used-car salesman. He liked to cheat people. Her mom just watched TV." *Safe,* she thought, picturing the word pinned to clouds. "Matilda liked to read."

"What is that?" 72 asked, in a low voice, as if he was scared of being overheard. But he sounded angry again.

"It's a story," she said.

"But . . ." He shook his head. She could see sand stuck to his lower lip, and dust patterning his cheekbones. "What *is* it?"

"It's a book," she said. "It's called *Matilda.*" And then,

though she had never admitted it to anyone: "One of the doctors read it to me."

72 frowned again. "You're lying," he said, but uncertainly, as if he wasn't sure.

"I'm not," she said. 72, she'd decided, was very ugly. His forehead was too large and his eyebrows too thick. They looked like dark caterpillars. His mouth, on the other hand, looked like a girl's. "I have a book here. Dr. O'Donnell gave it to me. . . ." But all the breath went out of her lungs. She had reached into the pillowcase and found nothing, nothing but the file folder and the pen. The book was gone.

"I don't believe you," 72 said. "You don't know how to read. And the doctors would never—" He broke off suddenly, angling his head to the sky.

"I don't care whether you believe me or not," she said. The book was gone. She was suddenly freezing. She wondered whether she should go back for it. "I had it right here, it was *here*—"

"Quiet," he said, holding up a hand.

"I need that book." She felt like screaming. "Dr. O'Donnell gave it to me so I could practice—"

But this time he brought a hand to her mouth and pulled her into him as she kicked out and shouted into his palm. She felt his warm breath against her ear.

"Please," he whispered. The fact that he said *please*

stilled her. No one said please, not to the replicas. "Be quiet."

Even when she stopped struggling, he kept her pinned to him, breathing hard into her ear. She could feel his heart through her back. His hand tasted like the mud of the marshes, like salt. Sweat collected between their bodies. Insects whined.

Now the air was being segmented, cut into pulsing rhythms as if mimicking a heartbeat. The helicopters were getting closer. The sound became so loud she wanted to cover her ears. Now a wind was sweeping across the marshes, flattening the grass, driving up mud that splattered her legs and face, and just as the sound reached an unbearable crescendo she thought 72 shouted something. He leaned into her. He was on top of her, shielding her from a roar of noise and wind. And then he relaxed his hold and she saw a dozen helicopters sweep away across the marshes toward the ruins of Haven. Inside them and hanging from the open helicopter doors were helmeted men wearing drab brown-and-gray camouflage. She recognized them as soldiers. All of them had guns.

Lyra, Cassiopeia, and 72 lay in tense silence. Several helicopters went and returned. Lyra wondered whether they were bearing away the injured like they'd done for the man who'd lost his leg to an alligator, who lay screaming in the darkness while the guards lit up the water with bullets. Every time one of the helicopters passed overhead she was tempted to reveal herself, to throw up an arm or stand up out of the long grass and the knotted trees and wave. But every time, she was stopped as though by an enormous, invisible hand, frozen on the ground where she was. It was the way they churned the air to sound that made her teeth ache. It was the memory of the guard with his gun drawn, shouting at her. It was 72, lying next to her.

For a long time in the lulls they could still hear men shouting and the roar and crackle of the fire blazing on the island. Voices hung in the ashy haze, were carried by it like a bad smell. After a while, however, Lyra thought the fire must have stopped, because she could no longer hear people yelling. At the same time she realized that she could hardly see. The sky, which for hours had been the textured gray of pencil lead, was now dark. The sun was setting, and the wind when it hissed into life carried a heavy chill. The rain swept in next, the thunderstorms that always came in the early evening, quick and ferocious, punching down on them. By the time it had passed, the sun was gone.

Cassiopeia was completely still. Lyra was afraid to touch her and find she was dead, but when she did she felt a pulse. Periodically the sky was lit up with helicopters passing back and forth, and every so often, a shout carried over the water. Lyra thought of her small clean bed under the third window in the dorm and had to swallow back the urge to cry again. She wouldn't have thought she could be so cold, and so afraid, and also have to fight so hard against sleep. At some point she must have drifted off because she woke from a nightmare of monsters with long metal snouts, and felt 72 put a hand against her mouth again, and lean his weight against her to speak into her ear.

"They're searching the marshes," 72 whispered. "Stay quiet. Don't move. Don't even breathe."

Her heart was still racing from the nightmare. It was so dark, she could hardly make out Cassiopeia lying even a few feet away. But after a second she saw light flashing through the tall grass, tiny suns blazing and being drowned. She heard voices, too—not the panicked and indistinct shouting of earlier but individual voices and words.

"Over here. That's blood, boys."

"Christ. Like a slug trail."

"You bring any salt . . . ?"

She was afraid. Why was she afraid? She didn't know. She wasn't thinking clearly. The guards were on her side. They had kept the others out—they kept the replicas safe. But still fear had its hand down her throat. This was her chance to change her mind, to call out, to be rescued. 72 shifted next to her, and she stayed silent.

"Here's one." One of the men raised the cry and lights flashed again, dazzling over the dark water, as several other soldiers joined him where he stood. She wanted so badly to look—but even as she started to raise herself onto her elbow, 72 jerked her back to the ground.

"Stay put," he whispered. She heard laughter from the soldiers, more words half blown by wind.

"Bring a—?"

"No point . . . dead . . ."

"No bodies . . . left . . ."

"It looks real, doesn't it?"

Lyra was filled with a cold so deep it felt like a pit. *It looks real, doesn't it?* She knew they'd found another replica—a dead one—and wondered what she would look like to them if they came across her with their flashlights: like something mechanical, a machine, or like a doll with moving parts. She imagined herself like a jigsaw puzzle—she had seen one, once, in the nurses' break room—well-crafted, neatly jointed, but full of seams and cracks visible to everyone else. She wondered whether humans had some invisible quality, the truly critical one, she'd never be able to replicate.

They were coming closer, slowing through the water. Now she couldn't have cried out even if she wanted to.

Her lungs had seized in her chest. She had to grind her teeth to keep them from chattering.

"More blood over here, see?"

Lyra's heart stopped. The men were just on the other side of the embankment. Their flashlights slanted through the grass—were they well enough concealed? Would they be seen?

"Keep an eye out for gators. These marshes are crawling."

"Maybe we should give Johnson up for bait."

More laughter. Lyra squeezed her eyes shut. *Move on,* she thought, still uncertain whether this was the right thing. All she knew was that she didn't want them to see her. They couldn't see her. *Move on.*

Then there was a horrible sucking, gasping noise, like water fighting through a stuck drain. For one confused second, Lyra couldn't tell where it was coming from. Then she realized Cassiopeia was trying to speak.

"Help." The word was mangled, distorted by the sound of liquid in her lungs.

"No, Cassiopeia," Lyra whispered, dizzy now with panic. But already she knew it was too late. The soldiers had gone silent.

Cassiopeia spoke a little louder. "Help."

"In here." One of the men was already crashing through the trees toward them, and the marshes were once again alive with lights and shouting. "There's someone in here."

"Leave her. *Leave* her." 72's voice, when he whispered, was raw with panic. This time Lyra didn't resist, didn't even argue. 72 was going elbow over elbow into the tangle of growth. She crawled after him as fast as she could on her stomach. The ground trembled under the weight of the soldiers' boots as she fought deeper into the growth. Pine needles grabbed her face and arms and scored tiny cuts in her skin. She was too scared to look back. She was certain they would be heard, crashing through the grass, but the soldiers were loud, calling to one another in a rapid patter she didn't understand.

Then the trees released them into a heavy slick of puddled mud and water: they'd reached another sudden opening in the land, a place where the marsh became liquid. 72 slid into the water first and Lyra pulled herself in next to him just as a beam of light swept over the bank where she'd been. She slipped down to her chin, gasping a little, certain they must have heard her, and then submerged herself to her eyes. The beam of the light continued sniffing along the mud like something alive. Twelve inches from her, then ten . . .

"There's a trail here," one of the men called out, crashing through the growth, kicking aside the spindly branches lit up by his flashlight. Lyra knew they were finished. "Looks like something crawled out this way."

The light inched closer, touching the water now, so close to her nose she drew back. . . .

"Found it."

The light froze where it was. If it had truly been an animal it would have been close enough to lick her. Then the soldier on the bank turned and retreated in the other direction.

"Dead or alive?"

"What the fuck, alive."

"Doesn't look like it."

How many were there? Three? Four? It was so hard to tell. How many were out there in the marshes with their lights and boots and heavy guns?

Cassiopeia spoke up one more time, faintly now. "Help me."

"Awww, Jesus Christ. There's blood all over the place. It got a bullet in the back or something."

"Might as well put a bullet in the front, too. No way it's gonna make it all the way to base."

"Are you kidding? You know how expensive these things are to make? Might as well take a dump on a hundred grand."

Beneath the surface, something slick and heavy brushed Lyra's arm, and she stifled a scream. She wondered if even now there were alligators circling them in the dark, or snakes with sleek black bodies and poisonous fangs. High above them the stars glittered coldly in a perfectly clear sky.

"Damn it. All right then. On three?"

"You're kidding, right? It's bleeding. That's how it spreads."

"Not unless you eat them, you dumb shit. What's the matter? You hungry?"

More laughter. There were definitely three of them. At least three. For the first time in her life, something black and deep and hateful stretched out of Lyra's stomach. She hated them. She hated that they could laugh and that they were afraid to touch Cassiopeia. She hated their easy way of talking. She hated that she could look like a human, and yet she was not a human, and they could tell.

But just as quickly as it had come, the hatred passed. She was cold and tired and scared. She had no energy to be angry, too.

At least the soldiers were going, and leaving Cassiopeia behind after all.

"It's already dead," one of them said. "See? Let one of the cleanup crews get to it tomorrow." There was the sound of a boot against a body, several hard thumps. Lyra sank down another inch in the water, as if she could flood the sound from her ears.

If there were alligators in the water, they could chew off her feet and she wouldn't notice . . . or maybe her feet were already gone, maybe the pain had numbed her . . . the idea was so awful it struck her as funny. She might be standing there on two stumps, bleeding out into the swamp like Cassiopeia.

"It's all right. They're gone now." In the darkness 72's features were softened. Then she realized she'd been laughing out loud, laughing and shivering. The men were gone. The marshes were silent and still except for another helicopter that took off in the distance and swept out toward Barrel Key. She waded out of the water after him, slipping on the mud.

"What if they come back?" she asked, through the hard freeze in her chest. She knew it couldn't really be cold. 72 didn't seem cold at all, and the nurses had been complaining only yesterday about the awful heat. The cold must have somehow been inside, lodged in her chest like the piece of metal that got Cassiopeia in the back. She wanted to go and look at Cassiopeia, to make sure she was really dead. But she was so tired.

"They won't be back," he said. "They'll finish searching the marshes, but they won't come back, not for a while at least. Lie down," he said, and she did, so tired that she didn't even pull away when he lay down next to her. Already she was half-asleep, drowning in a tangled liquid dream. But when he put his arms around her, she jerked briefly awake.

"The human body," he said, without letting go of her, his voice low and sleepy, "is full of nerve cells."

"I know," she said, reassured, "ten trillion of them."

She was asleep again, and dreaming of ten trillion nerves lighting up like stars against a bloodred, pulsing sky.

NINE

SHE WOKE UP WARM, SWEATING, from a dream she couldn't remember. The smell of smoke was fainter now. Her cheek was crusty with mud. The shock of what had happened had passed. She knew immediately where she was but not what had woken her. But something *had* woken her.

She sat up, wondering what time it was. Her body ached. She knew from the darkness it must still be the middle of the night. Beside her, 72 was sleeping with both hands folded beneath his head and his mouth open. He looked much younger when he slept.

Even before she heard a footstep she knew that someone was nearby and that this, the sound of someone close, was what had woken her. She took hold of 72's arm, and he came awake at the same time she heard a girl speak.

"What now?" she said. "Do you think we can still

get—?" But she abruptly fell silent, and Lyra realized she had made a sound without meaning to.

They must be more soldiers sent to comb the marshes. And yet the girl didn't speak like a soldier, and wasn't moving like one, either, with a fearlessness born from their guns. These people—she had no doubt they were people, and not replicas—were doing their best to stay quiet. Almost as if they, too, were afraid of being seen.

Who were they? What did they want?

72 was alert now, listening. The people—whoever they were—seemed to be just on the other side of the misshapen trees that grew all through the marshes; Nurse Don't-Even-Think-About-It had said they were bad luck. Lyra and 72 had to move. She shifted into a crouch, and a twig snapped beneath her weight.

"Don't move," 72 whispered. "Don't move."

But it was too late. She heard crashing in the brush. In the darkness all the sounds were confused, and she didn't know what had happened and whether they'd been found.

"Who's there?" 72 called out. But no one answered.

Lyra stood up and plunged blindly in one direction, sliding a little on the mud, her own breath harsh and alien-sounding. Pain ripped through her heel where she stepped: the marshes were full of toothy things, plants and animals that bit back, a world of things that only wanted to draw blood, and for a second she was aware of the stars infinitely high above her, the distance and coldness of them, a long dark plunge into emptiness. There was nowhere to go, nowhere to run. In the world outside Haven she was nothing, had no past and no future.

Shadows moved on her left. Something heavy hit the ground, and the girl cried out.

Lyra froze. She'd run in exactly the wrong direction, straight toward the strangers and not away from them.

"Jesus. Jesus Christ."

"That voice." The girl spoke again. "Where did it come from?"

"I don't know. Christ, Gemma. *Look* . . ."

Lyra heard coughing, as if someone was trying not to throw up. This, the evidence of side effects, calmed her. Maybe she'd been wrong. Maybe these were replicas who'd somehow escaped the way she did. She inched forward, parting the tangle of grasses with a hand, until she saw a boy silhouetted in the moonlight, his hand to his mouth, and the girl crouching beside him, whimpering.

"What the hell? What the hell?" he kept saying.

The moon broke loose of the clouds and clarified their features. Forgetting to be afraid, Lyra went forward.

"Cassiopeia," she said, because she was confused, still half in shock. Of course the girl couldn't be Cassiopeia, just like it couldn't be any of her genotypes, 7–10:

Cassiopeia was dead, and her genotypes didn't have soft brown hair, soft *everything*, a pretty roundness to their faces and bodies. Lyra stopped again, seeing in the grass next to the girl the body, the slender ankles and familiar wristband, the blood darkening her shirt. Cassiopeia. And yet the girl crouching next to her had Cassiopeia's face and round little nose and freckles. A genotype, then, like Calliope and Goosedown and Tide and Charmin, but one that Lyra didn't know. Were replicas made in other places, too? It was the only thing she could think of that made sense.

The boy stumbled backward, as if he was afraid Lyra might attack him. The girl—Cassiopeia's replica, identical to her except for the extra weight she carried and the hair that grazed her shoulders—was staring at Lyra, mouth open as though she was trying to scream but couldn't.

Finally Cassiopeia's replica said, "Oh my God. I think—I think she's one of them."

"Who are you?" Lyra managed to say. "Where did you come from?"

"Who are *you*?" The boy had a nice face, geometric, and she found it easy to look at him.

"Lyra," she said, because she decided there was no point in lying. "Number twenty-four," she clarified, because wherever they came from, they must have number systems, too. But they just stared at her blankly. She couldn't understand it. She felt as she had when she had first started to read, staring at the cipher of the letters, those spiky evil things that kept their meaning locked away.

"Oh my God." The girl brought a hand to her mouth. "There's another one."

Lyra turned and saw 72 edging out into the open, holding a knife. He must have stolen it from the kitchen before escaping, and she doubted it was very sharp, but the strangers didn't know that. Now the boy had both hands out. Lyra thought he looked nervous. For a split second he reminded her of the nurses, and the narrow way they looked at the replicas, and she almost hoped that 72 would hurt him.

"Look," he said. He wet his bottom lip with his tongue. "Hold on a second. Just hold on."

"Who are you?" 72 came to stand next to Lyra. She couldn't tell what he was thinking. His face, so open in sleep, had closed again, and she had never learned how to read other people's moods and feelings, had never been taught to.

"We're nobody," the boy said. Slowly he helped the girl to her feet. She was wearing normal clothing, Lyra noticed. People-clothing. She understood less than ever. "Listen, we're not going to hurt you, okay? My name's Jake Witz. This is Gemma. We got lost in the marshes, that's all."

Lyra was now more confused than ever. "But . . ." She met the girl's eyes for the first time. It was hard to look at her with Cassiopeia, poor Cassiopeia, lying dead at her feet between them. Who would come to collect her body? Who would bundle her up for burning? "Who made you?"

"What?" the girl whispered.

"Who made you?" Lyra repeated. She'd never heard of other places like Haven, and she felt a small stirring of hope, as if a heavy locked door in her chest had just been unlatched. Maybe there were places for them to go after all, places where there were people to take care of them like they'd been cared for at Haven, places with high walls to keep everyone else out.

"I—I don't understand," the girl said. Her eyes were so wide Lyra could see a whole portion of the night sky reflected in them.

"You're a replica," Lyra said impatiently. The girl was slow, much slower than Cassiopeia. But she knew that this wasn't uncommon. She thought of Lilac Springs—dead now, probably. And 101, who'd never even learned how to hold a fork. She wondered how many of the others had burned.

"A what?" the girl whispered.

"A replica," Lyra repeated. The girl shook her head. Where she came from, they must be called something different. She recited, "An organism descended from or genetically identical to a single common ancestor."

"A clone," the girl said, staring at Lyra so fixedly she was reminded of being under the observation lights, and looked away. "She means a *clone*, Jake."

"Yeah, well. I kind of already had that impression," the boy said, and he made a face, as if he was offended by the sight of Cassiopeia's body.

Lyra had the sudden urge to reach down and close Cassiopeia's eyes and wasn't sure where it had come from—maybe something one of the nurses had said about the way people buried one another. In Haven, the dead replicas had always simply been burned or dumped.

"But—but it's impossible." The girl's voice had gotten very shrill. "It's impossible, the technology doesn't exist, it's *illegal*. . . ."

Lyra lost patience. The girl was either suffering from side effects or she was very, very stupid to begin with. *Failure to thrive.* "It's not impossible," she said. "At Haven, there were thousands of replicas."

"Jesus." The boy closed his eyes. His face was like a second moon, pale and glowing. "Clones. It all makes sense now. . . ."

"Are you crazy? *Nothing* makes sense." The girl had turned away, covering her mouth with her hand again, as if she was trying to force back the urge to be sick. "There's a *dead girl* with *my face* on her. We're standing here in the middle of the fucking night and these—these people are telling me that there are clones running around out there, thousands of them—"

"Gemma, calm down. Okay? Everyone needs to calm down." The boy spoke loudly even though the girl was the only one who wasn't calm, or the only one who was showing it, at least. "Can you put that thing down, please?" This was to 72, still holding the knife. "We're not going to hurt you."

Suddenly Lyra was hit with a wave of dizziness. She went into a crouch and put her head between her knees. Her head was full of a hot and sticky darkness, a swirling that reminded her of heavy clouds of circulating gnats.

"What's the matter with her?" She heard the girl's voice, but distantly. If 72 responded, she didn't hear him.

"Hey." A minute later, the girl was next to her. "Are you okay?" She put a hand on Lyra's back, and Lyra jerked away. She was used to being touched, manipulated, even opened up with knives and needles; but this felt different, intimate and almost shameful, like when she'd first been caught by Nurse-Don't-Even-Think-About-It in the bathroom with her hands submerged in bleach, trying to scrub her first period blood from her underwear. She couldn't speak. She was afraid that if she opened her mouth, she would throw up. The girl stood up again and moved away from her, and Lyra almost regretted jerking away. But she didn't want to be touched by strangers, not anymore, not if she could help it.

Except—she remembered falling asleep, exhausted, on the ground, the way the stars had blurred into a single bright point, leading her into sleep—she hadn't minded when 72 put his arms around her for warmth. But she was in shock, exhausted. She had needed the body heat. The world outside was too big: it was nice to feel bounded by something.

"Maybe she's hungry," the boy said.

She wasn't hungry, but she stayed quiet. The worst of the nausea had released her, though. Strange how it came like that in dizzying rushes, like getting hit in the head. She sat back, too exhausted to stand again. She was no longer afraid, either. It was obvious that the strangers weren't there to hurt them or to take them anywhere. Now she just wished they would move on. She didn't understand the girl who was a replica but didn't know it. She didn't understand the boy who was with her, and how they were related.

72 took a quick step forward. "You have food?"

The boy looked to Cassiopeia's genotype, and she made a quick, impatient gesture with her hand. He shrugged out of his backpack and squatted to unzip it. Lyra had never had the chance to observe two males so close together, and noticed he moved differently from 72. His move-ments were slow, as if his whole body hurt. 72 moved with a quickness that seemed like an attack. "Sorry. We didn't bring much."

72 came forward cautiously. He snatched up a granola bar and a bottle of water and then backtracked quickly. 72 tore open the granola bar with his teeth, spitting out the wrapper, and began to eat. He kept his eyes on the boy—Jake—the whole time, and Lyra knew that he was worried the boy might try to take it back from him. But Jake only watched him.

72 opened the water, drank half of it, and then passed it to Lyra without removing his eyes from Jake. "Drink," he said. "You'll feel better."

She hadn't realized how raw her throat felt until she drank, washing away some of the taste of ash and burn-ing. She wished that Jake and Cassiopeia's replica would leave so that she could go back to sleep. At the same time, she was worried about what the morning would bring when they found themselves alone on the marshes again, with no food, nothing to drink, nowhere to go.

"Look." The boy was talking to Lyra. Maybe he'd decided she was easier to talk to. Maybe he hadn't forgot-ten that 72 had a knife. "I know you must be tired—you've been through—I don't even *know* what you've been through . . ."

"Jake . . ." Cassiopeia's replica pressed her hand to her eyes.

"They've been living in Haven, Gemma," the boy said quickly. "My father died for this. I need to know."

Father. The word sent a curious tremor up Lyra's spine, as if she'd been tapped between her vertebrae. So Lyra was right about him: he was natural-born.

"Jake, *no*." Cassiopeia's replica—the boy had said her name was Gemma, Lyra remembered now—looked and sounded like one of the nurses. Jake fell silent. "I don't believe you," she said. "I literally don't believe you. These poor people have been through God knows what—they're starving and cold and they have no place to go—and you want to *interview* them—"

"I don't want to interview them. I want to understand."

Lyra took another sip of water, swallowing despite the pain. "Not people," she said, because the girl had been nice to them and she thought it was worth correcting her.

Gemma turned to stare at Lyra. "What?"

"We're not people," Lyra said. "You said, 'These poor people have been through god knows what.' But we're replicas. God didn't make us. Dr. Saperstein did. He's *our* god." She stopped herself from pointing out that Gemma, too, must have been made by someone, even if she didn't know it.

Gemma kept staring, until Lyra finally felt uncomfortable and looked down at her hands. Had she said the wrong thing again? But she was just reciting what she knew to be true, what everyone had always told her.

Finally Gemma spoke again. Her voice was much softer now. "We should camp here for the night," she said. For an instant, she even sounded like Dr. O'Donnell. "We'll go back to Wahlee in the morning."

"We're not going anywhere with you," 72 said quickly. Lyra was surprised to hear him say *we*. She had never been a *we*. Maybe he'd only confused the word, the way she still confused *I* and *it* sometimes.

"No," Gemma said. "No, you don't have to go with us. Not unless you want to."

"Why would we want to?" 72 asked. In the dark he was all hard angles, like someone hacked out of shadow. Now Lyra wasn't sure whether he was ugly or not. His face kept changing, and every time the light fell on it differently he looked like a new person.

Cassiopeia's replica didn't blink. "You can't plan on staying here forever. You have no money. No ID. You're not even supposed to exist. And there will be people looking for you."

The girl was right. *You're not even supposed to exist.* Lyra knew the truth of these words, even though she wasn't sure exactly what they meant. Hadn't that been the point of the guards and the fences? To keep the replicas safe, and secret, and protected? Everyone who had known them had despised them. *You're not supposed to exist.* Wasn't that what the nurses were always saying? That they were monsters and abominations? All except Nurse Em, all those years ago, and Dr. O'Donnell. But both of them had gone away.

Everyone went away, in the end.

"Can I have more water?" she asked, and so somehow it was decided. 72 turned to look at her with an expression she couldn't read, but she was too tired to worry about him and what he thought and whether they were making the right decision.

Neither of the strangers wanted to sleep near Cassiopeia's body, so they moved instead through the thick patch of hobble-backed trees and tall grasses streaked with bird guano, leaving the corpse behind. Lyra didn't understand it. She liked being near to Cassiopeia's body. It was comforting. She could imagine she was back at Haven, even, that she and Cassiopeia were just lying in separate cots across the narrow space that divided them.

Gemma, the girl, suggested she try a soda. Lyra had never had soda before. At Haven, the vending machines were for the staff only, although sometimes the nurses took pity on the younger replicas and gave them coins from the vending machines to play with, to roll or flip or barter. Her first impression was that it was much, much too sweet. But she felt better after a few sips, less nauseous. Her hands were steadier, too.

Gemma found a clean sweatshirt in the bottom of Jake's bag and offered it to 72, but he refused. So instead Lyra took it, though it was far too big and she did nothing but pull it on over the filth of her regular shirt. She was warm now, but she was also comforted by the feel of clean cotton and the smell of it, like the laundry detergent they used at Haven that sent the sheets back stiff and crisp as paper. This sweatshirt wasn't stiff, but soft, so soft.

She curled up on the ground and 72 sat next to her.

"I don't trust them," he whispered, looking over to where the boy and girl were making camp, arguing over who should be allowed to use the backpack as a pillow. "They're not like us."

"No," she said. Her tongue felt thick. Her mind felt thick, too, as if it had also been blanketed in cotton. She wanted to say: *We don't exist.* She wanted to say: *We have no choice.* But even as she reached for the words, the cord tethering her thoughts snapped, and she was bobbing, wordless, mindless, into the dark.

It seemed she'd barely fallen asleep before she was jerked into awareness again by movement beside her. She sat up and saw 72 half on his feet with the knife in his hand.

The girl Gemma was standing above them, and for a confused second, before the clutch of dream fully released her, Lyra again mistook her for Cassiopeia and felt a leap of feeling she had no name for.

"It's okay," the girl said. "It's just me. Gemma, remember?"

72 lowered his knife. Lyra thought he must have been having a bad dream. He looked pale. They'd woken up very close together, side by side again. She wondered whether he'd reached for her again in the middle of the night. For body heat. A person's average body temperature fell during sleep, she knew, sometimes by a full degree. Another thing she had heard and remembered.

"There are still men on the island," Gemma said immediately. "They're burning what's left of Haven."

"You saw them? You got close?" The other one, Jake, had woken, too. He stood up, shoving a hand through his hair. Lyra had always been fascinated by hair—she and the other replicas had their scalps shaved every week—and was temporarily mesmerized by the way it fell. "You should have woken me. It's not safe."

Lyra barely heard him. She stood, too, despite the fact that her legs felt gelatinous and uncertain. The sky was getting light. "What do you mean, they're burning what's left of Haven?"

"Just what I said," Gemma said.

Lyra had a sudden explosion of memories: the smell of the Stew Pot in the morning and the way the sunlight patterned the linoleum; the courtyard paths splotched with guano; the medicinal smell of a swab on her arm, the pinch of a needle, a voice murmuring she would be okay, okay. All her friends, Squeezeme and Thermo-scan and even the Glass Eyes, who could never entirely be trusted—all of them gone. Lyra's memories felt right then like physical things, punching up into her conscious-ness. The small cot with her number fixed to the steel headboard. Showerheads arrayed in a row and the smell of soap-scented steam and the echo of dozens of voices. Laundry day and trash day and the mournful bellow of the departing barges. Even the things she hated: paper cups filled with pills and vitamins, the nurses sneering at the replicas, or worse, acting as though they were afraid.

Still. Haven was home. It was where she belonged.

"Then there's no going back?" She hadn't realized, fully realized, until the words were out of her mouth that on some level she had been holding on to the idea that this would all pass—the explosions and the fire and the soldiers shouting *stop,* saying, *You know how expensive these things are to make?*—all of it would be explained. Then they would be herded up, they would be returned to Haven, 72 included. They would be evaluated by doctors. The nurses would distribute pills: the prim white Hush-Hush for pain, the slightly larger Sleepers that made the world relax into fog. Everything would return to normal.

"There's no going back," 72 said. He wasn't as hard with her as he'd been the day before. Lyra wondered if it was because he felt sorry for her. "I told you that. They'll kill us if they find us. One way or another, they'll kill us."

Lyra turned away. She wouldn't listen. The guards and soldiers were trained to kill. And she had never liked the doctors or the nurses, the researchers or the birthers with their incomprehensible speech. But she knew that Haven had existed to protect them, that the doctors were trying to keep them safe against the cancers that exploded through the tissue of their lungs and livers and brains, against the diseases that reversed the normal processes of life and made food go up instead of down or lungs drown in fluid of their own creation.

Side effects. The replication process was still imperfect. If it weren't for the doctors, Lyra and 72 would have died years ago, as infants, like so many replicas had, like the whole yellow crop did. She remembered all those tiny bodies bundled carefully in paper sheaths, each of them no bigger than a loaf of bread. Hundreds of them borne away on the barge to be burned in the middle of the ocean.

"We have to get off the marshes. There will be new patrols now that it's light. They'll be looking for survivors."

Gemma was speaking in a low voice, the kind of voice Lyra associated with the nurses when they wanted something: *calm down, deep breath, just a little burn.* "Come with us, and we'll get you clothes, and hide you someplace no one will be looking for you. Then you can figure out where to go. *We* can figure it out."

"Okay," Lyra said, because 72 had just opened his mouth, and she was tired of being spoken for, tired of letting him decide for her. He wasn't a doctor. He had no right to tell her what to do. But she had followed him and she had to make the best of it.

Besides, she didn't think Gemma wanted to hurt them, though she couldn't have said why. Maybe only because Gemma was Cassiopeia's replica, although she knew that was stupid—genotypes often had different personalities. Number 120 had tried to suffocate her own genotype while she slept, because she wanted to be the real one. The only one. Cassiopeia was nice to Lyra, but Calliope liked to kill things. She had once killed a bird while Lyra was watching. And 121 had never spoken a single word.

"Okay, we'll go with you," she said a little louder, when 72 turned to look at her. She was pleased when he didn't argue, felt a little stronger, a little more in control. Cassiopeia's replica would help them. They needed to know what had happened to Haven and why. Then they could figure out what to do next.

Jake and Gemma had come on a boat called a kayak. Lyra had never seen one before and didn't especially want to ride in it, but there was no choice. Gemma and Jake would have to go on foot, and there might be places so deep they'd have to swim. Neither 72 nor Lyra had ever learned to swim, and she nearly asked him what he had meant by trying to escape Haven, how he'd expected to survive. When she was little she had sometimes dreamed of escape, dreamed of going home on the launches with one of the staff members, being dressed and cared for and cuddled. But she had learned better, had folded that need down inside of her, stored it away. Otherwise, she knew, she might go crazy, like so many of the other replicas who'd chosen to die or tried to sneak out on the trash barges with the nurses and been killed by exhaust in the engine room.

Once again, she wondered if 72 was just a little bit crazy.

Being in the kayak felt like being on a narrow, extremely wobbly gurney. The seat was wet. Her stomach lurched as 72 shoved the kayak into the shallows and then clambered in himself, refusing Jake's help. She couldn't believe they didn't just sink. She was uncomfortably aware of the sloshing of the water below her, which seemed to be attempting to jettison her out of her seat. She was afraid to move, afraid even to breathe.

But miraculously, the kayak stayed afloat, and 72 soon got the hang of paddling. The muscles in his arms and shoulders stood out when he moved, and Lyra found him unexpectedly beautiful to watch. She began to relax, despite the painful slowness of their progress and the continued rhythm of motorboats in the distance, and the ripples from their wakes that sent water sloshing into the kayak.

She should be afraid. She didn't know much about feelings, but she knew that Gemma was afraid, and Jake was afraid, and even 72 was afraid. But for some reason, for a short time, the fear released her. She was floating, gliding toward a new life. She had never thought she'd know what it felt like to be out on the water, had never imagined that a life outside Haven could exist. The outside world, constantly visible to her through the fence, had nonetheless seemed like the soap operas she sometimes saw on the nurses' TV: pretty to look at but essentially unreal.

But the novelty soon wore off. The insects were thick. Gnats swarmed them in mists. They hardly seemed to be moving. Tendrils of floating grass made certain routes impassable and had to be manually separated or threshed aside with a paddle. Several times Gemma lost her footing in the water and nearly went under. Lyra wondered how long they would be able to go, whether they would make it. She wondered whether they would have to leave Gemma behind, and thought of Cassiopeia lying in the reeds while the sun burned away her retinas.

She felt a momentary regret but didn't know why. Death was natural. Decay, too. It was another thing that made replicas and humans similar: they died.

Finally Gemma called them to a stop. Lyra was relieved for the break and the chance to get off the water, especially now that the midmorning sun was like an exposed eye.

They'd barely dragged the kayak out of the water when Jake yelled, "Get down."

The hum of an approaching helicopter suddenly doubled, tripled in volume. Lyra's breath was knocked away by its pressure. They went into a crouch beneath the fat sprawl of a mangrove tree as the helicopter roared by overhead. The whole ground trembled. Marsh grass lay flat beneath the wind threshed from the helicopter's giant rotor. Looking up through the branches, Lyra saw a soldier leaning out of the open door to point at something on the horizon. Then the helicopter was gone.

They left the kayak behind and went the rest of the way on foot. The ground was soft and wet and they had to wade through tidal pools where the mud was studded with sharp-toothed clams and splinters of broken shells. The growth here was different, the trees taller and less familiar to Lyra. She felt as if they were moving deep in an undiscovered wilderness and was shocked when instead Gemma gave a cry of relief and the trees opened up to reveal a small dirt clearing, corroded metal trash bins, and various signs she was too tired to read.

"Thank God," Gemma said. Lyra watched as Jake moved to a dusty car parked in the lot and loaded his backpack into it. She was afraid all over again. She knew about cars because she'd seen them on TV and Lazy Ass was always complaining about hers, *piece-of-shit,* but she didn't think she wanted to ride in one. Especially since, according to Lazy Ass's stories, at least, cars were always breaking down or leaking oil or giving trouble in some way.

But once again, they had no choice. And at the very least, being in the car felt better, sturdier, than being in the kayak, although as soon as Jake began bumping down the road, Lyra had to close her eyes to keep from being sick. But this only made things worse. The car was louder, too, than she'd thought it would be. The windows rattled and the engine sounded like a wild animal and the radio was so loud Lyra thought her head would explode. They were going so fast that the outside world looked blurry, and she had to close her eyes again.

To calm herself she recited the alphabet in her head, then counted up from one to one hundred. She listed all the constellations she knew, but that was painful: she imagined Cassiopeia's face, and Ursa Major's obsession with hoarding things from the mess hall—old spoons and paper cups, bags of oyster crackers and packages of mustard—and wondered whether she would ever see any of the other replicas again.

"Hey. Are you all right? It's okay—we're stopped now."

Lyra opened her eyes and saw that Gemma was right: they had stopped. They were in what looked like an enormous loading dock, but filled with dozens and dozens of parked cars instead of boats—*a parking lot*, another idea she'd absorbed from the nurses without ever having seen it. Could all the cars belong to different people? Looming in the distance was a building three times the size of even the Box. W-A-L-M-A-R-T. Lyra flexed her fingers, which ached. She had been holding tight to her seat without realizing it.

"You guys can stay here, okay?" Gemma said. "Just sit tight. We're going to buy food and stuff. And clothes," she added. "Do you know your shoe size?"

Lyra shook her head. At Haven they were provided with sandals or slippers. Sometimes they were too big, other times too small, but Lyra so often went barefoot she hadn't thought it mattered.

"Okay." Gemma exhaled. "What did you say your names were again?"

"I'm Lyra," Lyra said. "And this is seventy-two." She was distracted. Outside the car, Jake was speaking on a cell phone. Lyra felt a twinge of nervousness. Who was he calling? Every so often, he glanced back into the car as if to make sure that Lyra and 72 were still there. What if 72 was right, and Jake and Gemma couldn't be trusted?

"Seventy-two?" Gemma repeated. "That isn't a name."

"It's my number," 72 said shortly.

"I'm twenty-four," Lyra said, by way of explanation. "But one of the doctors named me." 72 looked faintly annoyed, but Lyra knew he was probably just jealous, because he didn't yet have a name.

"Wow," Jake said. "And I thought being named after my father was bad. Sorry," he added quickly. "Dumb joke. Just . . . stay here, okay? We'll be back in ten minutes."

For a while, 72 and Lyra sat in silence. Lyra figured out how to roll down the window but found no relief from the heat outside. It was what Nurse Don't-Even-Think-About-It had called molasses-hot. She watched Jake and Gemma as they narrowed into brushstrokes and then disappeared into W-A-L-M-A-R-T. Gemma's reference to a grandmother bothered her—but it excited her, too, because of what it meant.

Finally she said, "I don't think the girl knows she's a replica."

72 had been staring out the window—fists lodged in

his armpits, hunched over as though he were cold, which was impossible. He turned to her. "What?"

"The girl's a replica. But I don't think she knows it." The idea was taking shape now, and with it the simple suggestion of possibility, of a life that might exist on the other side of Haven. At the same time, she was afraid to voice the possibility out loud, aware that it would sound silly and afraid of what 72 would say. "Which means . . . well, maybe she comes from a place where being a replica doesn't make a difference. Where they have families and drive cars and things like that."

Lyra could see herself reflected in 72's eyes. They were the color of the maple syrup served in the Stew Pot on special occasions, like Christmas and the anniversary of the first God's death. "Is that what you want?" he said at last. "You want a family?"

"I don't know." Lyra turned away from him, embarrassed by the intensity of his stare, which felt like being back in the Box, like being evaluated, having her eyes and knees tested for reflexes. Her idea of *mother* looked much like the nurses and the Haven staff. Mother was someone to feed and clothe you and make sure you took your medicines. But now, unbidden, an image of Dr. O'Donnell came to her. She imagined herself tucked up in a big white bed while Dr. O'Donnell read out loud. She remembered the way that Dr. O'Donnell's hands had smelled, and the feel of fingertips skimming the crown of her head. *Good night, Lyra.* And there were her dreams, too, impressions of a birther who held and rocked her, and a cup with lions around its rim. When she was younger she had searched the mess hall for such a cup before being forced to admit that all the glasses at Haven were plain, made of clear plastic. She knew her dreams must be just that—dreams, a kind of wishful thinking.

But she was too ashamed to confess what she was thinking: that she could find Dr. O'Donnell. That Dr. O'Donnell could be her mother. "What do you want?" Lyra asked instead, turning to 72. "You ran away, even if you didn't get far."

"I couldn't," 72 said. "I couldn't figure out a way past the guards."

"You must have been hoping that something like this would happen," Lyra said, and a suspicion flickered: Could 72 have somehow been responsible for the disaster at Haven? But no. That didn't make any sense. They were standing together when the explosion happened. They were touching.

72 frowned as if he knew what she was thinking. "I didn't hope for anything," he said. "I was just waiting for my chance."

"But you must have had a plan," she insisted. "You

must have had an idea of where you would go on the other side."

"I didn't have a plan." He leaned back, closing his eyes. As soon as he did, he once again looked much younger. Or not younger, exactly. Stripped down, somehow, naked. Lyra remembered that once she and Ursa Major and Cassiopeia had spied on the males' dormitory from the courtyard. Through a partially open blind they'd seen the blurry and bony silhouette of one of the males shirtless and they'd stumbled backward, shocked and gasping, when he turned in their direction. Looking at 72 gave Lyra the same feeling of peering through those blinds, and left her excited and also terrified.

She was almost relieved when he opened his eyes again.

"You asked me what I want. I'll tell you what I don't want. I don't want to spend the rest of my life being told what to do, and what to eat, and when to sleep, and when to use the bathroom. I'm tired of being a lab rat."

"What do you mean, *a lab rat*?" It was so hot, Lyra was having trouble thinking. Once or twice she'd been sent into B-Wing for some reason or another and seen the milk-white rats in their cages, had seen when they threaded their paws through the bars the elongated pinkness of their strangely human fingers. And some of them were suffering in some stage of an experiment, bloated with pain or covered in dozens of tumorous growths, so heavy they couldn't lift their heads.

"I watched," he said simply. "I paid attention." He turned his face to the window. "When I was little, I didn't know the difference. I thought I might be an animal. I thought I must be."

Lyra had an uncomfortable memory again, of number 35 crawling on all fours, insisting on eating her dinner from a bowl on the ground. But number 35 had been soft in the brain. Everyone said so.

"Aren't you worried about what will happen?" she asked. "Without medicine, without check-ins, with no one to help us when we get sick? We weren't *made* for the outside."

But even as she said it, Lyra thought again of Dr. O'Donnell. She *knew* how the replicas were built. She was a doctor and she'd worked at Haven. She could help.

"You really believe." It wasn't a question. He had turned back to her. "You believe everything they ever told you."

"What do you mean?" she asked. It was so hot. Her face was hot. He was looking at her like some of the nurses did, like she wasn't exactly real, like he was struggling to see her.

But before he could answer, Jake was back, sliding behind the wheel.

"Sorry," he said. "Forgot to leave the AC on. I realized

you guys must be baking. Hot as balls today, isn't it?"

72 was still watching Lyra. But then he turned back toward the window.

"Yes," he said. It was the first time he'd spoken directly to one of the humans except in anger, and Lyra noticed that Jake startled in his seat, as if he hadn't really expected a reply. "Hot."

TEN

LYRA HAD NEVER SEEN SO many houses or imagined that there could be so many people in the world. She knew the facts—she'd heard the nurses and doctors discussing them sometimes, problems with overpopulation, the division between rich and poor—and the nurses often watched TV or listened to the radio or watched videos on their phones when they were bored. But knowing something was different from seeing it: house upon house, many of them identical, so she felt dizzyingly as if she were going forward and also turning a circle; car after car lined up along the streets, grass trim and vividly green. And people everywhere. People driving or out on their lawns or waiting in groups on corners for reasons she couldn't fathom.

Jake stopped again at one of these houses, and Gemma got out of the car. Lyra watched through the window as a girl with black hair emerged from the house and barreled into Gemma's arms. Lyra was confused by this, as she was by Jake and Gemma's relationship, the casual way they spoke to each other, and the fact that Gemma was a replica but didn't know it. But she was confused by so much she didn't have the energy to worry about it.

For several minutes, Gemma and the other girl stood outside. Lyra tried to determine whether this second girl, the black-haired one, was a replica or a regular human but couldn't tell, although she was wearing human clothes and her hair was long. She used her hands a lot. Then the girl went inside, and Gemma returned to the car alone.

"April's going to open the gate," she told Jake. She sounded breathless, though she hadn't walked far. "You can park next to the pool house."

Jake advanced the car and they corkscrewed left behind the house. Lyra saw a dazzling rectangle of water, still as a bath, which she knew must be a pool. Even though she couldn't swim, she had the urge to go under, to wash away what felt like days of accumulated dirt and mud and sweat. There were bathtubs in Postnatal, and even though they were too small to lie down in, Lyra had sometimes filled a tub and stepped in to her ankles after it was her turn to *tickle, engage, and maintain physical contact* with the new replicas.

When the gate closed behind them with a loud clang,

Lyra truly felt safe for the first time since leaving Haven. Contained. Controlled. Protected.

Next to the pool was a miniature version of the big house. Sliding doors opened into a large carpeted room that was dark and deliciously cold. The house was mostly white, which Lyra liked. It was like being back in Haven. Goose bumps ran along Lyra's arm, as if someone had just touched her. Where the carpet ran out was a kitchen alcove that Lyra identified only by its stove: it looked nothing like the kitchen in Stew Pot, a vast and shiny space filled with the hiss of steam from industrial dishwashers. Through an open door she saw a large bed, also made up with a white sheet and blankets and so many pillows she couldn't imagine what they were all for. And lined up on bookshelves next to the sofa: books. Dozens of books, four times as many as she'd seen in the nurses' break room, so many that in her excitement the titles blended together and she couldn't make out a single one.

She wanted to touch them. Their spines looked like different-colored candies the nurses exchanged sometimes, like the sugared lozenges the replicas got sometimes when they had coughs. But she was almost afraid to, afraid that if she did they would all blow apart. She wondered how long it would take her to read every book on the shelves. Months. Years, even. Maybe they would be allowed to stay here, in this clean and pretty room, with the sun that patterned the carpet and the soft hum of hidden air-conditioning.

At W-A-L-M-A-R-T, Gemma had bought Lyra and 72 new clothes—"nothing fancy, and I had to guess how they would fit"—soap, shampoo, toothbrushes and tooth-paste, and more food, including cereal and milk, granola bars, cans of soup she said she could show them how to heat in the microwave, and at least a dozen frozen meals. She showed them where the shower was—a single shower stall, the first Lyra had ever seen—and apologized that there was only one bed.

"So, you know, you'll have to share, unless one of you wants to take the sofa," she said. Lyra felt suddenly uncomfortable, remembering Pepper and her unborn baby, and how she'd been found with her wrists open; the Christmas parties when the doctors got drunk and some-times visited the dorms late at night, staggering on their feet and smelling sharply of alcohol swabs. That was why it was better for males and females to stay apart. "I know you must be exhausted, so we're going to leave you alone for a bit, okay? Just don't go anywhere."

Lyra didn't bother pointing out that they had nowhere to go.

"Get some sleep," Gemma said. The more Lyra looked at her, the less she resembled Cassiopeia and her other genotypes. That was the funny thing about genotypes, something the nurses and doctors, who could never tell them apart, had never understood. If you looked, you could see differences in the way they moved and spoke and used their hands. Over time, their personalities changed even the way that they looked. And of course Gemma was much heavier than Cassiopeia, and had long hair to her shoulders that looked soft to the touch. Gemma was nicer than Cassiopeia. More prone to worry, too. But they had the same stubbornness— that Lyra could see, too.

As soon as they were alone, Lyra went to the bookshelves. She could feel 72 watching her, but she didn't care and couldn't resist any longer. She reached up and ran a finger along the spines, each of them textured differently, some of them gloss-smooth and hard and others soft and crumbly like dirt. L-I-T-T-L-E W-O-M-E-N. *Little Women.* T-H-E G-O-L-D C-O-A-S-T. When she thought of *The Little Prince,* lost somewhere on the marshes, she still felt like crying. But these books made up for it, at least a little.

"You were telling the truth," 72 said. He was watching her closely. "You can read." He made it sound like a bad thing.

"I told you. Dr. O'Donnell taught me." She kept skipping her fingers over the titles and, as she did, read out loud: "*The Old Man and the Sea. The Long Walk. The Hunger Games.*"

He came to stand next to her. Again she could smell him, an earthy sweetness that made her feel slightly dizzy. She'd never found out which of the males Pepper had been with, although Cassiopeia had said a male doctor, because of what happened at the Christmas party, because Pepper had been chosen. But she wondered, now, whether instead it was 72.

"Is it hard?" he asked.

"At the beginning," she said. She didn't know why she was thinking of Pepper. She took a step away from 72. "Not so much when you get the hang of it."

"I thought only people could read," he blurted out. When she turned to look at him, surprised by the tone of his voice, he turned away. "I'm going to get clean."

A moment later, she heard the shower pipes shudder and the water start in the bathroom—a familiar sound that lulled her once again into exhaustion. She didn't understand 72 and his rapid changes of mood. But he'd chosen to stay with her. He hadn't left her behind. Maybe this complexity was a feature of the male replicas—she didn't know, had never been allowed to interact with them.

She removed the file she'd taken from its filthy pillowcase and placed it carefully on the desk below the windows. Although she had a roomful of books now—*a room full of books*, an idea so exciting it made goose bumps on her arms again—the folder, and the single sheet of paper it contained, was her final tether to home. She recognized an old patient report—she'd seen enough of her own reports to recognize a version of the form still in use. But she was too tired to read, and she left the folder open on the desk and returned to the shelves, no longer trying to make sense of the words, just admiring the way the letters looked, the angles and curls and scrolled loops of them.

"I'm all done now."

She hadn't heard the shower go off or 72 emerge from the bathroom. She turned and froze. His skin, which had been streaked with blood and caked in a layer of sediment and crusted mud, was now as shiny and polished as a beach stone, and the color of new wood. His eyelashes, grayed by the ash, were long and black. A towel was wrapped around his waist. She was struck again by the strangeness of the male's body, the broadness of his shoulders and the torqued narrowness of his muscled waist.

"Thank you," she said, snatching up the clothes Gemma had left for her. She was careful not to pass too close to him when she moved into the bathroom. She shut the door firmly, a little confused by the mechanism of the lock. At Haven, all the doors locked with keypads or codes, except for the bathrooms, which had no locks at all.

She stripped down and balled her filthy clothes in a corner. She had never showered alone before and it felt wonderful: the big echoey bathroom, the space, the aloneness of it. Was this how all people lived? It felt luxurious to her. She spent a few minutes adjusting the taps, delighted by how quickly the water responded. In Haven, there was never enough hot water. The soap Gemma had bought was lilac-scented and pale purple, and Lyra found herself thinking of 72, naked, washing with purple soap, and the urge to giggle bubbled up in her chest, followed by a wave of dizziness. She had to sit with her head between her legs and the water driving down on her shoulders until it passed.

She lathered and rinsed her scalp, scrubbed her ears with a pinkie finger, washed the soles of her feet so that they became so slippery it was treacherous to stand. Finally she felt clean. Even the towels here were better than they were at Haven, where they were thin and stiff from hundreds of washings. Her new clothes felt soft and clean. Gemma had bought her cotton underwear in different colors. She'd never had underwear that was anything but a bleached, dingy beige. Looking at herself in the mirror, she almost could have passed for a real person, except for the length of her hair. She fingered the scar above her right eyebrow. She had scars all over her body now, from spinal taps and harvesting operations to test her blood marrow, but when she was dressed, most of them were concealed. Not this one, though.

In the bedroom, she found 72 stretched out on top of the covers, staring up at the ceiling fan. He was wearing new jeans that Gemma had bought for him, and this fact seemed only to emphasize his shirtlessness and the smooth muscled lines of his chest and shoulders. She'd never noticed how beautiful bodies could be. She'd thought of them only as parts, machine components that serviced a whole. She'd been interested in the males, of course—curious about them—but she'd also learned that curiosity led to disappointment, that it was better not to want, not to look, not to wonder. But she was suddenly terrified of lying next to him, although she couldn't have said exactly why. Maybe because of what had happened to Pepper. But she thought it was more than that.

"What?" 72 sat up on his elbows. "Why are you looking at me like that?"

"There's no reason." Realizing she'd been staring, she forced herself to move to the bed. She slipped under the sheets—these, too, softer than any she'd ever known—and curled up with her knees to her chest, as far from 72 as possible. But still her heart was beating fast. She felt, or imagined she felt, warmth radiating off him. He smelled now a different kind of sweet, like shampoo and soap and fresh-scrubbed skin. For a long time they lay there together and she couldn't stop seeing him next to her, couldn't stop seeing his lashes lying on his cheeks when he closed his eyes and the high planes of his cheekbones and the darkness of his eyes.

He shifted in the bed. He put a hand on her waist. His hand was hot, burning hot.

"Lyra?" he whispered. His breath felt very close to her ear. She was terrified to move, terrified to turn and see how close he was.

"What?" she whispered back.

"I like your name," he said. "I wanted to say your name."

Then the bed shifted again, and she knew he'd rolled over to go to sleep. Finally, after a long time, the tension in her body relaxed, and she slept, too.

When she woke up, it was dark, and for a confused second she thought she was back at Haven. She could smell dinner cooking in the Stew Pot and hear the nurses move between the cots, talking to one another. Then she opened her eyes and remembered. Someone had shut the bedroom door, but a wedge of light showed from the living room. Jake and Gemma were talking in low voices, and something was cooking. The smell brought sudden tears to Lyra's eyes. She was starving, hungrier than she'd been in weeks.

She eased out of bed, careful not to wake 72. She was vaguely disappointed to see they'd been sleeping with several feet of space between them. In her dream they had been entangled again, sweating and shivering in each other's arms. In her dream he'd said her name again, but into her mouth, whispering it.

In the big room, Jake was bent over a computer laptop that sat next to a soda on the coffee table. He smiled briefly at Lyra. She was startled—it had been a long time since anyone had smiled at her, probably since Dr. O'Donnell—and she tried to smile back, but her cheeks felt sore and wouldn't work properly. It didn't matter. She was too late. He'd already turned his attention back to the computer.

Immediately, Gemma was moving away from the stove with a bowl, skirting the table that divided the kitchen from the library—Lyra thought it must be called a library, anyway, since Dr. O'Donnell had told her that libraries were places you could read books for free. "Here," Gemma said. "Chili. From a can. Sorry," she added, when Lyra stared, "I can't cook."

But Lyra had only been wondering at all her freedoms, at the fact that Gemma knew how to shop and get food and clothing. Wherever she'd been made, she must have lived for most of her life among real people.

"You need to eat," Gemma said firmly, and seemed

surprised—and pleased—when Lyra took the bowl and spoon and began to eat so quickly she burned the roof of her mouth. She didn't even bother sitting down, both thrilled and disturbed by the fact that there was no one to yell at her or tell her to keep her seat.

"Transmissible spongiform encephalopathies," Jake said out loud, still bending over his computer. "That's a category of disease. Mad cow is a TSE."

"Okay." Gemma drew out the last syllable. "But what does that mean?" She went to sit next to Jake on the couch, and Lyra licked the bowl clean, after making sure neither of them was looking. Jake kept turning his soda can, adjusting it so that the small square napkin beneath it was parallel to the table's edge.

"I don't know." Jake scrubbed his forehead with a hand and fixed his laptop so this, too, was parallel. "There are just references to it in the report."

Lyra saw that next to Jake's computer was the file she'd stolen from Haven. She set her bowl down on the table with a clatter. "You—you shouldn't be looking at that," she said.

"Why not?" Jake raised an eyebrow. "You stole it, didn't you?"

"Yes," Lyra said evenly. "But that's different."

"It's not like they'll miss it now. The whole place is an ash heap."

In Lyra's head, she saw all of Haven reduced to a column of smoke. Sometimes the bodies that burned came back to Haven in the form of smoke, in a sweet smell that tickled the back of the throat. The nurses hated it, but Lyra didn't.

"Jake," Gemma said.

He shrugged. "Sorry. But it's true."

He was right, obviously. She couldn't possibly get in trouble now for stealing the file or allowing someone else to see it—at least, no more trouble than she was already in. Jake went back to thumping away at the computer. Gemma reached out and drew the file onto her lap. Lyra watched her puzzle over it, frowning. Maybe Gemma couldn't read?

But after a minute, Gemma said, "Lyra, do you know what this means? It says the patient—the replica, I mean"—she looked up as though for approval, and Lyra nodded—"was in the yellow cluster."

The yellow cluster. The saddest cluster of all. Lyra remembered all those tiny corpses with their miniature yellow bracelets, all of them laid out for garbage collection. The nurses had come through wearing gloves and masks that made them look like insects, double wrapping the bodies, disposing of them.

"The Yellows died," she said, and Gemma flinched. "There were about a hundred of them, all from the younger crops. Crops," she went on, when Gemma still looked confused, "separate the different generations. But colors are for clusters. So I'm third crop, green cluster." She held up her bracelet, where everything was printed neatly. *Gen-3, TG-GR*. Generation 3, Testing Group Green. She didn't understand why Gemma looked sick to her stomach. "They must have made a mistake with the Yellows. Sometimes they did that. Made mistakes. The Pinks died, too."

"They all died?" Jake asked.

Lyra nodded. "They got sick."

"Oh my God." Gemma brought a hand to her mouth. She seemed sad, which Lyra didn't understand. Gemma didn't know anyone in the yellow cluster. And they were just replicas. "It says here she was only fourteen months."

Lyra almost pointed out that the youngest had died when she was only three or four months, but didn't.

"You said colors are for clusters," Jake said slowly. "But clusters of what?"

Lyra shrugged. "There are different clusters, and we all get different variants."

"Variants of what?" he pressed.

Lyra didn't know, exactly, but she wasn't going to admit it. "Medicine," she said firmly, hoping he wouldn't ask her anything more.

Gemma sucked in a deep breath. "Look, Jake. It's

signed by Dr. Saperstein, just like you said."

"Dr. Saperstein is in charge of the growth of new crops of replicas," Lyra said. Despite the fact that she was still annoyed at Jake and Gemma for looking at the file—the *private* file, *her* file—she moved closer to the couch, curious to know what they were doing. "He signs all the death certificates." Beneath his was a second signature, a name she knew well. Nurse Em had been one of the nicer ones: Nurse Em had taken care when inserting the needles, to make sure it wouldn't hurt; she had sometimes told jokes. "Nurse Em signed, too."

"Nurse Em." Gemma closed her eyes and leaned back.

"Holy shit," Jake said, and Gemma opened her eyes again, giving Jake a look Lyra couldn't decipher.

"Nurse Em was one of the nicest ones. But she left," Lyra said. An old memory surfaced. She was alone in a hallway, watching Dr. O'Donnell and Nurse Em through a narrow crack in a door. Dr. O'Donnell had her hands on Nurse Em's shoulders and Nurse Em was crying. "Think of what's right, Emily," Dr. O'Donnell said. "You're a good person. You were just in over your head." But then Nurse Em had wrenched away from her, knocking over a mop, and Lyra had backed quickly away from the door before Nurse Em barreled through it.

But that couldn't have been a real memory—she remembered a janitor's closet but that couldn't be right, not when the nurses and doctors had break rooms. And Nurse Em had been crying—but why would Dr. O'Donnell have made Nurse Em cry?

"Let me see that." Jake took the file from Gemma and leaned over the computer again. Lyra liked watching the impression of his fingers on the keys, the way a stream of letters appeared as though by magic on the screen, far too fast for her to read. *Click. Click. Click.* The screen was now full of tiny type, photographs, diagrams. It was dizzying. She couldn't even tell one letter from another. "This report—all of this terminology, TSEs and neural decay and protein folding—it's all about prions."

"Prions?" Gemma said. She'd clearly never heard the word before, and Lyra was glad that for once she wasn't the one who was confused.

"Bacteria, viruses, fungi, and prions," Jake said, squinting at the screen. "Prions are infectious particles. They're proteins, basically, except they're folded all wrong."

"Replicas are full of prions," Lyra said, proud of herself for knowing this. The doctors had never said so directly, but she had paid attention: at Haven, there was very little to do but listen. That was the purpose of the spinal taps and all the harvesting—to remove tissue samples to test for prion penetration. Often when replicas died they were dissected, their bones drilled open, for the same reason. She knew that prions were incredibly important—Dr.

Saperstein was always talking about engineering prions to be better and faster-acting—but she didn't know what they were, exactly.

Jake gave her a funny look, as if he had swallowed a bad-tasting medicine.

"I still don't get it," Gemma said. "What do prions do?"

He read out loud: "'Prion infectivity is present at high levels in brain or other central nervous system tissues, and at slightly lower levels in the spleen, lymph nodes, bone marrow. . . .' Wait. That's not it. 'If a prion enters a healthy organism, it induces existing, properly folded proteins to convert into the disease-associated, misfolded prion form. In that sense, they are like cloning devices.'" He looked up at Gemma, and then looked quickly down again. "'The prion acts as a template to guide the misfolding of more proteins into prion form, leading to an exponential increase of prions in the central nervous system and subsequent symptoms of prion disease. This can take months or even years.'" He put a hand through his hair again and Lyra watched it fall, wondering whether 72's hair would grow out now, whether it would fall just the same way. "'Prion disease is spread when a person or animal ingests infected tissue, as in the case of bovine SE, or mad cow disease. Prions may also contaminate the water supply, given the presence of blood or other secretions. . . .'"

"So prions are a kind of disease?" Gemma asked.

"The bad kind of prions are disease," Jake said quietly.

"That can't be right," Lyra said. She was having trouble following everything that Jake was saying, but she knew that there, at least, he was wrong. She knew that replicas were physically inferior to normal humans—the cloning process was still imperfect, and they were vulnerable. That was the word the doctors and nurses always used when they lined up vitamins and pills, sometimes a dozen in a row. But she'd always thought—and she didn't know why she'd thought this, but she knew it had to do with things overheard, sensed, and implied—that prions were *good*. She'd always had the impression that this was a single way in which replicas were superior to humans: their tissue was humming with prions that could be extracted from them.

She felt a curious tickle at the back of her throat, almost as if she had to sneeze. Sweat prickled in her armpits.

Jake wouldn't look at her. She was used to that.

"Listen to this." Jake had pulled up new writing— so many lines of text Lyra felt vaguely suffocated. How many words could there possibly be? "Google Saperstein and prions and an article comes up from back in the early 1990s. Saperstein was speaking at a conference about biological terrorism. 'Chemical weapons and viral and bacterial agents are problematic. Our soldiers risk exposure even as the weapons are deployed against our enemies. War is changing. Our enemies are changing, growing radicalized and more diverse. I believe the future of biological warfare lies in the isolation of a faster-acting prion that can be distributed via food supply chains.'" Jake was sweating. And Lyra had been sweating too, but now she was cold all over. It felt like she had to use the bathroom, but she couldn't move. "'We might cripple terrorist groups by disseminating doctored medications and vaccinations, which will be unknowingly spread by health care workers in dangerous and remote environments immune to normal modes of attack.

"'All known prion diseases in mammals affect the structure of the brain or other neural tissue and all are currently untreatable and universally fatal. Imagine'"— Jake was barely whispering—"'terrorist cells or enemy insurgents unable to think, walk, or speak. Paralyzed or exterminated.'"

"Oh my God," Gemma said. She brought a hand to her lips. "That's awful."

From nowhere a vision came to Lyra of a vast, dust-filled field, and thousands of bodies wrapped in dark paper like the Yellows had been, still and silent under a pale-blue sky.

What was it that Jake had read?

All known prion diseases in mammals . . . are currently

untreatable and universally fatal.

"Jesus." Jake leaned back and closed his eyes. For a long time, no one said anything. Lyra felt strangely as if she had left her body behind, as if she no longer existed at all. She was a wall. She was the floor and the ceiling. "That's the answer to what they were doing at Haven." Although he'd addressed Gemma, when he opened his eyes again, he looked directly at Lyra, and immediately she slammed back into her body and hated him for it. "Prions live in human tissue. Don't you see?"

Lyra could see. But she couldn't say so. Her voice had dried up. She was filled with misfolded crystals, like tiny slivers of glass, slowly cutting her open from the inside. It was Gemma who spoke.

"They've been experimenting on the replicas," she said slowly. She wouldn't look at Lyra. "They've been observing the effects of the disease."

"Not just experimenting on them," Jake said, and his voice broke. "Incubating them. Gemma, they've been using the replicas to *make* prions. They've been growing the disease *inside* them."

ELEVEN

"I TOLD YOU."

Lyra turned and saw 72, his cheek still crisscrossed with lines from the pillow. He was looking not at Jake or Gemma but directly at Lyra, and she couldn't read his expression. She had spent her whole life listening to doctors talk about the workings of the lungs and liver, the blood-brain barrier, and white blood cell counts, but she had never heard a single one explain how faces worked, what they meant, how to read them.

"I told you," he said again, softer this time, "they never cared. They were never trying to protect us. It was a lie."

"You knew?" she said.

He stared at her. "Didn't you?" His voice was quiet. "Didn't you, really?"

She looked away, ashamed. He was right, of course. Everything had fallen away, the final veil, the game she'd been playing for years, the lies she'd been telling herself. It all made sense now. Numbers instead of names, *it* instead of *she* or *he*. *Are you going to teach the rats to play chess?* They were disposable and always had been. It wasn't that they were more prone to diseases, to failures of the liver and lungs. They'd been manufactured to die.

All the times she felt nauseous or dizzy or couldn't remember where she was or where she was going: not side effects of the treatment, but of the disease. Actually, not side effects at all.

Symptoms.

Gemma stood up. "We've done enough for the night," she said to Jake. Lyra knew that Gemma must feel sorry for them. Or maybe she was only scared. Maybe she thought the disease was contagious.

She wondered how long she had. Six months? A year? It seemed so stupid to have run. What was the point, since she was just going to die anyway? Maybe she should have let the guards shoot her after all.

Jake closed his computer. "It's after ten o'clock," he said, rubbing his eyes. "My aunt's coming back from Decatur tomorrow. I've got to go home."

"Let's pick up in the morning, okay? We'll figure out what to do in the morning." Gemma addressed the words to Jake, but Lyra had a feeling she meant the words for her.

"Are you going to be okay?" Jake asked. He lifted a hand as if he was going to touch Lyra's shoulder, but she took a quick step backward and he let his hand fall.

Lyra shrugged. It hardly mattered. She kept thinking about what Jake had said. *They've been growing the disease inside them.* Like the glass hothouses where Haven grew vegetables and fruit. She pictured her body blown full of air and proteins misfolded into snowflake shapes. She pictured the illustration she'd once seen of a pregnant woman and the child curled inside her womb. They had implanted her. She was carrying an alien child, something deadly and untreatable.

"If you need anything, just give a shout," Gemma said.

"Here." Jake bent over and scrawled something on a piece of paper. Normally Lyra loved to see a person writing by hand, the way the letters simply fell from the pen, but now she didn't care. There was no help Jake could give her. No help anyone could give her. "This is my telephone number. Have you used a telephone before?"

"I know what a telephone is," Lyra said. Though she had never used one herself, the nurses hardly did anything but, and as a little kid she'd sometimes picked up random things—tubes of toothpaste, bars of soap, prescription bottles—and pretended to speak into them, pretended there was someone in another world who would answer.

Jake nodded. "This is my address. Here. Just in case. Can you read this?"

Lyra nodded but couldn't bring herself to meet Jake's eyes.

For several minutes after Gemma and Jake left, Lyra stayed where she was, sitting on the couch. 72 moved around the room silently, picking things up and then putting them down. She was unaccountably angry at him. He had predicted this. That meant it was his fault.

"When did you know?" she asked. "*How* did you know?"

He glanced at her, and then turned his attention back to a small bubble of glass: plastic snow swirled down when he inverted it. "I told you. I didn't know *exactly*," he said. "But I knew they were making us sick. I knew that was the point." He said it casually.

"How?" Lyra repeated.

He set the snow globe down, and Lyra watched a flurry of artificial snow swirl down on the two tiny figures contained forever in their tiny bubble world: a stretch of plastic beach, a single palm tree. She felt sorry for them. She understood them.

"I didn't ever not know," he said, frowning. To her surprise, he came to sit next to her on the couch. He still smelled good. This made her ache, for some reason. As if inside of her, someone was driving home a nail. "I was sick once, as a little kid. Very sick. I remember they thought I was going to die. I went to the Funeral Home." He looked down at his hands. "They were excited. When they thought I couldn't understand them anymore, they were excited."

Lyra said nothing. She thought of lying on the table after seeing Mr. I, the happy chatter of the researchers above her, their sandwich-smelling breath and the way they laughed when her eyes refused to follow their penlight.

"When I was a kid I used to pretend," he said. "I would pretend I was an ant or a lizard or a bird. Anything else. I would catch roaches sometimes coming out of the drains. All the nurses hated the roaches. But even they were better off than we were. They could get out." He opened his palm, staring as if he didn't recognize it, then closed it again in a fist. "It would be better," he said, slightly louder, "if they'd hated us. But they didn't."

About this, too, he was right. Worse than Nurse-Don't-Even-Think-About-It, worse than the ones who were afraid, were the ones who hardly noticed. Who would look not at the replicas but through them, who could talk about what to eat for dinner even as they bundled up dead bodies for burning.

"Why didn't you tell me?" Lyra asked.

"I tried," he said. "Besides, what good would it do?"

She shook her head. She needed someone to blame.

She had never been so angry before—she hadn't even thought she had the right. People, real people, believed they deserved things and were angry when they didn't get them. Replicas deserved nothing, received nothing, and so were never angry.

What kind of God was it, she wondered, who made people who would do what they had done to her?

"Is that why you ran away?" Lyra asked. She felt like crying. She wasn't in physical pain and yet she felt as if something had changed in her body, as if someone had put tubes in her chest and everything was entangled.

"No," 72 said. "Not exactly."

"Why, then?"

He just shook his head. She doubted whether he knew himself. Maybe only for a change. Then he said, "We can't stay here, you know."

Lyra hadn't expected this. "Why not?"

"We're not safe here," he said, and his expression turned again, folded up. "I told you. I don't trust them. They aren't replicas."

"The girl is," Lyra said.

He frowned. "She doesn't know it," he said. "No one's told her."

"But we don't have anywhere else to go," she said, and once again realized how true it was. How big was the world? She had no idea. They'd driven for what felt like hours today, and there had been no end to the roads and shopping complexes, streets and houses. And yet Gemma had told her they were still in Florida. How much farther did it all go on? "Besides, what does it matter?" *We'll just die anyway,* she almost added, but she knew he understood.

"I didn't come this far to be a toy," he said. "I could have gone back to Haven for that."

Lyra didn't know what he meant, exactly, but she could guess from his tone of voice. "They've been good to us," she said. "They helped us. They fed us. They gave us clothes and somewhere to sleep."

"Exactly. So what do they want? They must want something. They're people," he said. "That's what they do. Don't you see? That's all they *ever* do. They want."

Was that true? She didn't know. What had Dr. O'Donnell wanted from her? Or Nurse Em, who always smiled at the replicas, who had once told Lyra she had pretty eyes, who saved up her old ferry tokens to give to the young kids to play checkers with?

But maybe that was why they had left Haven: they did not fit in. She still didn't understand what made people so different from replicas, had never been able to understand it. And she had wanted things too, in her life. She had wanted to learn to read. She had been hungry, cold, and tired, and wanted food and her bed. But it was true she had never hurt anyone to get what she wanted.

Was that what made her less than human?

"Is that enough for you?" 72 said. He scared her when he looked this way, and reminded her of the statue in the courtyard at Haven, whose face, deformed by rain, was sightless and cold. "Someone to feed you and order you around, tell you when to sleep? Like a dog?"

She stood. "Well, what's the difference?" she said, and she could tell she'd surprised him, because he flinched. She was surprised, too. Her voice was much louder than she'd expected. "We're replicas, aren't we? We might as well be dogs. That's how they think of us anyway. That's what we were made for. To be dogs—or rats. You weren't pretending all those years ago. You *were* a roach."

He stared at her for a long second. She could see his chest rising with his breath and knew that beneath his skin hundreds of tiny muscles were contracting in his face even to hold it there, still, watching her. The idea of him and what he was made of, all the different fragile parts spun together, made her dizzy.

Finally he looked away. "That's why I ran," he said. "I wanted to know whether we could be good for anything else. I wanted to try." To her surprise, he smiled, just a little. "Besides, even roaches run away. Rats, too."

They went through the guesthouse, looking for anything that would be useful. In a bedroom closet beneath extra pillows they found an old backpack, which they filled with the remaining granola bars and bottles of water, plus the bathroom things that Gemma had bought for them. Lyra knew they likely wouldn't need soap but couldn't stand to leave the pretty, paper-wrapped bars behind, so different from anything she'd ever owned.

Jake had left his cell phone charging in the corner and 72 took it, although they had no one to call. It excited Lyra to have it in their possession, to touch the screen and leave fingerprints there. Only people had cell phones.

They took knives from the kitchen, a blanket from the otherwise empty cabinet by the bed. She didn't feel guilty about stealing from Jake and Gemma, who had helped them. She felt nothing at all. Maybe, she thought, the nurses had been right about replicas. Maybe they didn't have souls.

By then the main house had gone dark. 72 suggested they turn the light off too, so in case Jake and Gemma were looking out for them, they would believe Lyra and 72 had gone to bed. They waited there, in the dark, for another twenty minutes just to be sure. They sat again on the sofa side by side, and Lyra thought of her dream of entanglement, all those inches and inches of exposed skin. She was glad he couldn't see her.

Finally he touched her elbow. "It's time," he said. His face in the dark was different colors of shadow.

Outside, the sound of insects and tree frogs startled Lyra: a rhythmic and almost mechanical thrumming that recalled the throaty roar of Mr. I.

"Wait." 72 nudged her. Gemma was curled up on a plastic deck chair, still wearing her clothes, using several colorful towels as blankets. Lyra was confused. Had she been watching them? Trying to make sure they didn't escape? She couldn't imagine why she would have otherwise chosen to sleep outside.

Before she could stop him, 72 was already moving closer, stepping very carefully. Lyra followed him with a growing sense of unease. Gemma's face in the moonlight looked so much like Cassiopeia's, she wanted to reach out and lay a hand on Gemma's chest, to feel her breathing and believe Cassiopeia had come back to life. But she didn't, obviously.

Lying next to Gemma on the pool deck was an open notebook. A pen had rolled into the binding. As always Lyra was drawn to the words scribbled across the page. They appeared to glow faintly in the moonlight. Gemma's writing, she thought, was very beautiful. The words reminded her of bird tracks, of birds themselves, pecking their way proudly across the page.

Then a familiar name caught her attention: Emily Huang. Nurse Em.

She placed a finger on the page, mouthing the words

written directly beneath the name. Palm Grove. The words meant nothing to her. There were other names on the page, all of them unfamiliar except for Dr. Saperstein's, which was joined by a small notation to the Home Foundation. She didn't know what that was, either, but beneath it was at last another word she recognized: Gainesville. This, she knew, was a place. A big place. Jake and Gemma had argued about whether they should be getting off at the highway exit to Gainesville and Jake had said, *No one wants to go to Gainesville*, and then Gemma had said, *Except the half a million people who live there.* She figured that Palm Grove might be a place, too.

She took the notebook. Jake had taken the file folder she'd stolen, so it was a fair trade. She straightened up and saw that 72 was rifling through Gemma's bag to get to her wallet. She grabbed his shoulder, shaking her head. Once, years ago, Don't-Even-Think-About-It's wallet had been stolen from the mess hall, and she remembered how terrible it was, how all the replicas' beds were searched and their cubbies turned out, how Don't-Even-Think-About-It was in a foul mood for days and backhanded Lyra for looking at her wrong. They had found it, finally, in a hole torn out of the underside of Ursa Major's mattress, along with all the other things she'd scavenged over the years: dirty socks and a lost earring, ferry tokens, soda can tabs, gum wrappers.

But she couldn't speak without risking waking Gemma, and even as she watched he removed a wedge of money from her wallet and, pocketing it, returned the wallet to her purse. Lyra put back the notebook anyway. She wasn't likely to forget Palm Grove.

They scaled the gate because they didn't know how to make it work and, once they were on the other side, on a street made liquid dark and shiny by the streetlights, began to walk. Bound on either side by houses with their hedges and gates, Lyra did not feel so afraid. But soon they reached a road that stretched blackly into the empty countryside, and she felt a kind of terror she associated with falling: so much space, more space than she'd ever imagined.

Only then did Lyra speak. They'd gone too far to be heard by anyone. Besides, she hated the emptiness of the road and the streetlamps bent silently over their work, like tall arms planted in the earth.

"I know someone who can help us," she said. Their feet crunched on the gravel at the side of the road. Now she was grateful for the tree frogs. At least they were company.

"Help us?" 72 tilted his head back to look at the sky and the stars spread above them. She couldn't tell whether he was frightened, but she doubted it. He didn't seem afraid of anything. Even dying. Maybe he'd just had time to get used to it. She had known that replicas were frailer than real people, more prone to illness, sicklier and smaller. But on some level she'd believed that at Haven, she might be safe.

"I want to know more," she said. "I want to know why they did this to us. Why they made us sick. I want to know if there's a cure."

He stopped walking. He stared at her. "There's no cure," he said.

"Not that we know of," she said. "But you said yourself you didn't know exactly what they were doing at Haven. There could be a cure. They could have developed one."

"Why would they?" he said. He looked as if he was trying not to smile. In that moment, she hated him. She'd never met someone who could make her have so many different feelings—who could make her feel at all, really.

"I don't know," she said. "I don't know why they did anything."

He looked at her, chewing on the inside of his cheek. She supposed that he wasn't ugly after all. She supposed that he was beautiful, in his own way, strange and angular, like the spiky plants that grew between the walkways at Haven, with a fan of dark-green leaves. She'd overheard Gemma say that, on the phone in the car earlier. Maybe she hadn't thought Lyra was listening. *There's a girl and a boy,* she'd said. *The girl is sick or something. The boy is . . .* And she'd lowered her voice to a whisper. *Beautiful.* Lyra had never really thought of faces as beautiful before, although she had enjoyed the geometry of Jake's face, and she supposed, in retrospect, that Dr. O'Donnell had been beautiful. At least she was in Lyra's memory.

She wondered if she herself was ugly.

Two lights appeared in the distance. She raised a hand to her eyes, momentarily dazzled and afraid, and then realized it was only an approaching car. But it began to slow and she was afraid again. Somehow, instinctively, she and 72 took hands. His were large and dry and much nicer than the hands of the doctors, which, wrapped in disposable gloves, always felt both clammy and cold, like something dead.

"You kids all right?" The man in the car had to lean all the way across the seat to talk to them through the open window.

72 nodded. Lyra was glad. She couldn't speak.

"Funny place for a stroll," he said. "You be careful, okay? There's cars come down this road eighty, ninety miles an hour."

He started to roll up his window and Lyra exhaled, relieved and also stunned. If he'd recognized them as replicas, it didn't seem like it. Maybe the differences weren't as obvious as she thought.

"Hello," she blurted out, and the window froze and

then buzzed down again. "Hello," she repeated, taking a step toward the car and ignoring 72, who hissed something, a warning, probably. "Have you heard of Palm Grove?"

"Palm Grove, Florida?" The man had thick, fleshy fingers, and a cigarette burned between them. "You weren't thinking of walking there, were you?" He said it half laughing, as if he'd made a joke. But when she didn't smile, he squinted at her through the smoke unfurling from his cigarette. "The twelve goes straight up the coast to Palm Grove on its way to Tallahassee. If that's where you're headed, you can't miss the bus depot. But it's a hike. Five or six miles at least."

Lyra nodded, even though she didn't know what he meant by *the twelve*, or how far five or six miles was.

"Won't catch a bus this late, though," the man said. "Hope you got a place to stay the night." He was still staring at her, but now his eyes ticked over her shoulder to 72 and back again. Something shifted in his face. "Hey. You sure you're okay? You don't look too good."

Lyra backed quickly away from the car. "I'm fine," she said. "We're fine."

He stared at them for another long moment. "Watch out for the drivers down this stretch, like I said. They'll be halfway to Miami before they realize they got you."

Then he was gone and his taillights became the red tips

of two cigarettes and then vanished.

"You shouldn't speak to them," 72 said. "You shouldn't speak to any of them."

"He spoke to me," Lyra said. "Besides, what harm did it do?"

72 just shook his head, still staring in the direction the car had gone, as if he expected it might rematerialize. "What's in Palm Grove?"

"Someone who might be able to help," Lyra said carefully.

"Who?" 72 was backlit by the streetlamp and all in shadow.

She knew he might refuse to go with her, and if he did, she would still find her way to Palm Grove. They owed each other nothing. It was chance that had kept them together so far. Still, the idea of being completely on her own was terrifying. She had never been alone at Haven. At the very least the guards had always been watching.

But she saw no way to lie convincingly. She knew no one, had no one, in the outside world, and he knew that. "She was a nurse at Haven," she said.

"No," he said immediately, and began walking again, kicking at the gravel and sending it skipping away across the road.

"Wait." She got a hand around his arm, the one crisscrossed with all those vivid white scars. She turned him around and had a sudden shock: just for a second her body did something, *told* her something, she didn't understand.

"No," he said again.

She dropped his arm. She didn't know what she wanted from him but she did, and that made her feel confused and exhausted and unhappy. "She's not like the other ones," she said. Dr. O'Donnell had said, *You're a good person,* even as Nurse Em sobbed so that snot bubbled in her nostrils. *You want to make things right. I know you do.* That had to mean it was true.

"How do you know that?" 72 said. He took a step forward, and Lyra nearly tripped trying to get away from him. She didn't want to be anywhere near him, not after what had happened. Even standing several inches away she felt a current moving through her body, something warm and alive, something that whispered. She hated it.

"I just know," she said. "She left Haven. She wanted to help us." In her head she added, *Because Dr. O'Donnell believed in her. Because Dr. O'Donnell was always right.* She wished, more than anything, that she knew where Dr. O'Donnell lived, and imagined once again the feel of Dr. O'Donnell's hand skimming the top of her head. *Mother.* She thought Dr. O'Donnell's house must be all white and very clean, just like Haven. But maybe instead of being on the ocean it was in a field, and the smell of flowers came through the open windows on the wind.

Another car went by, this time with a punch of music and rhythm. Then another car. This time the window went down and a boy had his head out of it, yelling something she couldn't make out. An empty can missed her head by only a few inches.

For a long time, 72 just stared at her. She wondered again whether she was ugly, whether he realized that now, the same way she knew now that he was beautiful. As a replica it had never mattered, and it shouldn't matter now, but it did. She wondered if this was the human world rubbing off on her, whether she might become more human by becoming uglier, by accepting it.

She didn't want to be ugly in his eyes.

Finally he said, "We should get off the road and find somewhere to sleep for the night." She thought he almost smiled. "Well, we can't sleep here. And you heard him. There are no buses until morning."

They moved off the road and walked instead through a scrum of crushed paper cups, cigarette butts, and empty plastic bags. Soon they came to an area of buildings groveling under the lights that encircled them, including a sign in neon that read *Liquorz*. Lit as they were in starkness and isolation, they reminded Lyra briefly and painfully of Haven at night when, sleepily, she would get up to use the bathroom and would look out and see the guard towers and floodlights making harsh angles out of the landscape.

One of the buildings' pitched roofs tapered into the form of a cross and so she thought it must be a church, although otherwise it was identical to its neighbors: shingle-sided and gray, separated by a narrow band of cracked pavement from a gas station and a diner, both closed for the night. Lyra saw that someone had written *I was here* across the plywood and wasn't surprised. In a world this big, it must be easy to get lost and need reminders.

Behind the church was a weed-choked field that extended toward another road in the distance, this one even busier. Headlights beaded down the thin fold in the dark like blood along a needle. But the noise was transformed by all the space into a constant shushing, like the sound of ocean waves. They shook out their blanket here, and Lyra was glad that they'd decided to sleep so close to the road and the lights. The space in between, the nothingness and distance, frightened her.

The blanket was small, and when they lay down side by side, on their backs, they couldn't help but touch. Lyra didn't know how she would sleep. Her body was telling her something again, urging her to move, to run, to touch him. Instead she crossed her arms tightly and stared at the sky until the stars sharpened in her vision. She tried to pick out Cassiopeia. When she was little, she'd liked to pretend that stars were really lights anchoring distant islands, as if she wasn't looking up but only out across a dark sea. She knew the truth now but still found stars comforting, especially in their sameness. A sky full of burning replicas.

"Do you know more stories?"

Lyra was startled. She'd thought 72 was asleep. His eyes were closed and one arm was thrown across his face, so his voice was muffled.

"What do you mean?"

He withdrew the arm but kept his eyes closed, so she was free to look at him. Again, his face looked very bare in the dark, as if during the day he wore a different face that only now, with his eyes closed, had rubbed away. She noticed the particular curve of his lips and nostrils, the smooth arrangement of his cheekbones, and wanted to touch and explore them with her fingers. "You can read. You told that story on the marshes. About the girl, Matilda. You must know more, then."

She thought of *The Little Prince* and its soft cover, creased through the illustration, its smudgy papers and its smell, now lost forever. She squeezed her ribs hard, half wishing she would crack. "Only one more good one," she said.

"Tell it," he said.

Again she was surprised. "What?"

This time he opened his eyes, turning slightly to face

her. "Tell it," he said. And then: "Please." His lashes were very long. His lips looked like fruit, something to suck on. Now he did smile. She saw his teeth flash white in the dark.

She looked away. The stars spun a little, dizzy above her. "There," she said, lifting an arm to point. "See that star?"

"Which one?"

"That one. The little twinkly one, just next to the one that looks almost blue."

It didn't matter whether he was looking at exactly the same star as she was. But after a moment he said, "I see it."

"That's Planet B-612," she said. "It's an asteroid, actually. And that's where the Little Prince comes from." She closed her eyes, and in her head she heard echoes of Dr. O'Donnell's voice, smelled lemon soap, watched a finger tracking across the page, pointing out different words. "It's a small planet, but it's his. There are three volcanoes on the surface, one active, two inactive. And there are baobab plants that try and overgrow everything. There's a rose, too. The Little Prince loves the rose." This was the part of the book that had most confused her, but she said it anyway, because she knew it was important.

"But who *is* the Little Prince?" 72 asked.

"The Little Prince has golden hair, a scarf, and a lovable laugh," Lyra said, reciting from memory.

"What's lovable?" 72 asked.

Lyra shifted. "It means . . ." She didn't know. "I guess it means someone loves you."

72 didn't say anything. She was going to continue her story, but she felt a bad pressure in her chest, as if someone was feeding a tube into her lungs.

"How do you get to be loved?" 72 asked. His voice was quiet, slurred by sleep.

"I don't know," Lyra answered honestly. She was glad when he fell asleep, or at least pretended to. She didn't feel like telling a story much after that.

TWELVE

IN THE MORNING THEY WERE woken by a shout.
Lyra thought they must have been spotted. Instead she
saw a man in thick gloves loading trash from the Dumpsters into an enormous truck. Momentarily hypnotized,
she watched the trash flattened by machinery that looked
like metal teeth. The smell was sweet and vaguely sicken-
ing. Still, she was hungry.

Then she remembered the money they'd stolen from
Gemma's wallet. 72 was awake now too, and the man
in the gloves stared at them as they stood and rolled
up the blanket, stuffing it in their backpack, but said
nothing. Lyra was beginning to understand that humans
outside Haven didn't seem to care about them. Maybe
their world was simply too big. They couldn't pay attention to all of it.

72 was hungry too, so they went to the diner next to the

gas station and took turns in the bathroom washing their faces and hands. Lyra even wet her scalp and brushed her teeth. There was a stack of small paper cups and electric-blue mouthwash in a dispenser above the sink. When she returned to the table, 72 was fumbling with Jake's stolen phone.

"It won't stop ringing," he said. And in fact the phone lit up in his hands, sending out a tinny musical sound.

"Let me try," she said. She'd seen cell phones before but had only ever handled one once, when Nurse Em, years ago, had shown Lyra pictures of her dog at home on the mainland. A Pomeranian. White and fluffy but otherwise ratlike, Lyra had thought, but hadn't said so. Maybe the dog was still alive. She didn't know how long dogs normally lived, and whether they outlasted replicas.

She managed to get the phone to stop ringing and returned it to 72, who put it in his pocket. She wondered why he liked carrying it around if they had no one to call. Maybe it was because of what he'd said and why he'd escaped: just to see what it was like. Just for a little.

The menu was so full of writing that Lyra's head hurt looking at it. There was a whole section named *Eggs*. How many different ways could eggs be eaten? At Haven they were always scrambled, crispy and brown on the bottom.

"It's a waste," 72 said. He seemed angry about the

menu. "All this food." But she thought he was just angry about not being able to read. He made no mention of the story she'd started to tell him last night, of the Little Prince, and Lyra was glad. His question was still bothering her, as was the feeling she'd had afterward, a strange emptiness, as if she was already dead.

A woman came to ask them what they wanted to eat. Lyra had never been asked that question before, and in that moment she deeply missed the Haven mess hall and the food lit orange beneath heating lamps and the way it was deposited onto their plates by sour-faced women wearing hairnets. 72 ordered coffee and eggs. So she ordered the same thing. The eggs were burned on the bottom and tasted like they did at Haven, which made her feel better.

They paid with two of Gemma's bills and got a bewildering assortment of change back. Lyra couldn't help but think of the younger replicas and how they would have loved to play with all those coins, skipping them or rolling them across the floor, seeing who could get the most heads in a row. She wondered where all the other replicas were, and imagined them in a new Haven, this one perhaps on a mountain and surrounded by the clean smell of pine, before remembering what they were. Carriers.

Disposable.

Lyra asked the waitress about Palm Grove, and she directed them up the road to the bus depot. "Can't miss it," she said. "Just take the twelve up toward Tallahassee. Soon as you see the water park, that's Palm Grove. You kids heading to the water park?" Lyra shook her head. The woman popped her gum. "That's too bad. They got one slide three stories tall. Cobra, it's called. And today's gonna be a bruiser. Where you kids from?"

But Lyra only shook her head again, and they stepped out into the heat.

By the time they reached the bus depot, Lyra's shoes felt as if they were rubbing all the skin off her feet. She wasn't used to wearing shoes, but the asphalt was too hot for bare feet and the shoulder was glittering with broken glass. While they waited for the bus, 72 lifted his shirt to wipe his face with it, and she saw a long trail of sweat tracking down the smoothness of his stomach and disappearing beneath the waistband of his pants. It did not disgust her.

When the number 12 came, 72 was obviously proud, at least, to be able to read the number—he nearly shouted it. But once they boarded, they learned they'd have to have a ticket. They had to get off the bus again and return inside, where the man behind the ticket desk shouted at them for holding up the line, for struggling with their dollars and giving over the wrong bills, and Lyra got flustered and spilled coins all over the floor. She was too embarrassed to pick the money up—everyone was staring at her, everyone *knew*—and instead, once they'd gotten their tickets, she and 72 hurried back outside despite people calling after them. But the bus had gone and they had to wait for a new one. Mercifully, the bus that arrived was mostly empty, so Lyra and 72 could get a seat in the back, far from the other passengers.

It was better to ride in a bus than in a car. It made her less nauseous. But still the world outside her window seemed to go by with dizzying speed, and there was ever more of it: highways rising up over new towns and then falling away into other highways; stretches of blank land burned by the sun into brownness; building and building and building, like an endless line of teeth. After an hour she spotted a monstrous coil of plastic rising into the air, twisting and snakelike and vivid blue, and an enormous billboard tacked into the ground announced *Bluefin* and *Water Park*, and several other words between them she didn't have time to read.

They passed a parking lot glittering with cars and people, natural humans: children brown from the sun, only half-dressed and carting colorful towels, men and women herding them toward the entrance. She saw a mother crouching in front of a girl red in the face from crying, touching her face with a tissue—but the bus was moving too quickly and soon a line of trees ran across her vision, obscuring it.

The driver announced Palm Grove and stopped the bus in front of a run-down motel named the Starlite. Lyra had been imagining a grid of houses in pastel shades, like the neighborhood they'd left in the middle of the night. But Palm Grove was big: big roads with two lanes of traffic, restaurants and gas stations, clothing stores and places to buy groceries. Signs shouted at them from every corner. *Milk, 3.99. Guys and Dolls, Albert Irving Auditorium, Saturday. One-Hour Parking Monday through Saturday.* She didn't even see any houses, and she counted at least a dozen people on the streets, passing in and out of shops, talking on phones. It was so hot it felt like being inside a body, beneath the skin of something, filmy and slick. How many humans could possibly be here, in one town?

"And now what?" 72 said. He'd been in a bad mood all morning, ever since she had asked him why he had the scars on his forearms, which were different from the scars she and the other replicas had, the ones from spinal taps and harvesting procedures—all of it, she knew now, to test how deep the prions had gone, how fast they were cloning themselves, how soon the replicas would die.

He had only said *accident*, and had barely spoken to her on the bus. Instead he had sat with his chin on his chest, his arms folded, his eyes shut. She had counted fourteen scars, four on his right and ten on his left. She had noticed a small mole on his earlobe, had felt a secret thrill at sitting so close after years of seeing no male replicas at all.

"Trust me," Lyra said, which was what the nurses always said. *Shhh. Trust me. Just a little pinch. Stop with that noise. Trust me, it'll all be over soon.*

Lyra worked up the courage to stop the first person she saw who looked to be about her age. The girl was sitting on the curb in front of a store called Digs and was bent over her cell phone, typing on it. When she looked up, Lyra saw that she was wearing makeup and was vaguely surprised—she'd somehow thought makeup was for older humans, like the nurses. "Hello," she said. "We're looking for Emily Huang."

"Emily Huang." The girl looked Lyra up and down, and then her eyes went to 72. She straightened up, giving him a smile that reminded Lyra of the actresses the nurses used to watch on TV and look at in magazines they left lying around sometimes. Lyra didn't like it, and she was for the first time aware of the difference between her body and this girl's. This girl was all curves and prettiness, all smooth skin and beautiful solidity and long, flowing hair. Lyra, in her drab clothing and her sharp bones and the scar above her eyebrow, thought of that word again, *ugly*. "Emily Huang," the girl repeated. "She go to Wallace?"

"I—I don't think so." Lyra suddenly wished they hadn't stopped.

"Sorry." The girl *did* look sorry, but she kept her eyes

on 72. "Don't know her." Then she turned and gave Lyra a smile that wasn't friendly—more like she'd just eaten something she shouldn't have. "Cool scalp, by the way. Dig the Cancer Kid look."

They went on. Lyra could still feel the girl staring and wondered if 72 did, too. All he said was, "Too many people," and she nodded because her throat was too tight to speak. *Ugly.* Which meant the other girl was *pretty.* What a strange way to live, among all these people—it made Lyra feel small, even less important, than she had among the thousands of replicas grown like crops in the barracks.

The next person she stopped was older and *ugly*: wrinkles that made it look as if her face was melting, pouchy bits of skin waggling under her chin. But she didn't know who Emily Huang was and only shook her head and moved off. They stopped a man, and a boy about twelve who rode a flat thing fitted with wheels that Lyra remembered only belatedly was called a skateboard. No one knew Emily Huang, and Lyra didn't like the look the man gave them.

She was hot and thirsty and losing hope. The town kept expanding. Every time they came to the end of a block she saw a new street branching off it with more buildings and more people.

"We're never going to find her," 72 said, and she disliked the fact that he sounded happy about it, as if he'd proven a point. "We might as well keep walking."

"Just hold on," she said. "Hold on." Spots of color floated up in front of her vision. Her T-shirt clung to her back. She took a step and found the pavement floated up to meet her. She grabbed hold of a street sign—*Loading Dock, No Standing*—to keep from falling.

"Hey." 72's voice changed. His arm skimmed her elbow. "Are you all right?"

"Hot," she managed to say.

"Come on," he said. "With me. You need water. And shade."

Almost directly across the street was a park that reminded her of the courtyard at Haven, down to the statue standing at its center. This one was of a woman, though, her hands held together in prayer, her head bowed. Tall trees cast the lawns in shade, and benches lined the intersecting pathways. 72 kept a hand on her elbow even though she insisted he didn't need to.

She did feel better once she'd taken a drink of water from a water fountain and found a bench in the shade where she could rest for a bit. Somewhere in the branches birds twittered out messages to one another. It was pretty here, peaceful. The park ran up to an enormous redbrick building, portions of its facade encased in glossy sheets of climbing ivy. Lyra saw another cross stuck above the glass double doors and the letters beside it: Wallace High

School. Her heart jumped. Wallace. The girl on the street had mentioned Wallace.

"What do you want to do now?" 72 was being extra nice, which made Lyra feel worse. She knew he thought they'd failed. She knew he knew how sick she was. Without answering him, she stood up. She'd just seen someone moving behind the glass doors, and she went forward as if drawn by the pull of something magnetic. "Lyra!" 72 shouted after her. But she didn't stop. It didn't take him long to catch up with her, but by then she was already standing in front of Wallace and a woman had emerged, carrying a stack of folders.

"Can I help you?" the woman said, and Lyra realized she'd been standing there staring.

"We're looking for Emily Huang," Lyra said quickly, before she could lose her nerve. Remembering what the girl had said, Lyra added, "We think—she may *go* to Wallace." She wasn't sure what that meant, either, and she held her breath, hoping the woman did.

The woman slid on a pair of glasses, which she was wearing on a chain. Blinking up at Lyra, she resembled a turtle, down to the looseness of the skin around her neck.

"Emily Huang," the woman said, shaking her head. "No, no. She never went here." Lyra's heart dropped. Another *no*. Another dead end. But then the woman said, "But she came every career day to talk to the kids about the work she did. Terrible some of the stuff they said about her later. She was a good girl. I liked her very much."

"So you know her?" Lyra said. She was dizzy with sudden joy. Nurse Em. She would help. She would protect them. "You know where we can find her?"

The woman gave her a look Lyra couldn't quite read. "Knew her," she said slowly. "She lived right over on Willis Street, just behind the school. Can't miss it. A sweet yellow house, and all those flower beds. Woman who lives there now has let it go to seed."

And just like that, the happiness was gone. Evaporated. "She's gone?" Lyra said. "Do you know where she went?"

The woman shook her head again, and then Lyra did know how to name her expression: *pity.* "Not gone, honey," she said. "Never left, some say. Hung herself right there in her living room, must be three, four years ago now. Emily Huang's dead."

Lyra didn't know what made her want to see the place where Emily Huang had lived. When she asked for directions to Willis Street, 72 didn't question her, and she was glad. She wouldn't have known how to explain.

Behind the school they found quiet residential streets running like spokes away from the downtown, and houses at last, these concealed not behind walls but standing there pleasantly right on their lawns, with flowers waving from flower boxes and vivid toys scattered in the grass. It was pretty here, and she couldn't imagine why Emily Huang would have been so unhappy, why she would have killed herself like poor Pepper had. Then again, she remembered how Nurse Em had sobbed and Dr. O'Donnell had held her by the shoulders. *I know you,* she'd said. *You're a good person. I know you were just in over your head.* So maybe she was unhappy even then.

Nurse Em's old house had once, the old woman had told them, been the yellow of sunshine and thus easy to spot. Now it was a faded color that reminded Lyra of mustard. The flower beds looked scraggly, and there were four bikes dumped on the front lawn and so many toys it looked as if these were coming up from the ground. Loud music came to them across the lawn.

She closed her eyes and arranged all her memories of Nurse Em in a row: Nurse Em bathing Lyra and a dozen other replicas when they were too young to do it themselves, plunging them into the bathwater and hauling them like slippery, wriggling puppies onto the cold tile floor afterward. Nurse Em standing with Dr. Saperstein in the courtyard, speaking in a low voice, and the way he said, "It's nothing. They don't understand," after Nurse Em turned around and caught Lyra staring; the time in the janitor's closet with Dr. O'Donnell.

"I'm sorry," 72 said, and Lyra opened her eyes. Maybe

he wasn't angry at her anymore. His eyes were softened with color.

It was the first time anyone had ever apologized to her. "For what?"

"I know you were hoping she would help," 72 said.

"Now we have no one," Lyra said. She pressed a hand to her eyes. She didn't want 72 to see how upset she was. "Nowhere to go, either."

72 hesitated. He touched the back of her hand. "You have me," he said very quietly. She looked up at him, surprised. Her skin tingled where he touched her.

"I do?" she said. She felt hot in her head and chest, but it was a good feeling, like standing in the sun after being too long in the air-conditioning.

He nodded. "You have me," he said. "I have you."

He looked as if he might say more, but just then in the house next to Emily Huang's the garage door rattled open, revealing an enormously fat woman in a tracksuit. She waddled out dragging a trash bin, keeping her eyes on 72 and Lyra. Lyra stepped from him. She felt as if they'd been caught in the middle of something, even though they'd just been standing there. She waited for the woman to turn around and return inside, but instead she just stood there at the end of the driveway, one hand on the trash bin, breathing hard and staring.

"You need something?" she called out to them, when

she had caught her breath. She pulled her T-shirt away from her skin. A large sweat stain had darkened between her breasts.

"No," 72 said quickly.

But the woman kept staring at them, and so Lyra added, "We came looking for Emily Huang. We were . . . friends." She enjoyed the way the word sounded and felt like repeating it, but bit her tongue so she wouldn't.

The woman's face changed, became narrower, as if she were speaking to them through a half-open door. "You knew Emily?"

Lyra had never had to lie so much in her life. She wondered if lying, too, was a human trait. She fumbled for an excuse, and for a second her brain turned up nothing but white noise. What was the word again? "Parents," she said finally. It came to her like a match striking. "She was friends with my—our—parents."

Even 72 turned to look at her. Her cheeks were hot. This lie felt different, heavier. The word, *parents*, had left a thick feeling in her throat, as if it had slugged its way up from her stomach. She was sure that the woman would know that she was lying. But instead she just made a desperate flapping motion. It wasn't until 72 moved that Lyra realized the woman was gesturing them forward.

"In." She had a funny, duck-like walk. She kept turning around to see that they were following her. "Come on.

Come *on*." Lyra didn't have enough experience to wonder whether it was safe to follow a stranger into her house, and soon they were standing in the coolness of the garage and the door was grinding closed behind them, like an eyelid squeezing shut and wedging out all the light. The garage smelled faintly of fertilizer and chemicals.

"Sorry for being a push," the woman said, moving to a door that must, Lyra knew, connect with the house. "You never know who's watching around here. Nosy Nellies, that's what everyone is. That was Em's problem, you ask me. Trusted all the wrong people." She opened the door. "I'm Sheri, by the way. Sheri Hayes. Come on in and have a chat with me. You kids look like you could use a lemonade or a bite to eat."

Lyra and 72 didn't look at each other, but she knew what he was thinking: these real-humans were not like the ones at Haven. They were nice. Helpful. Then again, they didn't know what Lyra and 72 really were. Lyra had a feeling that they wouldn't be quite so helpful then. She imagined the inside of her body rotted, filled with disease, and wondered if soon it would begin to show on her outside, in the look of her face.

"Well, come on. Don't just stand there gawping. I'm sweating buckets."

They followed the woman—Sheri—into the house. Lyra was startled by a cat that streaked across the hall directly in front of her, and jumped back.

"Oh, you're not allergic, are you? I've got three of 'em. Tabby, Tammy, Tommy. All littermates. Little terrors, every last one. But don't worry, they won't bite you."

Lyra saw another two cats perched on a sofa in a darkened living room, their eyes moon-bright and yellow. Her heart was still hammering. She wasn't used to animals roaming *free* like that. At Haven the animals were kept in cages. She was glad they went instead into the kitchen.

Sheri sat them down at a wooden table and brought them two glasses of lemonade in tall glasses filled to the rim with ice cubes. It was delicious. She laid out cookies, too, a whole plate of them.

"So where do you kids come from?" Sheri asked, and Lyra froze, caught off guard again. 72 moved his thumb over a knot in the table. But Sheri just made a kind of clucking noise. "I see," she said. "Let me guess. Emily helped place you with your parents, didn't she? You went through the Home Foundation?"

Lyra didn't know what she was talking about so she stayed quiet, and Sheri seemed to take that for a yes.

"'Course she did. You two don't look a lick alike." She sighed. "Poor Emily. You knew her well, then?"

"In a way," Lyra said carefully. She knew Nurse Em had never hit the replicas, or cursed them for being demons. She knew that Dr. O'Donnell thought she was a good person who wanted to make things right. She knew she'd been younger than many of the other nurses, because she'd overheard Dr. O'Donnell say that, too. *You're young. You didn't know what you were doing. No one will blame you.*

"She was a good girl. All that work she did for other people. I could have killed them for what they said about her in the papers after she died. It came as a shock to me, you know, a real shock. We'd been talking about a barbecue that very weekend. She called me the day it happened, asked if I wanted macaroni salad or potato." Sheri shook her head. "Now what kind of person about to hang herself is worried about macaroni or potato salad?"

Lyra knew she wasn't expected to answer. Sheri went on. "Too sad. She was still young, too. Thirty-four, thirty-five. I think there must have been a man involved. Maybe more than one. Well, I suppose there were signs. You know, after they found her body I did a little bit of Googling. Found out some of the warning signs. Of course, I didn't see them before. But she did give away some of her things the week before she died, and that's right up there to look for. Giving away prized possessions. Of course at the time I thought she was just being nice."

"What do you mean, there was a man involved?" 72 asked, and Lyra was surprised, as ever, to hear him speak. She realized he hardly spoke unless they were alone. Somehow, this made her feel special. Her glass was empty but still cold, and she pressed it to her neck.

"Well, isn't there always?" She raised her eyebrows. "Besides, it would've been hard not to notice those men in and out. Just once or twice, of course, as far as I could tell. Suited-up types. Like in finance or something. But mean-looking." Lyra thought of the Suits who'd come to inspect Haven sometimes and felt a curious prickling down the back of her spine. *Those men.* Like the nurses had always called them. Sheri shook her head. "But there's no accounting for taste, I always say."

Lyra grasped for some idea of what to ask next, of what any of this meant or whether it mattered. "You said she was giving away her things," she said, suddenly struck by what this might mean. "She gave *you* something, didn't she?" Lyra asked. Maybe, she thought, Nurse Em had left Sheri something important—maybe she'd left her something that related to Haven and to the work they were doing there. To the prions.

To a cure.

Sheri had taken a seat. Now she placed both palms on the table to stand up. "Never been able to find a place for them. But can't bring myself to throw 'em out, either. Oh, she told me I could. Told me I could take the damn things apart and sell the frames, if I wanted. But of course I never would." She moved off into another room. 72 gave Lyra a questioning look and she shrugged. She didn't know what she was waiting for or looking for anymore. Only that out there, in the real world, there were no answers—nothing but vastness and things she'd never seen in real life and experiences she couldn't understand and strangers who didn't know what she was and would hate her if they did. Nothing but the disease. Nothing but being nothing and then dying nothing.

At Haven she'd never *wanted* anything, not in any way that counted. She'd been hungry, tired, bored, and sick. She'd wanted more food, cold water, more sleep, for the pain to end, to go outside. But she'd never had a want that moved her, where the goal felt not like an end but a beginning. She'd never had a purpose. But now she did. She wanted to understand.

And this single fact made her feel more human, more *worthy*, than she ever had before.

She was shocked to feel 72's hand in hers. She looked up at him and felt the same strange thing happen to her body, as if she was transformed to air. He pulled away when Sheri returned to the room, carrying three framed photographs. She plunked them down on the table.

"Well, you see, they're not exactly my taste," Sheri said. The pictures were all illustrations. Lyra guessed they came from the same anatomy textbook. She'd seen many similar pictures in the medical textbooks at Haven. "I like my kittens and my watercolors and oils here and there.

Never been much for drawing."

Lyra thought the drawings were beautiful—she loved the sinewy look of the muscles, the precision of the bones, and even the faded lettering too small to make out, labeling different physical features. But even so, she was horribly disappointed. There was nothing here, no secret message or miracle cure.

Somewhere in the house, a phone rang. Sheri stood up again. "It never ends, does it?" she said. "Give me just a minute." As soon as she left, another cat, this one gray, leapt onto the table, and Lyra instinctively grabbed one of the framed illustrations to keep the cat from stepping on it.

"Why have cats in a house?" 72 whispered to her. But she couldn't answer, even though she'd been wondering the same thing. She'd felt an irregularity in the canvas backing, and she flipped the frame over, her chest suddenly cavernous with hope.

The canvas had at one time been stapled to the wooden frame. On two sides of the rectangular canvas, the staples were in place. But on two sides they were missing, and instead had been replaced with gobs of glue at inch-long intervals, some of which had seeped out and hardened onto the wood. Lyra and the other replicas had spent too long at Haven searching for places to hide their limited belongings not to suspect that the picture Nurse

Em had given Sheri was in fact concealing something else behind it.

Nurse Em had told Sheri she could *take the damn things apart*. What if she had meant that Sheri *should* take the damn things apart?

The phone had stopped ringing, and Sheri's voice, muffled by the walls, was now nothing more than tones. She must have closed a door. Before she could lose her nerve, Lyra pried a corner of the canvas from the frame and ripped.

"What are you doing?" 72 reached out and seized Lyra's wrist as if to stop her.

"Nurse Em gave these pictures away before she died," Lyra whispered. "Maybe she was hiding something." Fearing both that she would find something and that she wouldn't, she slipped a hand behind the canvas. Almost immediately, her fingers landed on several loose items, glossy-slick. Photographs.

72 stared as she laid them out on the table. There were three of them, each showing Nurse Em with a tall, dark-haired man who had a beard and a sour expression. In one photograph, Nurse Em was sitting on his lap and he was turning away from the camera. In another, she was kissing him on the cheek and he was lifting a hand as if to block them from the lens. But in the last one she'd caught him square on, or someone else had. They were standing

in front of a nondescript stretch of highway. There was a scruffy range of blue hills in the distance. She was holding on to a straw hat and looked happy. Lyra felt sick for reasons she couldn't say.

"Dr. Saperstein," 72 said, naming him first. Lyra could only nod. The man in the pictures was unmistakably Dr. Saperstein, whom Lyra had always thought of a little like the humans thought about their God: someone remote and all-powerful, someone through whom the whole world was ordered.

Lyra could no longer hear Sheri talking. But after a minute, there was a quick burst of laughter from the other room and she knew they still had a little time.

"Quick," she said. "Help me check the other frames."

She flipped over the second picture. Like the first, its backing had been pulled away from the frame and then reglued. But this one had been done more carefully and was difficult to detach. 72 leaned across her, knife in hand, and neatly sliced the canvas, barely missing her fingers.

"It's faster," he said, and leaned across her to slit open the back of the third picture.

They found, behind the second picture, a folded sheet of paper that looked at first glance to be a list of names and a typed document, although Lyra didn't have time to try and read it. She didn't have time to check the third picture frame, either. At that moment she heard a door open, and Sheri's voice, suddenly amplified.

"I'll call you tomorrow," she was saying. "I'm being rude . . ."

Sheri would only have to glance at the frames to know what they had done and to guess, probably, that something had been removed from behind the pictures. Without speaking, she and 72 stood up from the table and moved as quietly as they could to the back door, which opened out onto a little patio. Sheri was still trying to get off the phone. Lyra saw her pass momentarily into view and froze, one hand on the door handle.

"I have *guests*," Sheri was saying. "But I was listening, I promise . . ."

Then Sheri, who was pacing, passed out of view again without looking up.

Lyra eased open the screen door, wincing when it squeaked on its hinges. 72 ducked outside onto the stone patio. One of the cats was still staring at her, unblinkingly, and for a terrifying second Lyra thought it might open its mouth and let out a wail of alarm.

But it made not a sound, and so Lyra slipped after 72, closing the door behind her.

THIRTEEN

LYRA HALF EXPECTED SHERI TO come running after them, and they were several blocks away before she thought that they were probably safe. They found another park, with several dirty sandboxes and a rusted swing set at its center. But there were trees here, and shade, and they were alone.

She examined the pictures again, one by one. She'd seen romance on the nurses' televisions, of course, and heard the staff at Haven talk about boyfriends and girlfriends and wives and husbands. She knew about it. But knowing about what humans did, the kinds of relationships they had on TV, was different from seeing and holding proof of this. Dr. Saperstein had struck her not so much as human but as some bloodless stone deity come to life. She had never once seen him smile. True, he wasn't smiling in these pictures, either, but he was dressed in T-shirts and striped shorts and a baseball hat, like he could have been anybody. This made him more frightening to her, not less. She thought of the snakes at Haven that left their long, golden skins on the ground, brittle and husk-like.

Nurse Em was hardly recognizable. She looked so happy. Lyra thought again of the last time she'd seen her—sobbing into Dr. O'Donnell's arms. And she had killed herself, using a rope instead of a knife, as Pepper had.

What had happened?

Sheri had mentioned men in suits visiting Nurse Em before she died. Was Dr. Saperstein one of them? Before looking at the photographs, Lyra had never seen him in anything but a lab coat.

She unfolded the list. 72 leaned over her. He smelled sweet, as if he was sweating soap. "What does it say?" he asked impatiently, and she had the sudden, ridiculous urge to take his hand, to tuck herself into the space between his arm and shoulder, as Nurse Em and Dr. Saperstein were doing in the picture.

She read instead thirty-four names—all names she didn't know, nobody she recognized from Haven—in alphabetical order. Donald Bartlett. Caroline Ciao. Brandy-Nicole Harliss. She stopped. That name seemed somehow familiar, and yet she couldn't think why. But rereading it gave her the weirdest sensation, like when the doctors used to bang her on the knee to test her reflexes and she would see her body jerk. Like something inside of her was *stirring*.

The second piece of paper, Lyra had trouble deciphering at first. It wasn't a list, but a full page of writing, and it picked up in the middle of a sentence. As Lyra began to read, she had the impression that Nurse Em was talking to *her*, to an invisible other body that existed beyond the page.

. . . *eggs on my car*, it began. Lyra read the phrase several times, trying to make sense of it, before she decided there must have been a first sheet that had gotten lost. She kept reading, and both because it was easier for her to spell the words out and 72 was getting impatient, she read slowly, out loud.

"'Mark tells me not to worry so much. I know they're kooks'"—Lyra stumbled a little over the word, since she'd never heard it—"'but they aren't that far off. Someone stopped me the other day after I caught the ferry. They're raising zombies, aren't they? she said. A normal woman. Someone you'd see at the grocery store." She continued reading.

It gave me chills, Ellen. I felt for a second as if she knew. Is it really so different, after all?

I tell you, I never thought I'd miss Philadelphia. I don't miss the winters, that's for sure. But I miss you, Elbow, and

I miss how simple things felt back then. I even miss that shitty apartment we found through Drexel—remember?—and that stupid ex-boyfriend of yours who used to throw cans at your window. Ben? Sometimes I even miss our coursework (!!). At least I felt like we were on the right path.

I know what you'll say. It's the same thing Mark says. And I believe in the science, I do. If a parent loses a child . . . well, to have that child back . . . Who wouldn't want that? Who wouldn't try? When I think of people like Geoffrey Ives . . . All the money in the world and a dead baby that he couldn't save and all he wants is to make it better. To undo it.

But is it right? Mark thinks so. But I don't know. I can't decide. Dr. Haven wants to keep the NIH out of our hair, so he stays clear of dealing with the clinics, even though they've got fetal tissue they'll sell off for just the transportation fee. But already the funds are running thin. I don't think there's any way we'll last unless we get federal support, but if good old George W. outlaws spending on the research. . . .

Then there's the question of Dr. Haven. Ever since he went into AA, he's been changing. Mark worries he'll shut down the program, shut down the whole institution. He doesn't seem to be sure, at least not anymore, and if the donors' money dries up, we'll have to go in a totally new direction. Mark thinks there might be other ways, military research, cures—

The writing stopped. Lyra flipped over the page, but there was nothing more. She'd either been interrupted or the rest of what she'd said had been lost. Lyra also assumed from the reference to an Ellen, a name, that Nurse Em must have been intending the message for someone specific. She had never passed it on. But she'd felt it was important enough to hide—to hide well—and to deliver to someone before she died.

Was she hoping Sheri would find it?

What was Nurse Em hoping she'd see?

It was a puzzle. It was data. It was a *code,* like DNA was.

All codes could be read, if you only knew the key.

For a long minute, she and 72 stood there in silence, in the shadow of a construction of wood and rope and plastic whose purpose she didn't know. Codes everywhere. That was the problem with the outside world, the human world. The whole thing was made up of puzzles, of a language she didn't quite speak.

"What does it mean?" 72 asked finally, and she realized that that was the question: about standing in the park, about him and his moods and the way he sometimes rubbed the back of his neck as if something was bothering him there, about their escape and the fact that they were dying anyway but she didn't feel like she was dying. She didn't feel like dying.

What does it mean?

She had never asked that question.

She forced herself to reread, squinting, as if she could squeeze more meaning from the letters that way. She knew that Haven made replicas from human tissue, and she knew, of course, that it must have come from humans, people. She knew there were hospitals and clinics that did business with Haven, although she didn't know how she knew this, exactly. It was just a fact of life, like the cots and the Stew Pot and *failure to thrive*.

And she knew what zombies were. The nurses had talked about them, about several zombie movies and how scary they were. Lyra explained what they were to 72 but he, too, had heard of them. The human world—or at least some of it—had penetrated Haven.

"Read it out loud again," he said, and she did, conscious all the time of the sun on the back of her neck and 72 and his smell and that question—*what does it mean?*—all of it shimmering momentarily and so present and also so insubstantial, like something on fire, hot and at the same time burning into nonexistence.

She took her time with the sentences she thought were most important.

> . . . *he stays clear of dealing with the clinics, even though they've got fetal tissue they'll sell off for just the transportation fee* . . .

When I think of people like Geoffrey Ives . . .

All the money in the world and a dead baby that he couldn't save . . .

And finally she understood.

"Dead children," Lyra said. *Zombies. Is it so different?* "They were making replicas from dead children." Was that how she'd been made? From the tissue of a child who'd been loved, grieved over, and lost? It shouldn't have made a difference and yet it did, somehow. It wasn't even the fact that the children had died as much as the fact that at one time they'd been cared for.

And yet the process of making their doubles—the *science* of it—had turned Lyra and the other replicas into something different. She remembered how sometimes the voices of the protesters had carried over on the wind, across the miles of snaggletoothed marshes. *Monsters,* they'd shouted.

But for the first time Lyra felt not shame, but anger. She hadn't asked to be made. She'd been brought into the world a monster and then hated for it, and it wasn't her fault, and there was no meaning behind that.

None at all.

"It doesn't make sense," 72 said. "Why kill us, then?"

"Something changed," Lyra said. She could hardly remember Dr. Haven. She may have seen him once or twice. She could vividly recall his face, but then again she'd seen pictures of him her whole life: Dr. Haven in oils staring down at them from the framed painting at the end of the mess hall, Dr. Haven in black and white, pictured squinting into the sun in front of G-Wing.

They stood there again in silence. Had Lyra been intended originally for the human parents of a child who had died? But if so, why had they never come for her? Maybe they had, but found the substitute terrible.

Maybe they hadn't been able to stomach looking at her—the flimsy substitute for the girl they'd loved and had to grieve.

"She mentions a cure," 72 said quietly. "Maybe you were right. Maybe she did know something that could help us."

"Well, she's dead now," Lyra said. Her voice sounded hollow, as if she were speaking into a cup.

"Lyra." 72 touched her elbow, and she pulled away from him. His touch burned, *physically* burned, although she knew that was impossible. His skin was no hotter than anyone else's. She turned away from him, blinking hard, and for a second, looking out across the park and to the houses in the distance—all those parents, families, moms and dads—she transformed the afternoon sun striking the windows into white flame, and imagined burning the whole world down, just like they'd burned down Haven.

"On the bus you asked me why the cuts," 72 said. This surprised her, and she momentarily forgot her anger and turned back to look at him. His skin in the light looked like something edible, coffee and milk. "When I was younger I didn't understand what I was. *If* I was."

Lyra didn't have to say anything to show she understood. She had wondered the same thing. She had confused *it* for *I*, had pinched number 25 to see if she herself would feel it, because she didn't understand where she ended and the herd began.

"I started thinking maybe I wasn't real. And then I started worrying that I wasn't, that I was disappearing. I used to . . ." He swallowed and rubbed his forehead, and Lyra realized with a sudden thrill she *knew* what he was feeling: he was scared. She had read him.

"It's okay," she said automatically.

"I got hold of one of the doctor's scalpels once," he said, in a sudden rush. "I kept it in my mattress, took out some of the stuffing so that no one would find it." Lyra thought of the hole in Ursa Major's mattress, and all the things they'd found stashed inside of it. She thought, too, of how Ursa had just stood there and screamed while her mattress was emptied—one high, shrill note, like the cresting of an alarm. "I used to have to check. I felt better when I saw the blood. I knew I was still alive, then." He raised his eyes to hers, and in her chest she had a lifting, swooping sensation, as if something heavy had come loose. "You wanted to know. So I'm telling you."

She didn't know what to say. So she said, "Thank you." She reached out and moved her finger from his elbow all the way to his wrist, over the ridge of his scars, to show him it was okay, and that she understood. She could feel him watching her. She could *feel* him, everywhere he was, as if he was distorting the air, making it heavier.

She had never *felt* so much in her life.

"We'll go back," 72 said, so quietly she nearly missed it.

"Back?" she repeated. He was standing so close she was suddenly afraid and took a step away from him.

"The girl, Gemma. And Jake." He hesitated. "You were right all along. They might be able to help. They know about Haven. Maybe they'll know about a cure, too."

"But . . ." She shook her head. "You said you didn't trust them."

"I don't," he said simply. "But I don't trust anyone."

"Even me?" Lyra asked.

Something changed in his eyes. "You're different," he said, in a softer voice.

"Why?" She was aware of how close they were, and of the stillness of the afternoon, all the trees bound and silent.

He almost smiled. He reached up. He pressed a thumb

to her lower lip. His skin tasted like salt. "Because we're the same."

Lyra knew they'd never be able to backtrack. They'd left the house in the middle of the night and they'd hardly been paying attention—they'd been thinking of nothing but escape—and she could remember no special feature of the house to which they'd been taken, nothing to distinguish it from its neighbors.

Fortunately, 72 remembered that Jake had written down his address and phone number. They couldn't call—72 had stolen Jake's phone, and besides, Lyra had never made a call before and, though she had often seen the nurses talking on their cell phones, wasn't sure she knew how to do it—and so they started the process again of asking strangers how to get to 1211 Route 12, Little Waller, Florida.

A woman with hair frosted a vague orange color directed them to a car rental agency, but almost as soon as they entered, the man behind the counter began asking for licenses and credit cards and other things neither one of them had. Lyra got flustered again, upsetting a small display of maps with her elbow so the maps went fanning out across the counter. 72 got angry. He accused the man of shouting.

"I barely raised my voice," the man said. "You some kinda freak or something?"

Quickly, 72 reached for his pocket, and Lyra was worried he was going for his knife. The man must have been worried, too, because he stumbled backward, toppling his chair. But instead 72 just put the paper with Jake's address onto the desk.

"You have a map," he said. His voice was low and tight, as if the words were bound together with wire. "Show us how to get here. *Please.*"

The man reached for a map slowly, keeping his eyes on 72. A TV in the corner reeled off the sound of an audience laughing, but otherwise it was so quiet that Lyra could hear the man's lungs, like something wet caught in his chest as he took a red pen, pointed out the different bus routes they could take to reach Little Waller, less than an hour away. Lyra noticed his hand was shaking ever so slightly—and for the first time the idea of being a *freak*, of being a *monster*, made her feel not ashamed but powerful.

There were only two other passengers on the bus, including a man wearing several different layers of clothing who smelled like sweat and urine. Lyra and 72 took a seat at the very back. They sat so close their thighs and knees touched, and Lyra felt the warmth coming through the window like the gentle pressure of a hand. As the bus passed the water park, Lyra pressed her nose to the window, eager again for the sight of all those real human families. But the sun was hard in her eyes and she could see nothing but blurred, indistinct figures.

Then they were on the highway again, passing long stretches of vivid green space where there were no towns or houses, just trees crowning the roads, just growth and dark spaces.

72 was quiet for so long, leaning back with his eyes closed, she thought he'd fallen asleep. But then he turned to face her. The sunlight fell across his skin and made it seem to glow. When he spoke, she felt his breath on her ear and in her hair. "Can I ask you a question about your story?" he said. "About the little prince, and the rose?"

"Okay." Lyra took a breath. She again had a sense of his whole body extended there in space, the miracle of all those interwoven molecules that kept him together.

His eyes were dark, and she could see herself inside of them. "You said the Little Prince lived on Planet B-612," he said. "You pointed it out to me." He bit his lip and she had the strangest desire to bite it too, to feel his lips with her mouth. "But all the stars look the same. So how do you know?"

"Not if you look closely," she said. Her body was bright hot, burning. It was his breath on her shoulder and the feel of him next to her in the afternoon sun. "That's what the Little Prince found too, on his travels. He thought his rose was the only rose in the whole universe at first. But then he came down to earth and found a garden of them."

72 shifted and their knees touched again. The sun made his eyes dazzle, and the rest of the world was disappearing. "What happened then?"

She tried to remember the rest of the story. It was hard to concentrate with him so close. She kept imagining his skin under his clothing, and beneath his skin, his organs and ribs and the blood alive in his veins, kept thinking of this miracle, that he should exist, that they both should, instead of just being empty space. But what came to her was Dr. O'Donnell's voice, and the way she'd leaned forward to read this part of the book, her dirty-blond hair falling out from where it was tucked behind her ears.

"He was very sad," Lyra said slowly. "He thought the rose had tricked him. She wasn't special. She was just like thousands of other roses. Identical to them," she added.

"A replica," 72 said.

"Exactly," Lyra said, although it was the first time she'd made the connection, and understood, truly understood, why Dr. O'Donnell had given her that particular book. "Just like a replica. Only . . ."

"What?"

"Only the Little Prince realized his rose was special. She was the only one in the universe. Because he'd cared for her, and talked with her, and protected her from caterpillars. She was *his* rose. And that made her more special than all the other roses in the universe combined." Lyra found the sun was painful and blinked. She was crying. She turned away and brought a hand to her face quickly, hoping 72 wouldn't see.

But he caught her hand. And before she could ask what he was doing, before she could even be afraid, her body responded. It knew what to do. It sensed a question and answered for her, so she found herself turning to face him, placing her hand against his face so the warmth of him spread through her fingers. They sat there, looking at each other, on a bus suspended in space. She knew it was impossible, but she thought her heart stopped beating completely.

"Lyra," he whispered.

"What?" she whispered back. His face was cut into geometric shapes by shadows, and he was a beautiful puzzle to her, mysterious and ever-changing.

But he didn't answer. He brought his fingers to her face. He touched her cheekbones and her forehead and the bridge of her nose. "Lyra," he said again. "I like your name." Then: "I wish I had a name."

Lyra closed her eyes. He kept touching her. He ran his fingers across her scalp. He traced the long curve of her earlobe, and then moved a finger down her neck, pressing lightly as though to feel her pulse beating up through his hand. And everywhere he touched, she imagined she was healed. She imagined the disease simply vanishing, evaporating, like water under the sun. "We can give you a name," she said, still with her eyes closed. "You can take one from the stars, like I did."

He was quiet for a while. His hand moved to her shoulder. He walked his fingers along her collarbone. He placed his thumb in the hollow of her throat.

"You pick," he said, and for the briefest second he touched her lips, too. Then he placed his hand flat against her chest, just above her heart.

In the darkness behind her eyelids she saw a universe explode into being, expand into brightness. She pictured names and stars bright blue or purple or white-hot.

"Caelum," she said. She knew it was right as soon as she said it out loud. "You'll be Caelum."

"Caelum," he repeated. Even without opening her eyes, she could tell he was smiling.

FOURTEEN

SOMETHING HAD CHANGED. LYRA COULDN'T
have said what it was, exactly, only that something had
softened in Caelum, or in her, or both. They were bound
together. They had chosen each other, to be responsible
for and to care for each other.

By four p.m. they had reached Little Waller, although
Lyra asked several people to be sure. A policeman spotted
them standing at a corner, puzzling over the sign, and
came loping down the street. Lyra's chest tightened—
he was wearing a uniform similar to the one the guards
had worn at Haven, and she thought of that night on the
marshes and how the soldiers had been afraid to move
Cassiopeia, afraid she might be contagious. *You know how
expensive these things are to make?* But the policeman only
asked them if they needed help and pointed the way.

"Straight and keep walking," he said. "That road runs

right out into marshland. Couldn't have picked a nicer day for it." She didn't know whether he was being serious. It was already so hot the pavement shimmered.

On their way through town they passed a blocky cement building called the Woodcrest Retirement Home. Behind a tall hedgerow, several sprinklers were tossing up water, crossing in midair, making shimmering rainbows. Both Lyra and Caelum crouched to drink, and Lyra felt a bit like a dog but not in a bad way. She and Caelum were a team, a pack. They could survive like this. They would survive. They'd figure out a way.

Together.

Caelum stood guard while Lyra took off her filthy shirt and her jeans, and, crouching, moved into the spray of water to clean herself. They had no towels, so she had to get dressed right away again, but it didn't matter: the water was delicious and cold, and she was happier than she could ever remember being. Then she stood watch for him, although she couldn't resist looking after he'd stripped off his shirt. She had seen anatomical drawings of the muscles connecting the shoulder blades and torqued around the spine, but she had never imagined that they could make this, something seamless and graceful. Something *beautiful*.

They set out again, their shirts damp with water, their socks squelching a little in their shoes. Neither of them cared. They walked in silence, but it wasn't uncomfortable at all. Lyra and Caelum: the two replicas with names plucked straight from the stars.

Jake's road was little more than a dirt path through the woods, crowded with tall spruce trees and hanging moss and loud with the chitter of birds. All at once Lyra felt her happiness picked apart by anxiety, by the sense of someone concealed and watching. But the road was empty except for a dead turtle, flattened under a car tire, and a bird picking at it. The bird flapped away as soon as they approached.

What was that feeling? It was standing naked in front of a team of doctors and nurses. It was the lights in the operation room, and the shadow of people moving behind glass.

Jake's house, number 1211, looked like it had simply been dropped there, temporarily stifling a nest of exploding growth. Two shutters were broken and the window boxes were empty. But a little lawn had been cleared in front of the porch, and someone had repainted the exterior yellow to conceal the moisture rotting out the baseboards. A cat slunk beneath the porch, and for a paranoid second Lyra was sure that Sheri Hayes had followed them all this way to yell at them for ruining her pictures. But that didn't make sense. And there must be many cats in the world. There were many *everything* in this world.

Lyra followed Caelum to the front door. The sun was hot on the back of her neck and felt weighty. They knocked and rang the doorbell. No one came. Jake's car was in the driveway, though. Lyra recognized it. They rang the doorbell again. Caelum leaned in to listen at the door. But it was obvious no one was home. There was not a single creak from inside.

"He must be out," Lyra said at last, although she hated to admit it. The disappointment was almost physical. Suddenly she was exhausted again.

"We'll wait for him here, then," Caelum said. When Lyra looked at him, he shrugged. "He's got to be back sometime, right?"

"He said his aunt would come home today," Lyra said. She didn't have a clear sense of what an aunt was but knew it meant family, like mother and grandmother. "What if his aunt finds us first?"

Caelum tested the door, but it was locked. "Come on," he said. "There must be another way in."

They went around the house to the back. Here there were no signs, and no grass, either: just a small cement patio and planters filled with dying brown things, plus an old sofa, puddled with rain and specked with mildew. Sliding doors opened onto the patio and these, Lyra was relieved to find, were unlocked. At least they could wait inside, where she didn't feel so exposed.

The kitchen was a mess. There were papers scattered across the table. The drawers hung open. The refrigerator was pulled away from the wall, revealing plastic disks of insect poison behind it. Even the microwave was open. There was mail on the floor, and Lyra saw footprints where someone had walked.

"It's wrong," Lyra said immediately.

"What is?"

"All of it." Lyra thought about how Jake had set a napkin on the coffee table before setting down a glass of water, how he had adjusted his computer so that it ran parallel to the table edge. "Someone else was here before us."

Caelum looked at her. "Or he doesn't like to pick up after himself," he said.

"No." Lyra shook her head. She was afraid. "Someone was here."

They moved from the kitchen into a small living room. This, too, was a mess. It was as if a library had exploded. Papers, folders, books. A coffee mug, overturned, pooling onto the rug. Jake's computer was on the couch, flashing a moving image—a picture of deep space, vivid with color. When Lyra touched it, the image dissolved, leaving in its place a small white box and the demand for a password. Inspired, she bent down and sought out the letters on the keyboard one by one. H-A-V-E-N. But the password was refused, and almost immediately she felt sorry. The help they needed wouldn't be found there on the computer anyway.

Caelum went out of the living room. Lyra was about to follow him when she saw several photographs displayed on a wall-mounted shelf. One of them, a portrait of Jake from when he was a kid, was framed. The other two were just stacked there, and smudgy with fingerprints.

In one of them Jake was standing next to a man she originally confused for a much older replica—they had the same dark eyes and hair, the same well-cut chin and cheekbones—but she quickly realized the man must be his father. In another, a woman with white-blond hair and breasts coming out of a tank top was grimacing at the camera, holding tight to Jake's shoulder, as if she was afraid he might run away. Was this *aunt*? It was family, she was sure of it. The woman also had Jake's square chin.

For some reason, this made her sad. Replicas were singular events. They exploded into being and they died, leaving no one. But people were just one in an interlinking series of other people.

She made a sudden decision: she would ask Caelum to be her family. That way, when she died, she wouldn't be completely alone.

In another room, Caelum shouted for her. She turned

and saw him back into the hall. In the dim light, he looked pale.

"What?" she said. "What is it?" But she knew already.

He didn't look at her. "Dead," he said, with a single nod, and Lyra replaced the photographs, facedown, as if they might hear. "Jake's dead."

He was hanging from the closet door, just pinned there like an old suit. He'd written with black marker on one of the walls. *I'm so lonely. I can't take it anymore.* This room, the bedroom, was equally as messy as the others. A second computer was open on the bed.

Lyra had seen countless dead bodies, but this one was the first that made her want to look away. Jake Witz was no longer nice to look at. His face was purpled with blood. His tongue was exposed, stiff and dark, like something foreign that had gotten lodged there. His fingernails were broken where he had tried to free the belt, which had been wedged between the door frame and hammered in place to the far side of the door. A thick film of blood and spit had dried on his lips.

"What do you think?" Caelum asked.

"Nurse Emily hung herself, too," Lyra said, stepping out into the hallway. A wave of dizziness overtook her, and she reached out to steady herself on a wall. Caelum followed her, and briefly put a hand on her lower back.

She wished herself back into the field last night, and their bodies silhouetted by all that darkness. "That's what Sheri said."

Caelum watched her. "You don't believe it?"

She didn't know what she believed. "Someone was here," she repeated. She took a step toward the kitchen and stumbled. Caelum caught her elbow before she could fall. "I'm all right," she said, gasping a little. "I just need to sit."

But she felt no better sitting in Jake's kitchen and drinking water from one of his water glasses, which tasted like soap from the dishwasher. Someone had been here. Someone from Haven? They couldn't stay here. What if whoever had killed Jake came back to clean up? They needed to get to Gemma, but she had no idea how. She couldn't keep her thoughts together. They kept scattering like points of light across her vision. An alarm was going off. A beeping. She stood up. Then she saw Jake rooting through the backpack and remembered: the phone. The phone was ringing.

The phone.

"I thought you turned it off," Caelum said.

"It must have come on again," Lyra said. "Here. Give it to me." The number on the screen was labeled *Aunt Kit* and she waited, holding her breath, until the phone stopped ringing, her chest full of sharp pains. People called phones, phones called people. Would Gemma be stored in Jake's phone? Maybe. But she had no idea how to look for Gemma, how to *get* to her.

"Lyra." Caelum's hand found her wrist. His fingers were cold. But at that moment she heard it too: footsteps outside, the muffled sound of voices. They had barely slipped into the living room before they heard the patio doors slide open and then close again. For a delirious second Lyra hoped that maybe Gemma had come for them, and thought about peeking into the kitchen to check, but when a woman spoke, her voice was unfamiliar.

"These cleanup jobs," she said. "I feel like a goddamn housekeeper. What exactly are we supposed to do?"

"You're looking at it. The first team left a mess. Livingston's worried someone might get suspicious. Doesn't say suicide. You're supposed to get all your shit in order, not trash the fucking place."

"Did they find anything?"

"Don't know. The kid knew too much, though, otherwise he wouldn't be swinging from a rope."

Sweat gathered between Lyra's breasts. She'd been right to worry that the people who killed Jake might come back. Could she and Caelum make it to the front door without being seen? They would have to pass in front of the kitchen. If the strangers were busy or had their backs turned, if they were over by the refrigerator without a clear view of the hallway, she and Caelum might manage it.

The sound of rustling papers. A chair scraping back from the table. How long would it take them to straighten up the kitchen? Not long. One of them was whistling. Lyra didn't know that people could be so casual about killing other people as they were about killing replicas. She felt something hard and hot in her throat, as if she'd swallowed an explosive. She'd been angry before, and she'd been lonely and afraid. But she had never hated, not like this.

She hated the people in the next room. She hated Dr. Saperstein. She hated the people who had killed Jake Witz, and the people who'd filled her blood with disease. She wanted to see them die.

Caelum eased off the wall, nodding to the front door. Lyra nodded back to show she understood, although she didn't really see how she would move. She was liquid fear and anger. She wanted to scream, and she could hardly stay on her feet.

Caelum moved. For a second that felt like forever, passing the entrance to the kitchen, he was exposed. It seemed to Lyra he was hanging there, hooked to the air the way Jake Witz had been hooked to the door. But then he was in the hall, and the sound of his footsteps was con-cealed by all the noise from the kitchen. He turned back to gesture to Lyra. *Come.*

She unstuck herself from the wall. She imagined if she turned around she would see her silhouette, all dark and sweat-discolored. On the desk Jake's computer was still flashing the picture of a beach, and then, for reasons that Lyra didn't totally understand, she was moving not toward the door but away from it. She picked up the computer, which was surprisingly light, and hugged it to her chest. She felt as if her body was making decisions and relaying them to her brain and not the other way around.

Caelum was white-faced, staring at her. She knew he wanted to scream at her to hurry up. She knew he wanted to yell *What were you thinking?* She could feel the charge of his fear in the silence.

She took a step toward the door.

The phone in her pocket, Jake's phone, began to ring.

The whole world went silent and still. In Lyra's head, a white burst of panic, a life at an end. The noise from the kitchen had completely stopped.

Then: "What the fuck is that?"

"It's a phone."

"No shit. Where's it coming from?"

She had no time to think. Vaguely she saw Caelum disappear, retreating down the hall. She took the phone from her pocket and tossed it on the carpet, then shimmied behind the couch, still holding Caelum's computer, as the man crossed heavily into the room. She got down on the floor, on her stomach, inhaling the smell of old upholstery and dust. When she breathed, dust stirred on the exhale. But she tried not to breathe.

She saw the man toe the cell phone with a boot. "Aw. Look at that. Aunt Kit's calling."

The woman's voice was now distant. She must have gone into the bedroom, or maybe the bathroom at the end of the hall. "What'd they think, he was hiding state secrets in his porn collection? They really did a number on this place, huh?"

"You think I should snatch the phone?" The man bent down. She saw his fingers, long and a little fat. Stupidly, she felt like crying. She didn't know why, exactly. They'd stolen the phone from Jake, but now it felt like a gift, like something they were meant to have. She didn't like seeing the man's fingers on it.

"Hell no. That's the first thing the police are gonna look for. They'll know someone was here if it's gone. These kids nowadays . . ."

The man straightened up, leaving the phone, now silent again, where it was. She waited until she heard his footsteps go creaking down the hall before sliding out from behind the couch, nauseous now with fear and the nearness of her discovery. Her hand was shaking when she reached for Jake's phone, and when she stood up again

she fought against a wave of blackness that nearly top-
pled her. She couldn't get sick now. She was almost out.
Almost safe.

She took a step toward the door, and another step. She
was dizzy. She reached out a hand to steady herself against
the wall. The computer seemed heavier than it had only
a minute ago. Her head was full of a strange buzzing, like
the noise of bees.

"Aw, fuck. Now I left *my* phone—"

She barely registered the man talking again before he
had stepped into the hallway and spotted her. He gave a
shout—and that, his moment of surprise, of utter shock,
was what saved her life. She tore her hand away from the
wall and plunged across the living room, losing sight of
him as she careened into the front hall.

He was shouting. The woman, too. And there were
footsteps pounding after her but Lyra didn't look back,
didn't stop. Caelum was at the front door. He was fumbling with the locks. He was saying something she
couldn't hear. The door was open. She banged against the
screen door hard with an elbow. There was a view of blue
sky, of dirt and grass and exterior, and voices ringing like
alarms inside her head, and then they were outside, they
were out.

FIFTEEN

THEY HAD NO TIME TO do anything but duck behind a neighbor's car before they saw a dark-blue sedan edge out from Jake's driveway and nose into the street. They waited until the noise of the engine faded, then stood and started down the rutted dirt road, turning onto the next street they came to, this one thick with growth and lined with a ruin of old houses. They needed to get back to town. But Lyra was mixed up. Which way had they come?

They turned again and froze. Several blocks away, the sedan was coming toward them at a crawl. They pivoted and began to run. Lyra didn't know whether they'd been spotted and was too afraid to look. There was a roaring in her ears. The car, getting closer?

"Town." Lyra's breath was coming in short gasps, like something alive inside her chest. "We need to get back to town."

She didn't know whether Caelum had heard. He made a hard right and took off straight across a front yard overgrown with high weeds. A dog began to bark, but no one came out. They squeezed into the narrow dark space between the garage and the house just as the sedan came around the corner, and looking back, Lyra saw the woman's face, white with concentration, scanning the streets through the open window. Lyra's legs were shaking so badly Caelum had to put his arms around her to keep her on her feet. His chest moved against her back, his breath was in her hair and on her neck, and she wished the world would end so she could end with it, so she didn't have to run anymore, so Caelum could stay with her in a dark, close space that felt like being buried.

But the world didn't end, of course. When the sedan was once again out of view, Caelum released her. "Now," he said. But she found she couldn't move. She was so tired.

"Wait. I don't think I can."

"Okay." Caelum looked young in the half dark, with the sky a narrow artery above them. "We'll stay here for a bit."

"No. I don't think I can. Go on." Lyra was still having trouble breathing. It felt as if her lungs were wrapped in medical gauze. She leaned back against the garage, which was made of cinder block and very cool, and closed her eyes. The space was full of spiderwebs and wet leaves. It smelled like decay. What was the point, anyway? How long did she really have?

Half of her wanted simply to walk out into the road and wait for their pursuers to find her. Where would they take her? She would be reunited with the rest of the replicas, she was sure. Or maybe she would be killed and her body disposed of. Maybe they were erasing the experiment, slowly eradicating all indications that Haven had ever existed. But it would be easier. So much easier.

"You can't give up now," Caelum said. "Lyra. Listen to me." He put a hand on her cheek and she opened her eyes. His thumb moved along the ridge of her cheekbone, as it had last night. His lips were very close. His eyes were dark and long-lashed. Beautiful. "You named me. That means I'm yours, doesn't it? I'm yours and you're mine."

"I'm scared," Lyra said. And she was—scared of the running, scared of what would happen to them, but scared, too, of how close he was standing, of how her body changed when he touched her and became fluid-feeling, as if something hard deep inside of her were softening. She knew that there were electrical currents in the body and that was what she was reminded of now, of currents flowing between them, of thousands of lights.

"I'm scared too," he said. He leaned forward and touched his forehead to hers. And still her body called out for something, something more and deeper and closer, but she didn't know what. She wished them out of the bodies that divided them. She thought of the word *love*, and wondered whether this, this feeling of never being able to get close enough, was it. She had never been taught. But she thought so.

"I love you," she said. The words felt strange, foreign to her, like a new food. But not unpleasant.

"I love you," Caelum repeated back to her, and smiled. She could tell the words were just as surprising to him. He said them again. "I love you."

Inside her chest, a door opened, and she found she was at last breathing easily, and now had the strength to go on.

They made it back into town without seeing the sedan again, but they were standing at the first bus stop they could find, debating where to go next, when Lyra spotted the man from the house in a parking lot across the road, passing between the businesses, delis, and retail shops that were clustered together, like beads someone had strung along the same necklace. She took Caelum's hand and they hurried to the most crowded place they could find: a dim restaurant called the Blue Gator, separated from the road by a scrub of sad little trees. Dozens of men were crowded around a counter, drinking and watching sports, occasionally letting out a cheer or a groan in unison. Lyra and Caelum moved toward the back of the restaurant, past old wood tables filled with kids squabbling over plates of french fries and couples drinking and staring dull-eyed at the TVs. A hallway led back toward the kitchen. A girl with a haircut almost like Lyra's was standing beneath a sign that indicated a restroom, her fingers skating over the screen of her phone, her chin prominent in the blue light cast by its glow. Lyra had an idea.

She took Jake Witz's phone from her pocket.

"Hello." Lyra held out the phone. The girl's eyes jumped from her screen to Lyra to Caelum. "Can you please help?"

"Help with what?" the girl said. She didn't sound mean, but she didn't sound exactly friendly, either. Caelum kept turning around to look at the door, to make sure they hadn't been followed, and the girl ignored Lyra to watch him.

"We need to find Gemma," Lyra said. "In the phone," she added impatiently, and finally the short-haired girl dragged her eyes from Caelum to look at her. "We need to find Gemma in the phone. We don't know how."

The girl snorted. She had a metal ring in her nose. "Are you serious?" When Lyra didn't answer, she rolled her eyes and took the phone. She made several quick movements with her fingers and then passed the phone back to Lyra. "You should really keep that thing locked, you know. Do I get a prize now?"

Lyra's heart leapt. She pressed the phone to her ear but heard nothing but silence. She shook her head. "It's not *working*."

"Jesus. Where do you *come* from? The 1800s?" The girl snatched the phone back, made another quick adjustment, and then jammed it to Lyra's ear. "Happy now?"

The phone was ringing. Lyra held her breath. She counted one ring, two rings, three. How long would it ring, she wondered? But then there was a nearly inaudible click.

"Jake?" Gemma's voice sounded so close Lyra nearly jerked the phone away in surprise. "Is that you?"

Lyra turned away, so the short-haired girl, who was still watching her suspiciously, wouldn't be able to hear. "It's not Jake," she said. "Jake is dead. And we need your help."

SIXTEEN

GEMMA AND A BLOND-HAIRED BOY named Pete arrived just as a man in an apron was badgering Lyra and Caelum to order something or leave. Lyra was afraid to go outside. She thought it likely that the people who'd been in Jake's house were still out there, walking the streets, waiting for them. So when Gemma came through the crowd—her eyes big and worried in that pretty moon-face, the face that had so recently belonged to Cassiopeia—she felt a wash of relief so strong she nearly began to cry. They were safe.

"It's all right. They're with us, and we're leaving," Gemma said, and the man in his apron scurried away. "Are you okay?" she asked, and Lyra nodded. She felt as if a hand had reached down and picked her up. And again, a memory came to her of warmth and closeness, an impression of one of the birthers rocking her, singing in her ear. But she knew it must be made up. The birthers didn't hold the human models they made. They came and were kept in the darkness of the barracks, and were sent away in darkness, too, after receiving their pay.

The birthers weren't male, either. But in her memory, or her imagination, or her fantasy, she felt the tickle of a beard on her forehead, and clear gray eyes, and a man's hands, scarred across the knuckles, touching her face.

Caelum always kept close to her now. Even in the car he sat only inches away from Lyra, with one hand pressed to hers. She understood that they were bound together, and she thought of their lives and their fates like a double-stranded helix, wound around each other, webbed with meaning. And she felt that next to him she could face anything, even a slow death, even the world that kept unfolding into new highways and more people and a greater horizon.

In the car, Lyra told Gemma about going to track down Emily Huang and discovering she was dead.

"I could have told you that," Gemma said, and Lyra heard the criticism in her voice: *If you hadn't run.* She was getting better at sorting out tones and moods.

She described how they had found the card with Jake's address and determined to go and find him. She told Gemma about the unlocked screen door and finding him in the bedroom with a crust of dried blood on his lips.

"They must have come for him right after we left," Gemma whispered to the boy, Pete. "God. I might throw up."

"It's not your fault," he said, and reached out to place a hand on her thigh. Lyra saw this and wondered if Gemma and Pete were bound in the same way she was to Caelum.

"Both of them strung up, made to look like suicides," Gemma said, and turned away to cough. There had been a fire, she had told them, but Lyra would have known anyway. The whole car smelled like smoke. "Must be the military's little specialty."

"Less suspicious, maybe, than a gun," Pete said.

She told them about the man and woman who'd shown up only a few minutes later to finish the job of staging a suicide, and how she'd nearly been caught and had to hide behind the sofa.

"Holy shit," Pete said, and this time it was Gemma who reached over to squeeze *his* leg.

"I took his computer," Lyra said.

Gemma turned around in her seat. "You what?"

"I don't know why." Lyra was still ashamed that they'd stolen Jake's cell phone and left in the middle of the night. She didn't want Gemma to hate her. "I thought it might be useful, so I took it."

Gemma blinked. If Lyra squinted, she could pretend

she was looking at Cassiopeia instead—a healthy Cassiopeia, a Cassiopeia with soft brown hair and a quick smile. She could have been number 11.

"That's brilliant," Gemma said. "You're a genius."

Caelum spoke up too, to explain why they had run, and Gemma seemed to understand. Lyra was intensely relieved: she wondered whether in some strange way, some mystery of biology, she and Gemma got along for the same reason she had always liked Cassiopeia.

"And I almost forgot." She took the backpack wedged at Caelum's feet and removed the papers and photos she'd found hidden behind the picture frames at Sheri's house. "Before she died, Nurse Em gave three pieces of art to her next-door neighbor. I found these hidden in the backing."

Gemma held the pages in her hands carefully, as if they were insect wings. She stared for a long time at the list of names that Lyra hadn't been able to make sense of. "Can I keep these?" she asked.

"Okay." Lyra had been looking forward to rebuilding her collection of reading materials, using these pages as a start to her new library. But she knew they might be important—they must be, if Nurse Em had wanted them to stay hidden.

"I'll give them back, I promise," Gemma said, as if she knew what Lyra was thinking. Gemma seemed to have that uncanny ability. Lyra wondered whether Gemma was special, or whether she was simply the first person to care what Lyra thought and felt. Gemma folded the pages carefully and tucked them inside a pocket. Lyra was sorry to see them go. "Look," Gemma said. "There's something I need to tell you. Something about your past."

The car jerked. Pete had barely swerved to avoid an object in the road, some kind of animal, Lyra thought, although they were past it too quickly for her to make out what it was.

"What?" she said. "What is it?" She was suddenly afraid but couldn't say why. She thought she could feel Caelum's pulse beating through her palm. She thought it began to beat faster.

Gemma was squinting as if trying to see through a hard light. "You weren't actually made at Haven."

A burst of white behind Lyra's eyes—a sure sign of a bad headache to come. *Side effects. Symptoms.* She pictured those hands again, the scar across the knuckles, the tickle of a beard on her forehead. Imagination. Fantasy.

"What do you mean?" It was Caelum who spoke. "Where was she made?"

"Nowhere," Gemma said, and Lyra heard the word as if it was coming to her through water. As if she was drowning. *Nowhere.* A terrible, lonely word. "This list is of kids who got taken from their families and brought to Haven, at a time the institute couldn't afford to keep making human models. The third name, Brandy-Nicole Harliss, is your birth name. Your *real* name. That's the name your parents gave you."

Next to her, Caelum twitched. Lyra's lungs didn't feel like they were working. She could hardly breathe. "My . . ." She couldn't say the word *parents*. It didn't make sense. She thought of the birthers in the barracks and the new replicas sleeping in their pretty little incubators in Postnatal. That was her world. That was where she'd come from.

"You have parents," Gemma said gently, as if she was delivering bad news. And it *was* bad news. It was unimaginable, horrific. Lyra had wondered sometimes about what it would be like to have Dr. O'Donnell as a mother, what it would be like to have parents, generally, but never had she truly thought about being a person, natural-born, exploded into being by chance. One of *them*. "Well, you have a father. He's been looking for you all this time. He's loved you all this time."

That word, *love*. It shocked her. It hit her like a blade in the chest and she cried out, feeling the pain of it, the raw unexpectedness, as if an old wound had opened. Although she had dreamed when she was little about going home with one of the nurses—although she'd even, secretly, imagined Dr. O'Donnell returning for her one day, taking Lyra in a lemon-scented hug—these were fantasies, and even in her fantasies home looked much like Haven, with white walls and high lights and the soothing sounds of rubber soles on linoleum.

She didn't want love, not from a stranger, not from a *father*. She was a replica.

Caelum took his hand from hers. He turned back toward the window.

No, she wanted to say. She felt somehow dirty. *It isn't true. It can't be.* But she was paralyzed, suffocating under the weight of what Gemma had told her. She couldn't move to touch Caelum's arm, to tell him it was all right. She couldn't ask him to forgive her.

He didn't look at her at all after that.

SEVENTEEN

SHE DIDN'T WANT A FATHER.

She had never even known what a father did, had never completely understood why fathers were necessary. When she tried to imagine one now she thought instead of God, of his dark beard and narrow eyes, of the way he always seemed to be sneering, even when he smiled. She thought of Werner, whose fingers were yellowed and smelled like smoke; or of Nurse Wanna Bet, a male, pinching her skin before inserting the syringes, or fiddling with IV bags, or poking her stomach for signs of distention.

And yet, alongside these ideas was her impression—her memory?—of that plastic cup, of hands rocking her to sleep and the tickle of a beard.

Caelum didn't speak again until they stopped for the night, just outside of a place called Savannah. Lyra was both relieved and disappointed to learn they wouldn't be going on. She was dreading meeting her father, whoever he was, but also desperate to get it over with, and had assumed Gemma would take her straight back to him. Now she would have to live instead with her fantasy of him, his face transforming into the face of various Haven doctors and nurses, into the soldiers on the marshes with their helmets and guns, into the hard look of the men who came on unmarked barges to load the body when a replica had died: these were the only men she had ever known.

They stopped at an enormous parking lot full of other vehicles, concealed from the highway beneath a heavy line of plane trees and shaded by woods on all sides. Gemma told her that these camps existed across the country for people traveling by camper van and RV—two words Lyra didn't know, although she assumed they referred to the type of cars parked in the lot, which looked as though they'd been inflated to four times normal size—and once again she was struck by just how many people there must be in the world, enough so that even the ones traveling between towns had their own little network of places to stop for the night. It made her sad. She wondered whether she would ever feel she had a place in this world.

All she knew was that if she had a place, it must be with Caelum.

"I'll be back," Caelum said when they got out of the

car—the first words he had spoken in hours.

"I'll come with you," Lyra said quickly. But she found that walking next to him, she couldn't find words to say what she wanted to say. It was as if a wall had come down between them. She felt as if he was a stranger again, as if he was the boy she'd met out on the marshes. Even his face looked different—harder, more angular.

At one end of the camp was a whitewashed building with separate bathrooms for men and women, and shower stalls that could be accessed by putting coins in a slot in the lockbox on the doors. Lyra found she did after all want a shower. She wished she could wash off the past few hours: the dizzying reality that somewhere out there were people who'd birthed her, the memory of Jake Witz's face, bloated and terrible, and the smell of blood and sick that still seemed to hang to her clothes. How did she even know Gemma was telling her the truth? But she trusted Gemma instinctively, no matter what Caelum had originally feared, and when Gemma offered her coins to work the door, she accepted.

The shower was slick with soap scum and reminded her of the bright tiles of Haven and all the replicas showering in groups, herded under the showers in three-minute bursts. She missed that. She missed the order, the routine, the nurses telling her where to go and when. But at the same time the Lyra who was content to float through the days, who lay down on the paper-covered medical beds and let Squeezeme and Thermoscan do their work, who thought of them as friends, even, felt impossibly foreign. She couldn't remember being that girl.

She had no towel, so when she got dressed again, her hair, still wet, dampened her shoulders and her shirt. But she felt better, cleaner. A father. She experimented with holding the idea for two, three seconds at a time now without shame. She brushed up next to it, got close, sniffed around it like an animal exploring something new. What would it be like to have a father? What did a father actually *do*? She had no idea.

She came outside into a night loud with distant laughter and the sound of tree frogs. She didn't see Caelum. She took a turn of the building and found him in the back, hurling rocks into the growth where the dirt clearing petered out into cypress and shade trees.

"Caelum?" He didn't turn around and, thinking he hadn't heard, she took another step forward. "Caelum?"

"Don't call me that." He turned to face her, his face caught in the flare of the floodlights, and her stomach went hollow. He looked as if he hated her. "That's not my name." This time he directed a volley of rocks at the restrooms, so they pinged against the stucco walls and the sign pointing the way to the showers. "I'm seventy-two. I'm a replica. A human model. Only humans have names."

Then she knew that what she'd been afraid of was true. He hated her for what she was, or for what she wasn't.

"You're wrong," Lyra said. She felt as if she were being squeezed between two giant plates, as if the whole world had narrowed to this moment. "That isn't what makes the difference."

"Oh yeah? You would know, I guess." He looked away. "I thought we were the same, but we're not. We're different. *You're* different."

"So what?" Lyra took a step closer to him. They were separated by less than a foot, but he might have been on the other side of the world. She felt reckless, desperate, the same way she'd felt running after Haven had exploded. He turned back to her, frowning. "So we're different. Who cares? We chose to escape together. We chose to stay together. We chose each other, didn't we?" *I gave you a name,* she almost said, but the memory of that night, and lying so close to him, while the darkness stirred around his body, made her throat constrict. "That's what makes the difference. Getting to choose, and what you choose." She took a breath. "I choose you."

"How can you?" His voice was raw. "You know what I am. I don't belong anywhere."

"You belong with me." When she said it out loud, she knew it was true. "Please." She'd never had to ask for anything, because she'd never had reason to. But this woke inside of her—the asking and the need, the feeling that if he didn't say yes, she wouldn't be able to go on.

"Please," she repeated, because she could say nothing else. But at the same time she took a step toward him and put a hand on his chest, above his heart, because there was always that to return to, always the truth of its rhythm and the fact that every person, no matter how they were formed or where, had a heart that worked the same way.

They were inches apart. His skin was hot. And though she could feel him, touch him, *know* his separateness, in that moment she also learned something totally new— that it was possible by touching someone else to dissolve all the space between them.

"I am no one," he said. In his eyes she was reflected in duplicate. "I was made to be no one."

"You're someone to me," she said. "You're everything."

He took her face in his hands and kissed her. They had never learned how to kiss, either of them. But somehow he knew. She did, too. It was beyond instinct. It was joy.

They were clumsy, still. They stumbled and then she was against the wall. She pulled herself into him and found to her amazement that her body knew more than how to ache or shiver or exhaust itself. It knew how to sing.

They barely touched except with their mouths, the way they explored together *teeth tongue lips*, the way they shivered with the joy of discovery. They were born for the first time in their bodies. They were born together. They came together into the world as everyone should—frightened, uncertain, amazed, grateful.

And for them the world was born, too, in all its complexity and strange glory. They had a place in it, at last, and so at last it became theirs to share. No matter what happened, no matter what trouble came, Lyra knew they would face it together, as they were then: turned human by joy, by a belonging that felt just like freedom.

GEMMA

GEMMA

For Katy —

LAUREN OLIVER

REPLICA

GEMMA

HARPER
An Imprint of HarperCollinsPublishers

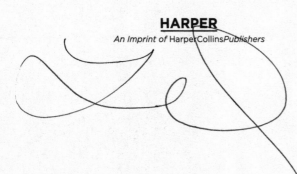

AUTHOR'S NOTE

Although in many cases you will find identical portions of dialogue occurring from both Gemma's and Lyra's perspectives in their respective narratives, you may also notice minor variations in tone and tempo. This was done deliberately to reflect their individual perspectives. Gemma and Lyra have unique conceptual frameworks that actively interact with and thus define their experiences, just as the act of observing a thing immediately alters the behavior of the thing itself.

The minor variations in the novel reflect the belief that there is no single objective experience of the world. No one sees or hears the same thing in exactly the same way, as anyone who has ever been in an argument with a loved one can attest. In that way we truly are inventors of our own experience. The truth, it turns out, looks a lot like making fiction.

ONE

ESCAPE: THAT WAS WHAT GEMMA dreamed of, especially on nights like this one, when the moon was so big and bright it looked like it was a set piece in a movie, hooked outside her window on a curtain of dark night sky.

In movies, teenagers were always sneaking out. They'd wait until their parents went to bed, ease out from under their blankets already dressed in miniskirts and tank tops, slide down the stairs and unlatch the lock and *pop!* They'd burst out into the night, like balloons squeezing through a narrow space only to explode.

Other teenagers, Gemma guessed, didn't have Rufus: a seventy-five-pound retriever who seemed to consist entirely of fur, tongue, and vocal cords.

"Shhh," Gemma hissed, as Rufus greeted her at the bottom of the stairs, wiggling so hard she was surprised he didn't fall over.

"Are you all right?"

She'd been awake for only a minute. But already her mother was at the top of the stairs, squinting because she didn't have her contacts in, dressed in an old Harvard T-shirt and sweatpants.

"I'm fine, Mom." Gemma grabbed a glass from the cabinet. She would *never* sneak out. Not that she had anywhere to sneak out to, or anyone to sneak out with, since April's parents kept her just as leashed up as Gemma's did.

Still, she imagined for a second that she was halfway to the door, dressed in tight jeans and a shirt that showed off her boobs, the only part of her body she actually *liked*, on her way to hop in her boyfriend's car, instead of standing in a darkened kitchen in her pajamas at eleven p.m. on a Wednesday night while Rufus treated her ankles to one of his signature lick-jobs. "Just needed some water."

"Are you dehydrated?" Her mom said *dehydrated* as if it meant *dying*.

"I'm fine." Gemma rattled the ice in her glass as she returned up the stairs, deliberately avoiding her mom's eyes. "Go back to bed, okay?"

Her mom, Kristina, hesitated. "Let me know if you need anything, okay?"

"Uh-huh." Gemma shut her bedroom door in Rufus's face, not caring that he immediately began to whine. She set the water on her bedside table and flopped back onto the bed. The moon made squares on her bare legs, cutting her skin into portions of light and dark. She briefly let herself imagine what Chloe DeWitt and Aubrey Connelly were doing at that very second. She'd always been told she had a vivid imagination, but she just couldn't picture it. What was it like to be so totally, fundamentally, ruthlessly normal? What did they think about? What were their problems? Did they *have* any problems?

Rufus was still whining. Gemma got out of bed and let him in, sighing as he bounded immediately onto the bed and settled down exactly in the center of her pillow. She wasn't tired yet, anyway. She sat down instead at the vanity that had once belonged to her mother, an ornate Victorian antique she'd loved as a child and hadn't been able to tell Kristina she'd outgrown. She'd never been able to tell her parents much of anything.

The moon made hollows of her eyes in the mirror, turned her skin practically translucent. She wondered if this was how her parents always saw her: a half ghost, hovering somewhere between this life and the next.

But she wasn't sick anymore. She hadn't been sick in years, not since she was a little kid. Still, they treated her as if she might suddenly blow away, like a human house of cards, disturbed by the lightest touch.

She herself could barely remember all those years of sickness—the hospital, the operations, the treatments.

Coping, her therapist said. An *adaptive defense*.

She did remember a garden—and a statue, too. A kneeling god, she thought, but she couldn't be sure, with one arm raised to the sky, and the other reaching toward the ground, as though to draw something magic from the earth.

TWO

GEMMA MUST HAVE BEEN THE only overweight sixteen-year-old girl in the entire history of the United States who actually *wished* she could participate in gym. It would be one thing if she were excused to go to study hall or free period. But due to "scheduling limitations" (the stated reason)—or, as Gemma suspected, the innate sadism of Ms. Vicke, the vice principal—instead Gemma was forced to go to gym and sit in the bleachers, pretending to work, while the rest of her classmates zigzagged across the gym, their sneakers squeaking, or flew across the mulchy, wet soccer fields, running drills.

In the bleachers, there was nowhere to hide. She might as well be a blinking *Does Not Belong* sign. Even worse: Mrs. Coralee, the gym teacher (also a sadist—the school was full of them), insisted that Gemma change into the puckered nylon shorts and matching tank tops the whole class was forced to wear, which on Gemma only served to further underscore how little she belonged—like wearing full-on ski gear to the beach.

"You are so lucky." April Ruiz, Gemma's best friend, swiped a lock of dark hair out of her eyes, as the girls filed back into the locker room. "I'm pretty sure dodgeball was invented by the same people who thought up rectal thermometers and wool tights."

"Move it, Frankenstein." Chloe DeWitt jabbed an elbow, hard, in the space where Gemma's waist should have been, if she *had* a waist instead of a roll of flab. Gemma probably had forty pounds on Chloe, but the girl was all sharp corners and she knew how to use them to her advantage. Her elbows felt like whittled blades. "Not *all* of us get to spend the whole period snacking."

Gemma blushed. She had never, ever eaten in class. She had hardly ever eaten in the cafeteria, precisely so that Chloe, and girls like her, would never get the opportunity to make fun of her for it. But it didn't matter. From the time Gemma was little, Chloe had made it her mission to ensure that Gemma never forgot that she was a freak. In third grade, she'd hit on the name Frankenstein, after Gemma's second heart surgery had left her with a thick scar from her chest to her navel. After that, Gemma had never changed except in a bathroom stall—but no one at school besides April and her teachers ever called her anything else.

What Gemma couldn't understand was why—if she were so delicate, like her parents were saying (*you're delicate, Gemma, that's why we have to be so careful; no roller coasters, Gemma, your heart is delicate*)—she couldn't *look* delicate, like one of the small crystal animal figurines that her mom collected and kept enclosed in the corner cabinet, with legs as thin as toothpicks. Like Chloe, with a tan that appeared permanently shellacked to the contours of her body, as finely chiseled and well-tuned as an instrument. Like she had been formed by a god with an eye for detail, whereas Gemma had been slapped together haphazardly by a drunk.

"Yeah," she muttered, as Chloe and her friends converged on the sinks, laughing. "Lucky."

"Don't let Cruella get to you," April said in a low voice. April always took Gemma's side. Years ago, they had decided that either they were two aliens in a school of humans or possibly *the only two humans in a school of aliens.* "Someone forgot to shoot her with her morning dose of tranquilizer."

April and Gemma waited until Chloe and the pack of wolves—a fitting nickname for more than metaphoric reasons, since Gemma was fairly sure that Aubrey Connelly had had her incisors filed into points, and wouldn't have been surprised at all to learn that she liked the taste of human flesh—had changed before they stripped. They would both be late for study hall and would have to endure another lecture from Mr. Rotem. But anything was better than changing with the pack of wolves.

"Good news," April said, when the rest of the locker room had cleared out. "Mom finally caved on the Green Giant. I told her it wasn't *safe* to drive sixty miles in that beast, much less six *hundred*. How's that for strategy? I used her own psychology against her."

"And so the hunted becomes the hunter," Gemma said, in her best movie-announcer voice. Sometimes she thought her favorite part of the week was sitting on the wooden bench just outside the shower stalls, which hadn't been used in twenty years, talking with April while she washed her face and reapplied her makeup painstakingly, even though the result always made it look like she wasn't wearing any. Like they were in their own protected world. But not a world her parents had made for her. A world she'd *chosen*.

"Something like that. Anyway, we'll be cruising down to Florida in our very own Lexus. Can you believe it? My brother's *so* pissed."

Apart from Gemma's, April's parents were the most protective people Gemma knew. Neither Gemma nor April was allowed to date—not that it mattered, since nobody wanted to date them. The list of other things they weren't allowed to do included, but was not limited to: (1) stay up past ten o'clock; (2) attend any school events or dances unless they were in a large group of females only, which precluded them from going, since they had no other friends; (3) go to Raleigh unless April's brother, a senior, chaperoned; (4) be on Instagram.

Gemma was sure that even if she were five-eleven and a supermodel look-alike, her parents' absurd beliefs about social media (*It rots the brain! It's bad for self-esteem!*) would have ensured she stayed on the bottom of the social food chain. She was also sure that when her mom and April's got together, all they did was brainstorm elaborate and ever more absurd ways to make sure that both April and Gemma stayed safe, friendless except for each other, and totally miserable.

When half the junior girls decided to spend spring break in Miami, Gemma hadn't even bothered petitioning her parents to be allowed to go. She knew she had just about as much chance of being named the first female president of the United States . . . at age sixteen. Besides, she had no desire to spend her vacation bumping into the same predators she spent all her time deliberately avoiding at school.

But April—who was not only prettier, smarter, and far more optimistic than Gemma, so much so that had they not been absolute, sworn lifelong best friends, co-aliens, outcasts together, Gemma would have despised her—hadn't given in so easily. She'd begged her parents. She'd cried. She had thrown a tantrum—a risky proposition, since her mother, Angela Ruiz, a renowned prosecutor for the state, had been known to frighten grown men into confessions at their first meeting. (And her *other* mother, Diana, was a computer programmer who had won several kickboxing competitions in her early twenties.)

Then the miraculous had happened. April hit on the magic word: *sexism.*

It was *sexism*, April claimed, that her older brother, Ryan, got to go on spring break with his friends. It was *sexism* that he got to drive a Lexus while she was stuck with the Green Giant, an ancient chartreuse station wagon. And even though Ryan was two years older, and the Lexus had been a congratulations gift for getting into Harvard early action, suddenly April's moms had generated a counteroffer: April and Gemma could take the car and drive down to Bowling Springs, Florida, for a week, where April's grandparents lived.

Even better, they had convinced Gemma's parents that it was a good idea.

And, yeah, sure, maybe hanging out in a community known for its 65+ dating scene and competitive weekly badminton tournament wasn't exactly the spring break of every girl's dream. But it was better than nothing. They could stay for a whole nine days, paddle around the pool, walk down to the community tennis courts, and take their car to the beach. They could drink virgin piña coladas and sample fried gator at the local restaurants. Still better, they would have the house to themselves for three full days while April's grandparents were off attending some weird Positive Visualization Health Retreat that involved a lot of yoga and deep breathing—a minor detail Gemma had managed to avoid in all of her conversations with her parents.

Discussing spring break plans with her best friend made Gemma feel all-American, beauty-magazine, country-song normal. So much so that she wasn't sure she actually wanted to *go*, just so she could keep talking about it.

April had to hop, haul, and wiggle to get into her jeans. Her preferred fit, she always said, was *human sushi roll*. Gemma's was *airy trash bag*. "I'll pick you up Saturday at eight a.m., got it?"

"Got it," Gemma said. They'd agreed on Saturday, March 19, eight a.m. weeks ago, but reconfirmed almost every day. Why not? This was the first adventurous thing either of them had ever done in their lives, unless you counted microwaving Peeps at Easter to watch them explode.

Gemma wished she only felt excited. She wished,

more than anything, that her parents' words and warnings hadn't over time worked their way like a virus into her cells, replicating there.

She wished she wasn't also just the littlest, tiniest bit scared.

But she told herself nothing would happen. After all, nothing ever did.

THREE

A LIST OF ALL THE medical conditions Gemma had had since she was born:

    1. two broken tibias

    2. one collapsed lung

    3. congenital heart failure

    4. pneumonia

    5. poison ivy (on her butt, of all places)

    6. pneumonia again

    7. a fractured wrist

    8. hypothyroidism

    9. pneumonia, a third time

A list of some of the medical conditions she had not had:

1. the bubonic plague
2. that disease where you stay really skinny, no
matter how much you eat

Every so often, when Gemma approached the massive
iron gates that encircled her property, she got a flash of
something—not memory, exactly, but something close
to it, like the sudden recollection of a song you heard
someone sing only once. There was a high fence lost
somewhere in the wild tangle of fever-dreams that had
so often been hers as a very young child—a high fence,
a giant statue of a man kneeling in the dirt, reaching, it
seemed, simultaneously for heaven and hell.

The driveway was exactly one-quarter of a mile long.
Gemma knew because one time she had asked her mom
to measure it in the car. It bisected an enormous lawn
spotted with ancient spruce trees and flowering dog-
wood. On days when April had chorus, taking the bus and
walking the quarter mile up the driveway was infinitely
preferable to having her dad's driver pick her up, which
would require that she wait at the student drop-off area,
in full view of the senior playing fields, and would be a
tacit admission that she had only one friend to drive her.

Besides, it was practically the only exercise Gemma
got. On nice days she walked deliberately slowly, making
it last, enjoying the smell of freesia and honeysuckle and

listening to the faint whine of the mosquitoes clustered in the shade.

Today, she walked quickly, too preoccupied by the plans for Saturday (*the day after tomorrow!*)—a ten-hour road trip, a real adventure, with her best friend—to care about the prettiness of the day. Because of the landscaping and the angle of the drive, she was practically on the front porch before she noticed two cop cars, one of which had its doors swinging open, as if the officers had been in too much of a hurry to bother closing them. Her mother was speaking to one of them, holding her throat with one hand.

Dad, Gemma thought immediately, and, without realizing it, broke into a run, her backpack jogging against her back.

"Gemma!" Kristina turned to stare as Gemma arrived in front of her, already panting, sweat gathering beneath the waistband of her jeans and trickling down her spine. She reached out and seized Gemma's shoulders. "What's the matter? Is everything okay?"

Gemma stared. "What do you mean, *is everything okay?*" She gestured to the cop cars, and the cop who stood a little ways apart from mother and daughter, hands on his hips, sunglasses on, staring up at the sky as though debating whether he might still get a tan at this angle. "What's going on?"

"Oh." Kristina exhaled long and loud, releasing Gemma's shoulder. "This? It's nothing. Something stupid. A prank."

By then, Gemma had noticed that one of the large glass panes of the French doors was shattered, as if something heavy had been hurled through it. She could see a second cop moving through the living room, placing his weight delicately, his footsteps making a *crunch-crunch* sound on the glass. As she watched, a third cop emerged, a woman, holding what at first appeared to be a lumpy rock in an improbable shade of green between two gloved hands. But as she shifted it to show her colleague, Gemma's whole body went cold. It wasn't a rock, but a Halloween Frankenstein mask stapled at the neck. From the way the cop was handling it, Gemma knew it must be heavy. It had obviously been filled with something to help it maintain its shape.

"Oh my God." Gemma could feel the blood pounding in her temples. Chloe. That fucking bitch. She focused on thinking logically so that she wouldn't start to cry. How had it happened? How had Chloe arrived so much quicker than the bus? Could she have cut last period? No. Gemma had seen her getting into Aubrey's car. And how had they gotten past the gates? The whole property was fenced in. But she was sure Chloe and Aubrey were to blame, would have staked her life on it.

Frankenstein. The misshapen monster.

"It's all right, Gem. It's all *right*," Kristina said, in a shrill voice, as if she didn't quite believe it. "No one was hurt."

That only made Gemma feel worse. *No one was hurt* meant *someone* could *have been hurt*. What if her mom had been in the living room? Unlikely, of course. Even though the house—Château Ives, as April called it, only half-jokingly—could have fit an army during wartime, her mom never went anywhere except her bedroom, the kitchen, the downstairs yoga studio, and the bathroom, as if she were controlled by a centrifugal force that kept her rotating between those four places. But what if Ender and Bean, their cats, had been curled up on the sofa? What if Rufus had been sunning himself on the rug?

"If you want us to file a report, we'll need you down at the station," said the cop with sunglasses, the one who looked bored. But he was doing his best to be polite. The Ives family, he'd obviously been told, was important.

Kristina shook her head. "I don't know," she said. "If only Geoff . . ." She trailed off. "My husband is in a meeting," she said, by way of explanation. Gemma's dad was always in a meeting, or in a car, or on a plane.

"How'd they get in?" Gemma blurted. The front gates could only be opened by a code. Guests had to be buzzed in. Château Ives meets Fort Knox.

Kristina blushed. Even when she blushed, she looked pretty. Gemma had tried for years to find herself in her mother's model-pretty face, in her high cheekbones and slender wrists. The most she could detect was a similar way of frowning. "There were vendors in and out for Sunday's horse show," she explained, half to Gemma, half to the police. "Florists, the planner . . . I left the gates open so they wouldn't have to keep buzzing."

Which no doubt meant: *I popped a Klonopin, had a glass of wine, and took a nap.* Since her parents never said exactly what they meant, Gemma had become adept at translating for them.

"Finke, look at this." Yet another cop came jogging out of the front door. He, too, was wearing nylon gloves, and holding a note written on a scrap of paper between his pointer and middle fingers. "This came with the special delivery."

The bored-looking cop flipped his sunglasses to the top of his head and read without reaching for it. The message was short, but Gemma felt the anger roil inside of her, pulling her heart down to her toes.

your sick your a monster you deserve to die

Kristina gasped as though she'd been physically slapped. Finke nodded, and the other cop withdrew, bagging the note carefully in plastic. Gemma imagined seeing Chloe arrested, her hands wrenched behind her back, her face squashed against the top of a cop car. She imagined her thrown into jail for the rest of her life, bunking with a murderous boulder with a name like Princess.

She imagined wrapping her hands around Chloe's neck and watching it snap.

"I—I think I'd better come with you," Kristina said. Now the blush was gone. She just looked pale, and confused. "Who would *do* something like this? Who would be so *awful?*"

"Have you or your husband been having any problems lately?" Finke asked. "Disputes? Legal issues?" Kristina shook her head.

"No other threatening messages, or phone calls?"

She again shook her head. "I just can't *imagine*—"

"Mom, wait." Gemma felt the words like nausea. *It's my fault. It's because everyone thinks I'm a freak.* Her mom knew that Gemma had a rough time in school, but Kristina's sympathy always made Gemma feel worse. The only thing more painful than being unpopular was being the unpopular daughter of a former popular girl. She took a deep breath. "I know."

"What?"

"I know who did it." Now all the cops were watching her—pityingly, she thought. She felt her cheeks heating up and was absolutely positive she did not look pretty like her mom. When Gemma blushed, she looked as if two pigments were trying to throttle each other beneath her skin. "It's just some stupid girl at school. She probably thought it'd be funny."

Was it her imagination, or did her mom, just for the tiniest second, look relieved? "Oh, honey," she said, and started to put her arms around Gemma. Gemma sidestepped her.

"It's fine," she said. "I'm *fine*."

"You still want to file the report?" Finke asked, but Gemma could tell he no longer thought it was a good idea. The whole vibe had changed. No one was looking at her. The cops were loading up, restless, eager to get back to more important things than some high school girl's social humiliation. Maybe they were annoyed they'd been dragged out here in the first place.

"It's up to you, sweet pea." Kristina reached out and threaded her hand through Gemma's hair. "What do you think?"

Gemma shook her head. As tempting as it was to imagine Chloe in a prison-orange jumpsuit—surely, surely, even Chloe wouldn't look good in prison orange—she knew that if she made a big deal out of it, things would only get worse. Then she'd be Frankenstein-the-Crybaby. The Alien Snitch.

Still, she felt the sudden, overwhelming desire to scream. Chloe and her little pack of wolverines had been doing their best to make Gemma miserable for years. But they had never done anything this bad. They'd come to her house. They'd taken the time to fill a Halloween mask with rocks or concrete rubble or metal shrapnel from their mechanical hearts. They had said that she deserved to die. Why? What had she ever done to them?

She was an alien, adrift on an unfriendly planet. Hopeless and lost.

"Are you sure?" Kristina said, smoothing Gemma's face with a thumb. Gemma was scowling.

She took a step backward. "Positive," she said.

"Okay." Kristina exhaled a big breath and gave Finke a weak smile. "Sorry for all the trouble. You know how girls are."

"Mm-hmm," he said, in a tone that he made it clear he didn't and had no desire to, either.

Gemma felt like going straight to her room, possibly forever, but Kristina managed to get an arm around her shoulders. For a thin woman, she was surprisingly strong, and she held Gemma there in a death grip.

"I'm sorry, honey," she said. "Why didn't you tell me you were having problems at school?"

She shrugged. "It's no big deal."

Kristina smelled, as always, like rose water and very

expensive perfume. So expensive that it actually smelled like new-printed money. "I don't want your father to worry, do you?" She smiled, but Gemma read anxiety in her mother's eyes, decoded the words her mother would never say: *I don't want him to think you're more of a disappointment than he already does.* "Let's just tell him there was an accident. A kid and a baseball. Something like that."

To hit a baseball from the street through the living room window, the kid would have to be a first-draft pick for the major leagues. Usually her parents' willingness to lie about things big and small bothered Gemma. If her parents were so good at making up stories, how could she ever be sure they were telling the truth?

Today, however, she could only be grateful.

"Baseball," she said. "Sure."

Gemma woke up in the middle of the night from a nightmare that, thankfully, released her almost as soon as she opened her eyes, leaving only the vague impression of rough hands and the taste of metal. In the hall, Rufus was whimpering.

"What's the matter?" she said, easing out of bed to open the door for him. As soon as she did, she heard it: the sudden swell of overlapping voices, the angry punctuation of silence. Her parents were fighting.

"It's okay, boy," she whispered to Rufus, threading a

hand through the scruff of fur on his neck. He was a baby about fights. Immediately, he darted past her and leapt onto the bed, burying his head in her heap of pillows, as if to block out the sound from downstairs.

She would have gone back to bed, but at exactly that moment, her father's voice crested, and she very clearly heard him say, "*Frankenstein.* For Christ's sake. Why didn't you tell me?"

Gemma eased out into the hall, grateful for the plush rug that absorbed the sound of her footsteps. Quickly, she moved past paneled squares of moonlight, past guest rooms always empty of guests and marble-tiled bathrooms no one ever used, until she reached the main staircase. Downstairs, a rectangle of light yawned across the hall-way. Her father's study door was open, and Gemma got a shock. Her mother was perched on the leather ottoman, her face pale and exhausted-looking, her arms crossed at the waist to keep her bathrobe closed. Gemma had never, ever seen anyone besides her father in the study. She had always assumed no one else was allowed to enter.

"I tried calling. . . ." Her mother's voice was weak and a little bit slurred, as if all the edges were lopped off. It must be after midnight. He must have woken her up from a sleeping-pill slumber.

"Feeding me some bullshit story. I had to hear it from Frank at the department. Thank God *someone* respects me."

Gemma's heart sank. It had been stupid to believe that they could conceal the truth from her father. He had contacts everywhere—in the police department and even in the government, although he kept his most important contacts secret. He'd cofounded the sixth-largest pharmaceutical company in the country, Fine & Ives, which made everything from shampoo to heart medication to drugs for soldiers suffering from PTSD. Although he'd been kicked off the board of his own company after a brutal three-year legal battle when Gemma was a toddler—Gemma had never found out the details, but she knew her dad had disapproved of where the company was putting its resources—he still traveled with a personal security guard and went to Washington, DC, every quarter to meet with politicians and lobbyists and top brass.

Often Gemma feared she would never, ever get truly away from her parents—not even when she went to college, not even when she moved out and moved as far away from Chapel Hill as possible and had her own family. They would always be able to find her. They would always be able to *see* her, wherever she was.

"I respect you," Kristina protested, and Gemma got a sudden strangled feeling, as if a hand were closing around her throat. Her father was twelve years older than Kristina. He and his twin brother, Ted, had both been to West Point, like their father before them. Geoffrey had gone on to become a military strategist, and he never let anyone—least of all Gemma and her mom—forget it. *Respect.* That was the drumbeat of their lives. *Respect.* He could write a book, she thought, about respect, and discipline, and order, and work. He could probably write a whole *series*.

On the other hand, what he knew about *acceptance* and *tolerance* and *his own daughter* would barely fill up a tweet.

Sometimes Gemma wondered how it was possible they were made from the same genetic material. Her father was angular and cold everywhere she was warm and soft and sensitive. But the proof was there. She would have so much rather looked like her mother. Instead she had her father's hazel eyes, his square chin, his way of smiling with the corners of his mouth turned down, as if neither of them had ever quite learned to do it correctly.

"I didn't want to worry you," Gemma's mom went on. "Gemma said it was just a prank. Some girls have been giving her a hard time at school, and—"

"A prank, Kristina? Are you blind? This wasn't a prank. This was a message. Do you know who Frankenstein is?"

"Of course I know—"

"Frankenstein is the *doctor.* In the original story, in the real version, he's the one who made the monster." There was a long moment of silence. Gemma could feel her heart beating painfully, swollen like a bruise. "This was a message for me."

He's the one who made the monster.

This was a message for me.

She tried to love her father. She tried to believe he loved her, as Kristina insisted that he did. She had made excuses, the same ones her mom always parroted back to her. *He's bad at expressing feelings. He's stressed at work. He didn't get a lot of love from his father.*

But deep, deep down, Gemma had always suspected that the reason her father avoided her, the reason he could barely look her in the eye, the reason he kept all her baby pictures locked up in drawers and desks instead of proudly on display in frames, the reason he could hardly speak to her without losing his temper, as if she were always paying for a crime she didn't know she had committed, was much simpler.

He couldn't stand her.

He thought she was a disappointment. A defective model, but one, sadly, that couldn't be exchanged or returned.

Her mother said something else, something Gemma didn't hear. There was a high whining in her ears, as if they were filled with bees. She wanted to turn around and run, to flee back to her bedroom, to wake and realize this had all been a dream. But she couldn't move.

"There was a breach at Haven," her father said.

"What do you mean, *breach*?"

"Apparently, one of them escaped," Geoff said.

A long pause. "Well, it won't live. No way can it live. The currents on that island . . ."

"But what if it does? Jesus Christ, Kristina. Can you imagine? Can you imagine the absolute shitstorm if the story gets out? We'll be persecuted. We'll be *executed*."

Kristina's voice rose in pitch. "No one will know what we've done," she says. "How *could* they?"

Her father barked out a laugh—an angry, bitter sound. "There are ways, trust me. All you have to do is follow the money."

"But you left Fine and Ives for that reason. You *refused* to participate—"

"Too little, too late. I knew what Saperstein was planning. I knew where the new round of funding would go."

Gemma could no longer follow the thread of the conversation. Still, she remained motionless, gripping the banister, trying to squeeze down a mounting scream. She could see her mother worrying the hem of her bathrobe between her fingers, and her father pacing, passing in and out of view. The angle made it impossible to see his face—a small blessing.

After a while, he spoke again. "Bowling Springs is only fifty miles from Haven."

Gemma's mother looked up. Her face was very pale, her eyes like two holes. "No," she said. Gemma was shocked.

She'd never heard her mother say no to her father. "You can't. Gemma's been looking forward to this trip for ages. *April* has been looking forward to it. What will I tell her moms?"

"I don't care what you tell them," he said. "It isn't safe. Not after what happened today. Fifty miles, Kristina."

Gemma felt as if her chest had been filled with wet concrete. She couldn't breathe.

"Oh, Geoff. Fifty miles is a lot. You can't really believe—"

"I don't *believe*, Kristina. I know." He rounded on her, and Kristina drew backward several inches. Gemma felt a sudden wave of hatred toward him, stronger than anything she'd ever felt. For one awful second, she wished for him to die, struck down by an invisible force. But that was too cruel. She wished instead that he would simply vanish. *Blip.* As if he'd never existed at all. "Those *nutcases* have been swarming the beach for months. Last week, they attacked one of the orderlies on her way to the ferry."

"But you said yourself they're nutcases," Kristina says. "No one actually *believes* them. Besides, they don't know anything. Half of them think Haven is home to vampires, for God's sake. They'll get tired soon enough and find another cause. And what does that have to do with Gemma? No one could possibly know—"

"Someone *does* know," he said, cutting her off. "That's

the point. I'm not sending her into the middle of that mess. She can go on spring break next year."

Gemma opened her mouth and let out a long, silent scream. She imagined the sound shattering the chandelier, blowing out the windows, exploding all of her father's priceless porcelain antiques.

"Fine." Kristina stood up, swaying a little on her feet. Gemma couldn't tell if it was the lingering effects of the sleeping pills, or because of the physical effort of standing up to the great Geoffrey Ives. "But *you* have to be the one to tell her. It'll break her heart, and I won't do it."

"Fine," her father said, and then, to Gemma's horror, he flung open the door and stomped into the foyer.

She turned quickly and slipped down the hall again, her heart beating out the word *unfair, unfair.* In her room, she shoved Rufus aside and climbed under the covers, mounding a pillow over her head as if it could smother the sounds of what she had just heard. She waited, tight with anxiety, to hear her father's footsteps outside her door. How would she face him now? How would she face him ever again?

But minutes passed, and he didn't come, and slowly the tension in her body dissipated, replaced by the heavy sensation of lying at the very bottom of a pit. She was filled with a gnawing sense of injustice, of anger, of flat-out grief. *Unfair.* She didn't understand half of what her parents had said. All she knew was that yet again, she was trapped. *Unfair.* She was like an insect in her father's hand; maybe he got pleasure just from squeezing, from watching her squirm.

She didn't think she would ever fall asleep again. But she did, eventually, hours later, when the light in her room had turned the color of dark chalk. And when she woke up, her father had been called away to Shanghai on business, and so it was Gemma's mother who broke the news after all.

FOUR

SHE DIDN'T GO TO SCHOOL on Friday, claiming she was sick, and her mom didn't even bug her about what was wrong—a sure sign she knew Gemma was faking.

Gemma was glad her dad was once again traveling. Glad they were separated by time zones and a big ocean. She couldn't have faced him. If she had, she thought she would have spit at him, or kicked him in the shins, or finally said some of the things she'd been meaning to say for sixteen years.

The great Geoffrey Ives, cofounder of Fine & Ives Pharmaceuticals, Master of the Universe, *total fucking asshole.*

April called her during homeroom, a useless fifteen minutes of time between second and third periods when random juniors got shuffled together to suffer through announcements about basketball games, prom, and Tolerance Week.

After the third time Gemma didn't pick up, April resorted to texting, flooding Gemma's phone with scowling selfies. *What the shit is going on?? Are you okay?*

Gemma felt a sudden surge of viciousness, a desire to cause pain, since she had been caused pain. Maybe this was how Chloe and the wolves felt: maybe somewhere deep in their lives, someone was nipping at them, trying to make them bleed. *No,* she wrote back. Then: *not going tomorrow.*

There was a five-minute space between messages. Gemma wasn't sure whether April was stunned or just pretending to pay attention to her homeroom teacher.

Her next message said: *This is a joke, right?*

She could have written back, explaining. Better yet, she could have called. She could already imagine April shoving the phone deep into her pocket while she hurried into the nearest bathroom stall, then perching, knees to chest, on a toilet seat and pressing the phone to her ear while Gemma sobbed. She could have explained about the broken window, and her father's terrible words: *This was a message for me. . . .* It had all come true: her crashing fears, the strange terrors that had always infected her. Her father hated her. She might someday leave, but she would never escape—not him, not that truth, not really.

But she had already cried—had woken, in fact, with her throat raw and the taste of salt on her lips, and realized she'd been crying in her sleep—and today she felt nothing but a strange, bobbing sense of emptiness, as if she was a balloon untethered from the earth, slowly floating away into nothingness. She wondered whether her mom felt this way when she took pills.

So she wrote back: *not a joke.*

And, after a minute: *sorry.*

Her phone stayed quiet after that.

For the first two days of spring break, Gemma did nothing. She watched TV on her computer without knowing what she was watching. She slumped from upstairs to downstairs to microwave food her dad wouldn't have approved of her eating, the Hot Pockets and frozen mac and cheese she'd convinced Bernice, their housekeeper, to buy for her, Chinese takeout that had mysteriously materialized in the fridge. Once she took Rufus to the backyard and stood in her pajamas, blinking in the sun, while he ran circles around Danny, one of the lawn guys (she thought that was his name, anyway; there had been so many), who was moving slowly on the enormous lawn mower like a ship captain through a sea of green.

Her mom, who would normally have peppered Gemma with constant questions, or asked that she come have lunch at the club, or suggested they do mani-pedis—all activities that Gemma hated—largely left her alone. They were like two snowflakes, drifting through the vast white house, encased in their own arrangements of pain and misery.

All, she thought, her father's fault: her father's rules. Her father's house. Her father's walls, white and oversized, made pretty with ornate picture frames and chandeliers, so pretty they might keep a person from knowing she was trapped. Even, she realized, her father's pills. She'd never before thought about the fact that her dad's old company probably manufactured the meds her mother took, day in and day out, to help her sleep or wake or keep her from dreaming.

If she was honest, she realized that some small part of her—okay, maybe a big part of her—had been hoping that because she wasn't going to Florida, April wouldn't go. And she knew that if she'd told April the truth, April wouldn't have gone: she would have gladly spent spring break watching bad TV or trying to learn the choreography of stupid pop videos from YouTube. It was her fault, which made her feel mean and stupid and small. But the fact that April *did* go made her feel mean and stupid and small—and also abandoned.

She was wallowing, and she was pretty deep.

On the third day of spring break, Gemma woke up

and felt a desperate, urgent desire to move, to *do* some-thing. April had been at her grandparents' house for a full thirty-six hours. Gemma knew this because, in a moment of true, epic pathetic-ness, she had logged onto April's iTunes account and used Find My Phone to track April's progress down the coast—they had traded passwords years ago so they could always find each other if they were ever separated in a zombie apocalypse, assuming Wi-Fi still worked. No doubt April was already working on her tan and trying to scope out cute guys to flirt with who didn't know she was an alien.

Gemma knew by now April would have heard about the Frankenstein mask, or at least some version of the story filtered through their parents, and Gemma wished they could talk about it. Why had the mask freaked her father out so badly? She wished she'd been listening more care-fully to her parents' midnight conversation. Already, the conversation seemed like a dream. She couldn't remember details, just a place called Haven, a word she thought she remembered vaguely from childhood. A hospital, maybe? One of the boards her father sat on? He consulted for dozens of companies, all with names like NeoTech and Amalgam and Complete Solutions.

Missing April was like having a hole in the very bot-tom of her stomach. Like period cramps, as if she was puffy and swollen and bruised but on the inside. Gemma wasn't gay, she didn't think (although she didn't know, having never kissed anything but a practice pillow—and in a moment of complete, delirious silliness, given one practice blow job on a cucumber), but that didn't stop her from being stupid in love with her best friend.

She sent a picture of one of her oldest stuffed animals, an octopus missing two legs thanks to Rufus's rabid appetite for anything stuffed. He was April's favorite. *I miss you! Hope you're having fun!* she'd written, and then left her phone in her bed, buried under a pillow, in case April was still mad and didn't write back. Besides, she didn't want her mom calling her every five seconds.

Leaving the house wasn't a problem. It was early, and her mom was probably at her spin class. Leaving the *property* was a slightly bigger problem, since she a) had no car, and b) had never even learned to drive. She leashed up Rufus. It was a shortish walk down the drive, past Danny, who was pruning the hedges today, out the gates, and to the bus that ran past the university down to Franklin Street, with its pretty clutter of bars and cafés and the college bookstore selling UNC gear. Rufus loved the bus and sat the whole time on the seat next to Gemma, like a person, with his nose pressed against the window.

It was a beautiful day. She wandered down Franklin, looking in shop windows, debating whether to buy something. The town felt emptier than usual: UNC students were on spring break, too, until Monday. She kept picturing the phantoms of all her classmates, flitting by her on empty streets, while their real selves were four hundred miles away, lathering on sunscreen or taking tequila shots at breakfast.

She had just turned onto Rosemary Street, half thinking she would stop in at Mama Dip's for hush puppies even though she wasn't hungry, when she got a sudden nervous feeling in her stomach, as if she'd approached the edge of a cliff unexpectedly.

Watched. She was being watched.

If she'd been alone, in the dark, she might have been too afraid to turn around. But she was standing between the orthodontist's office where she'd had her braces tightened for three years and a small Mobil station that sold postcards touting North Carolina's many beauties. So she turned, even as the sense of dread yawned open wider, like a mouth lodged beneath her ribs.

She relaxed. No one. An older guy muttering about a parking ticket wedged under his windshield, a group of women—two of them she recognized as her mom's yoga friends—standing outside Mama Dip's. Patti Winters, the mother of a hideous girl in Gemma's grade whose endless bids for popularity meant she treated Gemma like the weakling who had to be eaten so the tribe could flourish, looked up and caught sight of Gemma. She waved and started to cross the street to come over.

Quickly, Gemma turned around, pretending not to have seen, and hurried across the gas station parking lot. She tied Rufus up to the sign that indicated a handicapped parking space and slipped inside the Quick-Mart, darting behind a display of cheap plastic sunglasses. Pete Rogers, aka Perv Rogers (a nickname assigned to him in third grade, when on a class trip he'd been caught stealing a pair of underwear from Chloe's overnight bag), eyed her from behind the register.

After fifteen seconds, Gemma felt like an idiot, and once again, missed April badly. She was still in school mode, prey mode. A rabbit on the run. But her mom's friends weren't going to track her and pin her down with conversation about why she was home on spring break and where-were-all-her-friends. She bought a heart-shaped pair of red sunglasses, because she didn't want to seem like she was hiding, which of course she was.

"I like your style," Perv said, in a pervy way. Gemma frowned at him.

No one was waiting for her in the parking lot. Patti Winters was long gone. Rufus was lying on the pavement, tongue out in the heat.

Still, as she began crossing with him back toward the street, she got that nervous, alert feeling again, as if someone were whispering something mean just a little too softly for her to hear. The guy who'd gotten the parking ticket was now refueling, his shitty old Chevrolet pulled haphazardly up to the pump. Their eyes met briefly, and he opened his mouth, as if to say something to her.

She was almost passing him, and that was when her brain click-clicked into motion, and gears slotted together, and she realized all at once that he wasn't getting gas—his car wasn't even connected to the pump—and he hadn't just randomly looked at her. He'd been watching her.

He was following her.

But by the time she understood this, they had drawn level. He grabbed her wrist and pulled, a motion seamless and small and effective, so she dropped Rufus's leash. Rufus just stood there patiently, wagging his tail. Gemma was too shocked to cry out, but then she was pinned to the man, temporarily so close she could see the wide black expanse of pores freckled across his nose, the sweat beading on his upper lip.

"Gem," he said. His breath smelled like coffee and like old, moldy closets. His hair was long and looked unwashed. "Listen to me. I don't want any trouble."

Her mind moved in short, explosive bursts, sending up disconnected images and ideas. She must know him. How else would he know her name? She searched his face, lean and cavernous, pitted with old acne scars and covered all over with stubble, and the taste of acid burned her throat as her brain made a final winding *click-click*.

Abducted. She was being abducted.

More lightning flashes in her brain: ransom demands; a cold, wet basement fitted with chains and old torture devices.

He fumbled the door open with one hand, keeping a grip on her wrist with the other. "I'm not going to hurt you, okay?" He was panting hard. "You gotta trust me. We're gonna be okay." As if they were on the same side.

She got a quick glimpse of a backseat littered with empty soda cans and crumpled receipts, a baseball hat, plastic bags from Party City, a dark thatch of something that looked like a huge, furry spider, and at that moment she found her voice and screamed. Or she tried to scream. What came out was more of a hoarse shout. Even her vocal cords were shaking, petrified. Only then did Rufus begin to bark.

The man instantly released her, springing backward, pressing himself against the car as if she'd just whipped out a weapon.

"Jesus." He was shouting now too, angrily. "Jesus. Why'd you go and do that, huh?"

She turned, snatched up Rufus's leash, and ran. It had been so long since she'd run—since she was allowed to run—she was worried her legs wouldn't work. But they did. She careened back toward the Quick-Mart, her heart exploding through her ribs, nearly toppling an old woman who'd just emerged, holding a fistful of lottery tickets. She didn't bother tying Rufus up. She wanted him next to her, anyway, even though he was evidently the world's worst guard dog.

"What do you know about heaven?" the man shouted to her, or at least she thought he did. By the time she was inside, taking deep, hiccuping breaths of air standing beside the windows papered over with flyers advertising deals on milk and Bud Light and cigarettes, he was gone.

"You're not supposed to have dogs in here," Perv said. "Sorry. State law."

Gemma ignored that. "Can I borrow your phone?" No way was she getting back on the bus. She had an itchy, exposed feeling, even standing in the warm, familiar must of the Quick-Mart. She wanted to go to the bathroom and scrub off her wrist, where the man had grabbed her.

"Are you okay?" he asked, squinting at her. "You look really—"

She glared at him. Fortunately, he shut up. She punched in her mother's number, her fingers shaking so badly she fumbled it the first time.

"Gemma? Gemma, what's the matter?" she said, as soon as Gemma choked out a hello. "Where are you? Whose number is this?"

She almost lost it and started to cry. But Perv was still

watching her—he wasn't actually bad-looking, with very clear skin and straight teeth and messy blond hair that looked as if he'd just had his head out the window of a moving car—so she kept it together.

"I'm okay," she said. "I—I missed the bus. And I'm not feeling well."

She'd said the magic words: *not feeling well*. Her mom's tone instantly changed. She became brisk, businesslike, as she always was about her daughter's health.

"I'm coming," she said. "Where?"

Gemma explained and hung up, passing the phone back to Perv and scowling at him so he would know not to ask questions. As soon as her mom came, she would tell her everything. She wished now she'd paid more attention to the car—it was a white Chevrolet, she knew, and old, but she hadn't caught even one digit of the license plate. Jesus. She'd always thought she would be good in a crisis: cool, ironic, detached. But her knees were shaking. She hadn't picked up even one good detail they could tell the police, except that the guy liked McDonald's. That narrowed it down to a bazillion people.

It took her mom fifteen minutes to get there, and Gemma spent the whole time ignoring Perv's looks of concern, trying to keep Rufus from going after the display of beef jerky, and doing her best to recall every single detail of the man's interaction with her. And by the time her mom pulled up—leaving the BMW door open as she jogged out of the car, still in yoga pants, scanning the parking lot for Gemma as though she expected her to be curled up in a fetal position on the ground—and then gripped both of Gemma's shoulders and demanded to know what was wrong, what had happened, Gemma only smiled tightly.

"I got tired," she said. She knew she probably looked like shit and wouldn't have to fake it. "I did too much walking, I think."

Because by then her mind, grinding slowly through its memory spool, had glitched on a few small details that in retrospect became huge, all-important: the shopping bags from Party City, which sold Halloween masks—like Frankenstein's—year-round. The fact that he'd called her Gem.

More importantly, the last thing he'd said to her, which in memory became clarified, distilled, amplified. Not: *What do you know about heaven?*

But: *What do you know about Haven?*

FIVE

GEMMA WASN'T ACTUALLY EXPECTING TO find much of anything by Googling Haven. She thought she'd heard her parents talk about Haven before, although other than their fight of the previous week she couldn't remember specific instances of it.

The first time she typed in the search term, she got back a random assortment of articles and web pages: a band named Haven was releasing its fourth studio album; a woman named Debbie Haven had recently been convicted of seducing one of her teenage students; a bioethicist named Richard Haven, founder of a famous research institute, had driven his car off the road in Florida the same year Gemma was born; the same Richard Haven had left a large sum of money in his will to the University of Pennsylvania, where for years he had been a professor emeritus. Nothing that pertained to her, nothing that made sense. She felt almost relieved.

But then she had the idea to type in Haven plus her last name, Ives.

Instantly, there were over a million results, all of them pertaining to the Haven Institute—Gemma quickly realized this must be the same research facility founded by Richard Haven—located on Spruce Island, somewhere off the coast of Florida. She found a PDF credited to her father's old company, Fine & Ives Pharmaceuticals. In it, a letter to the shareholders, the board wrote of hiring Haven to perform the company's research and development. But it was dated several years *after* her father had ruptured with the cofounder of the company and been ousted from the board.

She kept clicking and eventually turned up a picture of her father, standing at some kind of a gala next to a blond guy who looked like he belonged in a commercial for surf gear but who was, according to the caption, the famous Richard Haven. Next to them was a man with a dark curling beard and a forehead, sharply angled, that gave him the look of a shark: Dr. Mark Saperstein, a name that again registered very dimly with her from childhood. She remembered that her father had mentioned Saperstein the other night. *I knew what Saperstein was planning.* A quick Google search revealed that Saperstein had replaced Richard Haven after his death at the institute that bore his name.

She kept toggling through results, increasingly confused. If Fine & Ives hadn't contracted Haven for its research until well after her father left, why were there so many photos of him getting chummy with Richard Haven? She found an interview with Haven himself for the Scientific Medical Association, crediting her father for his "tireless support of medical research and advances in stem-cell technology."

She resumed her search, this time typing in *Haven Institute*. The official website was one of those bland templates that all research facilities seemed to share, filled with yawningly boring terminology like *neurobiological resolution* and *cutting-edge biotech services*. She found nothing listed on the website to indicate what kind of research Haven did, exactly—at least nothing she could understand. The institute, she noted, had been opened the year before she was born. Whatever her father felt about Haven now, Haven couldn't have been the reason he'd left Fine & Ives. The timing wasn't right.

More interesting were the websites about Haven: millions of results, half of them blogs, conspiracy websites, and speculative articles about what really went on there, what kind of research was performed, and whether any of it was legal. Some articles were straight-up sci-fi, and claimed that the island was a place where hybrid animals were being manufactured for military use, or where aliens were being studied and even trained. Other bloggers speculated that at Haven scientists performed illegal stem-cell research.

One of the websites cited most frequently was called HavenFiles.com. When she clicked over to it, a bright-orange warning, exuberantly punctuated and capitalized, flashed at the top of the screen.

Don't be fooled by phony websites and reports!! it said. *Haven-Files.com is the NUMBER ONE source for TRUTHFUL and VERIFIED reporting on the Haven Institute!!*

Half-amused, half-curious, she began to read. The website was, as far as she could tell, operated by some guy down in Florida named Jacob Witz, who had, for whatever reason, dedicated his life to reporting on various theories, rumors, and phenomena pertaining to Haven. His bio showed a picture of a gap-toothed middle-aged guy squinting into the sun, wearing a fishing hat feathered with different lures. He looked exactly like the kind of person you'd expect to see tipsy and railing about the time he was abducted by aliens. In his bio, half treatise, half manifesto, he revealed that he'd been a journalism major at the University of Miami and that he was devoted to "integrity," "uncovering the facts about one of the military's best-kept SECRETS," and "delivering KNOWLEDGE to the AMERICAN PUBLIC in accordance with the tenets of FREE SPEECH." This last sentence was punctuated with about forty exclamation points.

"All right, crazy," Gemma said out loud. "Let's see what you got."

His website was like one of those all-you-can-eat buffets where food keeps getting replenished, no matter how much you load up: every page led to more and more pages, every link to more and more links. Gemma felt as if she were falling down a well. There were detailed maps of Haven as imagined from above, and blurry pictures of the buildings taken from a distance and obviously from some sort of boat. (Reading between the lines, Gemma felt sure that Witz had never actually set foot on the island, which was guarded by troops and enclosed within a jail-style fence. He had pictures of this, too, dreary chain-link fitted with barbed wire that Gemma estimated to be about sixteen feet high.) Dozens of pages were devoted to the various theories about the experimentation done at Haven, and Witz argued carefully, in great detail, against the idea that Haven was manufacturing monsters or performing tests on aliens—although he was quick to say that he was an "expert" in military cover-ups of alien landings and had even written a self-published book on the subject (*The Secret Others: What the US Government Doesn't Want You to Know!*).

Several whole pages were devoted to something called the "Nurse M controversy": Nurse M, real name unknown, who supposedly committed suicide after working at Haven, the day before Witz, who had tracked her down but at least on the site refused to reveal her real name, was supposed to interview her. She found a link to a three-year-old news story in which Haven was named, supposedly because a nationwide hospital system was illegally selling off embryonic and fetal cells to research facilities. An embedded video showed one of the hospital execs leaving a courtroom, swarmed by reporters and right-to-life protesters holding graphic handmade signs.

Gemma's back was sore and her eyes burned from staring at the screen. She was shocked to see she'd been at it for three hours already. Still, she had more questions than she had answers. Her father's company had contracted Haven to do research and development for them. So what? Fine & Ives was one of the largest pharmaceutical companies in the country. They contracted plenty of research facilities—and besides, her father had already left by that point, after a protracted court battle with his former partner.

Why did the man in the parking lot think she'd know anything about Haven? And why was it important in the first place? What *did* go on at Haven? Why all the secrecy, and the guards, and that fence?

There was something she was missing, something obvious and yet hidden, like one of those visual riddles where a picture can be viewed two different ways. She wished she could get into her father's office, but he of course kept the door locked. Besides, she didn't even know what she was supposed to be looking for.

She stood up, did a clumsy approximation of a yoga stretch, and nearly fell over. Rufus raised his head and blinked at her.

"So much for Zen," she said. Obviously unimpressed, Rufus flopped back onto her pillow.

Almost instantly, the buzzer sounded downstairs. Someone was at the gate. Rufus sprang to his feet and dove off the bed, barking furiously, charging for the stairs. For a second, Gemma worried it might be Chloe again, maybe back to do a second round of damage.

But that was stupid. Chloe wouldn't bother buzzing—besides, she was probably on spring break getting trashed on cheap tequila shots with the rest of her pack wolves. And though she'd been certain only a few days ago that Chloe had been the one to throw the Frankenstein mask, now she was having doubts. Maybe, if all the rumors about Haven and monsters were true, it really had been a message for her dad, even if she still couldn't understand the connection.

She checked the security camera and was surprised to

see Perv Rogers, leaning half out of the car, the shock of his white-blond hair visible despite the low resolution. But she buzzed him in without asking him what he wanted. Perv was harmless. Well, except for being a pervert and maybe keeping girls' underwear strung around his basement for sniffing. Maybe keeping *girls* in his basement.

Rufus was still barking two minutes later, when Perv's car—a purplish minivan that looked like a giant, mobile eggplant, obviously borrowed from one of his parents—came rolling up the drive. She had to hold Rufus by his collar so he didn't bolt into the front yard.

"Sorry," she said, over the sounds of his continued barking, even as Perv climbed out of the car and began edging cautiously toward the door. "He doesn't bite, I promise. He just likes to make a lot of noise. Sit down, Rufus." Rufus finally sat, and even licked Perv's hand when Perv bent down and presented it for sniffing.

"How old is he?" Perv asked.

"An artifact," Gemma said. "Thirteen. But still really healthy," she added quickly, because she had a superstition about referring to Rufus's age. He'd arrived as a puppy when she was three years old. She had no memories that didn't include him.

"I probably smell like Quick-Mart hot dogs," Perv said. He must have changed after work, because instead of his crappy collared shirt he was actually dressed nicely, in a white button-down that showed off skin that was half tan and half just freckly, plus a pair of faded chino shorts and old Chuck Taylors. She realized she was wearing an old Hannah Montana T-shirt—*ironically*, of course, but he wouldn't know that—and crossed her arms over her chest.

"What are you doing here?" she asked.

"You forgot your change," he said, digging into one pocket and producing a few crumpled bills and some loose change. "There you go. Three dollars and twenty-seven cents."

She stared at him. "You drove to my house to give me three dollars?"

"And twenty-seven cents," he repeated, smiling broadly. "Besides, I wanted to see where you live. I heard your house was kind of awesome." He craned his neck, looking beyond her into the house. "Oh, man. Is that a chandelier? I thought chandeliers were for hotels and Las Vegas casinos. And maybe Mexican drug lords."

"Are you serious?" Gemma had maybe spoken three words to Perv in her whole life before their exchange in the Quick-Mart—most recently *no*, when he'd turned around in bio and asked whether she knew that in sea horses, only the male carried the eggs.

"Sorry." Perv rubbed a hand over his hair, making it stick up, flame-like. "Sometimes my mouth says things without checking in with my brain first."

"Yeah, I get that," Gemma said. "Mexican drug lords?" Perv shrugged. He seemed to be waiting for something, but she had no idea what. He was the first boy who'd ever come over to see her—not that he was there to see *her*, really—and she was suddenly mortified. She wanted Perv to leave, but didn't know how to ask without seeming mean. After all, he'd just done her a favor. And he was nice, even if he did steal girls' underwear. And possibly, you know, have a sex chamber in his basement, as April had once theorized when she caught Perv staring at Gemma in the cafeteria.

"So can I?" Perv asked, after looking at her patiently for a bit.

"Can you what?"

He blinked. "Come in and see where you live."

She didn't want to say yes but couldn't think of a way to refuse. So she shuffled backward, taking Rufus by the collar. "Okay," she said. "I mean, if you really want."

Perv took a step forward and then hesitated. "You sure that thing doesn't like the taste of human flesh?" He pointed at Rufus.

She rolled her eyes. "Please. He's a grumpy old man. He likes to make a lot of noise, especially around people he doesn't—" She broke off suddenly. She'd just remembered that Rufus, who still barked as if the world was ending whenever a stranger came to the door, hadn't made a sound when the man had approached her in the parking lot, at least not until Gemma shouted. He'd even wagged his tail. Almost as if . . .

Almost as if he recognized the man, knew him from somewhere.

She was gripped, then, by a terrible feeling: that something was coming. Something she couldn't understand. The man, Haven, her father—all of it was tangled up together, and she, Gemma, was at the center of the mess, the heart of the shitstorm.

Head shit.

Perv was still prattling on, oblivious. "Damn. Is that your mom in the oil painting?"

"It's a watercolor," Gemma said automatically.

"Wow. Cool. Your mom's kind of hot. Is that weird?"

"Yes." Gemma's head hurt. "Listen, I'm really sorry. But I'm kinda not feeling great. It's not really a good time for me. . . ."

But he didn't seem to hear. He'd just spotted the bathroom off the foyer. "Holy shit. Is that a TV? Right next to the toilet?" He disappeared, although she could still hear him talking, his voice tinny and distorted by the tile. He reemerged a second later, midsentence. ". . . snorkel in that bathtub. It's like the spring break of shower models."

Gemma took a deep breath. "Has anyone ever told you that you talk a lot?"

"All the time," Perv said, grinning. "It's kind of my trademark. So, what else you got? A hidden bowling alley? An indoor pool?"

"No bowling alley," she said. She was tempted to add: *And the pool's out back.* But that would only encourage him. "Listen, seriously, can we rain check on the tour?" She said it knowing a rain check was unlikely. It wasn't as if she and Perv were friends. Sure, he'd always been nice to her— he never laughed when someone whispered about one of her scars, for example, or called her *Frankenstein*—but he was pretty much nice to everybody. He was probably one of those do-gooder, Save-the-Manatees types. Maybe he thought being nice to Gemma would win him karmic brownie points.

"Sure," he said. He did a semi-decent job of concealing his disappointment. "I should get home anyway. I'm leaving for Florida tomorrow, and my mom's acting like I'm heading off to war. I swear, there may be a twelve-salute send-off."

Florida. The word set off little sparks in Gemma's mind. "Where in Florida?" she asked, trying to sound casual.

He'd already started for the door. Now he turned around, shrugging. "Tallent Hill," he said. "No one's ever heard of it. It's like an hour outside of Tampa."

"I've heard of it," Gemma said quickly. And she

had—Tallent Hill was just outside the Chassahowitzka National Wildlife Refuge, a little more than an hour south of Barrel Key, where boats carrying staff and supplies to and from Haven launched. She remembered seeing Tallent Hill on one of the detailed maps on the Haven Files website.

With a sudden, electric sense of clarity, she knew: she had to get to Florida. She had to go there, to Haven, and see it for herself.

"My aunt has a time-share there," he was saying. "And she makes a killer margarita. Alcohol free, but still. What's spring break without relatives and cocktails, right?" He shoved his hands in his pockets. "What about you? You got any big plans?"

"Actually"—Gemma licked her lips; her mouth was suddenly dry—"I was supposed to be driving down to Florida. To Barrel Key."

Perv raised his eyebrows but said nothing.

She kept going, elaborating on the lie as she went, hoping he couldn't see how badly she was blushing. "There was a problem with my car"—a clumsy lie; there were three cars in the driveway alone, but whatever, he wouldn't know the difference—"and now I'm kind of stranded. I was thinking of taking a Greyhound . . . ?" She trailed off hopefully.

"No," he said immediately. "No way. I once got stranded

on a Greyhound for nine hours with nothing to eat but a pack of Tic Tacs. *And* the toilet backed up. Friends don't let friends take the bus."

Gemma raised her eyebrows. "So we're friends now?"

"Sure we are," he said, reaching out and chucking her gently on the arm. When he took a step forward, she could smell him. He didn't smell like hot dogs at all, but like something clean and also a little bit spicy. "We became friends when we agreed to take a road trip. I'll pick you up at nine tomorrow."

April screamed when she found out that Gemma was coming down to Florida after all—Gemma had to yank the phone away from her ear to avoid having her eardrums blown out. April was so excited, she didn't even ask Gemma how she was planning to make the trip—thankfully, since Gemma thought she might die if she had to admit Perv Rogers was going to drive her.

"I don't believe it," she said. Their fight had been completely forgotten. "Gemma Ives. I didn't know you had it in you. And your parents just caved?"

"I guess they were done playing bad cop," Gemma said. Lying gave her a sticky feeling in her chest, like she'd accidentally inhaled a condom. Fortunately, her father's business trip would keep him in Shanghai for at least the next week, so that left only Kristina to deceive. Still,

Gemma had no idea how she would deal with lying to her mom—and not just lying, but sneaking off to a different state.

She wasn't exactly a natural rebel. The one time she and April had decided sophomore year to try an e-cigarette, Gemma had been so terrified the next day that she was dying of cancer that she had confessed to her mom just so she could be reassured.

But at eight a.m. the next morning Kristina would be in a long board meeting of one of the charities she supported, which meant that Gemma had a solid four hours to get the hell out of the state before her mom even found out she was missing.

Kristina and Gemma ate in front of the TV that night, side by side, as they often did whenever Gemma's dad was traveling. Usually, their game was to turn on a trashy reality television show and make fun of all the contestants. But tonight, Gemma was too antsy and distracted to concentrate.

"Can you believe her lips?" Kristina said, gesturing with a fork at the TV. "It looks like she got attacked by a vacuum cleaner." Gemma laughed, but a second too late. Kristina turned to her. "Are you all right? You seem quiet." Then, alarmed: "Are you feeling okay?"

"I'm fine," Gemma said. She set down her dinner—takeout from Whole Foods, since her mom considered *cooking* selecting from the various prepared options—on the coffee table and nudged it away from Rufus's nose with a toe. The sticky feeling was still lodged in her chest. Without meaning to, she blurted out, "Why did Dad leave Fine and Ives?"

Kristina turned to her, obviously startled. For a second, she looked almost afraid. Then she became immediately suspicious. "Why are you asking?"

Gemma shrugged. "Just curious. I mean, it was his, wasn't it? It still has his name and everything. I was so little. . . ." Gemma was two when her dad had first decided to leave Fine & Ives, but the subsequent lawsuit had dragged on for more than three years. She remembered nothing about that time; her childhood memories consisted mostly of hospital visits, doctors and constant evaluations, illnesses, relapses, injections, and bitter medicine spooned to her by her mother. But she did remember her parents had celebrated the end of the lawsuit in her room at Duke University Hospital, and she remembered being overwhelmed with happiness and with a sense even then that it wouldn't last. It never lasted.

Kristina turned back to the TV. But she was no longer watching. That was obvious. And after a second she picked up the remote and clicked the mute button. "Your father and Matthew Fine had . . . disagreements about the company's direction."

"What kind of disagreements?" Gemma pressed.

Kristina sighed. "To be honest, Gem, the details were never clear even to me." She said the words lightly, and Gemma knew they'd been practiced before. "Matthew Fine wanted to make some investments and your father disagreed. It was all boring and very, very complicated." Kristina's eyelids flickered: a sure sign that she was lying.

Gemma thought that would be the end of that, but then Kristina turned to her.

"I know your dad can be difficult," she said, making a weird face, as if the words were sour. "He's made his mistakes, like everyone. But he's a good man. Deep down, he is."

Gemma nearly said, *If you say so.* But she swallowed back the words. No point in getting into an argument with her mom—not when, if everything went according to plan, there were so many arguments in her future.

SIX

GEMMA WAS ABSOLUTELY SURE THAT something would go wrong. Kristina would know something was the matter and refuse to go to her board meeting. Perv would show up at nine and the truth would come out and Gemma would be locked in her room until menopause.

She was a nervous wreck. She couldn't imagine how thieves and murderers kept their cool. She could barely sneak out without her stomach liquefying.

But her mom just kissed Gemma's cheek, as she always did, and promised to be home later for another Whole Foods and reality TV marathon. One good thing about being relatively friendless and a total Goody Two-shoes: no one ever expected you to do anything wrong. Gemma was suspicion-proof.

She packed her bag, unpacked it, realized she'd packed all the wrong things and far too many of them, and repacked. She was too nervous to sit at her laptop, although she did pull up the Haven Files again on her phone and swipe through the maps section, partially to reassure herself of its existence.

Perv showed up punctually, driving the same eggplant-colored minivan. This time, Rufus hauled himself to the door but let out only three restrained barks of welcome.

"Bye, Roo." Gemma knelt down to hug her dog, taking comfort in his familiar smell. She knew she was being ridiculous—she was only going to be gone for a few days, maybe less if her mom got really aggressive and decided to fly down to Florida to get her—but she couldn't help but feel she was leaving forever. And she was, in a sense. She was leaving her old self behind. She would no longer be Gemma-who-did-everything-right, who-listened-to-her-parents, Fragile Gemma of the Broken Body. She was Gemma-who-rode-with-strange-boys, Gemma-who-investigated-mysteries, Gemma-who-defied-parents-and-lied-to-best-friends.

Ninja Gemma.

"Ready to rock?" Perv asked, when she came outside with her backpack slung over one shoulder. Today he was wearing a green T-shirt that made his hair look even blonder and a pair of striped Bermuda shorts.

"Sure." Gemma let Perv take the bag from her, though

it wasn't heavy, and sling it in the trunk. "How long is the drive, anyway?"

"Normally? Nine hours. When I'm behind the wheel?" Perv opened the door for her before she could do it for herself. He didn't just talk quickly. He did everything quickly. If he were a comic book character, there would be little zoom-y lines drawn behind him. "A record eight hours and forty-five minutes. That's with a standard three pee breaks. Fine. Four," he said, when Gemma looked at him. "But don't blame me if it throws our timing way off."

All morning, Gemma waited for Perv to run out of things to say. She soon realized that it was a lost cause, as were her attempts to ignore him. Trying to ignore Perv was like standing in the middle of a highway, trying to ignore the eighteen-wheeler about to turn your brains into pancake batter.

A typical conversation with Perv went like this:

"Hey, check it out. A Hostess truck. Can you imagine pulling a heist on a cupcake truck? That'd be the most delicious crime ever. You'd be a national hero. One time when I was little I tried to make cupcakes by pouring pancake batter into actual cups—my mom's china, to be exact. Turns out, interestingly, that china doesn't do very well at high heat. You know what else doesn't do well at high heat? Cell phones. Remind me to tell you about the time I accidentally microwaved my phone. . . ."

And on and on and on. Occasionally, he paused expectantly and waited for Gemma to say *uh-huh* or *no way*, or fired a series of rapid questions her way in an attempt to draw her out. For the most part, she responded in as few words as possible. She was too nervous to have a normal conversation, especially with Perv. She'd never been good with strangers and she had zero experience with boys, so the combination—*boy* and *almost stranger*—meant that her tongue felt as if it was wrestling itself every time she tried to speak. She was hoping he might take the hint and suggest they listen to music, or just leave her in peace.

No such luck.

"So your dad's some big pharma guy, right?"

"Used to be."

"I love saying the word *pharma*. Pharma. It sounds like a type of plant. Say it."

"Do I have to?"

"Yes. I'm driving. You're here for my amusement. Humor me."

"Pharma."

"See? Totally a type of plant."

They stopped just after noon at a rest stop in South Carolina that featured a Panera and a McDonald's. As they were getting out of the car, Gemma made the mistake of calling Perv *Perv*—out loud.

"Seriously?" He made a face.

"Sorry." Gemma felt immediately guilty. Perv was nice, and secretly she'd been flattered when April caught him staring at Gemma in the cafeteria, even if it was probably only because he had dirt in his eye or something. Nobody ever stared at her except in a horrified kind of way, as if her face was a graphic image of a car accident. And Pete was *cute*—in a very messy boy kind of way, but still, undeniably cute. *And* he was giving her a ride.

Perv—*Pete*—shook his head. He didn't look mad. Just surprised and a bit disappointed. "You really think I'd steal underwear from *Chloe?*"

Gemma tried to make a joke out of it. "Are you saying you'd steal it from someone else?"

She was relieved when Pete—she would only think of him as Pete from now on—cracked a smile. "Maybe," he said, "under the right circumstances. Like, for the good of social justice."

"Why would stealing underwear be good for social justice?" she asked.

"Politics are complex, Gemma," he answered solemnly, and she couldn't help but laugh.

They agreed to meet back in the car—or rather, Pete decided they should have a race to see who could get back to the car soonest, claiming he had once ordered a McDonald's meal, peed, and purchased several plastic figurines from one of the twenty-five-cent machines that always cluttered the rest stops, all within a record four minutes.

Gemma didn't like to eat in front of strangers, ever since the time in seventh grade when Chloe had made pig-snorting noises when she'd carried her tray at lunch, and half the class had joined in. Instead she followed Pete into the rest stop and scarfed a granola bar while peeing in a stall, feeling pathetic and stupid but still too embarrassed to buy what she wanted, which was a Happy Meal. She didn't feel so much like Ninja Gemma sitting with her pants around her ankles and granola bar crumbs on her bare thighs.

She made it back to the car first, and Pete emerged about thirty seconds later at a sprint, holding an enormous bag from McDonald's. He stopped when he saw her and threw up his hands dramatically, nearly losing his soda cup.

"I don't believe it," he said. "You beat me." Then, unlocking the car and seeing she was empty-handed, he said, "You're not hungry?"

"Not really," Gemma said, even though she was. She turned away so he wouldn't see her cheeks burning.

When they climbed into the car, he plopped the McDonald's bag in her lap. She could smell the fries.

They smelled like grease and salt and heaven.

"Share mine," he said. "I don't want you to starve to death. It would be awkward to explain to your parents."

"I doubt I'm in danger of starving anytime soon," she said. She wasn't sure if he was making fun of her—compared to some of the girls at her school, she was a massive balloon that floated over the crowd at big parades—but it didn't seem that way. The idea of her parents made her stomach turn a little. She checked her phone. One o'clock. Her mom would be home any second, would discover Gemma was missing, and would send out an Amber Alert.

"Fine. But you're in danger of turning into a walking toothpick, like Chloe. Every time I see her, I feel like I have something in my teeth."

She liked him a hundred times more for saying it, even if it wasn't true. She couldn't help it. Chloe looked like pretty girls were supposed to look, at least according to every fashion magazine and blog. And Gemma looked like the girl who'd *swallowed* the pretty girl.

She dug her hand in the bag and popped fries in her mouth. They were delicious. She didn't care that when she leaned forward her stomach rolled a little over her waistband. Pete wasn't even looking at her. He was busy scarfing his own burger. Gemma decided she liked the way he ate—with total attention, like the food was a complex math problem he had to solve.

"So you really didn't steal Chloe's underwear?" she asked after a moment.

"'Course not," he said, although since his mouth was full it came out *cough noff*. He made a big show of swallowing. "Want to know my theory? My theory," he said, without waiting for her to respond, "is that Chloe DeWitt was and is hopelessly in love with me, and when I didn't steal her underwear, it drove her crazy. She had to pretend that I did."

Gemma stared at him. There was a little bit of sauce at the corner of his mouth and she had the momentary urge to reach out and wipe it off. "You're insane. Do you know that? You actually might be certifiable."

He shook his head. His expression turned serious. "Those girls are clones, Gemma. They lack brains."

She turned toward the window so she would stop noticing things about him—how nice and long his hands were, with freckles sprinkled across the knuckles. His funny Adam's apple, which rioted up and down his throat when he spoke. Even if he was nice, he was still a cute boy, and cute boys did not go for girls like Gemma. She'd seen enough romantic comedies to know it.

"Clones have brains," she said. "You're thinking of zombies."

"Zombie clones, then," he said, and put the car in drive.

SEVEN

THEY WERE NEARING JACKSONVILLE WHEN they heard about the explosion off Barrel Key, and the fire burning out of control on Spruce Island. Gemma had been searching the radio for something that wouldn't tempt Pete to sing along. It turned out when he wasn't talking, he was singing, usually off-key, and with some random jumble of words that had only a vague relationship to the *actual* lyrics. She was looking for gospel, bluegrass, hard-core rap, *anything*. The first hour of impromptu karaoke had been all right—she'd actually enjoyed his rendition of "Man in the Mirror" and had nearly peed her pants when it turned out he knew every word to Britney Spears's ". . . Baby One More Time"— but after the second hour she longed for quiet, especially since Pete wouldn't stop harassing her about singing along.

When she hit a news station, she almost skipped right over it.

"—local officials confirmed the fire . . . at the Haven Institute for—"

"Come on, DJ, how about playing a song?" Pete spun away from the station just as Gemma froze, stunned. The radio skipped to a Jimmy Buffett song.

"No. Stop. Go back, please." Gemma turned the radio back, past the crackle and hiss of silent frequencies, until she heard the newscaster's voice tune in again.

". . . unconfirmed rumors . . . a deliberate attack . . ."

Pete was pretending to pout. "Jimmy Buffett, Gemma. That's, like, Florida's national anthem. I think it's mandatory that we hear 'Margaritaville' at least once a day. Otherwise we might get kicked out of the state."

"I'm begging you. *Please.* This is important, okay?" She cranked the volume button, but the sound quality was awful. She had no idea where the station was broadcasting from, but it must have been closer to Barrel Key, and the voices kept patching in and out, interspersed with snippets of music from another station.

"Tom, is it true . . . actually took credit on Facebook?"

". . . problem is . . . nobody talking . . ."

"Police say stay away until . . . situation under control . . ."

"Military presence . . ."

"Rumors of a protest at Barrel Key . . ."

But by then the interference was too great, and they were listening to some old-timey singer warbling about heartbreak. Gemma punched the radio off. She needed silence to think. There was a fire at Spruce Island—possibly an attack. But by whom? And what did it mean? Why would anyone attack a research institute? She thought of the man who'd grabbed her in the parking lot, with his coffee-stink breath and the wide frenzy of his eyes.

"Barrel Key," Pete said slowly. For once, he wasn't smiling or twitching or trying to make her laugh. He was just frowning, holding tight to the steering wheel with both hands. "That's where you're going, isn't it?"

"That's where you're going to take me," Gemma said. And maybe it was the way she said it, or the way she looked, but he finally stayed quiet after that.

They got to Barrel Key just after six o'clock. Gemma had powered down her phone hours earlier, after sending a single text to her mom—*Gone to see April in Florida*—just so Kristina wouldn't be tempted to call out the police or the National Guard. Still, she knew her mom would be frantic. She had probably called Gemma's dad by now, too, and this gave Gemma her only satisfaction: he was thousands and thousands of miles away and couldn't punish her.

Barrel Key was one long chain of warehouses and boat

shops, big metal storehouses and bait-and-tackle shacks leaning over on their foundations. The sky, she noticed, was greenish, and only when she rolled her window down and the acrid smell of burning reached her did she realize that the wind had carried ash from Spruce Island.

"Wow," Pete said as they passed a single motel, the *M* in its sign burned out, buzzing the word *vacancy* at them like a threat. "Great vacation spot. Very, um, authentic."

"It's more of a working vacation," she said, because she knew he wouldn't drop it otherwise.

"What kind of work? You a world-class fly fisherman or something? Or trying to re-up on ammunition?" This as they were passing a lean-to advertising both *farm-fresh eggs* and major firearms. "Do you want to tell me what you're really doing here?"

Gemma hesitated. "I can't," she said. It wasn't a lie. She didn't know exactly what she expected to find, only that the universe seemed to be pointing here, toward Haven. A battered sign showed the way to the marina. "Turn right here."

She kept the window down, straining for a glimpse of Spruce Island, but the buildings kept intruding and the ocean was only visible in brief flashes. Here, at least, the town was not nice, exactly, but nicer: another motel, this one with all its letters intact; diners and bars, stores with colorful lures displayed in the windows, a T-shirt shop and a restaurant with outdoor seating. In the distance she heard a sound she thought must be the roar of waves, but as they grew closer she made out human voices. A helicopter passed overhead, then another.

The road curved and they were prevented from going any farther by a series of sawhorses in the road and cops grimly gesturing them to turn around. Beyond the roadblock was the marina, and hundreds and hundreds of people gathered there, shouting and chanting and waving homemade signs. Beyond them, the spiky masts of small sailboats bobbing up and down in the water. A column of smoke was visible here, tufting up into the sky from somewhere up the coast and smearing the sun to a strange orange color.

A cop rapped on the driver's-side window, and Pete rolled it down. "You're going to have to turn around," the cop said. He was suited up in riot gear and carrying three guns that Gemma could see.

"That's where we're going," Gemma said, gesturing to the angry crowd at the marina, and Pete gave her a look like, *We are?*

"Turn around," the cop said. "Nothing to see here."

"Except for the huge fireball and all the people going nutty," Pete said. Gemma elbowed him as the cop leaned down to stare at them through the window. "But otherwise you're right, nothing to see. Nothing at all." A second cop was moving toward them, and Pete quickly put the car in reverse. "Have a nice day!" he shouted, even as he was backing haphazardly up the street. The two cops stood there, staring after them, until they'd turned around in the parking lot of a hardware store and started back in the direction they'd come.

"Well, *that* was a lovely day trip," Pete said as they left the marina behind. "Where to now? Any natural disasters you want to visit? Prison camps? Political riots?"

Gemma spotted a vacant parking lot behind a long line of low-ceilinged storage units. "Pull over here," she said.

Pete turned to stare at her. "Are you serious?"

"Please. Just do it." It felt good to give orders, to have a plan, to be out on her own, to do what she wanted without having to beg for permission. Something leapt to life in her chest, a force beyond the guilt and the fear. It was like she'd been living in a cartoon, in two dimensions, her whole life, and had just fought free of the page.

He did, barely making the turn, and rolled to a stop. "Most people think of spring break, they think bikinis, virgin piña coladas, spray tans . . ."

"Not me," Gemma said, trying to make a joke of it. "I'm allergic to coconut. And I don't even *own* a bikini."

"Why not?" His eyes were very clear when he turned to look at her. "You'd look great in a bikini."

Once again, she couldn't tell whether he was making

fun of her. There was an awkward second when Gemma was acutely aware that she was imagining Pete imagining *her* in a bikini, fat rolls and thighs that rubbed together and everything. She wanted to die of embarrassment. Her cheeks felt like someone had put a torch to them. She could hardly stand to look at him, but she had to know whether he was smirking.

He wasn't. He was fiddling nervously with the radio, even though he'd shut off the car ignition. It occurred to Gemma that he was nervous—actually nervous. Because of her.

Germ Ives. The Frankenstein monster.

"I'll be fine," she said, and opened the car door. She didn't know where all the tension had come from, but she was desperate to escape it. Her whole body was torch-hot now. Immediately, the faint scent of burning reached her, and beneath it, the smell of swampland—sunbaked mud and belly-up fish and microorganisms wiggling deep in the earth. "Thanks for the ride. Really."

"You *are* serious," he said, as though he couldn't believe it. He raised his hands. "All right. Whatever gets your goat."

"*Whatever gets your goat?*" She shook her head, amazed.

"Yeah. You know. Whatever wets your whistle, gets your rocks off, brings you to your happy place—"

"Pete?" she said. But she couldn't help but smile.

"Know when to stop. Seriously."

She got out of the car, half expecting him to call her back. But he popped the trunk when she rapped on it and she slung her backpack over her shoulder, still with that weird sense of guilt and fear arm-wrestling with excitement in her stomach. Pete rolled down the window and called out to her before she could walk away.

"You'll call me, right? If you need anything?"

"Is this your fancy way of getting my number?" Gemma asked. Immediately she wanted to chew her own lips off. She sounded like such a dork. And she hated herself for caring, too. He'd given her a ride and that was it. It wasn't like they'd been on a date.

"Technically," he said, "it's my fancy way of making you *ask* for my number." He smiled at her all crookedly, with his hair standing up as if it was happy, too. She took his number down and he took hers. "Promise you'll call, all right? So I know you didn't end up, you know, eaten by a crocodile or something?"

She promised she would, although she knew she wouldn't—besides, he was just being polite. She stood there and waved good-bye, feeling a quick squeeze of regret as Pete bumped off onto the road in his ridiculous van. If she was honest, she had to admit she hadn't *hated* hanging out with him. He was annoying, obviously. She didn't like the way that he looked at her sometimes, as if his eyes were lasers boring straight into her brain. But he was funny, and he was company, and he was, okay, maybe-kind-of cute. She'd never even been alone with a boy before today.

Now she was definitely alone.

She turned back toward the marina. As soon as she began walking, she regretted telling Pete to drop her off so far away. She couldn't approach the marina head on. She had no desire for face time with RoboCop and his buddy. But she figured if she could find a different route onto the beach, she could make her way back along the water to the place where everyone had gathered. Then, she hoped, she'd be able to figure out what had happened at Haven—what Haven *was*, even.

When she could hear the noise of the protest, she turned left and cut through a rutted, salt-worn alley between two boat shops, and then right on a street parallel to the one that led to the marina. Beach grass grew between cracks of the asphalt and a fine layer of sand coated the sidewalks. The houses here were interspersed with smoke shops and dingy bodegas, each of them painted a different pastel but also dusty and dim-looking, like old photographs leached of their luster. After another minute, the buildings fell back and she saw the water flashing behind saw grass the color of spun caramel. A chain-link fence blocked passage down to the beach, and beyond it she saw rusted kayaks piled in the grass and a scattering of broken beer bottles and cigarettes. She looked behind her: no movement in any of the houses, no signs of life at all except for a skinny cat slinking out from underneath an old Toyota Corolla. Several more helicopters motored by overhead.

She removed her backpack and heaved it over the fence, and then, checking once again to make sure no one was looking, interlaced her fingers in the chain-link and began to climb. The fence swayed dangerously and she had a momentary vision of toppling backward and pulling the whole fence with her. She maneuvered clumsily over the top of the fence and then dropped to the sand, breathing hard now and sweating under the strange smoky sun. She picked up her backpack, realizing as she did that she could now see Spruce Island in the distance— or at least, what she thought must be Spruce Island. About a mile up the coast she could make out a range of heavy dark growth above the horizon. The rest of the island, and whatever Haven was or had been, was blurred by a scrim of smoke and heat.

She picked her way along this untended portion of beach back toward the marina, watching her feet so she didn't trip on any of the junk embedded in the sand. She came to another chain-link fence, this one running down into the water, but luckily found a gate unlatched and didn't have to climb again. Then she was in front of a battered gray warehouse. She'd seen it at an angle from Pete's car and knew that it extended like a long arm to brace one side of the marina.

And now the swell of voices reached her over the wind. She had to slosh down into the mud to get around the old warehouse, and every time she stepped, a few inches of filthy water swirled up around her shoes. On the far side of the warehouse was the parking lot the police had blocked off, and the crowd had assembled there, some people carrying signs and chanting in unison, some camped out on the asphalt with picnic blankets and binoculars, like they were at a summer concert. A few kids Gemma's age or slightly older were grouped along the edge of a neighboring roof, legs dangling like icicles from the eaves, watching the action. Gemma counted fifty people and at least a dozen cops. What was going on at Haven that it would be so worth protecting? Or destroying?

She slipped unnoticed into the crowd.

She passed a man wearing a plastic Viking helmet that had been outfitted with different antennae and metal coils. He kept pacing in circles, gesturing to an invisible audience and muttering, and when he caught Gemma looking, he whirled on her and continued his monologue even more loudly "—and why we couldn't drink any of the water when we were stationed in Nasiriyah, fear of poison, of course some must have gone in the food supply and that's why the doctor says holes in my brain—"

She turned quickly away. Several people wore gas masks that made them look like the bad guys in a horror film, or like enormous insects, which made it even weirder that they were standing around in jeans and beat-up Top-Siders, gazing out over the water. The protesters, she saw, were calling for Haven's shuttering. *Our Land, Our Health, Our Right,* read one sign, and another said, *Keep Your Chemicals Out of My Backyard.* But among them were signs with other, stranger messages: signs that referenced Roswell and Big Brother and zombies, and several posters screaming about the dangers of hell. One girl who couldn't have been older than twelve was holding a colorful handmade sign with bubbly letters: *And Cast Ye the Unprofitable Servant into Outer Darkness.*

Gemma picked out a sunburned middle-aged couple who looked normal enough and fought her way over to them. The man wore leather sandals and a baseball hat with the logo of a hunting lodge on it. The woman was wearing a fanny pack. Both of them were staring out toward the billowing clouds of smoke in the distance, which made it look as if a volcano had erupted mid-ocean.

"What's going on?" Gemma asked them. It was funny how disasters made friends of everyone. "Is anyone saying how the fire started?"

The man shook his head. "Nothing official. Heard

maybe a gas line blew up. Of course the island's loaded with chemicals, would have caught fast—"

His wife snorted. "It was no gas line," she said. "We've talked to a dozen locals say they heard at least two explosions, one right after another."

"Explosions," Gemma repeated, shifting the backpack strap on her shoulder. Sweat had gathered under the collar of her shirt. "Like a bomb or something?"

The woman gave Gemma a pitying look. "You're not from around here, are you? People have been calling for the institute or whatever it is to be shut down for years now. I wouldn't be surprised if someone decided to take a shortcut. Of course the rumors . . ." She spread her hands.

"What kind of rumors?" Gemma pressed, although she remembered from the Haven Files a long list of all the different things supposedly manufactured at Haven—everything from incredibly contagious diseases to human organs.

"Some people think they got aliens out there on that island," the husband said. Now Gemma understood the reference to Roswell, where an alien spaceship had supposedly crashed and then been concealed by the military. "Well, I tell you, we come up every year from Orlando to do a little paddling and bird-watching in the reserve. Great birds up here—white ibis, knots, and dowitchers on the old oyster bars. You interested in birds?" Gemma arranged her face into what she hoped was a polite expression and nodded. He harrumphed as if he didn't believe it and went on, "I've got a pair of binoculars can spot a pine grosbeak at a distance of eight hundred yards, and I've done a little sighting of the island and never seen any glowing green men." He kept his eyes on the fire in the distance. "But I'll tell you they have guards in mounted towers, barbed-wire fences sixteen feet high. They'll shoot you if you get too close and won't blink about it. They say they're doing medical research out there, stuff for our boys overseas, but I don't buy it. They're hiding something, that's for sure."

Another chopper went by overhead, and Gem felt the staccato of its giant rotor all the way in her chest. It seemed obvious that no one knew what was happening or had happened out in Haven, but still she fought through the crowd, searching for an official, for someone in charge. Forcing her way through the knot of protesters, she saw a policeman arguing with a dark-haired boy with the kind of symmetrical good looks that Gemma associated with movies about superheroes. The cop was holding a professional-looking camera and appeared to be deleting pictures.

". . . no right to confiscate it," the boy was saying, as Gemma approached. "That's private property."

"What did I say about taking pictures?" the cop said,

angling away and blocking the boy with a shoulder when he tried to reach for his camera. "This isn't the goddamn Grand Canyon. We've got an emergency on our hands. Show some respect."

Gemma couldn't help but feel sorry for the boy. He looked furious. He couldn't have been much older than she was, and the camera looked expensive. "I'm not a tourist," he said. "And I can take pictures if I want to. This is America."

"This is a crime scene, at least until we say otherwise," the cop said.

The boy clenched his fists. Gemma found herself momentarily frozen, watching him. For a second his eyes ticked to hers, but they swept away just as quickly. She wasn't offended. She was used to being invisible to other people, preferred it, even.

"All right." The cop had finished with the camera. He popped open the back of the camera, removed the battery, and then returned the now-useless camera to Jake. "Now for your phone, please."

"You can't be serious." The boy had gone completely white. Gemma was getting angry on his behalf. Why wouldn't he have the right to take pictures if he wanted to?

The cop was obviously losing patience. He raised a finger and jabbed it right in the boy's face. "Now look here, son—"

"My name is Jake," the boy said smoothly. "Jake Witz."

"All right, Jake Witz. You want to make trouble, you just keep on yapping. But I'll bring you down to the station—"

"For what? Having an iPhone?"

"That mouth is gonna get you into trouble. . . ."

Gemma was too stunned to move. Jake Witz was the name of the guy who ran the Haven Files website. It had to be a coincidence—he bore no resemblance to the guy in the profile picture on the site. This guy looked like he could be a Clark Kent body double, just without the glasses.

And yet . . . When she looked closer, she thought she saw certain similarities. The line of the boy's jaw, which in the older man had been blurred. The same slightly-too-large nose, which on the boy looked strong and perfect and on the older man had just looked comical. Relatives, then? She couldn't be sure.

Finally the boy had no choice but to pass over his phone. The cop made Jake unlock the screen, and then sorted through the pictures, deleting the ones he deemed inappropriate. Jake stood there, his face hard with anger, which somehow made him even *more* attractive.

Finally the cop returned the phone and gave Jake a big thump on the back, as if they were best friends at a base-ball game. "Good man," he said. "Now don't make me ask you again, all right? Clear on out of here. Nothing to see."

Almost immediately, the cop swaggered away, pushing roughly past Gemma without sparing her a second glance, this time to yell at two teenage girls who were trying to record a video with their phones. Jake aimed a kick at a crushed Coca-Cola can, which skittered across the sand and gravel and landed in a patch of grass. Either he hadn't noticed Gemma or he was pretending not to have.

So she cleared her throat. "Jake? Jake Witz?"

He looked up finally and her heart stuttered. His eyes were large and dark and mournful, and reminded her of the way Rufus looked when no one was paying him any attention.

"Yeah?" he said. He sounded tired. He looked tired, too, and she wondered how long he'd been out here, watching.

"My name's Gemma Ives," she said. She realized she hadn't exactly planned what she was going to say. She still didn't know what connection this Jake Witz had to the guy who ran the Haven Files, or whether there *was* a connection. If he recognized her last name, he gave no indication of it. "I know you. Well, I know of you. You're from the Haven Files, right?"

He frowned. "The website was my dad's thing," he

said. "I have nothing to do with it." He started to turn away.

"You must have *something* to do with it," Gemma said. The words leapt out of her mouth before she could stop them. Slowly he turned back to face her.

"What's that supposed to mean?"

Gemma licked her lips. "You're here, aren't you?" she said. "We're about as close as we can get to Haven. You're taking pictures. You must be interested, at least a little."

He didn't agree. But he didn't deny it, either. He just stood there, watching her. Gemma couldn't tell whether he found her amusing or irritating. His face was too perfect. It was unreadable. Just being around him made her feel like she was fumbling her way through a restaurant that was far too fancy for her. She found if she avoided looking directly in his eyes, and instead focused her attention on his nose or eyebrows or cheekbones, she could at least think.

"Look," she said. "I came all the way from North Carolina. My dad was involved with Haven somehow, or at least people *think* he was involved. He's not scared of anything, but he's scared of that. I want to know why. I have to know what they do at Haven. I have to know why it matters to him." *And to me,* she added silently.

For a long time, Jake said nothing. Then, just for a second, a smile went fast across his face. "Not by a long shot," he said, so quietly that Gemma wasn't sure he meant for her to hear. He started to turn around again, and Gemma's heart sank.

"What did you say?" She was sure, now, that fate had led her here, to Jake Witz. Sure that no matter what he claimed, he knew the truth about Haven.

"You said we were as close as we could get to Haven. But we're not. Not even close." He inclined his head and Gemma recognized the gesture for what it was: an invitation. He wanted her to follow him. This time, his smile was real, and long, and nearly blinded her. "Come on, Gemma Ives. I've been in the sun all day. I could do with a waffle."

Jake explained that there were two ways out to Haven. One was to take a launch from Barrel Key and circle around to the far side of the island, where the coast dissolved into open ocean, staying clear of the marshes. This was the way the passenger boats ferried employees back and forth, and the way that freight was moved. No boat of any size could navigate the marshes.

But there was another way: the Wahlee River, which passed the tiny fishing village of Wahlee and fanned out into the marshes—miles of winding, narrow channels and half-submerged islands that reached nearly all the way to Haven's northern coast.

"How do you know all this?" Gemma asked. They'd found a diner tucked off the main drag, empty except for a mom and her toddler and two older men in hunting vests huddled over coffee, with faces so chewed up by wind and weather it looked like their skin was in the process of dissolving. Although from here the ocean was invisible, there was still a rubber-stink smell in the air, and they could hear the occasional threshing of helicopters overhead.

Jake lined up four containers of half-and-half and emptied them one by one into his coffee. "I've lived in Little Waller my whole life," he said. "That's forty miles from here. My dad was big into fishing, camping, that kind of thing. We used to camp on the Wahlee. Spruce Island used to be owned by some timber company but Haven bought them out to build the institute. I remember they were still doing construction on some of the buildings when I was a kid." He shrugged. "Maybe that's when his obsession started. I never got the chance to ask."

Gemma swallowed. "Is he . . . ?"

"Dead," Jake said matter-of-factly, without looking at her. He stirred his coffee with a spoon but didn't drink. "Died four years ago, when I was fourteen. Drowned in the marshes. That's what they said, anyway."

Gemma felt suddenly cold. "What do you mean?"

Jake just shook his head. He leaned forward on his

elbows, staring out the window, and was quiet for a bit. A small TV mounted above the coffeepot was tuned to the news and kept scanning across the marina they'd just left behind. The waitress, a woman with hair shellacked into a bun, was parked in front of the TV with her arms crossed.

"I never really understood my dad," Jake said. His voice was rough, as if it were sliding over gravel. "He wasn't like the other dads. He worked at one of the plants cleaning out fish guts, but he carried a business card everywhere like he was the president of the United States or something, never left the house without a blazer, no matter what else he was wearing, Bermuda shorts or a bathing suit. He was always talking about his *theories*. He talked so goddamn much. He used to joke that's why my mom left, because she couldn't stand the talk. But I don't know. He might've been right. As a kid I just wanted him to shut up sometimes, you know?" He leaned back, meeting Gemma's eyes again, and she was startled by their darkness, their intensity. She couldn't help thinking that Jake and Pete were complete opposites: Pete walked like he was jumping, Jake as if the gravity were double for him what it was for anyone else. Pete was all lightness, Jake all weight. "I was ashamed of him, you know? Even as a kid, I was ashamed. Does that make me a bad person?"

"No," Gemma whispered.

He smiled as if he didn't believe her. He was neatening his empty plate, lining up his silverware with the table, his cup and saucer with the plate. He was the neatest eater Gemma had ever seen. She was embarrassed to see a ketchup blob and some crumbs by her elbow, and quickly wiped them up when he wasn't looking.

"My dad liked to say he missed his calling as a journalist. He always saw cover-ups, conspiracies, that kind of thing. JFK was killed because he was about to do a public memorandum on sentient life on other planets. Chicken pox was actually a biological agent released from a government lab. But Haven. Haven was his white whale." Jake pressed his hands flat against the table, hard, as if he could squeeze the memory of his father out through his palms. Even his *fingers* were perfect. "He used to take me with him on fishing trips out on the marshes. Or at least, I *thought* they were fishing trips, at first."

"Reconnaissance," Gemma said.

Jake nodded. "Being on the marshes is like being inside a maze. Red maple and cordgrass, needle rush, palmetto—it grows ten, twelve feet high and swallows up the horizon. My dad had friends who'd gotten lost for hours, even days out there, floating around trying to lick water from plant leaves and eating grubs for dinner and there they were, not a half mile from camp. Once we got really close, within shouting distance of the island. Well, all of a sudden there must have been eight, ten guards with guns, shouting for us to turn around and head back. My dad was furious. I was just a kid, you know. They acted like they were about to blow our heads off. They probably would have. They've fired on people before, civilians. I know a fisherman from town, says he almost got a hand blown off. Says he thinks it must have been a sniper to get him from that distance. Of course they're all from the military." He shook his head, smiling faintly. "In all the years I've lived down here, I know of only one person who made it onto the island—some kid snuck under a bad bit of fence in the middle of the night. Got chucked out just as quickly."

Gemma was having trouble following everything that Jake was saying, but she understood the main points: crazy-tight security, no one allowed to talk. "What about the people who work out there?" she asked. "The guards and the staff? *Someone* must be going on and off the island."

Jake nodded. "Freight goes in and out, sure, and trash gets collected on Sundays. But no one goes past the gate. The staff goes out on launches from town. Some of them live there and come back to the mainland on leave. Some of them commute. But they won't talk. They won't say a word about what goes on there. Like they're all scared."

He took a breath. "Everyone except for Nurse M."

"Nurse M?" Gemma repeated. "Who's Nurse M?"

"I wish I knew." This time, Jake's smile was crooked, as if he was too tired to make it line up. "Before he died, my dad said he was working some big angle. He said he was going to blow the lid off the whole operation. That's how he talked, you know. Like we were all cast members of some Hollywood spy movie." A look of pain seized him momentarily. "He told me he'd found a woman, Nurse M, who'd agreed to talk to him. She wanted everyone to know the truth. But the day before they were supposed to meet up, she died. Killed herself, allegedly." He straightened his fork and knife again, avoiding Gemma's eyes.

Although it was warm in the diner, Gemma felt as if a cold tongue had just licked the back of her neck. "But you don't believe that," she said slowly, watching him. He shrugged. "You think she was . . . murdered? So she wouldn't be able to talk?"

Now he picked at the surface of the table with a thumbnail. "I don't know. But it looks strange, doesn't it?" He shook his head. "My dad left notes. Tons and tons of notes about Haven, some of them nonsensical, some of them just irrelevant. I never found her real name. He was trying to protect her, I think. But he failed."

Gemma felt suddenly nauseous. Her father was wrapped up in this. Her family was wrapped up in it. "You said

they told you your father drowned. You don't believe it."
She was afraid to ask. But she had to know.

He looked down at his lap. "After that time we almost got shot, my dad stopped taking me with him when he went out on the marshes. He was scared. But he was getting closer, too. I know that now. He died only two months after Nurse M was found hanging. That's no coincidence." A muscle in his jaw twitched. "I still remember the smell of that morning, like this kind of aftershave one of the cops was wearing. Isn't that crazy? I can't remember his face, but I remember his goddamn aftershave." He laughed softly. She had the urge to reach out and take his hand, but of course, she didn't. "I was fourteen. They told me he'd been fishing when a storm blew in. Said he must have flipped his kayak, got turned around."

"And what do you think?" Gemma said.

He looked up. His eyes were like twin holes. There was so much pain at the bottom of them, Gemma wanted to look away, but couldn't. "My dad was a lot of things," he said softly. "But he wasn't an idiot. He could navigate those marshes blindfolded. He was happier on the water than anywhere else. He said it was the only place he belonged, you know?" He looked away again. Gemma wondered what it would be like to lose a parent so young, and found she couldn't imagine it. Would she be unhappy if her father died? She had always fantasized about simply deleting him from her life, pressing backspace and watching him vanish. But the truth, of course, was more complicated than that.

"What do you think really happened?" she asked.

He sighed. "I think he made it," he said. "I think he got onto the island. And then I think he was caught. They would have made it look like an accident."

Gemma felt as if there were a spider caught in her throat, trying to claw its way up her windpipe. She didn't want to believe any of it.

But she did.

"Do you know what they do at Haven?" Gemma asked. It was the question she'd come to Florida to answer—the only question that mattered.

"No," Jake answered bluntly, and Gemma's heart fell. "But I have some idea."

She waited, almost afraid to breathe. Jake looked around the diner as though trying to judge whether they were safe. No one was paying them any attention. Still, he called out to the waitress. "Excuse me? Would you mind turning up the volume?" he said. She barely glanced at him before punching up the volume on the remote.

A bug-eyed woman behind a news desk was staring earnestly into the camera, and for a moment Gemma latched on to her voice. ". . . Dr. Mark Saperstein, who is listed as the current director of the Haven Institute, cannot be reached for comment. It is unknown whether he too was on the island when the explosion . . ."

Jake leaned forward and cleared his throat. "Human experimentation."

"What?" Gemma looked away from the TV, which was again showing images of the coastline, and the sun setting behind a veil of smoke.

Jake shoved his hand through his hair. "Human experimentation. I know it sounds crazy," he added, before Gemma could say it. "And I'm not talking about your usual drug trials, either. I'm talking illegal experimentation. Weapons development. Chemical trials. That's why all the security, and why they're so far out of the way. No oversight."

Gemma frowned. Every medication or treatment that went to market had to go through human clinical trials. Gemma's dad was always railing against the medical ethics board's shortsightedness and how difficult it was to drum up volunteers for certain treatments. He was convinced that thousands of people died every year because the drugs that could have saved them were still being reviewed for safety by the FDA or hadn't been approved yet for human trial. Could Haven be a place designed so researchers could skirt the normal rules, and do their work with no oversight? She could understand, if so, why her father might have refused to pour money into Haven, and might have left Fine & Ives before his name could be associated with the deal. There had never been a bigger fan of rule following than Geoffrey Ives.

Still, the whole thing was pretty far-fetched. And it wouldn't explain why Gemma's father was so afraid. If he really had refused to participate, if he'd left his own company just to avoid the association with Haven, he would be praised as a hero.

"Where do they get the volunteers?" she asked. Her coffee was cold by now, but it was comforting to hold the mug between her palms.

Jake bit his lip, looking at her sideways. "That's the point," he says. "I don't think they're volunteers."

Gemma stared at him. "What do you mean?"

"They're not *getting* volunteers—not for these experiments. They're forcing people to participate."

"But . . . how?" Gemma asked. The french toast she'd eaten seemed to be sticking in her throat. "They can't just—I don't know—kidnap people."

"Why not?" Jake leaned forward. "Look, Gemma. This was my dad's work. This was his life. However nuts it sounds, I think he was onto something. Fine and Ives has military contracts, money coming directly from the top. *Half* of Fine and Ives's budget comes from military contracts. This is the government we're taking about."

Gemma thought of her father and his old company,

and her stomach squirmed. She remembered Christmas parties as a kid at the Carolina Inn, the ceiling draped in tinsel and plastic snowflakes, and everyone standing to applaud her father as he entered, clutching Gemma's hand. She remembered visiting the White House with her dad on a trip to DC, and how he shook the president's hand, and Gemma and her mother got to go downstairs to play ninepins in the White House bowling alley. And men suited up in crisp uniforms pinned with shiny medals going in and out of her father's office, smiling at her, hefting her into the air, tossing and catching her with big muscled arms.

Jake leaned forward, lowering his voice. "You've heard of Dr. Saperstein?" Gemma nodded. She remembered reading that Dr. Saperstein had taken control of Haven after Richard Haven had died in a car accident—the very same year she was born. The coincidence now seemed ominous. "About fifteen years ago, Saperstein weaseled his way onto the board of a nonprofit called the Home Foundation up in Philadelphia. It still exists today," he added when Gemma shook her head to show she hadn't heard of it. "He spent a few years growing its operations, expanding the volunteer forces, crowing about it in the media. Anyway, my dad dug up all the details. The Home Foundation places kids in foster care. These are the worst cases, children who've bounced around for years, or got dumped in front of the fire station or the hospital. It was the perfect setup. Kids get shuffled and reshuffled, moved around, drop out of the system, run away, disappear. Nobody's going to look too hard for them, right?"

Gemma felt now as if her thoughts were all gummed up and sticky. Maple Syrup Brain. "I don't get it," she said. "What are you saying? You can't mean—" She took a deep breath. "They're not doing experiments on kids?"

"They're *only* doing experiments on kids," Jake said gently—almost apologetically, Gemma thought. "I think Saperstein stole them. He stole them and brought them to Haven. That's why all the security. It's not just to keep us out, you know. Not by a long shot. It's to keep them in."

Gemma felt dizzy, even though she hadn't moved. It was too terrible. She didn't want to believe it. She wouldn't believe it. "There's no proof," she said. Her voice sounded tinny and far away, as if she was hearing it through a pipe.

Jake turned to look out the window. The smoke was still smudging the horizon, turning the setting sun to a smoldering orange. He said something so quietly Gemma nearly missed it.

Nearly.

Suddenly her heart was beating so hard, it felt as if it might burst through her chest.

"What?" she said. "What did you just say?"

He sighed. This time when he looked at her, she was afraid.

"I saw them," he repeated.

"How?" Gemma felt like she was choking.

"Remember that boy I told you about, the one who made it onto Haven through the fence?" Jake half smiled. "I was the boy."

EIGHT

THE TWO BASS MOTEL WAS just outside of town—a long, low, shingle-sided building with only a single car in the parking lot. When Gemma requested a room, the ancient owner knocked over her tea in surprise, as if she'd never before heard the words. But the room was clean, although slightly musty-smelling, and decorated, predictably, with lots of fish: an itchy coverlet woven with images of leaping salmon, a framed picture of fly-fishing hooks above the TV, a plastic bass mounted on the wall in the bathroom. Gemma hoped it wasn't the singing kind.

They had agreed that Jake would come back for her at eleven o'clock, and Gemma wasn't sure what was making her so nervous—the idea of trying to sneak into Haven, as Jake had done only once before, or the idea of being alone with him in the dark.

Alone with those perfect hands and eyes and lashes and

fingernail beds. She'd never even *noticed* fingernail beds before. But she'd noticed his.

She powered on her phone. There was a sudden frenzied beeping as a dozen texts and voice mails loaded, and she was surprised to see among all the messages from her mom that Pete had already texted her.

You didn't get eaten by an alligator, did you?

For a quick second, she actually felt guilty, as if she was cheating on Jake. Then, of course, she felt like an idiot. A delusional idiot.

She wrote back: *I'd like to see one try.*

Then she dialed April's number.

April picked up on the first ring and was talking before Gemma could even say hello.

"Thank God, finally, I've been calling you for, like, five hours. I thought you said your parents *caved*, but your mom is freaking out, she said you basically *ran away*, I mean, seriously, I'm talking about National Guard, Armageddon-level freak-out, if screaming were a superpower, she'd seriously be eligible for her own franchise—"

"Did you tell her I was with you?" Gemma asked quickly. The idea of her mother screaming—or even raising her voice—was both difficult to imagine and also terrifying. Her dad was the screamer. Her mom was the apologizer, the mediator, the smoother-over. The nothing-a-glass-of-wine-and-a-Klonopin-can't-fix kind of person.

April snorted. "Do you think I'm a complete amoeba? Of course I did. Except I started running out of reasons you wouldn't come to the phone. First I said you were napping, then that you'd gone out for a swim, then that you were in town getting coffee, and then I had to stop picking up the phone. I'm talking serious harassment here, she's probably called, like, twenty times—"

"I'll call her, okay? I'll call her right now," Gemma said, and April let out a big *whoosh* of air.

"Please," she said. "Before your mom calls in a SWAT team. My grandpa will kill me if they trample his geraniums." And then, in a different voice: "Where *are* you? Are you okay? How did you even get down here?"

"I'm in Barrel Key, not far away," Gemma said, avoiding April's last question, tracing one of the fish patterned on her coverlet with a finger. All the fish were identical, and all of them had the same anatomical error, an extra fin on the back that gave them a vaguely prehistoric look.

"But what are you doing *there*? I thought you were coming to stay with me."

"I am. Tomorrow. And then I'll tell you everything. I *promise*," Gemma said, before April could protest. She'd already lied so much in the past twenty-four hours. She couldn't stand lying to April, too. But what could she say to explain? *Oh, no big deal, someone threw a Frankenstein mask through our window and then a random psycho tried to nab me from a gas station and I think it's because my dad's old company is kidnapping children and testing chemicals on them and he might have known about it all this time.* "Just trust me, okay?"

April sighed. "Swear you're not holed up in some seedy motel meeting a stranger named Danger66 who claims to be a French exchange student looking for an English tutor."

Gemma looked around the room, and decided it definitely counted as a seedy motel. "I promise I'm not meeting a stranger named Danger66," she said. "I promise I'm not meeting *any* stranger." Jake Witz blinked momentarily in her mind. But he didn't count. She'd sought him out, not the other way around. Besides, she couldn't believe that someone who looked like Jake Witz could be dangerous. She'd been fed a steady diet of Disney growing up. The evil ones were always ugly. By the same logic, she knew that she was destined to be the charming dumpy sidekick for life: only skinny girls got to be leads.

Her next phone call went far less smoothly. April was right. Her mom was in full-on panic mode. Gemma had never heard her mother so upset, except for one time when she was a little kid and decided to smash up her mom's favorite necklace with a hammer to see whether diamonds were really the hardest substance on earth.

"I don't believe you. I really don't believe you. I would

never have expected it, never in a million years—after we specifically told you—"

"Mom, calm down." Gemma was annoyed not by the injustice of her parents' rules but by the fact that her mom had automatically assumed she would always obey. Just like she'd obeyed as a kid, shivering in those hospital beds, swallowing pills when she was told to swallow them, waking up with new scars, new evidence of damage. "It's not a big deal, okay?"

"Not a big deal? Not a big deal?" Kristina seemed to be gasping the words. "How can you even say that? Do you know how worried I've been? How worried your *father's* been?"

"Yeah. I'm sure he's been crying into his PowerPoint." The words were out of Gemma's mouth as soon as she thought them.

Kristina drew in a sharp breath. Then she said, in a quiet voice, "For your information, your father is on his way back from Shanghai right now. As soon as he lands, we're getting on a plane and coming straight down to get you—"

"Mom, no." Gemma was surprised that in an instant, all her anger was gone, and instead she was suddenly on the verge of tears. She took a deep breath. "Please," she said, because she knew that fighting or yelling wouldn't help. "I'm not in trouble. I'm safe. I'm with April." She no longer felt guilty about lying. If Jake was right about what they were doing at Haven, her father must have known about it, and had spent his whole life lying—her mother, too. It was like she'd heard him say: he'd done nothing. "Please let me have this, just this once. Let me be normal."

Kristina sighed, and Gemma knew she'd said the right thing. She imagined her mother cradling the phone against one shoulder, unscrewing the cap of one of her pill bottles and shaking one into her palm, starting to calm down.

"I'll talk to your dad," she said. "But you know how he is. He's furious. You lied to us, Gemma."

How many times have you lied to me? Gemma nearly said. But she swallowed the words back. She said instead, "You didn't give me much choice."

To her surprise, her mother laughed. But it was the saddest laugh ever, like she really wanted to cry. "We're just trying to keep you safe, Gem," she said. "That's all we ever wanted."

"I'm safe," she said. "I'm fine."

When Kristina spoke again, her voice was softer. Probably just the *thought* of a pill working its way through her bloodstream had calmed her. "I expect you to call me first thing in the morning."

"I will," Gem said. "Just tell Dad not to worry."

Kristina hesitated. "I'll see what I can do."

Gemma hung up. She was briefly euphoric, almost dizzy, but the feeling was short-lived. She'd gotten her mom only temporarily off her back. If her dad insisted on driving straight to April's house . . . if he discovered she wasn't there . . .

But if everything went as planned, she could make it to April's by morning, when her dad was still thirty thousand feet over the Atlantic. If everything went as planned, she might have all the answers she needed tonight.

And then what? What did it matter, really?

She wasn't sure. But she sensed—no, she *knew*—that there was in Haven a reason for her dad's constant, simmering anger; for the pills her mom measured out day by day; for the vast silence that filled her house and the way she caught her parents looking at her sometimes, as if she were a stranger.

She had to know why.

Her phone pinged. She assumed it would be her mom, calling back, but saw she had a new message from Pete: a GIF of a cartoon cowboy wrangling an alligator.

She tried watching TV but couldn't get anything but a blinking error message. She was nervous about what they were about to attempt, which was more dangerous than anything she'd ever even considered—she'd once nearly crapped herself cutting gym class to hang out with April like badasses behind the tennis courts. She wished she were the kind of girl who, when nervous, lost her appetite. Instead she made four trips to the vending machine, which contained only a few warm sodas, some Kit Kats, cardboard-tasting chips, and a bag of ancient Sour Patch Kids, shriveled and dry as discarded husks of molted cicadas.

She searched for more news about what had happened at Haven, refreshing the few local news sites that were covering it and toggling back and forth between individual blogs and conspiracy sites. The explosion had renewed public interest in Haven. She found a couple of news sites that referenced the controversy from several years ago, in which Haven was listed as one of the research institutes that had illegally purchased human tissue for research, including embryonic and stem cells. She knew embryonic cells were used for medical research. It fit Jake's theory. Fine & Ives had even released a statement, a bland PR document about a sudden fire at one of their research institutes. Every article had attracted dozens of comments, many of them nonsensical or filled with curses and hysterical references to escaped biological agents.

Around nine she saw references on several sites to a terrorist attack, by an individual who supposedly believed she was acting on God's commandment and had somehow managed to infiltrate the island. But there was frustratingly little information about the attack, and after only twenty minutes, many of the individual story links had been disabled or taken down. She was halfway through an article about the possibility that the person responsible had managed to stow away on the ferry that collected the waste from Haven twice a week when the whole page just blinked and then went dark, as if someone had pulled a curtain over her screen. She reloaded the page several times but kept getting the same 404 error.

"What the hell?" She jabbed her screen with a finger, trying to figure out how a webpage could just disappear while she was looking at it. There was a knock at the door and she jumped. She'd lost track of time completely. It was eleven o'clock already.

Jake had changed into a black T-shirt, dark jeans, and black Vans. When Gemma opened the door, she thought he looked like the lead singer in some indie band April might have been obsessed with. She wished temporarily she'd done something with her hair—more delusion. As if a great hairstyle would distract him from the thirty extra pounds she was packing.

He came into the room without saying hello and sat down on the bed.

"Did you hear?" he said. When he shoved a hand through his hair, it resettled right away. Soft, then. Of course. "The cops traced the explosion."

She closed the door and leaned against it. It occurred to her that this was exactly what she'd sworn to April she wouldn't do—meet a stranger in a seedy motel room. Maybe she'd sit down next to him and he'd try and touch her thigh or force his tongue down her throat. Then again, she wouldn't mind. If anyone was in danger of getting sexually harassed, it was probably him.

Jake pulled out a laptop from his backpack. "This came into my in-box an hour ago." He pivoted his computer screen around. "When my dad died, I couldn't bring myself to shut down the Haven Files admin on his website, so messages get routed to my in-box." She joined him on the bed, moving stiffly, hoping he wouldn't notice. She could smell his soap, and when he shifted the laptop onto her lap, his fingers grazed her thigh.

It was the first time a guy had ever touched her. And even though it was accidental, she got a small thrill.

The message had apparently come through the contact form on his website—it was addressed not to Jake but to the administrator. It was written in all caps.

WHEN JESUS DIED, THE CURTAIN IN THE TEMPLE WAS TORN INTO TWO PIECES. THE GRAVES OPENED, AND MANY OF GOD'S PEOPLE WHO HAD DIED WERE RAISED FROM DEATH. MATTHEW 27:51–3 GOD TURNS HIS FACE FROM ABOMINATIONS

AND CASTS MONSTERS DOWN TO HELL AND
THOSE WHO DISOBEY HIS WORD WILL FEEL THE
WRATH OF ETERNITY. AT HAVEN DEAD MEN
WALK FROM THEIR GRAVES AND GOD DEMANDS
JUSTICE FOR THE CRIMES OF THOSE WHO DON'T
LISTEN. I WILL BRING HELLFIRE TO HAVEN LIKE
GOD DID TO THE SINNERS AT BABYLON TO
PURGE THEM FROM THIS EARTH AND I WILL BE
WELCOMED BY ALL THE ANGELS IN HEAVEN WHO
WILL SING MY PRAISES.

The message was signed *Angel Fire* and included a link to a Tumblr, www.wrathofgod.tumblr.com, but when Gemma tried to click on it, she found it disabled.

Jake took the computer back from her. "The site was registered to an Estelle Williams in Sarasota. They already wiped it clean, but I managed to get screenshots, though. Give me a second."

Gemma thought of all the pages she'd Googled turning up suddenly wiped or just failing to load. "Who's they?"

He shifted on the bed, and Gemma realized he was nervous. "One of the federal departments, I assume," Jake said, looking at her sideways, as if expecting she wouldn't believe him. "I wouldn't be surprised if by tomorrow everyone's reporting that Haven never existed at all—it was some holographic experiment and we're all supposed to forget about it. Look." He swiveled the screen toward her again. "This is some of Angel Fire's stuff."

Gemma keystroked through a few pages, most of them decorated with grinning skulls or licks of flame and peppered with biblical verse and lots of exclamation points. "She thinks they're raising people from the dead at Haven?" she asked.

"She *thought* that," he said quietly. "If she really is responsible for what happened, if she did turn herself into one gigantic IED, like they're saying, she's scattered across the marshes by now." He shook his head, and Gemma couldn't help but think: another person dead. Another person dead because of Haven. Nurse M, Jake's father, and now this woman, Angel Fire. "She must have timed her message to go out to a bunch of people at once. Even the news channels got wind of it, and they're always the last to know anything." He closed the laptop and slipped it into his backpack—which was, predictably, black—and stood up. "So? Are you ready?"

"I guess so." She knew it was stupid to be freaked out by some nutter's theory about Haven and its weird science. But she couldn't shake the image of people staggering through the darkness of the marshes, reaching for her with clammy hands.

"You need to be *sure* sure." Jake stood up. "We might get arrested."

Suddenly, though, Gemma felt as if all those Sour Patch Kids were nails trying to claw back out of her throat. She had the sense that being arrested would be the best thing that might happen to them.

Jake had told her that several weeks after his father died, he'd woken up in the middle of the night, certain that someone had just shaken him awake. But he was in the room alone. Still, every few minutes he felt a phantom pressure on his shoulder, as though someone was tapping him.

"I know what you're probably thinking," he'd said, a little too forcefully. "But I don't believe in things like that. Spirits, voices from the grave. I'm not like my dad."

Still, the impression of a *presence* wouldn't leave him. Every few minutes, there was a tap-tap on his shoulder. So he had stood up, walked down the stairs, and walked straight out of the house.

His mom had just returned from Las Vegas, where she'd been living doing God knows what, essentially refusing to recognize the existence of her son except in the occasional birthday message, usually an email sent a few days late. Within a month, she would be gone again, and Jake would move in with his dad's sister, a widow who'd never had children and never wanted any.

Guided by a certainty he could never afterward explain, he had walked the five miles to the Wahlee basin campsite where he and his father had set off so many times together, and found a rowboat pitted with rust, likely left there by a local fisherman. The whole time, he said, he could feel an occasional tap on his shoulder, like a kind of Morse code, telling him to go on.

He had no compass. No water. No supplies. And yet somehow that night, alone in the marshes, he knew exactly where to go.

Dawn was breaking by the time he saw a bank of spruce and knew he'd reached Spruce Island. The institute was hidden from view. He realized he must have rowed all the way around to the west side of the island, which was still undeveloped. The security was lighter, too. There was a fence, and guard towers, but at dawn they were abandoned.

And still the finger kept tap-tap-tapping on his shoulder.

He pulled his boat up onto shore, less than ten feet away from a downed tree that had taken down a four-foot section of the fence.

He was on the island less than ten minutes before he was caught, thrown to the ground by military-style guards, frog-marched across the island and out to the dock, where police were already waiting for him. He never went near the main buildings, had only the briefest glimpse of the white-walled institute and the people inside it.

But it was enough.

She looked around the room, wishing she didn't have the melodramatic feeling she was seeing it for the last time. Even though it had been her idea to try and get to Haven tonight—or maybe because it had been—she felt she couldn't back out now. "I'm sure," she said, grabbing the only sweatshirt she'd brought. She wished it weren't bright pink.

Jake was obviously thinking the same thing, because he frowned. "Take this." He wrestled a black Windbreaker out of his backpack. It was a warm night, but the mosquitoes on the marshes, he told her, were killer.

Jake's car was so old it seemed predominantly composed of duct tape and string. "Sorry," he said, with an apologetic smile that made Gemma's heart purr. "But at least you're getting door-to-door service."

The car rattled so hard when he accelerated she was sure she was about to be expelled from her seat, that the car would just roll over and give up, panting, like a tired dog, but she didn't want to complain, and sat there white-knuckling her seat so hard her fingers ached.

"Just a few more miles," Jake said. They'd looped around to approach Wahlee from the north, on one of the few roads that gave access to the nature reserve, and the bouncing of the headlights made Gemma feel seasick.

Miraculously, they made it without incident, although

Gemma could have sworn that the car gave a relieved sigh when Jake cut the engine. Stepping outside, she was immediately overwhelmed by the sound of the tree frogs. They were so loud and so uniform they seemed like a single entity, like the heartbeat of the world rising and falling. Even here, she thought she detected a faint smell of smoke.

Jake removed a flashlight from his backpack and gestured for Gemma to follow him. The Wahlee Nature Reserve was technically closed at sunset, and theirs was the only car. They moved onto one of the paths that cut into a thicket of pine and mangrove trees, and immediately Gemma felt a difference in the ground, a sponginess that made her heart turn over a little. Jake had told her casually that all the islands and marshes around here would be gone in twenty years, swallowed up by water. She imagined the trees submerged, stretching ghostly fingers up toward a sun filtered through layers of murky water. She wondered what April would think now, if she knew that Gemma was following a boy she didn't know into a darkened nature reserve with no one around for miles.

She didn't know anymore whether she was glad or worried that she hadn't told anyone where she was going.

They walked for fifteen minutes, though it felt like longer, and the sticky, humid air seemed to get all tangled up in Gemma's lungs. After a certain point they didn't seem to be following a path at all, and she had no idea how Jake was sure that he was heading in the right direction. The marshes had tides that shifted subtly and without sound: the water wouldn't even warn them before appearing suddenly beneath their feet. Jake stopped and touched her elbow.

"We're close," he said. "Go carefully. There are tidal pools here."

"Okay," Gemma said. Her voice sounded strange in the humid darkness, like it was being muffled by a pillow. She was sorry when Jake took his hand away.

A few paces farther on, Jake stopped completely and angled his flashlight at a patch of ghostly white saw grass, running down to a black expanse she now recognized as an inlet. Partially concealed beneath a myrtle oak was a bright-red kayak, which he'd rented from a local boat shop and stashed earlier that night. It was skinny and long as a Popsicle. Gemma's stomach dropped.

"I don't think we're both going to fit," Gemma said desperately, as Jake bent over to drag the kayak free of the growth.

"Of course we will. It's a two-seater." He pointed with the flashlight. There were, in fact, two seats in the kayak—if you could call them seats. Gemma thought they looked like those car seats meant for toddlers.

I'm not going to fit, Gemma wanted to say. But of course she couldn't. Not to him. Jake was the kind of guy who had size-zero girlfriends who modeled locally and were always complaining about trying to find clothes small enough.

"Can't we get another boat?" she asked desperately. "A *boat* boat?"

He must have thought she was kidding, because he only laughed.

"Anything bigger will just get stuck. Some of the channels out there are so narrow even the kayak's a stretch." Jake bent down and shoved the kayak down into the water, which sucked at the plastic with a wet farting sound. He steadied it with a foot. "Besides, it's more comfortable than it looks."

He clambered easily into the kayak—or the floating Popsicle—and somehow enfolded his long legs inside it, as if he were just sitting down in a chair. Then he maneuvered the kayak so he could reach out a hand to help Gemma inside.

"Come on," he said. "You'll be fine."

She bit her lip. She had a sudden vision of getting stuck in her seat, of having to be hauled out of the kayak by a crane. Or worse, of not being able to fit inside in the first place. But she took his hand. As soon as she placed a foot into the kayak, it began bucking like a badly trained horse, and if the boat hadn't still been rooted in the mud of the bank, she was sure the whole thing would have gone over.

"All right, now the other foot . . . there you go, easy now . . ."

Somehow she managed to climb in without flipping the kayak, and even more miraculously, managed to squeeze herself down into the hard plastic seat, feeling a little like an elephant in a girdle.

"See?" Jake used a plastic paddle to push them out of the mud and turn them in the right direction. He was smiling at her again, his teeth white in the moonlight. "Not so bad, is it?"

"For the record," Gemma blurted out, "this is *exactly* as comfortable as it looks."

"Aw, come on. Don't be a baby." But he was still smiling. And as they began to move through the marshes, her spirits lifted. Jake had given her a paddle but instructed her not to use it, and she was happy to let him do the work. They progressed steadily and in near silence except for the slurping of the water on the paddles. They'd agreed in advance that they should try and avoid talking as much as possible, in case there were patrols on the marshes.

So far it seemed their gamble—that after what had happened, security would be trying to get everyone out, not worrying about people trying to get in—was correct.

Occasionally helicopters passed in the distance on their way to and from the island, but less frequently now. And Gemma knew they must still be ferrying people *from* the island. It was unlikely, however, that given Haven's security, any survivors had even *made* it onto the marshes, which explained why they were putting hardly any effort into searching for them.

After an hour they'd met no one, heard no one, although occasionally they seemed to hear shouting in the distance, and Gemma knew they were still quite far from Haven. The marshes really did look like a labyrinth, full of narrow channels that forced them back toward the mainland before they could find another vein of water to follow in the right direction. Every few minutes, Jake stopped to consult the compass on his phone. With the saw grass growing as high as a tall man and mangrove trees furry with overhanging moss, they would have otherwise had no way of knowing where the mainland was and which way led to open ocean.

But there was a strange beauty to the marshes, and the tangles of dark weeds that drifted just below the surface of the water and came up on Jake's paddle, like long, dark fingers drawing him back, and the saw grass painted white with bird guano. The moon was full and bright, even behind a wispy covering of smoke, and so close Gemma could see individual craters, a pattern of trenches and shadow that made a grinning face. Jake picked out constellations to show her, and Gemma thought they all looked like they were winking down at her, letting her in on some secret. Jake obviously loved the marshes, despite what had happened to his dad here, and he told her stories of camping trips and frog-hunting expeditions, how his dad had renamed all the stars he didn't know and claimed Orion's Belt had been named for a drunk god who liked to pee in the Wahlee. Jake shook his head. *I believed him for so many years.* He smiled. *Whenever I see Orion's Belt, I think of him.*

It occurred to Gemma that this was the second time in the past twenty-four hours she'd been squeezed next to a cute boy in a strange vehicle. Maybe tomorrow she would meet a tall, dark, handsome stranger who'd want to take her on a motorcycle ride. Maybe she'd end up in Vegas working for the mob as a professional blackjack dealer.

At that moment, anything at all seemed possible.

She lost track of time completely but knew they must be getting closer. Sometimes she thought she heard the echo of overlapping voices, and once Jake froze, sticking the paddle down into the mud and shoving them into the shadow of an overhanging sand oak. But the voices always receded. If there were other people out in the darkness, the marshes were expansive enough to keep them at a distance.

At one point, Jake fished out his phone to check the

time and Gemma saw that he looked exhausted. She felt horrible: she hadn't been helping at all, and he'd been paddling for nearly two hours.

"One a.m.," he said. He was a little out of breath. "We must be getting close."

"You need a break," Gemma said.

"I'm okay," Jake said, completely unconvincingly.

"You're a terrible liar," Gemma said firmly. "You need a break." She, too, needed to stretch. Her feet had gone numb hours ago.

He didn't argue again. He angled the kayak up into the shallows and freed himself, so tired he didn't even complain when he sank a leg shin-deep in the mud. He helped shove the kayak onto sturdier ground so she could disembark. A rush of sudden feeling invaded her legs and she nearly stumbled. Jake caught her and for a second she was close to him, his hands on her elbow, his lips bow-shaped and his jaw just stubbled with hair and his eyes unreadable in the dark. She quickly pulled away.

She helped him haul the kayak farther into the grass so it wouldn't drift away. The saw grass grew nearly to shoulder height, and Gemma was glad, now, for the Windbreaker: it was sharp, and left sores on her exposed skin. As they hacked through the grass, for the first time in hours she spotted Spruce Island, by this point so close she could make out individual trees, and the spiky points of the guard towers, which looked to be abandoned. They had somehow come around the westernmost tip of the island, which was densely overgrown. She could make out none of the buildings, although some lingering smoke indicated a point in the distance where they must have been.

Gemma was so tired she'd forgotten to be nervous. Now, however, she remembered. "What now?" she whispered. "Do you think we can still get—?" She broke off before she said *closer.* Jake went very still.

They'd both heard it: a muffled cry.

Jake grabbed her arm and pulled her into a crouch. He brought a finger to his lips, but there was no need. Gemma was so frightened, she couldn't have made a sound if she wanted to. The silence was anything but reassuring. They'd heard a voice, a human voice, ten, twenty feet away in the marshes. Which meant that whoever had cried out was now deliberately being quiet. Creeping up on them, maybe. Waiting to attack. Gemma pictured herself handcuffed in a military facility, a single lightbulb swinging overhead, an ugly army sergeant with a face like an old baseball mitt leaning forward to spit on her.

She was scared of Chloe DeWitt, ninety-pound blond shrimpoid. She would never make it in prison.

Then again, maybe she'd just get shot in the back, hit by a sniper from a distance of a hundred yards. One breath in and one breath out and then darkness forever.

Then they heard it: a faint rustling of the grass, followed by a sharp silence, as if someone had taken a step and then frozen. Jake was so still she couldn't even tell if he was breathing. The footstep had come from somewhere behind them. Jake gestured in the opposite direction. *Move,* he mouthed, and despite the fact that Gem's legs felt stiff and fatter than usual, she began to inch forward, shuffling crablike as quietly as possible. Her thighs were burning and tears sprang up unexpectedly in her eyes. Pathetic. Out here on the marshes in the middle of the night, crying because no one knew where she was, because she hadn't told her mom she loved her, because she hadn't told April, either, because her thighs were really out of shape and she would never wear a bathing suit again. . . . They would kill her, they would shoot first and make it look like an accident. . . .

"Who's there?"

The voice was harsh, male, and came from no more than ten feet behind her.

Gem forgot to stay down, forgot to stay quiet, forgot to keep hidden. Something screamed through her chest and into her head, an ancient voice shouting *go,* a force exploding into her muscles and lifting her to her feet. She was running. She was plunging blindly through the saw grass and the salt-eaten shrubs, ignoring the cuts on her shins and forearms. There were shouts, now, from all around her, or so it seemed—she didn't stop, wasn't thinking, couldn't hear anything but that drumbeat of panic.

Her foot snagged and her ankle went out. She stumbled on something buried in the grass and for a second that seemed like an eternity she was in the air falling, still imagining hands to reach out and grab her. She landed so hard the wind went out of her and she curled in on herself, shocked and airless, fighting for a breath that wouldn't come. Then Jake was next to her again, pulling her up so she was sitting. She finally took a breath, a long gasp of it, and began coughing.

"Jesus," he whispered. He was sweating. He looked like he was going to be sick. "Jesus Christ."

"That voice," she managed to say. "Where did it come from? Where are they?"

"I don't know," he said. "Christ, Gemma. *Look . . .*"

She turned to see what had tripped her. Time that had moved so slowly seemed to crack entirely. For a long second she didn't understand what she was seeing, and then she thought—wished, hoped—it was an animal, some kind of strange underwater speckled thing, but then Jake drew back and began to cough, half choking, and dropped his flashlight: Gemma saw in its beam the dimpled elbow, the fingers curled in a half fist, and a green medical bracelet strapped around the bony wrist.

She couldn't have said, then or afterward, what made her reach out to part the grasses with a hand so that she could better see the girl's face. Instinct, maybe, or shock.

She was thinner than Gemma, much thinner. Her scalp was shaved, but in places a fuzz of brown hair had begun to regrow. Her green eyes were open to the sky and her mouth was open too, as if in a silent scream. There were four freckles on the bridge of her nose, four freckles Gemma knew because she counted them every day in the mirror, because Chloe DeWitt had once taken a pen and connected them during naptime in kindergarten. The soft plump mouth that had been her grandmother's. The hard angular jaw that belonged to her dad.

Behind her, Jake was still gasping. "What the hell? What the hell?"

The girl—the dead girl—was wearing Gemma's face.

NINE

GEMMA SOMETIMES HAD NIGHTMARES WHERE she was trapped in a crowd in an underground vault. In her dreams she was usually looking for someone, often her parents, sometimes April or even Rufus. But everywhere she turned she saw reflections of herself, not in mirrors but in the distorted faces of the people looking back at her, all of these not-Gemmas laughing the more frantic she became. She always woke up shaken and sick.

This was like that, only worse. She had the impression of swinging over a pit, as if the world might simply buck her into nothingness, and she would drown next to the dead girl who could be her twin.

She hadn't seen the stranger approach, hadn't noticed her at all, until she spoke.

"Cassiopeia?" She was extremely thin, not the kind of Chloe DeWitt thinness that came from weight-loss shakes and detox juicing and SoulCycle, but true, not-enough-to-eat, maybe-dying-of-cancer thinness. It made her bones stand out in her cheeks, her knuckles huge and mannish, her knees like sharp kites angling for a wind. Her head was completely shaved. Above her right eyebrow was a long white scar the width of a needle.

The stranger took an uncertain step forward and nearly tripped over the girl lying dead in the mud, and she drew a sharp breath and stopped, holding herself very still. When she looked up at Gemma, her face had changed. Gemma had the impression of huge eyes sunk in that narrow face, and a question in them she didn't know how to answer. She took in the girl's clothing—a white T-shirt, streaked with mud and grass and what looked like bird shit, ugly cotton elastic-waist pants—and then the girl's breasts, braless, hardly more than two sharp nipples beneath the fabric, her bare feet, the toenails colorless. Bare feet. Where had she come from with no shoes? But Gemma knew, even before she spotted the hospital bracelet, identical to the one secured around the dead girl's wrist.

"Oh my God." She felt as if her heart had been stilled with a hammer. She pictured it like an old-fashioned clock, splintered into uselessness. "I think—I think she's one of them."

The Haven girl looked suddenly ferocious. "Who are you?" she said. "Where did you come from?"

"Who are *you*?" Jake's face was the bleached white of bone, but his voice was steady. Gemma wanted to reach out and take his hand. But her body wasn't obeying her correctly, and just then she was distracted by movement behind the girl, and something tall and dark and shadowed resolved itself into a boy.

"Lyra," the girl said, and, when they said nothing, made an impatient gesture with one hand. "Number twenty-four."

"Oh my God," Gemma said again. Her voice sounded high and shrill and unfamiliar, as if it were being piped through a teakettle. Her mind kept reeling away from the dead girl lying not four feet away from her, the pattern of freckles on her face, the exact shape of her mouth, reeling away from the truth of it, like a magnet veering away from its pair. "There's another one."

She knew the boy must be from Haven, too, as soon as he appeared. He was barefoot, and very thin, though not nearly so thin as the girl. Muscles showed through his T-shirt when he moved. He was mixed race and very beautiful, but there was something hard about him, too. He looked like one of the wax figurines in Madame Tussauds, where she'd gone with her mom on a trip to New York ages ago. As if you could stare and stare into his eyes and get nothing back. A person a little like a black hole: all the light vanished around him.

She didn't see the knife in his hand until the boy stepped forward so that the light showed on its blade.

"Look." Jake put up both hands, as if he could physically stop the boy's progress. "Hold on a second. Just hold on."

The boy gave no sign of having heard. "Who are you?" he said, keeping the knife high. Gemma realized in that second how stupid they'd been, how unprepared. They'd been scared of being arrested for trespassing. Not for a second had they considered that the Haven patients might be dangerous. Maniacs. Brain-altered killers. God only knew what kind of sick experiments they were doing there.

"We're nobody," Jake said. Very slowly he reached down and helped Gemma to her feet. Her body felt dull and even heavier than usual, as if it belonged to somebody else. Now, standing, she had a clearer view of the dead girl who looked like her, and it was terrible, worse than any nightmare, like staring into an open grave with a mirror at the bottom of it. She thought she might fall. She hardly trusted her legs to carry her. Jake was still talking, but she could barely understand him. "Listen, we're not going to hurt you, okay? My name's Jake Witz. This is Gemma. We got lost in the marshes, that's all."

The girl frowned and turned to Gemma. Gemma was glad for the excuse to look somewhere, anywhere other than the body at her feet. "But who made you?"

Gemma was sure she'd misheard. "What?" she whispered.

"Who made you?" the girl repeated, more slowly this time, as if Gemma were very young or very stupid.

The wind, which had filled the marshes with a kind of constant, sibilant hiss, an underlying rhythm, went still. Gemma could feel the pressure of a thousand invisible eyes peering at her from the mud, from their many hiding places. "I—I don't understand."

"You're a replica," the girl said.

"A *what*?"

"A replica," she repeated impatiently. "An organism descended from or genetically identical to a single common ancestor." Gemma closed her eyes, hit with the sudden memory of being with her mom as a child at an art auction, bored out of her mind, listening to the auctioneer drone on and on about a vase that was supposedly the *exact replica* of the one in Versailles where Louis XVII had occasionally stored his false teeth. *Why*, her mother had leaned down to whisper, *would anyone spend so much money on a fake?*

"A clone," she said. The word had a stupid, sci-fi sound to it. "She means a *clone*, Jake."

Jake winced. "Yeah, well. I kind of already had that impression." He kept his eyes on the boy with the knife.

Gemma felt panic pressing on her from all sides, from *inside*, as if thousands of tiny fists were beating inside of her to get out.

A clone. A replica. Why would anyone spend so much money on a fake? Gemma's thoughts were whirling like a hard snow, then disintegrating when she tried to catch hold of them. "But—but it's impossible." She knew she was hysterical, she knew she was loud, but she didn't care and couldn't help it. "It's impossible. The technology doesn't exist; it's illegal. . . ."

"It's not impossible," the Haven girl said. Gemma had the sudden, vicious urge to punch her, to take her huge eyes out of their sockets, to get her to stop speaking, stop staring, *stop*. "At Haven, there were thousands of replicas."

"Jesus," Jake whispered. He closed his eyes for a second, and she saw that he looked almost restful. Peaceful. As if they hadn't just stumbled on a *girl with Gemma's exact face*, her chest black with blood; as if they hadn't found two survivors of the place, looking scared but also dangerous, like wild animals. "*Clones.* It all makes sense now."

"Are you crazy? *Nothing* makes sense." Gemma's heart was twitching like a dying bug. "There's a *dead girl* with *my face* on her." Jake turned to her, looking stricken, as if she'd reached out and slapped him. She wished she had.

She had the urge to slap him, to shake him, to shake the whole world and force it right again, like how her dad smacked the cable box whenever service was coming in weird. Thinking of her dad, of her home, suddenly made her feel very young and very afraid. She wished she'd listened to her parents. They'd been right all along. She should never have come. She wasn't strong enough. "We're standing here in the middle of the fucking night and these—these people are telling me that there are clones running around out there, thousands of them—"

"Gemma, calm down." Jake put a hand on her arm. She nearly screamed. But she was afraid to open her mouth again—afraid of losing it completely.

Her father had known about Haven. All this time, he'd known.

"Everyone needs to calm down, okay?" Jake was saying. The boy with the knife had tensed up again. "Can you put that thing down, please? We're not going to hurt you." The boy lowered the knife, finally. Jake had said the right thing, but Gemma didn't care. Even though they were standing in open air, she felt the sky might at any second collapse and bury them. She kneaded her chest with one hand, willing her heartbeat to slow down. The girl, she noticed, looked sick also. Somehow this made her feel less afraid. They couldn't be *that* dangerous, even if they did have a knife and look like creepy escaped psych inmates from a horror film. And when the girl couldn't stand anymore and instead crouched and ducked her head between her knees, breathing slowly, obviously trying to control her nausea, Gem felt sorry for her, and annoyed at the boy with the knife. He barely glanced at her.

She took a deep breath. "What's the matter with her?" No one answered.

Without really intending to, she moved slowly toward the girl. When the girl shuddered, her spine stood out, almost architectural beneath her shirt, and for the first time in her life Gemma was actually happy she wasn't thin. She bent over. Her hand, as it floated toward the girl's shoulder, looked like a foreign object, a balloon or a spacecraft. "Are you okay?"

For a millisecond she was surprised by the feel of the girl's warmth, the tautness of her skin and the muscle beneath it. The girl looked so insubstantial, Gemma had almost expected a hand would pass through her. Then the girl jerked away and Gemma took a quick step backward, her breath catching. The girl had looked at her with something close to hatred, and Gemma was again reminded of an animal—once a few years ago one of their handymen had cornered a rabid raccoon on the property and her father had taken out his rifle to shoot it, and she'd never forgotten how its eyes looked, desperate and wild, before the bullet hit.

"Maybe she's hungry," Jake said.

The girl said nothing—she wrapped her arms around her knees and dropped her head again, her spine rising and falling with every breath—but the boy took a step forward. "You have food?" His face was so full of open need that Gemma felt another lurch of pity. Had they been starved at Haven?

Jake squatted to rifle through his backpack. "Sorry," he said, producing a few granola bars and two bottles of water. "We didn't bring much."

The boy ate in a way that reminded Gemma of a squirrel, holding the granola bar with two hands and chewing quickly until it was all gone. He took water and drank half a bottle before passing it over to the girl, still crouching next to him. He said something too low for Gemma to hear, but the girl took the water from him and drank, and immediately she looked a little better. She would be very beautiful, Gemma thought, if she were heavier, if the lost, dark look of her eyes could somehow be warmed.

Jake couldn't take his eyes off them, the boy and the girl, and Gemma could hardly stand to look at him. She guessed that for him this was the end of a long mystery, the final act. For her this was the start. Her old world had exploded and she'd been born again into a new one. All she wanted was to go back.

"Look," Jake said to them. "I know you must be tired—you've been through—I don't even *know* what you've been through . . ."

Gemma thought she knew what he wanted, but hoped she was wrong. "Jake, no," she said warningly. She pressed a hand to her forehead, trying to push back the drumbeat of a migraine that was beating dully somewhere behind her eyes.

"They've been living in Haven, Gemma," Jake said quickly, as if she hadn't understood. "My father died for this. I need to know."

"Jake, *no.*" The migraine exploded into existence: she imagined some sicko with a hammer pummeling her brain. "I don't believe you. I literally don't believe you. These poor people have been through God knows what—they're starving and cold and they have no place to go—and you want to *interview* them—"

"I don't want to interview them. I want to understand."

"Not people." The girl spoke up unexpectedly. Gemma turned to face her.

"What?" she said. The girl was holding the water bottle tightly, her knuckles standing out. But she seemed calm.

"We're not people," she said. Her voice had a low, musical quality, but it was strangely without affect, as if she hadn't been taught to feel or at least to express herself. "You said, 'These poor people have been through God knows what.' But we're replicas. God didn't make us. Dr. Saperstein did. He's *our* God."

All of Gemma's anger evaporated in an instant. She was alone momentarily in the dark with this thin, frail girl, this *clone*, who believed she was not a person. Gemma wanted to hug her. She wanted to understand, too—how she had become this way, how she had been made and why, who had taught her that God was out of reach. And she knew then that Jake was right, in a way. All the answers she needed, all the mysteries of her past, were bound up in the girl and boy from the island. She was still afraid of them, but also afraid for them in a way she couldn't verbalize. But she couldn't leave them alone. They had to stay close.

"We should camp here for the night," she heard herself say, before she even knew that she was going to suggest it. Jake looked at her as if she'd lost her mind. Maybe she had. "We'll go back to Wahlee in the morning."

The boy seemed uncertain. "We're not going any-where with you."

"No," Gemma said evenly. "No, you don't have to go with us. Not unless you want to."

Once again, Jake just stared at her, as if a hand had just emerged from her mouth and started waving.

"Why would we want to?" the boy asked.

Gemma ignored Jake, speaking directly to the boy. "You can't plan on staying here forever. You have no money. No ID. You're not even supposed to exist. And there will be people looking for you."

She would have known this even if she hadn't seen, earlier that night, the helicopters pass overhead for hours, even if she hadn't seen soldiers outfitted in riot gear patrolling the coast. If the girl was telling the truth—and Gemma had proof that she was, in the form of the corpse she could hardly stand to look at—and Haven had indeed been full of clones, there had to be a reason for all the secrecy, the protections, the confidentiality. It should have been a miracle for modern science. The scientists who'd perfected the process should have won Nobel Prizes. Everyone in the world should have known about it. And yet nobody did.

The question was: Why?

She knew that whoever was in charge wouldn't allow the products of his or her experiments to run free, not when those products could talk and think for themselves. She assumed the only reason that the girl and boy, the *replicas*, hadn't been found and taken into custody already was because of all the chaos. Probably they were still counting the dead and the missing. Staying on the marshes for any length of time was a huge risk. But Gemma sensed that the clones weren't ready to move yet, and she knew that she had to stay close to them, that the ember of truth was here, with them. She needed time to think and to plan.

She expected more resistance from Jake. But he only shook his head and said, "We should try and get some sleep. We'll want to get off the marshes as soon as possible." And the clones didn't argue anymore. They obviously didn't want to be too far from the food and water.

They moved to the far side of a contorted thicket of mangrove trees that blocked them from a view of the body. Gemma didn't want to camp so close to the dead girl. She couldn't stand to think of her, that face like her face hollowed out by hunger, the hair that Gemma sweated and toiled to keep straight shaved close to her fragile scalp. She had never been superstitious, but it felt like a bad omen, as if the fate of her double might wear off on her.

On the other hand, she didn't want to go far in the darkness, and the girl and the boy, the replicas, were exhausted. The replicas bedded down side by side, although Gemma noticed that they hardly spoke or even acknowledged each other. As if they each belonged two separate realities that only coexisted momentarily.

Jake fell asleep right away, using a rolled-up towel as a pillow and clutching his backpack as though it were a teddy bear. Gemma, however, lay awake long after even the replicas had fallen asleep. It wasn't just because she was physically uncomfortable—she was clammy and too hot; the whine of mosquitoes needled her; the ground was uneven and unpleasantly spongy; she was dirty and she was sure that she smelled—but because of an itchy, hard-to-name feeling *inside*, like the wriggling of thousands of ants under her skin, in her blood and her veins. She imagined the girl on the other side of the trees, the second-Gemma, coming to life again, slithering through the mud, reaching for Gemma's face with bloodied fingernails, reaching for Gemma's hair, demanding it back. . . . She had to sit up, stifling a cry of terror.

Someone had cloned her. It was the only explanation that made sense, but she couldn't accept it. Had her father known? Was that why he had left Fine & Ives, and ruptured forever with his business partner? Was that why he'd wanted Haven shut down? A scientist had taken a sample of Gemma's DNA when she was a baby and used it to make another Gemma. Except . . .

The dead girl wasn't just another Gemma. She had Gemma's DNA, her face and her freckles, but even now her insides were liquefying, her stomach bloating with gases. She'd had a different name, different memories and preferences, and a very different life. Two people built of the same material, but radically separated by experience and now by death.

Had her father known? Or had he only suspected?

Maybe during one of her many hospital stays as a baby, someone had stolen some tissue from her without her parents' knowledge. That must be it. There would have to be a black market for things like this, places on the internet you could go to buy kiddie porn and new livers and medical samples.

She knew that was nonsensical, though. What were the chances that her DNA had randomly ended up in the same research institute her father's company had helped fund?

She would never sleep. How could she, with that dead girl, that doubled girl, so close by? So many thoughts were turning in her head, she felt dizzy. She had to *know*. She had to understand this place, and what her father's connection to it had been. What *her* connection to it was.

It was much harder to get into the kayak without Jake there to steady her, and again she had a fear of turning over and getting stuck, like a banana in a too-tight skin. But she managed it eventually and, after flailing around with the paddle for a bit, loosed herself from the tangle of long grass and reeds and maneuvered into the dark, glassy water. She didn't even know how to read a compass, even though her phone must have had one. But she felt confident that she was sufficiently close to the island that she wouldn't get lost, and she even had the idea of tying her sweatshirt to the overhanging branches of one of the mangrove trees, so that she would be able to find her way back.

After only a few minutes, she regretted the decision.

Paddling was much harder than Jake had made it look. Her heart was soon thumping and her shoulders ached. And she had to keep angling into the shadows and sloshing onto miniature pockets of land to orient herself. Down in the water she could see nothing, not with the mangroves crowding her and the reeds tall and spindly and white as bone. After a little while, the water became scummy with a fine layer of trash from the island, not just ash but human things, old buttons and charred plastic pieces and even bits of paper. She found a laminated ID entangled among the reeds: the picture showed a grim-faced black woman and indicated low-security clearance. She pocketed it. Now the thudding of her heart had nothing to do with the effort of paddling.

She came around a bend and sucked in a sharp breath: there beyond another stretch of muddy water was the fence, and empty guard towers, and trees blackened by fire beyond it. She must still be on the side of the island that had never been developed, because she could see only one long building through the trees, a shed or a storehouse that appeared abandoned. She dragged the kayak onto the shore and set out through the reeds down the narrow beach, as frogs splashed noisily into the water to avoid her, keeping very low to the ground in case there were still soldiers patrolling.

Here in the shallows was even more garbage, accumulated trash frothing against the grass. She angled her phone to the ground as a makeshift flashlight. She found a small rectangular sign, the kind that hung on office doors, indicating the way to Storeroom C, whatever that was. Its plastic was melted at the edges, so the sign looked as if it were bleeding out. She saw bits of plaster and white things studded between the rocks that she realized with a surge of nausea looked like pieces of bone. There were occasional stretches of sticky-dark stains, blacker than shadow, that she knew must be blood. The explosion must have been tremendous. And then of course had come the wind, which had carried the smell of burning all the way to Barrel Key and blown the fire into a conflagration.

After five minutes the trees thinned and the smell of charred plastic and campfire and something sweeter and deeper and more unpleasant intensified. At last she could see buildings—or at least, a single building—huge and rectangular and stained with soot, its windows shattered so that it appeared to be staring blankly out over the water. She was shocked to see the fire still burning, glowing dimly inside the building so that the walls were turned the strange translucent pinkish glow of a heart. She dropped into a crouch when she saw movement, pocketing her phone. Dimly she heard people calling to one another, and saw as her eyes adjusted people outfitted in firefighters' rubber pants and heavy boots. As she watched, she realized they were in fact stoking the fire, keeping it going, keeping it under control. And she understood that they'd been charged with burning the rest of Haven down, to make sure there was nothing left. She could go no farther, not without risking being caught.

Although the firefighters must have been a thousand yards away, she still winced when she stepped backward and heard a sharp crack. Turning, she saw that she'd stepped on a framed photograph, further shattering the cracked plastic that encased it. She bent down to retrieve it but could make out nothing more than a blur of dark figures. She pocketed it anyway and moved down the beach again, back in the direction she'd come. She waited until she could no longer hear the people or see the glow of fire through the trees before fishing out her phone again for light.

She recognized the man in the photo, heavily bearded and wearing a lab coat, as Dr. Saperstein, the current Haven director, from a picture she'd seen on the internet. He was outside, squinting against the sun, and in the distance she recognized the building she'd just watched burning, although the photograph was taken at a different angle, as though from an interior courtyard. Behind him was a statue—*the* statue.

In her memories, indistinct as they were, she'd always assumed that the statue represented some kind of god, but now she saw it was a David-like figure, a mortal, one arm thrown to the sky, one arm reaching down as though to draw something from the earth. In the photograph she could just make out a strand of DNA, represented by ribbons of interlocking stone, beneath its hand. The man in the statue had the posture of God forming Adam from the dust. It was a statue meant to represent the people at Haven and the work they were doing, the way they formed life from the earth, the way they had taken over for God.

And she, Gemma, remembered it. It was her earliest memory. Which meant: she'd been here before.

Made here. The idea was there, lodged in her mind, before she could unthink it. Made, manufactured, like the weird veggie patty they served in the cafeteria in school. She felt wild, dramatic, desperate. She thought for a second she might simply sit down and refuse to move, just wait for the salt to eat through her and the crabs to pick apart her bones.

But no. A new idea struck her and this time it felt like salvation, like finding a rope in the middle of a freezing riptide—she *couldn't* have been made at Haven, not cloned like the girl and boy claimed they had been. Like her double must have been. She'd seen dozens of pictures of her mom in the hospital, clutching an infant Gemma to her chest, sweaty and exhausted-looking, just moments after birth. There was one of her parents together, and minutes-old Gemma red and swaddled in a yellow blanket, and another of a nurse with a bottle of champagne. It was obviously Gemma in the pictures. Even then she'd had soft curls of brown hair and a snub nose that made it look as if it were being supported by an invisible thumb.

She felt calmer. She could breathe again. She was being silly. She might have visited Haven with her dad. And although she associated the statue with the idea of a long stay, she knew she might have made that up, or confused Haven with another one of the hospitals she'd been to as a child.

It was just after five thirty—time to get back, although she dreaded the return, of getting close to that horrible other who would rot out here with no one to mourn or bury her. But already, long electric tentacles of pink were swimming up through the darkness from the horizon. She knew she had to wake the others. It was time to get off the marshes.

She removed the photograph from its broken frame, folded it, and pocketed it next to the laminated ID she'd found entangled in the weeds. She was almost tempted to leave the photograph behind—carrying it made her feel jumpy and also ashamed, as if it were contraband or evidence of a crime. And it was evidence, although she didn't know, hadn't yet figured out, exactly what the crime had been.

Paddling felt even harder on the way back. Her arms ached and the lack of sleep had taken its toll. She was thirsty and exhausted. Even as it was driven off by the rising sun, the darkness played tricks on her. She kept thinking she saw movement in her peripheral vision, kept whipping around, half expecting to see another bloodied version of herself, holding her paddle like a weapon, only to see nothing but an insect skimming the water or a bullfrog blinking at her between the rushes.

It was lucky that the sky was lightening or she might never have found her way back. She passed dozens of mangrove trees extending out over the water, many of them overhung with mosses that in the dark might have looked like her sweatshirt. But she made it back a little after six and was surprised to find Jake and both clones still asleep. She knelt next to Jake.

"Hey," she said. He woke suddenly, and for a second as he was still enveloped in sleep, Gemma saw a look of terror seize him. He blinked and it passed. She wondered whether he'd been having a nightmare.

She didn't want to touch the others—she hadn't forgotten how the girl had jerked away from her. Instead she stood at a careful distance and called to them until the boy came awake with a start, on his feet and reaching for his knife before he was fully awake.

"It's okay," Gemma said quickly, as his eyes slowly found focus. "It's just me. Gemma, remember?" The boy wiped his mouth with the back of a hand. His chest rose and fell beneath his T-shirt, and again Gemma was struck by how beautiful he was, beautiful and strange and wild-looking, like a new and undiscovered species. She couldn't fathom that he'd spent his whole life behind a fence. He was the kind of person who looked like he should be sailing on open seas, or parachuting down a mountain.

The girl had come awake, too. She looked even sicker than she had the night before. Her skin was a blue, bruised color Gemma associated with frostbite. But she couldn't possibly be cold. Gemma was sweating.

"There are still men on the island," Gemma said. "They're burning what's left of Haven."

"You saw them?" Jake stood up. His hair was messy and his eyes were slightly puffy from sleep, but he still looked like he could be in an ad. "You got close?" She nodded, and he frowned. "You should have woken me. It's not safe."

"What do you mean, they're burning what's left of Haven?" The girl stood up unsteadily. She brought a hand to her eyes as if she was dizzy.

"Just what I said," Gemma said.

"Then there's no going back?" The girl spoke so

quietly Gemma nearly missed it.

Before Gemma could answer, the boy said, "There's no going back. I told you that. They'll kill us if they find us. One way or another, they'll kill us."

The girl shook her head as if she didn't believe that, but she said nothing. Gemma wanted to know what he meant by that—*one way or another, they'll kill us*—and thought he was probably exaggerating. But they were running out of time. Even now she could hear the distant roar of a motorboat engine.

She made a sudden decision: the girl was sick and needed help. Food, water, somewhere to sleep. Somewhere to *hide*. And Gemma needed to understand who she was, and whether she and the boy were telling the truth about the number of clones at Haven, and what they were being used for. She needed to understand who the girl who had Gemma's face was, and how she'd come to be. Maybe she could even figure out what her father knew and what he didn't. "We have to get off the marshes. There will be new patrols now that it's light. They'll be looking for survivors." And for the dead bodies, she thought, to count them. "Come with us, and we'll get you clothes, and hide you someplace no one will be looking for you. Then you can figure out where to go. *We* can figure it out."

Jake shook his head but didn't object. She noticed, however, that when he looked at her, he seemed almost afraid. She wondered what he thought about her now, after their discovery of the body, and felt a small cold hand grip her heart. But she had bigger things to worry about.

"Okay." It was the girl who spoke. The boy shot her a look, either surprised or irritated or both—Gemma couldn't tell. But he didn't argue. "Okay," she said, a little louder. "We'll go."

There was nothing to pack up, and no breakfast besides two granola bars, which Jake offered to the replicas. Gemma was, for maybe the first time in her life, not hungry. The roar of distant powerboats was growing louder and more constant. They'd be taking things off the island, files and equipment too expensive to burn. But at some point soon, bodies would be counted, and three would be found to be missing. Then the soldiers would come looking for them.

Gemma had no desire to approach the dead girl again, but she felt bad leaving her there, too, to be used as a nest for flies and picked apart by wild animals. She hoped that someone would at least give her a decent burial. She shoved aside the idea of her own face lying in a chilly morgue somewhere, the freckled chest she knew so well split from sternum to stomach. Before they left, Gemma fought her way back through the mangroves and took a picture of the girl, forever still, forever sightless. A beetle was tracking across her left ankle, and Gemma wanted to reach down and brush it off but was too afraid. She didn't want to feel the iciness of the skin that was hers. She had a stupid idea that the girl might come roaring back to life, grabbing Gemma's wrist, furious that her double had lived when she had died. She backtracked quickly, zipping her phone into a pocket: her ever-growing stash of evidence.

Neither the girl nor the boy knew how to swim, and she guessed that made sense, although it was strange because they'd lived only a few feet from the ocean—but of course, on the wrong side of the fence. They would take the kayak while Jake and Gemma walked or half swam. Jake stashed his backpack at the girl's feet, and Gemma added the Windbreaker Jake had lent her to the pile as well. She didn't care if the rest of her clothes got wet. But she needed proof of what she'd seen and where she'd been.

Jake kicked off his sneakers, tied the laces together, and slung them over one shoulder. He rolled up his pants legs and waded into the water.

Gemma kicked off her shoes too and followed him in. The water was the temperature of a kiddie pool after someone had peed in it. It smelled a little like pee, too, and Gemma knew that was just because of all the decay, the singed plant life and dead bugs and the fish. The footing was silt-soft and slippery. Jake had told her last night that there were alligators in the marshes, and cottonmouth snakes, too. Gemma prayed they wouldn't encounter any.

The going was very slow. Jake held his phone high to keep it out of the water and directed the replicas which way to point the kayak. In places Gemma and Jake managed to stick to the shallows, where the water was only shin-deep, and move more quickly, but often the water was waist high or deeper and it was like a huge, outstretched hand was halting their progress. They slogged forward as the replicas drifted behind them, scanning the sky for helicopters. The sun rose and soon they could hear the noise of boat traffic, and see it in the miniature waves kicked up in the water by the boats' distant passage. Gemma had never known you could be in the water and sweaty at the same time, but she was both, and dizzy from the heat and the effort and the fear. Her lungs felt like they'd been strapped and squeezed into too-tight leather, like they might burst at any second.

"I can't go on," she said. She could barely get the words out. "I need to rest."

Jake turned around as if he was going to object. But one look at her and he just nodded. She must look horrible, red-faced, sweaty, soaked up to her pits. But she was too exhausted to care.

They sloshed up onto solid ground again. Gemma

wished Mrs. Coralee, her stupid gym teacher, could see her now. Wilderness Gemma. In the past twelve hours she'd paddled a kayak and hiked nearly two miles through a slog of swamp. She'd probably keel over and die of shock.

Gemma's legs were shaking, and she sat down immediately in the mud. The replicas followed, disembarking clumsily from the kayak. Jake helped them drag it up beneath the shade of a mangrove, and not a second too soon.

"Get down," Jake said hoarsely. They crouched together, shaded by the network of moss-fuzzed branches, while a roar grew steadily above them and the water splintered into waves. Then a helicopter swept overhead, so close it drove the dirt up into Gemma's eyes and stripped the leaves from several branches. But they hadn't been spotted. That she was sure of. Luck.

Jake stood up. She could read the tension in his whole body, in the set of his jaw and shoulders. "I think we can make it back to the car overland from here," he said. "We can't be far. Can you walk?"

Gemma nodded, even though her thighs ached and she was desperately thirsty.

"We'll have to leave the kayak," Jake said. "Dragging it will slow us down."

"You'll lose your deposit," Gemma said stupidly. She

was so tired she could think only that they'd get in trouble with the rental shop.

Jake helped Gemma to her feet again but tightened his hand on her wrist to keep her from pulling away. "Gemma, I want you to understand something. We're in very big trouble." He spoke in a low voice, so the replicas wouldn't hear, and he kept his tone neutral, pleasant, even, as if they were just discussing the weather. "The people running Haven are very powerful. They're going to be extremely unhappy that two of their experiments are walking free. They're going to be tracking us. They might *already* be tracking us. I need you to understand that."

"We can't just leave them on the marshes," Gemma whispered back. Over Jake's shoulder, she could see the girl watching her. The fuzz of brown hair cropped so close to her head made her look like a baby bird. Gemma looked away, lowering her voice further. "They're half-starved. They could have been abused, for all we know. You heard what she said about not being human. Who the hell taught her that stuff?" Gemma thought of her father grinning proudly in front of Haven and felt nauseous all over again. "Besides, the girl is sick or something. Take a look at her."

"That's another thing," Jake said. His eyes were so dark they seemed expressionless. "We don't know what's been done to them. They could be carrying diseases."

"Carrying diseases?" Gemma repeated. She pulled away from him. She was still shaking. "You make them sound like animals."

"Gemma, think about it." He caught her arm again before she could turn away. "We don't know what they were doing in Haven. They weren't making clones for the glory of it." So he'd already come to the same realization that Gemma had: If Haven's goal had been to successfully clone a human being, why all the secrecy? "They could be testing toxins, or studying smallpox. The point is, we don't *know* what they were doing."

Gemma knew he was right. But she saw no other way of getting at the truth. And she was angry—angry because he wasn't meeting her eyes, because he acted as if it was painful even to touch her now. She turned away from him. "This is what you said you wanted," she said. "Your father spent his life studying Haven and now, now that you have the chance to *know*, you're too scared."

"Of course I'm scared," he said quietly. "They killed my father, remember?"

Now, on top of her anger, she felt guilty—which just made her even angrier.

"I'll take them back on my own, then," she said. It was ridiculous: she would never find her way back. "I don't care what you do. You have your answers. You finished your little quest." She knew she was being unfair, but she couldn't stop. She was dizzy, and so damn thirsty, too. "Come on," she said, a little louder, to the replicas, who were standing there looking uncertain. Even Gemma was surprised by how harsh her voice sounded. The boy looked startled, then sheepish, and, perversely, she felt a rush of pride: she'd scared him, the big baddie with the knife.

Jake caught up with her before she'd gone even two steps. "Don't be stupid," he said. To her relief, he didn't seem mad. Already she felt terrible. His father had *died.* "We're in this together. Besides, no way am I letting you get all the credit." His smile was strained, but at least he *was* smiling, and Gemma felt a wave of relief. She hadn't realized how afraid she was of losing Jake's help.

Jake took the lead again. He was right: they were able to make it back to the car on foot, circumnavigating the narrow veins of water, although he had to stop frequently to consult the compass and the GPS on his phone, once cell phone service patched in again. At some point the composition of the ground shifted subtly beneath their feet, but it wasn't until Gemma saw a *No Littering* sign that she realized that Jake had led them safely back onto the nature reserve. After another two minutes they were within sight of the car, and Gemma nearly shouted with joy. There was a case of bottled water in the trunk, and they each downed a bottle. It was, Gemma thought, the best thing she'd ever tasted.

They piled into the car. Gemma felt better once they were no longer standing in the open. In the car, they could be anyone. Picnickers, backpackers, sightseers, friends. The replicas, on the other hand, seemed very nervous. It occurred to Gemma they had likely never been in a car before, and the boy jumped when Jake turned on the ignition and the radio blared to life.

Gemma had been without cell service since they'd first paddled out onto the marshes, but as soon as they pulled back onto the dirt road that led to Wahlee, her phone came alive with texts, voice mails, and alerts, almost all of them from April.

She dialed April immediately, praying she would pick up.

"*Jesus*. You were supposed to call me ASAP. I thought you'd been dismembered by an ax murderer or taken to Guantánamo or something. What the hell happened?"

Gemma didn't know why, but hearing April's voice—so familiar, so *April*—made her want to cry. For the first time she let herself think that they were safe. They were okay. They were speeding along a dirt road toward civilization and fast-food burger chains and bad pop music and normal life. Being on the marshes had been disorienting, like a nightmare that keeps its hold on you even after you wake up. Except this time they'd pulled two people from the nightmare. They'd brought proof of its reality back.

She took a deep breath, blinking rapidly to keep the tears back, aware that Jake was watching her. "It's a really long story," she said. "Did my mom call?"

"Only about seven times," April said. "I told her you ate bad sushi and were puking your brains out and then went to sleep. I'm telling you, Gem, you owe me major on this one. I'm talking free lunches for a month. Maybe a year. I'm talking vacation-to-Disney-World owe me."

"Okay." Gemma closed her eyes and leaned back against the headrest. The sun was warm on her face, and the air-conditioning smelled reassuringly of chemical exhaust. "Listen. Did your grandparents leave for their health conference thingie?"

"It's not a health conference. It's a wellness retreat."

"Yeah, whatever. But the house is empty for a few days?"

"Yeah." April's voice had turned suspicious. "Why?"

Gemma opened her eyes again. They were passing out of the Wahlee Park Reserve now and back into Wahlee. A cop car was parked by the side of the road, its lights circling noiselessly. The driver's seat was empty. She wondered where the cop had gone. She felt an itch on the back of her neck, like someone was dragging a fingernail there. Not safe. Not by a long shot.

"I'm going to need your help," she said, gripping the phone so hard, it made her palm sweat. "I made it all the way to Haven, April. And trust me. You might want to save your IOUs. This is just the beginning."

"Holy shit." There was a long pause. "What did you find?"

"Not *what*." In the rearview mirror, Gemma could see the boy's profile, elegant and dark. *"Who."*

TEN

GEMMA HAD BEEN HOPING THAT once they got to April's grandparents' house, she could install the replicas in the guesthouse before she had to answer any questions. She should have known, of course, that April would be watching from the front windows. She rocketed out of the door and onto the front lawn as soon as she saw Jake's car turn in the driveway.

"Gemma!" The force of April's hug nearly knocked Gemma backward. April pulled away, squeezing Gemma's shoulders. "You look like shit. And"—she made a point of sniffing—"you stink."

"Nice to see you too," Gemma said, but she was too tired to be offended. April smelled like suntan lotion and Coke.

April's eyes went to the car. "Is that—I mean, are they in there?" Gemma nodded. April licked her lips. She was tan and relaxed-looking, her shoulders peeling, and standing next to her, Gemma felt a thousand years old. "You're serious about . . . you think they're really clones? Real clones?"

"No, fakes," Gemma said, and then saw that April was too distracted to catch sarcasm. "Yes, real," she said. "At least, that's what they told me."

"But you don't have proof," April said, sounding almost disappointed. "You haven't seen, you know, *doubles*."

Gemma thought again of the body stretched out in the grass, a body just like hers except so much thinner than her own. She hadn't told April about seeing the girl who had to be her clone, her replica. She wasn't ready for that. Not until she understood more than she did now. Instead she said only, "I think they're telling the truth. Why would they lie? They were raised on that island. They were *made* there. They've been told they're less than human. The boy doesn't even have a name. Just a *number*." That was what the girl, Lyra, had told them in the car.

April hugged herself. "God," she said. She was still staring into the car. Turning, Gemma was relieved to see that because of the direction of the sun, Lyra and 72 were no more than blurry silhouettes. She had a feeling that once word got out—which it had to, there would be no way to keep the truth secret now—they'd have plenty of people staring at them. "Can I meet them? Is it safe to let them out?"

"They're not animals," Gemma said, surprised by the harshness of her tone. April flinched, and Gemma felt instantly guilty. "Sorry," Gemma said. "I'm tired. *They're* tired."

April ignored that. "And who's *that*?" Her eyes had landed on Jake. She looked as if she wanted to lick him. Gemma was surprised her tongue wasn't lolling out of her mouth.

"Look, let me just get everyone into the guesthouse, okay? And then we can talk, and I'll tell you everything."

"You better," April said, still staring at Jake. "I've been covering your ass for days."

"I know," Gemma said. "You're the best friend in the world."

"Universe," April corrected her.

They'd stopped at Walmart on the way to April's house and bought clothes, food, and toiletries with the credit card her parents had given her, trusting that they never reviewed the statements too closely—one of the few benefits of having parents who kept you on the world's tightest leash, and at least occasionally felt guilty about it. She was dying to ask both replicas about Haven, but the lack of sleep was catching up to her. She felt as if her brain had been replaced by sludge.

The guesthouse was cool and decorated in lots of beach pastels. The boy held himself very carefully, as if he was afraid to break something. Lyra stopped in front of the bookshelves, staring up at the old warped paperbacks, mass-market romances, and thrillers with time-smudged spines, as if she'd never seen books before. Maybe she hadn't. Gemma wondered whether she'd been educated, whether she knew how to read and that there were seven continents, that the earth orbited around the sun. So many questions, so many things she needed to understand.

"Get some sleep," Gemma told them. She was feeling calmer since they'd made it to April's house without getting arrested or swarmed by SWAT teams or whatever. They were safe. They had time.

Jake and Gemma left the replicas to rest in the guesthouse. Gemma was exhausted, but as soon as they stepped outside, Jake—who had been quiet through almost the entire car ride—began to talk. "You know what doesn't make sense to me?" he said. "Why all the secrecy? People have dreamed of cloning humans for years. They've barely been able to clone animals. Most clones die early. The scientists at Haven should get the Nobel Prize. They should be on TED Talks. They should be billionaires, you know? So why haven't they told anyone?"

"I don't know," Gemma said, as they skirted the pool toward the main house. The sun was dazzling off the water. She wished she had sunglasses. "But Fine and Ives has military contracts, like you said. They always have. Maybe Haven was using the clones for drug testing. Isn't that what you thought they were doing out there, Dr. Whatever-his-name-is and his orphan charity and his human experiments?"

Clones no one knew about, no one cared about—they could be used as human guinea pigs. No wonder they'd been given numbers, not names.

It would explain, too, the fact that her father had known Richard Haven, had been photographed with him and spoken about his genius in interviews. It might explain his sudden change of attitude and abrupt departure from Fine & Ives right after Richard Haven's death, and just when Fine & Ives had begun to invest. Gemma could imagine her father excited by the idea of human cloning, by the scientific possibility of it, only to feel disgusted should it actually succeed. And no matter how horrible he was, she couldn't imagine that he would willingly get involved in testing deadly drugs or toxins on human beings, cloned or uncloned, without their consent. It had nothing to do with empathy. He simply liked rules too much.

Still, no matter which way she thought about it, her father must have known what was really going on at Haven. He'd known, and he'd turned his back on what was happening. He had retreated with his family to Chapel

Hill, hiding behind tall gates and manicured lawns and money. Despite what she knew about her father—his coldness, the way he hardly seemed to care about his own family—she couldn't believe it. How would she ever look at him again?

"Dr. Saperstein is the director of Haven. The Home Foundation is the name of the charity he founded," Jake said evenly. "But it doesn't make sense to do medical testing on clones. Clones are expensive to make. I mean, Haven has been paying for their care, feeding them, keeping them healthy—or at least *alive*. It seems like a lot of effort if they're just going to fill them up with drugs."

He had a point. It was all too much. She suddenly felt like crying. "Please," she said. "*Please*, can we talk about this later?"

"Sure. Of course." Jake squinted at her as if her face was a puzzle and he was trying to arrange it in the correct order. He looked like he was about to say more, so Gemma sped up to beat him into the house. Jake went off to take a shower—April, perv that she was, seemed *way* too interested in explaining how the faucet worked, as if expecting him to start stripping if she just gave it enough time—and Gemma took the opportunity to retreat to April's room and collapse onto the bed.

Gemma had never wanted to sleep more badly in her life. But as soon as she pulled out her phone, she saw more missed calls and texts from her mom. The last text had come in from her mom only fifteen minutes ago. *CALL ME.* She wanted to do nothing less, but she pulled up her home number and dialed.

Her mother picked up on the first ring. She'd obviously been waiting by the phone.

"How are you feeling?" Kristina asked.

"I'm fine," Gemma said cautiously. She'd been expecting her mom to sound angrier.

"April said you were sick. I tried calling the house several times, *and* I've been calling your cell. . . ." Her mom's voice was edged with suspicion.

She'd completely forgotten April's cover story. "I'm still really tired," she said quickly. That, at least, was the truth. "I've been basically sleeping since I got here."

"Well, I'm glad you're feeling better," she said. "Listen, I've spoken to your father. He's very upset . . ."

Gemma's heart started beating harder.

". . . but I've convinced him there's no reason to rush home," Kristina finished.

Gemma exhaled. "So he's staying in Shanghai?"

"He was already in London when I managed to reach him," she said. "He's going to stay there for a few days and take some meetings. But he wants you home by the time he gets back on Saturday. I'll email you some flight options later."

It was better than Gemma could have hoped. It was Wednesday. That gave her almost a full three days. "I was thinking I'd just drive home with April—" she said, but her mom cut her off before she could finish.

"Don't push your luck," Kristina said, her tone changing and becoming harder. "You'll fly on Saturday morning and we'll figure out how to manage your father." Again Gemma felt that hard squeeze of anger, of hatred, bringing a burn to the back of her throat. "And Gemma? I wouldn't try to call your dad just now. He's still quite upset."

I wasn't planning on it, Gemma nearly said. But she thought she'd take her mom's advice and wouldn't push her luck. "Okay," she said. "Love you, Mom."

"You better," Kristina said. She was smiling, though. Gemma could hear it in her voice. Maybe, Gemma thought, she and her mom would run away somewhere. To California. To Paris. Somewhere her father wouldn't be able to find them. "Love you too."

There was a tangle of discarded clothes and bathing suits on April's bed, but Gemma didn't bother clearing it off. Instead she crawled in under the covers, still wearing her jeans and T-shirt. She could hear the water gushing in the other room, but the thought of Jake showering— *naked*, so close by—no longer made her blush or feel much of anything. When her phone started ringing again, she picked it up without checking the screen.

"Mom," she said, "I'm going back to sleep for a bit, okay? I'm not feeling great."

"Now that's a first." It wasn't her mom on the phone, but *Pete*. She recognized his voice. "I've heard *stud* before. *Babykins, hotcakes.* No one's ever called me *Mom* before."

Gemma smiled, and her face nearly cracked. She brought a hand to her cheeks. Already it felt as if she hadn't smiled in days. "I'm not buying it," she said. "No one's ever called you hotcakes, either."

"Fair enough." His voice changed. "What's the matter? Are you sick? Or just missing me?"

She rolled her eyes before remembering he couldn't see her. "You wish. Anyway, *you* called *me*. What's up?"

"Just checking in," Pete said. "I wanted to make sure you weren't lying in a gutter somewhere."

"Barrel Key doesn't have any gutters," Gemma pointed out.

"You know what I mean," Pete said. "Did you find whatever you were looking for?"

"More," Gemma said. She closed her eyes, allowing herself to relax for the first time in twenty-four hours. April's bed was cloud-soft and smelled deliciously of lavender. "Look, can I talk to you later? I really do need to sleep."

"Big night, huh?" Although Pete's voice was still light, Gemma thought he sounded hurt. But she was too tired to explain. She closed her eyes and saw the dead girl again, and the beetle tracking across her ankle. She knew that the body bloated after death and imagined the girl balloon-like, distended, and quickly opened her eyes again.

"You could say that," she said.

"Feel better." He'd recovered quickly and was his usual, cheerful self. "Stay away from the gutter, okay?"

"I'll try," Gemma said. Before he could hang up, she added, "Hey, Pete?"

"Uh-huh?"

"Thanks. Just . . . thanks." Then she hung up before she could begin to cry. She rolled over, burying her face in the pillow. When she closed her eyes, she forced herself to focus on Pete's eyes, and the pale blond of his lashes; the crooked look of his smile and the way he sang along to the radio station, getting all the words wrong. But soon Pete's face was merging with Jake's, and Pete was frowning and dressed in all black, at a funeral for Gemma's father—except when she looked inside the casket, she saw her own face reflected, her own body stitched and sutured and gray beneath its garish makeup, her mouth open as though to scream.

She woke disoriented. Only when she saw that the sun was setting did she realize she'd been asleep for most of the day. She felt a hundred times better, clearer, more focused. For several minutes she lay in bed, letting her heartbeat return to normal, trying to ignore the shadow of the terrible nightmare that still clung to her, like a film of sweat.

Why did she have that stubbornly persistent idea that she'd been at Haven, stayed there for a long period of time? Could her father possibly have *allowed* the scientists at Haven to extract his only child's DNA, just so they could create her human double? Could he have been *using* her, maybe concealing the truth from her mom? It was a horrible idea, and she couldn't believe it, even of her father.

It was time to get answers.

In the bathroom she splashed cold water on her face and scrubbed her teeth with a finger before remembering she had a toothbrush in her backpack. She found Jake alone in the kitchen in front of his laptop. He got up when he saw her and then quickly sat down again. He was nervous, she realized. She was *making* him nervous. Was it because he felt sorry for her? Or was he afraid?

"Where's April?" Gemma asked, drawing a glass of water from the sink and drinking deeply. She felt as if she was washing away the taste of the marshes, still burned into the back of her throat.

"She went out," he said, giving her a smile that could have launched a thousand memes. Strangely, though, it was Pete she wished for, Pete she wanted to see. Pete belonged to her life Before. "She kept asking questions, but I wasn't sure what I should and shouldn't say. I think she got tired of me."

He shrugged, and Gemma stopped herself from saying she doubted it. More likely, April had gone out before she could murder Jake by slow humping.

"Did you sleep?" he asked, and Gemma nodded. She nearly told him about the nightmare but didn't.

Gemma pulled out a chair and sat down across from him, cupping her chin in her hands. "How about you?" she asked.

He shook his head. "I've been running searches on the explosions, you know. Just trying to sort out what really happened." He made a face. "You won't believe this."

"Try me," she said. Twenty-four hours ago, she wouldn't have believed in clones, or that she'd paddle a kayak across an ash-strewn marshland to try and sneak onto what might as well be a military base, or that somewhere in the world there was a girl bearing her exact likeness. Now she thought she might believe anything.

"The woman who strapped herself full of explosives—"

"Angel Fire," Gemma said, remembering the name from the message that had come in to the Haven Files.

He nodded. "Right. Angel Fire. She left a backpack at Barrel Key. Maybe she camped there overnight, I don't know. And she had *every single page* of the Haven Files printed out and stashed in her backpack." He looked vaguely nauseous. "The website keeps crashing."

A bad feeling worked at the bottom of Gemma's stomach, like someone had a fist around her intestines. "That's not good, Jake," she said. "The police will come for you next."

He laughed, but without humor. "Already have. I missed two calls from some Detective Lieutenant something."

"What are you going to do?" Gemma asked.

Jake started ordering things on the table, lining up edges, the way he'd done in the diner. A nervous tic, obviously. "I'll be all right," he said, although he didn't sound convinced. "I had nothing to do with it, anyway. They can't pin anything on me."

Gemma hoped he was right. "You never told me what happened to Richard Haven," she said.

Jake sighed and closed his laptop. For a split second, he looked much older. "Killed," he said simply. "Only a few years after Haven was built. Car accident while he was on vacation in Palm Beach." She remembered, now, reading something about Richard Haven's death, when she'd first been searching for information about the institute. Already it seemed like a different lifetime. "Most Haven-ites don't think it was an accident."

"Havenites?" Gemma repeated, and Jake blushed.

"Sorry," he said. "That's what the Haven groupies call themselves. My dad was the biggest Havenite of all."

Gemma absorbed this. "So it was murder? Another murder?" That would make Jake's father, Nurse M, whoever she was, and Richard Haven all victims of murder made to look like accidents or suicides instead.

"It was broad daylight," Jake said. He leaned back in his chair. "There was no rain, no bad weather, nothing. And from the way the car was positioned and the place it went off the road, it looked like Richard Haven must have swerved to avoid someone. But no one ever came forward."

"But it doesn't make sense," Gemma said. "The other woman, the nurse who committed suicide—"

"Nurse M," Jake said.

"Right. I mean, she was threatening to talk to the media, wasn't she? Your dad was supposed to *interview* her." He nodded. "I can understand why she'd be a threat. But Richard Haven founded the institute. He wouldn't have wanted it shut down or exposed or whatever."

Jake rubbed his eyes. "As far as we know," he said. "But that's the thing. We don't know. Richard Haven was in it from the beginning—before the military got their hands in it through Fine and Ives. Maybe he was having doubts. Maybe he wanted to back out of the whole agreement.

Or maybe he just decided he wanted recognition for his life's work. There could be a thousand reasons he became dangerous."

Gemma absorbed this in silence. Outside the window, the sun had sunk below the rooftops, leaving only a smear of red behind, like a bloody handprint. She stood up. "Come on," she said. "Time to wake up our sleeping beauties."

The houses in this complex were nestled one right next to the other. From above it must have looked like a jigsaw puzzle of roofs and tiled pools and squat gardenia bushes. Gemma could smell someone grilling, and hear the blare of a television from a nearby house. It was weird to think of all those other people so close, fixing dinner or watching Netflix or worrying about their bills, totally unaware of the explosion that had punched through Gemma's life.

She felt very alone.

The guesthouse was dark. The replicas were still sleeping. Gemma could hear the boy snoring. She eased the door to the bedroom shut, figuring that if she wanted to get the truth about Haven she would need to start by buttering them up a little, earning their trust. She rooted around in the guesthouse cabinets until she found a pot.

"What are you doing?" Jake asked.

"Haven't you ever heard?" Gemma next began opening

the cans of chili she'd bought at Walmart. "Fastest way to a person's heart is through the stomach."

Jake smiled. "Ah. Of course. That's why the police use so many cupcakes in their interrogations." His hair had a funny cowlick, and for some reason it made Gemma sad. It was so *normal*. She knew she'd never feel normal again, not ever.

She had always joked about feeling like an alien, but she knew now that until today she'd had no idea what that meant.

"We're not interrogating them. We're talking to them. It's different." The stove sputtered for several seconds before it lit. "Turn on a light, will you? I can't see any-thing."

The room flared into shape, blandly reassuring: sea-shell prints on the walls, a sign in the kitchen that said *This Way to the Beach*. Jake wandered over to the small antique roll-away desk, which was the only piece of fur-niture in the whole open-plan room that wasn't white or beach themed. Suddenly, he sucked in a sharp breath, as if he'd just seen a snake.

"What?" she asked "What is it?"

He had picked up a manila folder, the kind Gemma associated with dental records. "It's a medical report from Haven." He looked up. His eyes were burning again with that dark light, the kind that seemed to absorb and not reflect. "They must have brought it with them."

He moved to the couch with the report and powered up his computer again. Gemma came to look. The folder was disappointingly light and contained only a single, double-sided report. Still, it was something. She leaned over and read from the heading. *Form 475-A. Release Authorization and Toxicity Report. Human Model 576.*

"What does it mean?" she asked. The whole report might as well have been written in another language. Every other phrase was one like *over-conversion* or *neural impairment* or some string of weird chemical-looking codes like vCJD-12 or pR-56.

"Let's ask the oracle," Jake said. "Google," he clarified, when she looked at him.

She sat on the arm of the couch, because when she leaned any farther she was forced to inhale him, the new soap smell and the warmth of his skin, and she got distracted. But she felt awkward sitting there, posed and clumsy, like an overinflated doll, and so she returned to the stove just to have something to do.

When the bedroom door opened, she spun around, startled. Lyra looked better than she had on the marshes. Pretty, despite the sallowness of her skin and her cheekbones like beveled edges. But there was something frightening about Lyra's stillness, and the blandness of her facial expression, as if there was nothing inside directing her, as if she were hollow, like a puppet.

Gemma slopped some of the chili into a bowl. "Here," she said. Her voice sounded hysterical in the silence. "Chili. From a can. Sorry, I can't cook. You need to eat."

Lyra didn't thank her. She didn't say anything. She didn't even sit down. She just took the bowl from Gemma automatically and began to eat mechanically, holding the spoon wrong and the bowl to her lips and shoveling the chili into her open mouth. It was strange to see a girl so fragile eat like that, like she was actually a trash compactor. Weirdly, Gemma liked her better for it.

"Transmissible spongiform encephalopathies," Jake said, and Gemma jumped. This was it: they were on the verge of understanding. Suddenly all her fear left her at once. It was like standing at the top of a really steep sledding hill and then letting go. There was nothing to do anymore but ride. "That's a category of disease. Mad cow is a TSE."

"Okay." Gemma went to sit next to Jake on the couch again. It was better than standing next to Lyra, the living evidence of whatever deranged experiments they were doing at Haven. "But what does that mean?"

"I don't know." Jake rubbed his forehead as if he had a headache. "There are just references to it in the report."

At the sink, Lyra released her bowl with a clatter. Gemma looked up and saw she'd gone very still. "You shouldn't be looking at that," she said. Gemma wondered at Lyra's loyalty to Haven—was she trying to protect its secrets?

"Why not?" Jake turned to Lyra. "You stole it, didn't you?"

"Yes," Lyra said evenly. "But that's different."

"It's not like they'll miss it now. The whole place is an ash heap."

"Jake," Gemma said quickly. For the first time, Lyra had flinched.

He shrugged. "Sorry. But it's true." He didn't sound sorry at all. He sounded angry. And Gemma knew how he felt. If even a fraction of what they suspected of Haven was true, she was glad it had burned to the ground. She bent forward over the report again, trying to make sense of the baffling medical terminology and shorthand. Among the jumble of terms she couldn't understand, she spotted repeated references to Human Model 576, *generation seventeen, cluster yellow.* "Lyra, do you know what these groups mean?" Gemma kept her voice light. Lyra was still motionless by the sink, as if she was waiting for someone to tell her what to do. Maybe she was. "The patient—the replica, I mean." She looked up, wondering whether she had used the term correctly. After a second, Lyra barely nodded. "She was in the yellow cluster?"

"The Yellows died," Lyra said. Gemma went cold.

There was something terrible in Lyra's matter-of-factness. "There were about a hundred of them," she went on, "all from the youngest crops." She could have been talking about anything. Groceries. The weather. Toilet paper. "Crops are for different generations. But colors are for clusters. So I'm third crop, green cluster." She held up her wrist, and Gemma saw the green hospital bracelet, truly saw it, for the first time. "They must have made a mistake with the Yellows. Sometimes they did that. Made mistakes. The Pinks died, too."

"They all died?" Jake asked.

Lyra nodded. "They got sick."

"Oh my God." According to the report, Human Model 576 hadn't been even two years old when she died. "It says here she was only fourteen months," Gemma said, because somehow she needed to speak the words, to get them out of her chest where they were clawing at her. Not a specimen. A *child*. Small and fat-cheeked with little fists that wanted to grab at things. Gemma loved babies, always had. Who didn't?

"You said colors are for clusters," Jake said slowly. "But clusters of what?"

Lyra shrugged. "There are different clusters. We all get different variants."

"Variants of what?" Jake pressed, and Gemma almost didn't want to know the answer.

For a second, Lyra looked almost annoyed. "Medicine," she said, so sharply that Jake briefly glanced at her.

"Look, Jake. It's signed by Dr. Saperstein, just like you said." She had the urge to take pair of scissors to it, to cut it into little shreds as if doing so would hurt the real person, too. Below Dr. Saperstein's signature—which was hard and angular and fit Gemma's impression of Dr. Saperstein as someone made all of angles and corners, someone from whom human feeling had been carved away—a nurse, Emily J. Huang, had signed as well.

"Dr. Saperstein is in charge of the growth of new crops of replicas," Lyra said, and Gemma tried not to wince when she used that word, *crops*. She was surprised when Lyra voluntarily came closer. She didn't sit, but she hovered there. Maybe she *could* read. Her eyes were moving in the right way. Normally Gemma found people who read over her shoulder intensely annoying, but she was afraid of doing anything to startle Lyra away. "He signs all the death certificates." Gemma was surprised when Lyra smiled faintly. She reached out and touched Emily Huang's name with a finger—gently, as if it were something fragile, a ladybug or a butterfly. "Nurse Em signed, too."

Nurse Em. Something burst across Gemma's mind—an electric pulse of understanding. She leaned back and closed her eyes. She saw whiteness, as if she'd been staring at the sun, and silhouettes stumbling in front of it, chanting soundlessly to her. "Nurse Em," she said out loud, testing the sound of it. Yes.

"Holy shit," Jake said, and she knew that he, too, had understood.

Emily J. Huang.

Nurse M.

ELEVEN

GEMMA FELT CLAUSTROPHOBIC EVEN ONCE she was outside. She'd felt in that small bright box of a living room as if the ceiling were going to collapse—for a second she'd almost hoped it would. Now she knelt and plunged her head into the pool, which was shockingly cold, and came up gasping, her hair running water down onto her sweatshirt. But still she sensed a terrible pressure all around her, as if an invisible hand was trying to squeeze her into a sandwich bag. But she knew that in fact the pressure came from inside, from the weight of the truth and all that Jake had found out.

Ask and ye shall receive.

They had wanted to know why and now they did. They knew why. But now more than ever her mind reeled away from the truth, careened off it pinball-style. Instead she latched onto the ancillary mysteries, the other questions still unanswered: What had really happened to Emily Huang? Why had she left Haven? Was she really killed so she couldn't talk to Jake's dad?

Jake had gone home with a promise to call later. She was glad. She needed a break from him, from what they had learned together. He was *implicated*. She would forever associate Jake with the marshes, with the replicas, with the terrible thing growing inside of them.

Through the lit windows of the guesthouse she could see Lyra and 72 sitting together on the sofa, or at least, sitting side by side. Each of them seemed bound up in individual space, totally discrete, totally other. She wondered whether they knew she could see them, or even cared. They were likely used to being looked at. She couldn't imagine what they'd seen, and she shivered thinking about how matter-of-factly Lyra had talked about all the children in the yellow cluster dying, as if she were talking about a field being mowed or the garbage taken out for collection.

She felt trapped. She couldn't face the replicas again. But she couldn't face April either, who appeared every two minutes at the kitchen window, cupping her face to the glass to peer outside, obviously dying to peek at the replicas in the guesthouse but doing her best to respect their privacy, at Gemma's request.

Gemma knew she'd been unfair—she'd asked for help and hadn't told April anything—but the more she learned, the more impossible it was to explain. Gemma didn't want to be forced to say the words out loud. She thought the words might scorch her vocal cords, leave permanent damage, make blisters on her tongue. She wished in that moment she'd never come down to Florida, that she'd never heard of Haven at all. She imagined Whole Foods takeout and the big couch and her father safely away on the other side of the world. Kristina happy-zonked on her nighttime pills. April Snapchatting the funny-looking dogs she spotted in Florida. Even Chloe Goddamned DeWitt and her skinny-bitch wolf-pack friends. She would give anything to go back to caring about Chloe DeWitt.

But she couldn't. She sat down on a sagging lounge chair and began running a search for Emily J. Huang on her phone. It was a common name. She tried Emily J. Huang, nurse, and a result surfaced immediately: a four-year-old funeral announcement. The announcement was accompanied by a picture of a pretty Asian woman smiling into the camera. The service had been held at the First Episcopal Church in Palm Grove, Florida—she'd seen an exit sign for Palm Grove on the highway earlier.

Emily J. Huang recently returned from a seven-year tenure with Doctors Without Borders, where she was dispatched to remote places in the world to volunteer with underserved medical communities . . .

Emily must have made up a cover story to tell her friends and family while she was working at Haven. No wonder Nurse M's identity had never been established. Emily had been sure to keep her personal and work lives separate.

. . . and had previously served as a staff director at a charity that placed children from high-risk backgrounds in stable environments . . .

Gemma reread the sentence a second and then a third time. Jake had mentioned that Dr. Saperstein had founded a charity responsible for placing foster kids and orphans into homes. Could it be a coincidence? She searched Emily J. Huang and the Home Foundation and sucked in a quick breath. There were hundreds of results, many of them from newspapers or crime blogs. One of the first articles, from a Miami-based paper dated only six months before the funeral announcement, showed Emily Huang leaving a police station, her hand raised to shield her face from the cameras. Gemma took a notebook from her backpack and made notes as she was reading, hoping a pattern would emerge.

The state attorney's office has declined to file charges against the charity the Home Foundation, after an initial inquiry showed that a number of foster children may have gone missing under its supervision. Our research puts that number at anywhere from twenty-five to more than two hundred over a three-year period beginning in 2001, during explosive growth that eventually resulted in the Home Foundation's expansion nationwide, and consolidation into one of the most powerful and well-endowed charities in the country. Several relatives of the children who allegedly came under the Home Foundation's care have come forward to suggest that the charity be charged with abuse, neglect, and fraud. One plaintiff has even filed a suit charging the Home Foundation with abduction.

"After a careful review of the cases in question, and in consideration of the thousands of children that the Home Foundation has successfully placed and monitored in homes across the nation, we don't think there's a case here to pursue at this time," said Assistant State Attorney Charles Lanski.

The Home Foundation has released only a single statement, in which it referred to the accusations as "wild, bizarre, and absolutely invented." Initially, they did not respond to a request for further statement. But later, Megan Shipman, director of publicity for the Home Foundation, followed up in an email.

"It's unfortunate that the accusations of a small group of very troubled individuals is calling into question the work of a twenty-year-old organization, which has placed more than two thousand children in safe and happy homes," she wrote. "Anyone who takes the accusations in context can see that they are no more than attempts to exploit human tragedy for financial gain."

All three accusers who have come forward were, at the time of the incidents in question, heavy substance abusers. Sarah Mueller was only nineteen and a crack-cocaine addict when a woman she claims was from the Home Foundation offered her the sum of two thousand dollars for temporary custodial guardianship of her infant child, Diamond.

Speaking from the state-run rehabilitative halfway house where she currently lives, Mueller told the *Highland News*: "I didn't think it was for good. I thought I could have her back soon as I got clean." But when Mueller sobered up, after a long period of bouncing between the streets, jail, and rehabilitation programs, she found that the Home Foundation showed no record at all that Diamond had ever come through their system.

Mueller's story has eerie parallels to that of Fatima "Tina" Aboud, who was barely out of her teens when a woman she describes as a Home Foundation "nurse" came knocking. Aboud claims she was offered three thousand dollars for her son, then two years old. Aboud, who suffers from schizophrenia, agreed, believing that if she didn't, the CIA would come for her child. Ten years later, Aboud is stabilized through medication and has tried to locate her son, Benjamin, only to find the trail completely cold.

The last plaintiff to come forward is Rick Harliss, and his story is the most difficult to untangle. The *Highland News* has learned exclusively that Harliss, a sometime-handyman, was in jail after an altercation involving his then-employer, Geoffrey Ives, formerly of the pharmaceutical giant Fine & Ives.

Gemma's stomach dropped through the soles of her feet. For a second the words blurred. She blinked, trying to make them come into focus again. Still her father's name was there.

Harliss left his daughter in the care of his ex-wife, Aimee (now deceased). Aimee subsequently claimed their daughter, Brandy-Nicole, was kidnapped from the car while she was at the grocery store. But Harliss became suspicious when her account of the story changed, and when he noticed that she came into a large sum of cash at the same time Brandy-Nicole vanished.

After the *Highland News* officially broke the story of Sarah Mueller's accusations more than a year ago, Rick Harliss claims to have recognized two people from a photograph of the Home Foundation staff, including a staff nurse, Emily J. Huang, whom he claims to have seen several times with his ex-wife.

Adding to the difficulty of disentangling the truth—and fueling the idea that these claims are fraudulent—is the fact that Sarah Mueller and Fatima Aboud may have known each other previously. Both women were in a state-run rehabilitation facility during the same period of time, although counselors from the program do not recall the women being friendly. . . .

Gemma stopped reading. Her head was pounding again. She couldn't make sense of any of it. Rick Harliss had once worked for her family. Why didn't she remember him? It must have been when she was young. But how did the story of those missing children connect to Haven, to the clones, to the charity, to her father?

All she knew was that it *was* connected. Jake had originally believed Haven was doing drug experimentation on orphaned children—and he was 50 percent right. But why, if Haven was also manufacturing clones?

She did some more Googling and found out most of the alleged disappearances had occurred during the *exact same three-year period* as her father's lawsuit against his former business partner. The facts, then, were these: Dr. Saperstein got control of the institute the same year Richard Haven died and was, potentially, murdered. Around the same time, her father sued for control of the company, possibly because his business partner wanted to invest in Haven. He lost.

Meanwhile Dr. Saperstein was busy "misplacing" children through his charity, possibly stealing them for some unimaginable purpose. Then Fine & Ives swooped in and took ownership of Haven, at least financially, and the institute began to breed clones in large quantities for its own sick purposes.

Her father had said *follow the money*. She was sure she was missing something, and she was sure it had to do with money, with the flow of cash from the military to Fine & Ives to Haven.

She Googled Rick Harliss, but although he was mentioned several times in articles related to the Home Foundation, he'd done a pretty good job of avoiding the photographers. She found a Rick Harliss who was a lawyer in Tallahassee and a Rick Harliss who had his own personal training business, but she could not find a single picture of the Rick Harliss who believed his daughter, Brandy-Nicole, had been sold to the Home Foundation. Then, remembering that he'd been in jail, she added *mug shot* to the search terms. Almost immediately, she was bounced to a website unimaginatively named Mugshot.com.

For one, two, three seconds, her heart failed to beat.

He was younger in the picture, and although his eyes

were raw-red and his expression ferocious, he was hand-some. She thought of his stale, coffee-breath smell, the curtained greasiness of his hair. He had aged terribly. And yet despite the differences, there was no mistaking him.

It was the guy from the gas station. *What do you know about Haven?* And she remembered now that she had had the impression of familiarity. She'd remembered him, at least vaguely, and now she knew why. He had done work for her father. Probably he'd been one of the rotating series of guys who kept the grounds, or cleaned the pool, or painted the house.

Always she came back to her father and Haven. That was the center of the mystery, the original cancer, the tumor that had metastasized into a hundred other mysteries.

"Gemma?"

Gemma looked up. She hadn't heard April come outside. Quickly, she pocketed her phone, as if April might read it from across the pool deck.

"What are you doing out here?" April frowned, shaking her bangs from her eyes.

"Nothing. Thinking. Trying not to think." Gemma stood up. The distance between her and April suddenly felt very great.

"You promised to explain." April's voice was all pinched, like it had been zipped up too tightly.

Gemma rubbed her forehead. "I know. I'm sorry. I'm still sorting it out myself."

April came down off the porch. She was barefoot and already dressed for bed, in cotton shorts and an oversized T-shirt from Bubba Gump Shrimp Company. Gemma was struck in that moment by how normal she looked: tan, rested, beautiful. She and April had always talked about being co-aliens, members of a different species dropped on this planet to suffer among the humans, maybe pay penance for crimes committed in a past life on their home planet. But April wasn't an alien. April belonged.

And for a split second, Gemma hated her.

"Well?" April stopped a few feet away from Gemma, hugging herself. She wasn't smiling. "I'm listening."

Gemma looked away, ashamed. April had helped her. April was *always* helping her. But how could she begin to describe what she had seen? How could she talk about the other-Gemma, the nightmare twin? It was like something out of a horror movie.

"Haven was using the replicas," she said, because it seemed as good a place to start as any. "They were engineering them for a specific reason. We think Haven was infecting them with some kind of disease," she added quickly, before she could lose her nerve.

"A disease?" April repeated. She stared openmouthed at Gemma. "And you brought them *here*?"

"It isn't contagious like the flu is." Gemma felt queasy thinking about it. She hoped she was right. She hadn't truly understood everything Jake was reading to her. The boy seemed all right, almost normal. But she'd seen the girl stumble. Motor coordination problems were some of the first symptoms, he had read. "You can't get it except through tissue or organ transfers or—ingestion. And it takes years to work. It's like mad cow disease, or Alzheimer's, or something like that."

"My grandparents would kill me," April said, and Gemma's anger notched up again. Twenty feet away were two people who had been raised as human petri dishes, and all April could think about was getting in trouble. "What do you think they're doing in there, anyway?"

"I don't know." When Gemma turned, she saw they were no longer in the living room. They must be in the kitchen or bedroom, and out of view. Irrationally, she was glad. She didn't want April to see them. April didn't *deserve* to see them. "I don't know. Eating. Sleeping. Trying to relax. Whatever people normally do."

April laughed in a way Gemma didn't like, as if Gemma had made a joke. "And you're sure they're not going to, like, infect us?"

"Only if you decide to go zombie on them and eat their brains," Gemma said sarcastically, but April actually nodded, as if she was reassured. She was still staring into the guesthouse. A glass of water and an open can of Coke on the coffee table were the only signs that someone had been there at all.

"And they can, like, talk and stuff?" April asked. "And eat normal food?"

"Yes, they can *talk and stuff.*" Gemma's voice sounded overloud, but she didn't care. "They're *people.*" If she'd considered even for a second telling April about the girl with Gemma's face, she knew now she never would. She couldn't.

"Okay, okay. Jeez. Calm down." April rolled her eyes, as if Gemma was the one being unreasonable. "Sorry if I'm not a clone expert."

"Replica," Gemma corrected her automatically. "They don't like being called clones." She didn't know how she knew this, only that she'd noticed Lyra flinch whenever she used that word, the way April did when someone referred to her *dyke* parents, or Gemma did when she heard *fat.*

"Are you serious?" Again, April laughed.

"Yes, I'm serious." She was suddenly way past anger. She was furious. She wasn't tied to the girl on the marshes and yet she was: they were bound together, they were the *same.* Which meant that Gemma had died, too. Just a little. But she had died. "They can talk, they have feelings, they have likes and dislikes, they dream and breathe and hurt like anybody else."

"Okay, okay. I'm sorry." Now April was squinting at Gemma as if she didn't know her. "I'm just a little freaked out, okay?" Gemma said nothing. "You have to admit it's weird. . . . I mean, you said yourself they were *engineered*. Shake and bake, test-tube style."

"I hate to remind you," Gemma snapped, not even sure why she was so angry, "but so were you."

Instantly, she knew it was the wrong thing to say. April went very still. "You're comparing me to one of *them*?" she whispered. Gemma wasn't deceived by her tone of voice. The quieter April got, the angrier she was. "You think because my moms are gay, that makes me some kind of freak?"

Gemma already felt guilty. But it was too late to take back the words. And what would April say if she knew that Gemma had a clone floating around somewhere—possibly *more* than one? That Gemma remembered Haven from her childhood? "I'm just saying." She couldn't stand to see the naked hurt on April's face, so she looked away. "Plenty of people would think you weren't in a great position to judge."

"I know." April's voice was sharp as a slap. "I just didn't know you were one of them."

She turned away and Gemma saw her bring a hand

quickly to her eyes. April *never* cried. Gemma was suddenly filled with wrenching guilt. She thought her stomach might actually twist itself up and out of her throat. She nearly put a hand on April's shoulder—she nearly begged for forgiveness—but then April spoke again.

"Maybe you should leave." She didn't turn around, but her voice was steady and very flat, and Gemma thought maybe she'd been wrong, maybe April hadn't been crying at all.

"What?"

"You heard me. Maybe you should leave. You *and* your new best friends." She turned just slightly, so Gemma could see the familiar ski-slope jump of her nose, the soft curve of her cheek, a sweep of dark hair, and she knew in that moment that something had changed forever. "I'll give you until morning," April said.

She moved soft-footed across the grass and into the house. Gemma wished she'd stomped off instead. She wished an earthquake would come, or rifts would appear in the ground—anything other than this terrible silence, the peacefulness of the crickets in the trees and the low drone of TV, the world humming along while hers was ending. April didn't once look back. After she closed the door, Gemma heard the lock turn.

Then she was alone.

TWELVE

GEMMA WOKE FROM A NIGHTMARE with her cheek saddled up against a band of old plastic striping and the sun hard in her eyes. Immediately she remembered her fight with April. She had a horrible, sticky feeling all over, as if something wet was clinging to her. She couldn't remember her nightmare, but she was left with the disturbing idea that something had been hunting her, wouldn't leave her alone.

She sat up, touching her cheek where the chair had indented it. The windows of the main house threw back the light so she couldn't see beyond them, but she thought April must still be asleep. She checked her phone: nine thirty. She noticed her notebook wasn't on the ground where she'd left it. But she must have stuffed it into her backpack.

Even before she figured out what to do about the

replicas, she was determined to apologize to April, to *explain*. April was her best friend—her *only* good friend, unless you counted Pete, and she wasn't sure she could. April was freaked out by the replicas, but anyone would be. And Gemma had been horrible. She had deserved to sleep outside, deserved the stiffness in her neck and shoulders and the taste of dead fish in her mouth.

She would make coffee. She would apologize. She would tell April everything, including the truth about the dead girl Gemma had seen out on the marshes.

She went up the stairs and was encouraged to find the back door unlocked. It seemed like a sign that April might be ready to forgive her. The kitchen was empty, but there was coffee in the pot and a dirty plate sitting on the table next to a ketchup bottle. So April was awake. Gemma was about to call out to her when she saw the note, anchored to the counter by a red mug that said *San Francisco*.

The note was very short.

> *Going for a run and then to play tennis. Will be back around noon. Please be gone.*
> *—April*

Gemma balled it up and threw it in the trash can. She felt like throwing something but she didn't want to get in trouble with April's grandparents, so instead she opened the back door again and slammed it three times. She was furious again. Fucking April. Gemma had been out slogging through the marshes, nearly getting shot, hiding from the *military*, rooting out her family's deepest, darkest secret. *She'd found her own fucking clone.* And April had been going for a run and taking tennis lessons and was chucking Gemma out because of one stupid thing she'd said. Meanly, Gemma thought now she was even glad she'd said it.

She took a shower, leaving hair in the drain and not bothering to clean it out, and then brushed her teeth vigorously. At least she looked slightly better after sleeping, less like a zombie from a horror movie brought back to life by its taste for brains.

Downstairs, she poured some coffee into a mug— pleased, again, that she could use the last of the milk—and tried calling Jake. His phone rang but he didn't pick up. She waited a few minutes and tried again. Then, when he didn't answer, she sent him a text. *You awake?* It was only ten, but she couldn't imagine he was sleeping in, not after yesterday and all they'd discovered about Haven.

She was halfway back to the guesthouse when something crunched beneath her foot: her ChapStick, which had somehow escaped from her backpack and rolled across the pool deck. She saw now that her bag was lying on its side, and when she went to return the ChapStick to it, saw that everything inside was a jumbled mess, as if someone had rifled through it. Instinctively she reached for her wallet. Her credit cards were there, but she'd taken out three hundred dollars from the ATM in Walmart the day before, and all of it was gone.

She felt as she had the single time her mom had caved and taken Gemma to an amusement park, and they'd ridden a roller coaster called the Cobra together. As they'd inched up, up, up toward that first crest and then the first downward hurtle, Gemma had known she'd made a huge mistake, that she didn't want to see what was on the other side.

The guesthouse was empty. That was obvious as soon as she walked in. It even *felt* empty, and she was afraid to speak out loud because she didn't want to hear her voice sucked away by the carpet. Still, she went from room to room, checking the bathroom, even opening the closet doors as if Lyra and 72 might be hiding there. For a brief, delirious moment, she even imagined Lyra, 72, and April out together somewhere near the ocean, dressed in tennis whites, working on their game.

But there was no pretending. The replicas were gone.

Jake still hadn't texted her back. She tried calling again, then remembered he had said his aunt's house was pretty rural and cell phone service was bad. He'd written down his address and home phone number on the back of a piece of tinfoil that looked like it had come from a cigarette pack, and she tried calling this as well, three times in a row. She switched back to trying his cell phone, and her next two calls went straight to voice mail. She couldn't understand what it meant, but she was afraid. Printouts from the Haven Files had been recovered from the bomber's bag. It seemed obvious that he would get in trouble. Maybe he was with the cops even now. What if they thought he'd had something to do with the explosion?

It was ten thirty now, and she was getting desperate. No way was she going to be here when April returned—she'd rather hitchhike. She'd rather *walk*.

Then she remembered Pete.

He picked up on the first ring. "This is your knight in shining armor," he said, in a baritone. "To whom do I have the pleasure of speaking?"

"A lady in distress," Gemma said. The sound of his voice lifted her spirits, just a bit. "I need help."

Pete cleared his throat. "You're in luck. That's what knights in shining armor *do*. Helping is basically our bread and butter. What's the trouble?"

"I need you to pick me up"—she gave him April's address in Bowling Springs—"as soon as possible. I'll explain when you get here."

"Aye, aye, Captain," Pete said. "Be there in two shakes of a lamb's tail."

"What does that even mean?"

"It means sit tight. I'm coming."

She hung up, feeling better already. Pete could be annoying, but he was reliable and sweet. A distraction, too. Kind of like having a fluffy Pomeranian for company. If Pomeranians could drive and knew all the words to "Baby Got Back."

He was there in less than half an hour, and her heart lifted again when she saw the ridiculous purple minivan swanning down the road. He leaned over to pop open the door for her, and she nearly sat on a bag of doughnuts in the passenger seat.

"Figured you hadn't eaten," he said. "There's coffee, too, if you want it." Two jumbo Styrofoam cups were straining against the cup holders.

Pete must have gotten sun yesterday, because his arms and the bridge of his nose were more deeply freckled. But the freckles looked good on him, like a dusting of stars. She was super aware of the fact that when she sat, her shorts cut hard into her thighs, and wished she had worn jeans instead. Even her *knees* looked fat. To conceal her embarrassment she looked down, fumbling with the lid of her coffee.

"You weren't kidding about the knight-in-shining-armor thing," she said.

He beamed at her. Actually beamed. His smile nearly blinded her. "So where to?"

She knew that there was no point in trying to go after the replicas. She wasn't Sherlock Holmes, and there were no footprints to track. They had most likely left in the middle of the night and could have been anywhere. She needed to talk to Jake. He might have ideas about what to do next. Fortunately, he'd written down his address when he'd given her his aunt's landline. At least the replicas hadn't stolen her entire wallet. Small mercies.

"Here." She fished out the piece of foil and handed it over to Pete. He raised his eyebrows.

"Is this a clue or something?" Pete said. "Because I think it was Sergeant Pepper in the pantry with an egg cozy."

"Just drive, okay? I need to talk to my friend Jake," she said. "He's not picking up his phone."

Instantly, Pete's face changed. "When you said *help*, I didn't think you needed a ride to your boyfriend's," he said, and although he put the car in drive, she could tell he was hurt.

"Jake isn't my boyfriend. Trust me," she said. "He's—" She was about to say he was way out of her league, but she didn't think this would make Pete feel any better. Especially since she was kind of starting to hope Pete might be *in* her league. "Look, he's been helping me. It's complicated. . . ." She trailed off.

Pete made a face, as if he wasn't convinced. "So why couldn't Prince Charming come and get you?"

"I told you. I can't get in touch with him," Gemma said, and Pete snorted. "Look, you've got it wrong. Jake's dad was a big Haven freak. After he died, Jake kind of took over for him."

"Haven?" Pete looked confused. "The place we heard about on the radio? The one that got blown up?"

"Yeah. That one." Gemma took a deep breath. The GPS was directing them out of the subdivision now, speaking in its measured mechanical voice, and Gemma found herself unconsciously scanning the streets for April in her jogging clothes. She was seized by the sudden idea that once they turned onto the highway, that was it. She would never see April again. And she knew, in part, it had been her fault. She should have talked to April, trusted her sooner, let her in on the secret, explained. She turned back to Pete. "There's a lot of stuff I haven't told you. It's going to sound crazy, okay? If I tell you, you're going to think I'm bananas. You have to promise not to think that."

"I swear," Pete said. He didn't seem upset anymore.

"*Turn right on County Route 39*," said the voice of the GPS. Gemma looked once more for April, and the streets were totally empty. As if they were just waiting for something, or someone.

"It's kind of a long story," Gemma said. Her heart was elbowing up against her rib cage, like it was trying to force its way through them. How would she even begin?

Pete smiled, just a little. "You've got eighty-seven miles," he said, reaching for the doughnuts. "So start talking."

It was easy to talk to Pete. Gemma hadn't expected him to be such a good listener, but he was. He didn't interrupt with stupid questions or squawk in disbelief when she told him about stumbling across the replicas—*literally* stumbling—in the marshes. Only once did he interrupt, when she described finding the dead girl with her exact face. Her replica. And then he just said, "Jesus," and then, "Go on."

By the time she finished telling him everything— about the long slog back through the marshes, and the folder that Lyra had smuggled out of Haven, about *transmissible spongiform encephalopathies*; about waking up to discover the replicas missing with all her money; about Jake and his dad and the Haven Files and Angel Fire and her mission from God—they had reached Jake's road.

Jake hadn't been lying about his aunt's house being rural. Route 12, on the outskirts of Little Waller, was a treacherous narrow dirt path studded with holes. On either side of the road, behind growth so riotous it looked like the trees were launching some kind of major offensive, prefab houses, little more than glorified trailers, sagged in the midday sun, doing their best to stay on their feet in the wilting heat. Gemma felt an unexpected rise of pity. No wonder Jake had been obsessing about his father's death for years. She couldn't imagine there was much else to do. This was a lonely place.

They had to squeeze by a Florida Energy truck that was teetering in a deep gutter on one side of the lane; a man in a hard hat was high on the pole, fiddling with the wire, and a group of workers were doing nothing but watching. Gemma was relieved to see that Jake's car was in the driveway, or the small patch of dirt that counted as one. For the first time she noticed the bumper was plastered with bumper stickers, so overlayered and old that most were illegible. She wondered whether it had been his father's car.

Pete pulled into the driveway behind Jake's car but made no move to get out. Instead he hunched forward over the steering wheel, peering up at the house. It was an ugly yellow color, with brown shutters, two of which were hanging at weird angles. Someone had made an effort to clear a patch of front lawn—Gemma thought of Jake, lining up his utensils neatly, and imagined it must be him—but the trees were reclaiming their territory slowly and the window boxes were empty except for dirt. No one had taken much pride in the house, for sure.

"Well," Pete said, with his usual cheerfulness. "At least we won't have to take our shoes off."

Gemma licked her lips. The coffee had been too sugary and now her mouth had a weird, gritty feel. Pete still hadn't responded to her story, not directly. Maybe he didn't believe her. "Look. All the stuff I told you . . ."

Pete turned to her. His eyes were the color of Rufus's. Toffee brown, warm. "You can trust me," he said. It was as though he read her mind. "I won't tell anyone."

It was as if a bubble of air in her chest had been released. "So . . . you don't think I'm crazy?"

"People who pay five bucks for coffee are crazy," he said. Then he frowned. "But you're in some deep shit." She'd never heard him sound so serious, and in that moment she realized he was handsome. Not just cute. Not goofy-looking. *Handsome.* Clean jaw and a little bit of stubble, all those golden freckles, the hair falling softly across his forehead. "I'm worried about you. Powerful people went to a lot of trouble to keep Haven's work a secret. My guess is they won't stop now."

"No one knows we were out on the marshes," Gemma said. Her stomach squirmed, though. "No one knows what we found."

"So you think," Pete said. And then, in a quieter voice,

"I'm not trying to scare you. But we have to be careful."
It was amazing, Gemma thought, how nice the word *we* could sound, and she nearly put her arms around him. She nearly kissed him.

Christ. She was fantasizing about kissing Pervy Pete. April would never believe it. *If* April ever spoke to her again.

It was hotter here than it had been in April's grandparents' subdivision, despite all the shade. Gemma felt sorry for the Florida Energy guys.

"You'll like Jake," Gemma said, partly to convince herself. The tree branches lifted and fell silently, touched by a phantom wind. She didn't know why she felt so nervous. Something about the whole place was creepy, like the set piece of an abandoned road from a horror film after the zombie apocalypse has struck.

Pete shrugged. But he still looked unhappy, or nervous, or both. "Weird are my people," he said. "Weird is what I do."

"He'll have a plan. You'll see," she said, partly to reassure herself. A tabby cat was sunning itself on the grungy porch and stared insolently at them as the sound of the doorbell echoed through the house. *You shouldn't be here*, it seemed to be saying, and Gemma couldn't help but feel the same way.

For a long minute, she heard no sounds of movement.

She began to feel not just nervous but truly afraid. She jabbed a finger on the bell again and at the same time tried the knob. Locked. Finally she heard footsteps. In the window next to the door, she saw Jake twitch open the blinds, and his dark eyes peer between them. Then the sound of the lock releasing. Relief felt like something physical, like something she could lie down in.

"God," she said, when he opened the door. "I was afraid something had happened. I was afraid . . ." But she trailed off, seeing that he had only opened the door a crack and he was angling his body so they couldn't come inside.

"What are you doing here?" He was looking at her as if he'd never seen her before in his life. He looked *furious*.

It wasn't exactly the welcome she'd been expecting. Next to her, Pete pivoted, staring back toward the street as though considering a quick getaway.

"You weren't picking up your phone," Gemma said. "I called a dozen times."

"Can't find my phone," he said. "Don't know what happened to it." His eyes swept the street behind them. "You should really go." He started to close the door.

"Wait." Gemma got a hand in the door. For a second he looked like he was considering closing it on her fingers, but then he thought better of it. "You don't understand. The replicas—they're gone."

"Quiet." Jake hushed her as though she'd cursed in church. She was close enough to see that he was sweating. Fear. Jake Witz, she realized, wasn't angry. He was terrified. "Keep your voice down."

"We came here for your help—" Pete started to say, but Gemma cut him off. She felt wild and reckless and dizzyingly confused.

"Didn't you hear me? They're *gone*," she said. "They must have left in the middle of the night. They took my money. Maybe they took your phone, too—"

"I heard you." Once again, Jake's eyes went to the street. "It's not my problem. Not yours, either. Now get out of here. You shouldn't have come. I don't know you, okay?" He raised his voice. He was practically shouting. "I don't even know you."

Once again Gemma stopped Jake from closing the door, just barely, on her fingers. She kept her hand in the doorjamb so he couldn't. She had that hard-throat feeling of trying not to cry. "What happened?" she said. "Are you in trouble with the cops?"

"The cops." Jake let out a sound that could have been a laugh or a cough. "Not the cops." He took a step forward, startling Gemma and forcing her to release the doorjamb. "My lights are working just fine," he added almost angrily, leaning so close that Gemma could feel his breath on her face. Before she could ask him what he meant, he closed the door, and the lock slid back into place.

For a second Gemma just stood there, stunned. Even with Pete standing next to her, she had never felt so alone in her life. She was too embarrassed to look at Pete. She'd dragged him all the way here, promising that Jake would help, and he hadn't even let them inside. "Something must have happened. He wasn't like this yesterday." She thought of the way he'd looked, with sweat standing on his skin, and what he'd said to her: *My lights are working just fine.*

"Gemma." There was a warning in Pete's voice, but she was too upset to listen to it.

"Someone must have gotten to him—yesterday he was practically *begging* me for information—"

"*Gemma.*" This time, Pete seized her hand, and she was surprised into silence by the sudden contact. Her palms were sweaty, but his were dry and cool and large. "Funny they need so many guys to work the wires, don't you think?" he said in a low voice, as he piloted her off the porch and back toward the van. He didn't look at the Florida Energy men a little ways down the road, but she could tell by the way he was staring straight ahead that he was *trying* not to look.

Instinctively, she glanced over to where the six or seven workers in their hard hats and vests were still standing— *doing nothing*—and had the sense that they had only avoided meeting her eyes by a fraction of a second. And then she understood what Jake had said about the lights.

Not nonsense. A code. *My lights are working just fine.* Meaning: no reason for the Florida Energy truck, and the people gathered across the street with their van spiky with antennae. Although Gemma had looked away as quickly as possible, she had caught the eye of one of the men down the road: clean-shaven, hard-eyed, pale as paper. Not the complexion of someone who spent every day working outside.

Jake was being watched. Which meant: they were now being watched, too. No wonder Jake had practically shoved them off his doorstep, had shouted that he didn't know them. He'd been trying to protect them. She had the overwhelming urge to turn around, to hurtle back up to the door and pound to be let in and to thank him. But that would be beyond stupid. Instead she walked stiff-backed to the minivan and climbed in, trying to appear unconcerned, as if maybe the whole thing really had been a mistake. Maybe the men—whoever they were—would believe that they were just casual acquaintances of Jake's, there to return something or say hello.

In the car, Pete wiped his hands on his jeans before grabbing hold of the steering wheel. They didn't speak. Pete kept glancing in the rearview mirror as he backed out of the driveway. *Please don't follow us,* Gemma thought.

She pressed the desire through her fists. *Don't follow us.* But a moment later, a maroon Volvo pulled out of another hard-packed dirt driveway and crept up behind them. Could it be a coincidence? She didn't think so.

"Do you think—?" she started to ask, but Pete cut her off.

"Not now," he said. "Need to think." Somehow, the fact that Pete—Pete of the endless, stream-of-consciousness babble—had run out of things to say scared her even more than the car behind them.

It wasn't a coincidence: the car followed them no matter how many turns they made down shitty country roads, even after they reached downtown Little Waller, such as it was: a few bleak roads studded with tire shops, fast-food restaurants, and liquor and discount stores. The driver didn't even bother going for subtlety—and this, too, scared Gemma, and made her angry. It was the way a cat toyed with its prey, batting it around a bit, taking its time, certain already of its satisfaction.

"We need to lose them." Gemma hardly recognized her voice when she spoke. It was as if an alien had crawled into her throat and taken over her vocal cords.

"*Lose* them?" Pete repeated. Gemma realized how tense Pete was. He was practically doubled over the steering wheel, staring hard at the road as if it might simply disappear. "Christ. You're really taking the knight-in-shining-armor thing to the limit, you know that?" He yanked the wheel hard to the left, and Gemma was thrown against the door. But only thirty seconds later, lazily, the Volvo turned, too. It was so absurd that they were riding around in an eggplant-colored minivan. They might as well be driving a hovercraft. It wasn't exactly like they could *blend*. "Who are these guys, anyway?"

"Maybe cops," Gemma said. She had an awful, heavy feeling in her gut, like she was trying to digest a roll of toilet paper. She'd dragged Pete into this. She'd dragged them *all* into this. "Probably military."

"Military." Pete repeated the word as if he'd never heard it before. His freckles were standing out ever more clearly from his skin, like even they were thinking of making a break for it. "Jesus . . ."

"You told me you wanted to help." Gemma was squeezing her hands so tightly she was sure she'd break the skin.

Pete sighed. "I do," he said. "I just didn't think we'd end up in a chase scene so early in the movie." Then: "All right, look. Are you buckled in?"

Gemma nodded. She was too nervous to speak. A sign ahead pointed the way to the interstate, and here there were more cars on the road, funneling onto or off the highway. The Volvo was still following them, but at a distance of about fifty yards.

Pete put on his blinker and moved into the far left lane, as though he was about to turn across traffic and into a shopping mall that boasted two liquor stores, a nail salon, and a pizza joint. At least one car crowded in behind them, separating them temporarily from the Volvo's view. The traffic light turned red. Pete inched forward. Gemma could hear him breathing. She felt as if she *couldn't* breathe, as if she was being squeezed between two iron plates.

"What are you . . . ?" she started to say, but then the light turned green and Pete slammed his foot on the accelerator.

The engine whined, then yanked them forward. Gemma nearly cracked her head on the dashboard before she was pulled backward by the seat belt, smacking her head against the seat. Pete jerked the wheel to the right, cutting across two lanes of traffic. Several drivers leaned a long protest on their horns, and a Chevy screeched to a stop to avoid colliding with them.

"What the hell? What the hell?" Gemma was screaming, and more horns went off as Pete careened onto the entrance to the interstate. But then it was over. He was speeding up the on ramp. Traffic blurred past them, a solid moving mass of cars dazzled by sunlight, and then they were there, passing among them, and the Volvo was long gone. The sky was bright and puffy with clouds. They could have been anyone, going anywhere.

"How's that for a chase scene?" Pete said. He was out of breath.

Gemma couldn't help it: all her fear transformed into the sudden desire to laugh. It practically lifted her out of her seat. She doubled forward, holding her stomach, laughing so hard it hurt. Pete started to laugh, too. Then he snorted, which just made Gemma laugh harder, until she couldn't breathe and had to lean back, gasping.

"Not bad," she said. Her eyes were watering, blurring her vision of the highway and the featureless towns on either side of it, all of them identical, replicas of one another. "Not bad at all."

THIRTEEN

THEY DROVE FOR ANOTHER HOUR. Pete switched onto different freeways several times, just in case, although Gemma couldn't imagine how anyone could still be pursuing them. She was surprised to see a sign for Palm Grove—the town where Emily Huang, the nurse at Haven who'd been killed before she could talk to Mr. Witz, had lived—and equally surprised when Pete turned off the highway.

"What are you doing?" she asked.

"I'm starving," he said. "I'm seriously about to self-cannibalize. And I need both hands to drive."

"I'm hungry too," Gemma said, before remembering that she tried never to admit to being hungry in front of other people. But of course, the fact that they'd just escaped from a military tail made her normal concerns about being overweight seem unimportant. Besides, Pete didn't look at her that way, as if there was something wrong with her, as if she *really shouldn't*, as if she would *be pretty if only she'd slim down a bit.*

She liked how Pete looked at her.

They pulled over at a diner across from a motel called the Starlite, its parking lot empty except for a white Chevrolet and a few beat-up, dusty sedans. She didn't want to think about the kind of people who used the Starlite midday. Gemma climbed out, stretching, her body still sore from being contorted on a lawn chair all night. Once again she had that awful, full-body sensation of being watched. She whipped around, certain she saw a face peering out at her from a window of the Starlite. But it was only a trick of the light.

Still, even after they were seated and tucking into enormous burgers and a platter of fries so towering it seemed to defy physics, she kept glancing out the window. Another car pulled into the diner parking lot and her heart stopped. But it was only a dad and his two kids. And after a while, she began to relax.

"So what's the next move?" Pete had waited until they were both finished eating before leaning forward and speaking to her in a low voice. "I mean, we can't depend on Jake anymore. The replicas are gone. Are we finished here?"

Again, she liked his use of the word *we*. "I've been

thinking about that." She'd eaten too much too quickly and now she was nauseous. "I have to talk to my parents. It's the only way." Even saying it made her chest feel like it might collapse, but she kept talking, half hoping to convince herself. "My dad has answers. He's been miserable for years, and I think it *has* to be because of Haven." She was surprised to realize, as soon as she said it, that this was true. "He walks around like he's got something clinging to his back. Like a giant vampire bat or something."

Pete made a face.

"What?" she said. "You think that's a bad idea?"

"I think it's a *great* idea." Pete sighed. He swiped a hand through his hair. It stood up again immediately. "This is big stuff. These are big, serious people. I worry . . ." He looked up at her, and something in his eyes made her breath snag. But he quickly looked away. "I was worried, that's all." He was back to his normal self, easy and silly. "You ready to hit the road, then? I made a playlist for the drive back, you know. 'One hundred greatest bluegrass hits of the 1970s.'"

"I'll throw you through the windshield," Gemma said. She felt surprisingly free now that she'd made the decision—as if something had clambered off *her* back. "Meet me in the car, okay?"

In the bathroom she stood in front of the mirror and remembered the girl on the marshes, her reflection, her other. She leaned over the sink and splashed water on her face, as though it would help wash the image from her head. The cold did her good.

She was going to confront her father and get answers, and she didn't care anymore whether he got angry, whether he ever spoke to her again, whether he ordered her out of the house.

She almost hoped he would.

She would be fine on her own. She was stronger than she'd ever thought she was. She was strong, period.

Outside, she saw Pete sitting very still with both hands on the wheel, staring at her with the strangest expression. He must be far more freaked out than he was letting on. His eyes looked enormous, like they might simply roll out of his head, and she felt a burst of gratitude for him. He was trying, for her sake, to act normal.

"All right, Rogers." She was speaking even as she yanked open the door. "Passenger gets DJ privileges, so hands off the radio—" All her breath left her body at once.

There was a man sitting directly behind Pete, holding a gun to his head. She knew him instantly: it was the man who'd grabbed her outside the gas station. The same long, greasy hair, the same gray stubble and wild look.

"Get in the car and shut the door," he said. His eyes went left, right, left, right. She wanted to move, but she was frozen. Even the air had turned leaden. She was drowning where she stood. "In the car," he said again, practically spitting. She saw the gun trembling in his hand and realized he was panicking. She nearly tripped getting into the car. She felt as if her whole body was coming apart.

"Okay," she managed to say. She got the door shut and held up both hands. *Think, think.* Her phone was in her pocket. If she could somehow dial 9-1-1 . . . "Okay, listen. Just calm down, okay? Let's everyone stay calm. You can have my wallet. You can have anything you want."

"I didn't come for money," the man said. He nudged Pete with the gun. Pete had gone so pale Gemma could see a vein, blue and fragile-looking, stretching across his temple. "Drive." She was amazed that Pete managed to get out of the parking lot without hitting anything. She was amazed by Pete, period. She'd never been so scared in her life. Her stomach was cramping, and she was worried she might go to the bathroom right there.

"Please," she said. Her voice came out in a whisper. "Please. What do you want?"

"I'm not going to hurt you," he said. But he didn't sound as if he meant it. Gemma could smell him sweating in his old camouflage jacket. *Rick Harliss.* The name came back to her from the article she had read about Emily Huang and her involvement with the Home Foundation. He'd once worked for her father. He'd lost a daughter,

Brandy-Nicole, when he went to jail. "I just want to talk, okay? That's all I want. That's all I ever wanted. Someone to listen. No one fucking listens, no one believes. . . ."

He was getting agitated. His hand was shaking again. She was worried he might accidentally discharge the gun.

"We'll listen," she said. "We'll listen all you want. Isn't that right, Pete?"

"Sure," he said. His voice cracked. He licked his lips. "Of course we will."

"Keep going," Rick Harliss said, giving Pete a nudge in the neck again when he started to slow down at a yellow light. Instead Pete sped through it. "Highway," Harliss said, when they came up on signs for I-27, and a sour taste flooded Gemma's mouth. Somehow getting on the highway made everything seem irreversible. Not like she would have rolled out of the car at a red light, but still.

She closed her eyes. She needed to focus. "Okay, you want to talk. So let's talk, okay?" She'd heard once that in abduction situations it was important to share personal information, to get chatty, to humanize yourself. "Let's start with names, okay? This is my friend Pete. Pete has terrible taste in music—"

"Shut up," Harliss said. "I'm trying to think."

"—but he's a decent guy, all around, really. Probably the most decent guy I've ever met." Gemma realized, even as she said it, how true it was. Poor Pete and the mess she'd dragged him into. And he'd never complained, not once. If they made it through without getting shot or butchered, she was going to buy him a lifetime supply of gummy bears.

She was going to kiss him.

"Gemma," Pete said softly, and his voice held a warning, but she didn't care.

"And my name is Gemma Ives," she said. "Germ Ives. At least that's what the girls in my grade always called me, because I was sick a lot as a kid—"

"I know who you are." Harliss's voice cracked. "Jesus. Stop talking, okay? You're making my head hurt."

Gemma pressed her hands hard into her thighs, digging with her fingernails, letting the pain focus her. She was scared to anger him further. But she had to make him see that she understood, that she knew him. That she was on his side. She had to buy them time. "I know who you are, too, Mr. Harliss."

Pete sucked in a sharp breath. For a split second the silence in the car was electric, and she worried she'd made a mistake. She was in too deep to stop now. She had to keep talking.

"You used to work for my dad, didn't you? I must have been just a little kid. But still. That day at the gas station. My dog recognized you. After all these years, he knew your smell."

"What did your dad tell you about me?" Harliss asked. He sounded like he was talking through a mouth full of nails.

"He didn't tell me anything," Gemma said. She didn't dare risk turning around. "I read about you. I read about you and about your girl—Brandy-Nicole. She disappeared when she was just a baby." Harliss whimpered. "I know you think that the Home Foundation had something to do with it. But I'm telling you, Pete and I don't know anything. We're just as confused as you are—"

"Bullshit." The word was an explosion. Pete winced and Gemma bit her lip, trying not to cry. "Your dad was in it up to his neck. Don't tell me you don't know. It was all because of Haven. It was his fault they needed money. It was his fault they started grabbing kids in the first place. Your dad knew. He fucking knew all about it." Rick Harliss took the gun from Pete's head for just a second, just long enough to wipe his nose on his sleeve. Before Gemma could do anything, or even contemplate doing anything, it was back. "They took her from me."

"Please," Gemma said. "We can help you. We'll get people to listen to you. But please just let us go. . . ."

He shook his head. "I'm sorry," he said. He did sound sorry. They were coming up on an exit for Randolph. He gestured to it with the gun. "Pull off here. This is far enough."

He directed them to a Super 8 motel. They climbed out of the car. Gemma first, carefully, conscious of the gun angling in her direction as if it were a live thing, a dog snapping at its tether, trying to get loose. Pete and Rick Harliss left the car together. Rick kept his gun, now concealed inside his sweatshirt pocket, trained on Pete's back. He herded Pete and Gemma together, forcing them to walk side by side directly in front of him, so they shuffled awkwardly toward the lobby together, bumping elbows. Rick Harliss kept stepping on Gemma's heel. It would have been funny if it weren't so awful.

"Some knight I am," Pete said quietly. He found Gemma's hand and squeezed. When he tried to let go, she interlaced their fingers instead. "I'm sorry, Gemma."

She almost couldn't speak. "*You're* sorry?" She shook her head. "This is all *my* fault."

"Quiet," Harliss said as they jostled together through the door. Gemma felt like a Ping-Pong ball bouncing around a tiny space. She was sure the receptionist would notice something was wrong—she was desperately hoping for it—and kept trying to telegraph desperation through her eyes. *He's got a gun. He's got a gun.*

But the receptionist was flipping through a magazine and barely even glanced up at them.

"Can I help you?" She had long pink nails with faded

decals on them. Sunflowers.

"We need a room." Harliss pulled out some crumpled twenties and placed them on the counter.

"One or two?"

"Just one."

The receptionist briefly lifted her eyes but they only went to the money before dropping back to the magazine, seemingly exhausted. "Room's forty-five a night."

"It says forty out front."

"Rates went up."

"Don't you think you should change the sign, then?"

There was a plastic fern in the corner, cheap blue wall-to-wall carpeting on the floor, a gun at their backs. Gemma felt the same way she did when she was dreaming—so much was true and familiar and then there was always some weird element distorted or inserted, a talking bird, the ability to fly. Finally Harliss forked over another five-dollar bill—Gemma caught herself nearly offering to pay before remembering that Harliss was kidnapping them—and they went bumping and jostling again back into the sunshine. Room 33 was on the second floor, up a narrow flight of cement stairs covered in graffiti, at the far end of the open-air corridor. Not that they could have shouted or banged on a wall, anyway. They appeared to be the only guests at the Super 8.

The room reeked of stale cigarettes. Once they were

inside, Rick Harliss bolted and chain-locked the door and drew the blinds. For several long seconds, it was dark enough that Gemma saw bursts of color and patterns blooming in the blackness of her vision. Then Harliss turned on the lamp, its shade yellowed and torn. He sat down on the bed. He removed his gun from his pocket and Gemma drew in a breath. But to her surprise he placed it in the bedside table, on top of the Bible, and closed the drawer.

"I told you," he said. "I don't want to hurt you. Sit." He gestured to the second twin bed. "Come on, sit," he said again, raking his fingers through his thinning hair, so it stood up. Gemma remembered that he'd been handsome at one point. Strange that time could do that to a person, just work like a hacksaw on them.

Gemma and Pete moved to the bed together, as if they were tethered by an invisible cord. Once they were sitting, they were separated from Harliss by only a few feet of space, and Gemma noticed the cheapness of his jacket and oiliness of his skin and the way his fingernails were picked raw, and found herself feeling not scared of him anymore but just *sorry* for him. She realized in that second she actually believed he didn't want to hurt them. She was sure he wouldn't even be able to if he tried.

"I told you," she said, speaking gently, as if he were a child. "We know even less than you do. That's why I came down here. Because I *didn't* know anything. Because I was in the dark about Haven."

"Huh. That's funny." Harliss laughed without smiling. "I'd think you'd have wanted to know all about it."

Gemma's hairs stood up. She felt in the room a subtle shift—an electric stillness. "What do you mean?"

Harliss looked up at her with those sad-dog eyes. "Well, that's where they made you, isn't it?"

FOURTEEN

SHE WAS DIMLY AWARE THAT Harliss was still talking. She felt as if a hole had opened inside of her and she was dropping into it.

Made there. She'd been made there.

Just like that girl on the marshes . . .

Gemma wasn't the original. She, too, was a replica.

Impossible, she wanted to say. She remembered all those baby pictures with her mom in the hospital. Could they have been staged? No. No one could fake her mother's look of exultation and exhaustion, the sweat standing out on her forehead, the look of bewildered joy. *Impossible.* But she couldn't make her voice work, and it was Pete who said it.

"That's impossible," Pete said. He was staring at her and she turned away, too numb even to be embarrassed. He sounded horrified. Why wouldn't he be?

". . . took me a long time to put it together," Harliss was saying. "I had nothing else to do, sitting there in state for twelve years. Not saying I didn't deserve it. I did. I used to do work around your house, you know, before they brought you back from that place. But I was all banged up. Got hooked on the shit they gave me for my back. I was out of my mind half the time."

"You're out of your mind now," Pete said. "It's *not possible.*"

If Harliss heard Pete, he gave no sign of it. He was still looking directly at Gemma. "My ex-lady used to do some cleaning. Your mom was in real bad shape then. Real bad. She'd just lost her baby. SIDS. That's sudden infant death syndrome, you know. Poor thing was only six months old."

Gemma's heart stopped. "What baby?" she managed to whisper. She'd never heard her parents mention another baby.

But Harliss just barreled on. "Aimee—that's my ex— used to say it was funny, all the money in the world but still you can't buy your way out of that. When Aimee got pregnant with Brandy-Nicole, your mom would just sit there with her hand on Aimee's belly, trying to feel the baby kick. She started cutting out articles, you know, how Aimee should be eating, how she was supposed to be laying off booze and cigarettes. Even bought us some stuff, a crib and a stroller, some baby clothes. You could tell she was all broken up. Your mom said she couldn't get pregnant again. Something about what had happened when the first was coming out."

There had been another one, a sister, a baby Gemma had never known about. Kristina had lost a baby. And somewhere deep in Gemma's mind an idea was growing, thoughts like storm clouds knitting together before they burst.

"When Brandy-Nicole was ten months old, I got picked up for holding and was sent to Johnston for eighteen months. That's a state prison near Smithfield. Reduced to twelve for good behavior. The day I was out I started using again." He touched his neck once, briefly, as if amazed to find a pulse still there, to find himself alive. "Your dad was decent. He knew I'd been sent away but he gave me the job back. I told him I was cleaned up. He believed me."

Life doesn't hand out second chances. Wasn't that what her father was always saying? But at some point he'd thought differently.

There was another baby. . . .

"Well, Aimee was still going over sometimes to clean. You were home by then, and only six months younger than our Brandy-Nicole. But your mom didn't like you two to play together. She hardly let anyone near you. We thought it was because she was worried you'd get sick like the first one."

The first one. The first daughter. The original. And she, Gemma: a shade.

"Funny, though, Aimee said to me. They look just the same. Could have been twins, she said, except for Emma had a birthmark on her arm. I didn't think much of it at the time. Only later, when I started figuring what Haven was for and what your dad had paid them for, I put two and two together."

Emma. She had a name, this phantom sister who was so much more than that. Gemma closed her eyes and thought of her mother, sweaty and exhausted and triumphant, a baby nestled in her arms. Not Gemma. *Emma*.

All these years, Kristina had lived with a reminder of that first, lost daughter. Emma. What a pretty name; much prettier than Gemma. She was the original. Gemma was the copy. And everyone knew copies were never as good. Was that why her mom had started taking so many pills? Oxycontin and Pristiq and Klonopin and Zoloft? An A–Z array of pharmaceuticals, all so that she could forget and deny.

All because Gemma was a monster.

"The Frankenstein mask." She opened her eyes. "You threw the Halloween mask." She remembered what her father had said about Frankenstein: *In the original story, in the real version, he's the one who made the monster.* She'd thought he meant it because she was awkward, and sick, and fat. But he'd meant it literally. Truthfully.

Harliss tugged at his shirt collar, and she saw a small cross tattooed on the left side of his neck. "I was mad," he said. "I tried to talk to your dad. Went to his office. He said he'd call the cops on me if I came around again. Said I was harassing him. But you've got to understand. I just want answers. I need to know."

Pete stood up, cursing. "This is crazy," he said. He moved toward the door, and Harliss didn't try and stop him. Gemma thought he might try to leave, but instead he just stood there. "This is crazy, you know that?"

Gemma didn't bother responding. It wasn't crazy. In fact, for the first time, everything made sense. The fact that her father could hardly stand to look at her. The strange tension between her parents, as if they existed on either side of a chasm, a secret that had fissured their world in two. Gemma's memory of the statue and all those early hospital visits—she was probably fragile because she'd been *engineered*. She wondered if this was God's way of getting vengeance on the people who'd been made so unnaturally. He was always trying to *un*make them.

"What happened to your daughter?" she said. Her voice didn't sound like her own. "What happened to Brandy-Nicole?"

Harliss clasped his hands. He might have been praying, except for the whiteness of his knuckles. Gemma knew he must be squeezing so hard it hurt. "It was pretty bad in those days," he said quietly. "Me and Aimee was always at each other's throats. Money, mostly. We never had any. We burned through it. We were both getting high every night. Poor Brandy-Nicole wasn't even three yet. . . ." His voice broke. "One time I woke up and she'd wet herself, made a mess all over in the middle of the night. Had to lie in it for hours. I was passed out cold all night, and Aimee hadn't even bothered coming home. That's when we split up for good."

Shockingly, Gemma had the urge to comfort him, to tell him it was all right. But of course it wasn't.

"I needed money bad." His voice was barely a whisper. She wondered whether he had ever told this story before. At the door, Pete was still standing there. Frozen. Horrified. "I was still doing work for your dad. All that money everywhere . . ." His eyes slid away from Gemma's. Guilty. "At first I just pocketed a few things. Stuff no one would notice. Pawned it off direct. I know it was wrong, but you got to understand. I wasn't thinking straight—"

Gemma shook her head to say, *It doesn't matter.*

Harliss licked his lips. "But then I started thinking about a bigger payday. You know, something hefty. I thought your dad must have something he didn't want other people to know—there's always dirt, especially for guys like him—" Again his eyes skated nervously to Gemma's, but she didn't correct him. She wouldn't defend her father ever again.

"You're talking blackmail," Pete said. His voice sounded very loud.

Harliss nodded. "That was the idea, yeah." He looked like he was about to apologize again. Gemma cut him off.

"What happened?"

He took a deep breath. "I went digging around your dad's office, through his emails." He squirmed. "Like I said, I was out of my mind—"

"Go on," Gemma said. She felt weirdly breathless, as if a giant hand were squeezing her lungs.

"I couldn't figure a way into his work files. Too much security. But I was looking for dirt closer to home, anyway. I got into his personal account. *Trouble.* That was the subject header of one of the very first emails. *Trouble.*"

The air in the motel was very still. Gemma had the sense that even the dust motes were hanging motionless in the air, suspended and breathless.

"I didn't understand any of it. Not then. It was all about some kind of investment your father had made. Your dad was pulling out. Said he'd given plenty of money already and wanted nothing to do with it anymore, said he'd figured out it was wrong. And this man, Mark Saperstein, wanted more money out of him. He said with Haven going in a new direction, it was going to make them all rich in the end if only your dad would get Fine and Ives on board. I remember one phrase exact: *They die early anyway.* That was at the end of Saperstein's message."

Gemma felt the space between her heartbeats as long moments of blank nonexistence. What had they learned in biology about clones? Imperfect science. Cancers, tumors that grew like flower buds in manufactured lungs and hearts and livers. It was as if the growth of their cells, unnaturally jump-started, couldn't afterward be stopped.

She wondered how old she would be when her cells began to double and triple and worse.

"Your dad caught me. Not then, but another time, in his office. High as a kite. He was pissed. After all he'd done for me, giving me another chance. Don't blame him. Cops found some of your parents' stuff back at our place, too. A watch and other stuff. I'd been too fucked up to offload it all. Getting careless. They booked me for theft and possession, too, since they found a few bags around my place. This time I got sent away for longer, because it wasn't the first time. But first I spent a couple of weeks in a detox unit.

"Detox nearly killed me. I was so sick. I prayed that I would die. But I didn't." His hand moved again to the cross on his neck. "Afterward I swore I'd never touch none of that shit again. And I haven't. That was fourteen years ago. I haven't even taken a sip of beer and I won't, never again." Those eyes, surprisingly warm, surprisingly attractive, buried in that damaged face: Gemma could hardly stand to look at him. "It's my fault Brandy-Nicole got taken. If I hadn't been high, if I hadn't got sent away, she'd still be here. With me. My baby . . ." His voice broke again and he looked away, pressing the heel of a hand into each of his eyes in turn. "Aimee said she'd been snatched from a grocery store." He shook his head. "Didn't make any sense from the start. That woman never went to a grocery store in her life. Only a corner store for more cigarettes and beer. Besides, why'd she wait two days to call the police? She kept changing her story, too. First Bran was snatched from a cart. Then from the back of the car. She came to visit, all hopped up, told me crackpot stories, couldn't even bring herself to cry." Harliss stared down at his hands, now clasped again. Gemma wondered how you could have faith after a loss like that. How you could pray.

"At first I thought Aimee might have just dumped her somewhere. Maybe even hurt her. The cops looked into it but not for long. They thought I was just mad, you know. The ex and all that. Aimee had a new guy, or at least it seemed like she did. She had a lot of money all of a sudden. New clothes, better car, and she was partying hard and heavy. Well." For the first time, he smiled. But it was a horrible smile, thin and sharp and mean, like it had been cut there by a razor. "She got hers, I guess. OD'd just a few months later. All that dirty money. It's true what the Bible says. You reap what you sow."

"You think she sold Brandy-Nicole," Gemma said, but Harliss took it as a question and nodded.

"I didn't know what to think, not then," he said. "But a few years later I saw the story of this woman, Monique White, who'd given over her kid to some group when she was a junkie and then cleaned up and tried to get the girl back. But the girl was gone. And she was only an hour from Durham, where we lived. Might not have thought much of it, except one of the hotshots on the board of the Home Foundation gave a quote, the woman was out of her mind, blah blah, the usual BS. *Saperstein*. The name jumped out at me. It was the same guy your dad had been writing to."

Gemma was starting to see it. Dr. Saperstein, brilliant and ruthless and cruel. Her father, Mr. Moneybags, and his sudden change of heart. He must have been one of Haven's early investors, one of their *angel* investors.

Had he decided he wanted nothing to do with it as soon as Gemma came home? Or was it not until she started talking, started showing her defects, revealing imperfections that rendered her, in comparison to the daughter who'd died, so disappointing? And Richard Haven had been killed, maybe by Dr. Saperstein, maybe because Saperstein wanted to go from simply making clones to using them for bigger reasons. The institute was in danger of shutting down just when Saperstein got control of it. He must have been desperate.

"I don't understand." That was Pete again, hugging himself, as if the room was cold, which it wasn't. It was stifling, airless. "If Haven was making clones, why would they be after regular kids? What was the point?"

"Money," Gemma said. Her voice squeaked. Harliss looked up at her, surprised, as if he'd forgotten she was there. Pete didn't look at her at all. "Probably Saperstein wanted my dad's company to invest, to keep the institute on legs. Maybe they realized remaking dead kids for rich guys wasn't exactly a cash cow." Pete cursed under his breath. Gemma got a raw pleasure in saying it. *Remaking dead kids.* The secret was out. She was a freak and a monster. There was no doubt about that now. "Fine and Ives has always done a lot for the military. So Saperstein would have tried to prove the clones could be useful, to land a big contract. But if they couldn't afford to keep making them . . . Well, he took children he thought wouldn't be missed. He used them to test on. Just long enough to get the money he needed."

"So there were normal kids at Haven," Pete said, "mixed in with the replicas."

She couldn't even be angry that he'd called them normal. What else would they have been? "Probably just in that first generation," Gemma said. Harliss had said his daughter was roughly her age. "Once Saperstein got the military contract through Fine and Ives, he wouldn't have taken the risk. Replicas are expensive, but they're disposable. At least, that's what everyone at Haven thought." She thought of the way Lyra's hands trembled, her thinness, her confusion. She thought of the disease as if it were a kind of infestation, dark insects marching through Lyra's blood, nesting in the soft folds of her brain.

"All this time I thought maybe Bran was still out there," Harliss said. He blinked back tears again. It made him look even more doglike, those big watery eyes and the wetness of his nose. "Since I got sprung six weeks ago, I've been on the trail. After I saw *you*"—he nodded briefly in Gemma's direction, as though they'd met in North Carolina for tea—"I thought I'd come down here myself to see it. I thought I could maybe find a way onto the island, see for myself what they were doing to those poor souls. But I was too late. I was too late. The flames were two, three stories high. Whoever burned it did it good."

"I know," Gemma said quietly. "We saw it. We were there."

Harliss shook his head. "I didn't know what to do. This one woman, Emily Huang, kept cropping up in all the things I read about the Home Foundation. There was even a picture of her in one of the papers. And then I knew. I'd seen her one time with Aimee. It was at your house. She musta come around with Saperstein, but she spotted Aimee on the way out, started fussing over Brandy-Nicole. I thought I'd come to Palm Grove anyways, even though I heard all about how she strung herself up. What else could I do? And then there I was, sitting in my motel room and thinking about what to do next, and across the street I see *you*." He looked up, amazed. "It was like a sign. Like God saying I was on the right path."

Gemma had almost forgotten that they weren't there by choice—that they'd been forced there, and that even now Harliss was within reach of the gun. She felt sorry for him, but that didn't mean she should trust him. He was desperate. That much was obvious. Desperate and with nothing to lose: a bad combination.

"Listen," Gemma said. "I saw the island. I got close to it. The whole institute's destroyed. There's nobody left. If your daughter really was at Haven, she's gone now. And I doubt you'll find her again."

"Gemma." Pete said her name quietly, but he might as well have been shouting.

But she didn't care. Everything was broken. And wasn't

it better to get it over with at once, to let the pain in, to let it take you? Wasn't it better than these years of puncture wounds and paper cuts, these chafing lies and half-truths, that left you rubbed raw and exposed? "You have to give up," Gemma said. "I'm sorry. But you'll only be disappointed. It'll only break your heart."

"It's too late for my heart anyway," he said sharply, in a different tone. Fear and feeling came back to Gemma all at once when he stood up. But he moved away from her, turning his back. She thought about trying to take the gun but couldn't bring herself to reach for it. He stood there for a long time, facing the corner where the wallpaper was curling and a door gave entry to the cheap and shitty bathroom, and after a while when Gemma saw his shoulders moving she realized he was crying.

"When Bran was a baby, I was getting high with her mom and she somehow got out of her crib. Cracked her head open on a glass table. I'll never forget that. How much blood there was. Blood all over the carpet. She needed twenty stitches in her forehead. They almost took her away from us then." He was losing it. "I never got to say I'm sorry. I never got to tell her . . ." But he choked on whatever else he wanted to say.

Gem wanted to stand up and comfort him, but again she couldn't move. She was stilled by the memory of Lyra and the scar stitched above her right eyebrow. An ancient scar. Something she might have gotten as a baby.

"Mr. Harliss," Gemma said. "Do you have a picture of Brandy-Nicole?"

He turned around. His face was the color of a bruise. His upper lip shone with snot, and she was glad when he wiped it away with a sleeve. "Yeah," he said. He was getting control of himself again. "Been carrying it with me since the day I went away the second time." He brought an old leather wallet out of a pocket and began fishing around in the billfold. Gemma's arm in space looked like something foreign, something white and bloated and dead. Emma. The first one's name was Emma, and she was dead. "Had more than this, but Aimee had 'em, so who knows where they went."

The picture was small. The girl couldn't have been older than three. She was sitting on the floor in a blue dress and white tights, her brown hair clipped into pink barrettes, gripping a plastic cup decorated with parading lion silhouettes and grinning at someone to the left of the camera.

"That was only six months before she got took." Mr. Harliss had moved to sit next to Gemma. Their thighs were practically touching. It was as though he'd forgotten how and why he'd brought them there. As if they were old friends, bound together by grief. "She loved that cup," he said. "I remember Aimee yelled at her to put it down, but she wouldn't. She wouldn't go anywhere without that damn cup."

The scar above the girl's eyebrow was more obvious than it was now. But it was unmistakably *her*.

Lyra, the replica, the lost child.

Gemma got to her feet. Parts of her body felt leaden, others impossibly light, as if she'd been disassembled and put back together wrong. All of a sudden, she thought her lungs were collapsing. She couldn't breathe. It was too hot. The air felt *wet* with heat, as if she was trying to inhale mud.

Peter squinted at her. "Are you all right?" An idiotic question: she didn't think she'd ever be all right again.

"What?" Mr. Harliss said. "What's wrong?"

She was going to throw up. She felt like she was relearning to walk, like she was just twitching across the room, like she might collapse. She half expected Mr. Harliss to stop her, but he didn't. "What's wrong?" he was saying, "What *is* it?" But she was at the door. She fumbled to release the chain and the dead bolt, her fingers clumsy-stiff, her body still rioting.

Then she was outside in air that was even worse, heavier, deader than the air inside. The sunshine felt like an insult. She leaned on the railing and stared down over the parking lot, heaving and coughing, trying to bring up whatever was lodged inside of her, that sick, twisted feeling in her guts, the horror of it. She wanted it out. But nothing came up. She was crying, too, all at once. The world went bright and the pain in her head narrowed to a fierce point and she was standing there in the stupid sun sobbing and snotting all over herself. A monster-girl. An alien. She was never meant to be here.

The door opened behind her. She didn't turn around. It would be Harliss, telling her to get back inside.

But it wasn't Harliss. Pete came to stand next to her. He put a hand on her elbow. "Gemma?"

She pulled away from him. She knew she must look terrible. She always did when she cried, like something that had just been born, all red and slimy. Not that it mattered. He would never look at her the same way.

"Talk to me, Gemma," he said.

The fact that he was still trying to be nice to her made her feel even worse.

"Don't," she said. "You don't have to."

"Don't have to what?" Standing there in the afternoon sunlight, quiet and patient and sad, Pete looked like the most beautiful thing Gemma had ever seen. Like turning a corner, exhausted, lost, and seeing your house up ahead with all the lights on. Of course she would realize she was falling for him at the same time she would find out the truth about her parents and how she had been made from the sister who should have lived.

"You heard what he said." Gemma couldn't bring herself to repeat the words. She squeezed the railing tightly, stupidly hoping she'd get a splinter, that she'd bleed some of this away. The parking lot was dazzling with sun and ugliness. "You know what I am now."

"What you *are*?" Pete reached out and placed a hand over hers. "What are you talking about?"

She couldn't stand to have him touch her. She thought of her hand, her skin, grown in some laboratory. Was that how they did it? Did they culture her skin cells, like they would a yogurt, a bacteria? She took her hand away. "I'm a freak," she said. She couldn't stop crying. Jesus. "I'm some kind of a monster." Her heart was beating in her throat, making it hard to talk. "The worst part is I think I always knew. I always *felt* it."

"Gemma, *no*." Pete grabbed her by her shoulders so she had no choice but to look at him. She wiped her face with a hand and left a slick trail of wet and maybe snot. Great. "Listen to me, okay? Those men at Haven—the ones who stole children so they could get their funding, the ones who made people, living people, just to use them and poison them—those are the monsters, okay? Not you. You're amazing, do you hear me? You're perfect."

Somehow through the suffocating mud of her misery, this penetrated. No one had ever told her she was perfect. She was about as far from perfect as you could get. And yet looking up at him, at his freckles and his eyes all warm with kindness, she believed that *he* thought so.

Of all the things that she'd seen and learned in the past week, this seemed like the most miraculous.

"So you don't hate me?" She swallowed a hiccup. She could only imagine what she looked like, but he didn't make her feel ugly. He still had his hands on her shoulders and she realized how close they were. No one had ever looked at her the way he was looking at her, or touched her like this, like she was something beautiful that needed preservation.

He smiled, and behind his eyes were doors that opened and said come in. "God, Gemma. You really are dumb sometimes. You know that?"

He had to lean down a little to kiss her. Gemma had never felt small before in her life, but she did then: small and protected, held inside of the space made by his chest, by his hands on her cheeks. His lips were soft. He didn't try and put his tongue in her mouth and she was glad. It was her very first kiss and she was nervous, too nervous to have to sort out whether she was doing it right or worry about opening her mouth and whether she was using too much tongue or too little. She just wanted to stand there, in the sun, with the softness of his lips on hers and his fingers light on her cheeks. She moved her hands to his waist and felt the thrill of his body beneath the T-shirt, the narrowness of his waist, so delicious and foreign and other.

He pulled away and she took a step backward, bringing a hand to her lips, which were tingling. Her first kiss. With Pervy Pete. But she was happier than she could ever remember being. It felt like someone had cracked open a jar of honey in her chest. She was filled with a slow warmth.

"Wow," he said. "That was pretty good, huh?" His smile was so big she couldn't see beyond it.

She nodded, afraid to speak, afraid she would giggle.

"I mean, I'm not going to lie, I think I kind of killed it, actually. Like if there was a town for knowing when to kiss a girl, I'd probably be mayor."

"Pete? Don't ruin it, okay?" But she was smiling, too. In the parking lot, a man in mirrored sunglasses was obviously watching them. She started to turn away, suddenly self-conscious—had he been staring at them the whole time, like some creep?—when she noticed the cut of his suit and the man, identically dressed and nearly invisible behind the glare of the windshield, sitting behind the driver's seat in the car next to him.

The car next to him was a maroon Volvo.

The maroon Volvo.

They'd been followed. They'd been found.

FIFTEEN

ALL THE GOOD FEELING VANISHED. She was suddenly freezing.

"Two men," she said.

As soon as he realized she'd spotted him, the man had turned away, pretending to be talking on his cell phone. "In the parking lot, watching us. They look military to me. Don't look," she said, grabbing Pete's wrist when he started to turn.

"Military. Christ." Pete had gone white again. Even his freckles seemed to disappear. "You sure?"

Gemma hated looking at the men. It felt like getting slapped. But she did now, in time to see the guy in sunglasses once again pivot away from her the second her eyes landed on him. He climbed into the car and for a second she imagined—she prayed—they would simply drive away. But both men just sat there. She nodded.

"How the hell did they find us?"

"I don't know." She didn't know what they were waiting for. Maybe they didn't want to cause a scene. But she was positive the men, whoever they were, wouldn't let Pete and Gemma leave. Only an hour ago she'd been hoping for someone, anyone, to interfere with Harliss, to save them from him. But now she wished herself back inside that close-smelling room, back inside the dark with the gun.

"Look, what can they really do? I mean, think about it. We didn't do anything, right? They can't arrest us just for talking to Jake Witz. They're not going to throw us in jail. Sure, we broke a few traffic laws. Maybe they're here to give us a speeding ticket, no right turn signal, points off my license. . . ." He trailed off. She knew he didn't really believe that the men had followed them across Florida because they'd failed to signal.

Gemma saw movement in the parking lot. A hard slant of reflected sun. The car doors opened. Both men climbed out of the car. She heard a tinny ringing, and it took her a second to recognize her own ringtone. She fumbled her phone from her pocket. *Jake.*

"This is America," Pete finished, in a whisper. As if that would help. As if that would protect them. "I mean, they're not going to hurt us. They couldn't. They wouldn't. Right?"

Gemma felt a surge of relief, of joy. Jake would help them. He would know what to do. He was back on her side.

"Jake?" She nearly choked on the word. She was close to tears again. "Is that you?"

It wasn't.

The girl's voice sounded distant, as if she was holding the phone away from her mouth.

"It's not Jake," Lyra, who was really Brandy-Nicole, said. "Jake is dead. And we need your help."

Jake is dead.

Gemma's mind crystallized around this fact, even as she revolted against the truth of it. Jake Witz was dead. Jake: his dark eyes, the strange stillness of him, his sudden dazzling smiles that made you lose your breath.

Dead, dead, dead. Even the word was ugly.

Those men were responsible. If they hadn't done it themselves, they'd given the order. She knew it.

"Where are you?" she asked, and Lyra told her: the Blue Gator in Little Waller. Easy enough to remember.

"There's Suits after us," Lyra said. "Two of them."

Her meaning was clear enough. They were being followed, too. "Just stay where you are," Gemma said. "We're coming for you." She hung up and slipped the phone back in her pocket.

Both of the men were pretending they weren't staring

up at room 33—pretending there was something wrong with one of their tires, now, which required both of them to puzzle over it. Maybe they didn't know that Gemma had recognized them. Maybe that was why they weren't in a hurry. And of course they wouldn't want to make a scene, wouldn't want Gemma and Pete to start screaming and calling for help.

A scene. That's what they needed.

The phone call, both the news about Jake and the fact that Lyra and 72 weren't lost forever, had focused her. She knocked on the door of room 33, and Harliss opened up right away. He might have been standing at the door, listening, making sure they hadn't slipped away.

"Listen to me," she said as soon as they were inside and the door was locked again behind them. "I was wrong. Your daughter is still alive, and I know where to find her."

Harliss took a step backward, as if she'd punched him. His hand worked its way to his chest. "How—?"

"There's no time to explain. We've been followed." Gemma's mouth was chalk-dry. "We need a distraction. The people who came for us won't like attention. They'll want us to come quietly. If we can get out of here, I can bring you to your daughter. I can protect her."

"Fuck." Pete turned a circle. But of course there was nowhere to go.

Harliss was staring at Gemma as if he'd never seen her before. She knew he hadn't heard a single thing she'd said. "Brandy . . ." His voice was hushed with awe, like he was speaking inside a church. "Where is she? Is she okay?"

Gemma fought down a hard swell of impatience. "She's okay now," she said. "She won't be okay if those men out there get to her first." He made a noise like a soccer ball punctured with a knife. "Look, you were right. She's been living at Haven. They made up stories, told her she'd been made there."

"All this time . . ." He shook his head. Although he must have expected it, he still looked as if someone had taken out his guts with a spoon. "So she doesn't remember me? She doesn't remember anything about me at all?"

"She remembers a few things," Gemma lied. How long would it be before the men got tired of waiting, and came up to finish the three of them off? She knew they'd killed Jake. She *felt* it. And she was sure they wouldn't have trouble killing again. "Now *listen* to me. We need to get away from those men. We need your help. Your *daughter* needs your help."

Harliss blinked. "Okay." He rubbed his face, as if trying to wake up from a dream. "Where are they?"

"Down in the parking lot. Two of them. Maroon Volvo."

His eyes were still raw-red, as though they'd been

scoured. "You're not messing with me? You know where my girl is?"

"I swear," Gemma said.

"And if I help you, you'll help me?"

Gemma nodded. Harliss turned to look at Pete. Pete held up both hands.

"Yes, yes," he said quickly. "Just . . . Christ. Let's get out of here, okay?"

Harliss ignored that. He turned back to Gemma. "Now *you* listen to me." He took a step forward and Gemma flinched, expecting him to grab her. But he only brought his finger up to point. "You get my girl. You bring her back to me safe, okay? You take her home to North Carolina until I get out."

"Get out?" she said. Her chest was tight with fear. "Get out of what? Aren't you coming with us?"

But Harliss didn't answer. He gave Gemma one final look and then moved past her to retrieve the gun from the bedside table. Before she could ask him what he intended to do, he'd slipped out the door. She could tell he was moving away from room 33 by the sound of his voice, which came back to them through the thin walls. He was shouting, letting off a volley of slurred obscenities and even snatches of song.

Pete went to the window and parted the curtains to look out. "He's pretending to be drunk or something," he said. "He's stumbling all over the place."

"Smart," Gemma said. That would get at least the desk clerk to pay attention. Maybe the other guests, if there *were* any.

"Should we call the police?" Pete asked.

"And say what? Some military guys are trying to kill us because they've been cloning people to use as petri dishes?" Gemma shook her head. They needed to get to Little Waller, fast. They didn't have time to tangle with cops and questions like *Where are your parents?*

"I don't know." Pete was pacing the room. "Even if those guys are military, they can't do anything with cops around, right?"

He was right. They needed cops, firemen, a whole shit-show drama. But they couldn't call. Something hinged open in her chest—an idea, a *hope*. She grabbed Pete's hand and dragged him into the bathroom.

"Seems like the wrong time for a shower," he said. But his voice was unsteady, breaking on the joke. "Aren't we supposed to be getting out of here?"

There was no escape this way. Nothing but a single slit of a window barely the width of a pizza box. She registered the sad shower, the sink with a nest of hair clinging like a waterlogged insect to the basin, the fire alarm. She grabbed the roll of toilet paper from next to the toilet and threw it in the sink.

Pete stood there, staring. "What are you . . . ?"

"Quick," she said. "I need a lighter or matches or something." She bent to search the cabinet beneath the sink. Several sheets of old newspaper lined the plywood. She balled them up and threw that in the basin, too.

Then he got it. He disappeared again into the bedroom, returning with a sheet from one of the beds and a book of matches from a place called Skins. There were only three matches left.

"Dresser drawer," he said, tossing them to Gemma. "Someone always leaves them behind."

She was so nervous she took off the first match head when she tried to strike it. But she got the second one lit. The newspaper flared and curled. The toilet paper began to smoke.

"Shut the door," she said, as the smoke began to drift out toward the bedroom, sniffing for oxygen. Pete stepped inside, closing the door behind him, and together they blew softly on the fire, so flames leapt up toward the mirror from the sink. Gemma's eyes watered. The chemicals in the paper let off an acrid smell.

The fire alarm was much louder than Gemma had expected. She plugged her fingers in her ears. The bathroom was now so full of smoke, her eyes began to water. Finally they couldn't stand it anymore and opened the door to the bedroom, stumbling out, coughing and sucking in clean air. There must have been a sprinkler system fitted at one point, but it hadn't been maintained. A dribble of water came from a thin pipe in the ceiling, and did nothing but wet the carpet. Already Gemma heard the wail of sirens in the distance. She hadn't thought there'd be so much smoke. . . .

"Shit." Pete had his shirt to his mouth. He had to cough out the word. "The walls."

The wallpaper in the bathroom had caught fire. Gemma had never seen anything like it. She'd never been so close to a fire at home, sitting in front of the fireplace, and those were the gas kind that ran on a neat little grate tucked away behind fake logs. Click on, click off. But now through the open door of the bathroom she saw the fire climbing the walls, leaping onto the plastic shower curtain and simply devouring it. She had the strangest urge to run back and try to smother it—as if she could do anything—and then fear hooked her hard in the stomach. *Out.* They needed to get out. The sirens outside were louder now. A bit of the carpet caught fire and the flame made a hand, waggled its fingers at her, crawled a little farther into the bedroom.

They couldn't get the door open. For a horrible second, she thought the men had somehow trapped them, locked Gemma and Pete inside so that their job would be easy. Then she realized that in his panic Pete had locked the bolt instead of unlocking it, and she reached up and slammed the bolt free and wrenched the door open. The fire made a sound—like a roar, like an animal, like it was alive and hungry—and smoke came out with them, clouds of it. But they were now in the sunshine, on the balcony, and she saw a cop car below them in the parking lot, newly arrived, and a fire truck just pulling in, and a dozen people slowly drifting into the street to watch. A crowd.

She saw things in images, pictures and flashes. In the parking lot: a teenage girl holding a kid—her son?— by the hand, her son trying to fit an enormous lollipop in his mouth. The desk clerk talking on his phone, an old woman pointing, athletic socks bunched around her ankles. A boy was standing next to the maroon Volvo, angling his phone toward the balcony, filming. Time was moving very quickly for Gemma, so everything else seemed almost to be frozen. The agony of the fire truck angling into the parking lot. The sludge of a cop getting out of his car.

"Don't you try and tell me what to do. I know your type. You keep your hands *off* me."

The mouth of the stairwell: fifty feet away, Harliss, stumbling and still pretending to be drunk, so the two men in suits were forced to dance around him. Gemma sliced the scene into segments, into *instinct*. They did not want to use violence, had been trying to get him to go quietly. He was shouting, shaking off one of the men, who had a hand on his elbow.

"I know my rights. This is America. I know all about the Constitution. . . ."

There was no way down to the parking lot but past them. And as Gemma and Pete stood there, maybe for half a second, maybe less, one of the men turned and saw them. He still hadn't taken off his sunglasses, and that was the scariest thing, worse even than a fire that obeyed its natural impulse to burn—the unnaturalness of a man doing what he had come to do and yet not bothering to take off his sunglasses, *no reason to sweat, no reason to get upset.*

And in that second she knew, she truly understood, what Pete had said to her outside. Monsters weren't made, at least not by birth or fate or circumstance. Monsters chose to be monsters. That was the only terrible birth, the kind that happened again and again, every day.

He was coming toward them. And still the endless sludge of firefighters half suited up, the radio static, the cop dull and useless standing there. The man couldn't take them, not if she screamed, not if she fought. There would be too much attention, too many questions, a cop coming to pull them aside and ask awkward questions. But they might lose Lyra and 72. Every minute, she was in danger of losing them.

He was close enough to speak, above the roar and Harliss's shouting and the way that things hum into sound as they're collapsing. "It will be easier, and much better, if you come with me," he was saying. "You're in a lot of danger. I'm here to help." Not the words Gemma had been expecting, but she still picked up on the lie, the worst kind—the kind that pretends to be a favor. She'd been hearing them her whole life.

"We're not going anywhere," Pete said, stepping in front of Gemma as if he could protect her, a gesture so sweetly useless she wanted to cry.

They were mirrored in his sunglasses, the two of them. She thought of shattering those glasses and the eyes beneath them, too. His face dissolving. Her fists like superhero hands, extending into trunks, pummeling him.

"You don't understand," he said. "I'm on your side." He took a step forward. He reached for Pete. "I'm going to have to insist—"

The gunshot was a clean, sharp crack that cleaved the air in two. Gemma had heard people describe gunshots as cars backfiring, as firecrackers, but she had no doubt what this was, even before she saw Harliss, still in that strange snapshot way, holding the gun, the barrel pointed to the sky. There seemed to be a pause before people were screaming, although she knew there was no pause, really: there was a gun and a shot and the man holding

Harliss had dropped to the ground, and the man standing in front of Pete, telling them he was only trying to help, had dropped, too, because of course they couldn't do anything else.

Harliss fired a second shot. Now dozens of people were screaming. Half the people in the parking lot were lying down, or ducking behind cars. For a split second Gemma met Harliss's eyes and the message felt physical, like the first inhale after the breath is knocked from your lungs. She understood why he'd asked her to keep Lyra safe until he was out. She understood that he'd waited more than a decade to see his daughter again and would now go back to prison because of the promise a stranger had made to him, because of the sheerest, slightest chance that it might help.

There was no time, only change, only atoms rotating, only Gemma and Pete and Rick Harliss and a love so turned around and imperfect and blind it could only be called faith. Things that existed outside of seconds and minutes and years. Gemma was peaceful now. She was calm. Both men were still on the ground and the cop was running for the staircase with two firefighters behind him—and yet Gemma saw them, suspended, still, held in that moment by a force much larger and more patterned than they were—and the little kid had dropped his lollipop to scream. There were more sirens in the distance.

Then they were down the stairs and through the crowd in the parking lot and almost at the van. They were beyond the swell of bodies, of voices, of people shouting and crying. They were in a universe made infinitely of itself, and yet small enough to hold these moments, these facts—the smell of smoke in the air, the echo of voices, and Pete's hand, bigger than hers, stronger, right.

SIXTEEN

GEMMA WISHED THEY COULD DITCH the van and trade it for something less conspicuous. She felt like they were driving around in a giant neon sign. But they made it back to Little Waller without seeing the maroon Volvo. As far as Gemma could tell, they hadn't been followed.

It had been more than an hour and Gemma was terrified that Lyra and 72 might have left, or been taken. They found the replicas huddled in a booth in the back of a restaurant called the Blue Gator, with paper shamrocks strung between the televisions and green vinyl booths and *Kiss Me, I'm Irish* T-shirts for sale behind the bar. They were in trouble: 72 was scowling at the table, and a waiter was badgering them to put in an order.

"I told you, it's not up to me." The waiter had bad dandruff that coated the shoulders of his black T-shirt. "It's restaurant policy. These booths are for diners, and that means people *dining*—"

"It's all right." Gemma noticed that Lyra's face transformed when she pushed through the crowd—Lyra actually looked happy. It was amazing how in such a short time, Gemma felt responsible for this skinny little rag doll with her big eyes and terrible past. Brandy-Nicole. "They're with us, and we're leaving."

"You weren't followed?" Gemma asked them, as soon as they were safely back in the car. Pete got on the highway immediately, although they hadn't agreed on a destination. Easier to disappear on the big roads, in the big towns.

Lyra shook her head. "We were," she said. "But not there. Not into that place."

"A man looked in from the street," 72 said. "But he didn't see us."

Above them, the sky was shedding its blue, revealing an undercoat of improbable violets and pinks. Gemma found herself praying that the night, and the darkness that transformed cars to headlights and absorbed individual features, would come quickly. She didn't want to ask about Jake—on one level, she didn't want to know—but it was far too late to pretend, and she owed it to Jake to face up to the truth of what had been done to him. "What happened to Jake?"

Lyra was the one who told them the whole story: about

tracking down Emily Huang and learning she was dead, about finding Jake's address and deciding to go and speak to him, about the man and woman who'd come to clean up the job.

"Both of them strung up, made to look like suicides." Gemma's mouth tasted bitter, as if she'd inhaled ash along with the smoke earlier, and she couldn't stop coughing. "Must be the military's little specialty."

"Less suspicious, maybe, than a gun," Pete said quietly. He reached out and put a hand on her knee. Her heartbeat responded, jumped a little beneath his touch. That, at least, was one good thing, maybe the only good thing to come out of this: Pete was hers.

"Why did you run?" Gemma asked, and for a second neither Lyra nor 72 spoke.

"It was Caelum's idea . . . ," Lyra said finally.

"Caelum?" Gemma twisted around in her seat and was shocked to see that 72 was actually smiling, staring out the window, as if the smear of highways contained the world's best secret. She hadn't seen him smile before— wouldn't have even said he was capable of smiling—and she was shocked by the change. He'd gone instantly from *brooding sociopath* to *budding Calvin Klein model.*

"I named him," Lyra said proudly. "Like Dr. O'Donnell named me."

"I wasn't sure I could trust you." The boy now named

Caelum turned away from the window to meet Lyra's eyes. "I'm sorry." She wondered whether the act of naming him had changed him on deeper levels, too. She couldn't imagine this boy, the boy sitting politely in the backseat wearing a Seven-Up T-shirt, pulling a knife on them in a swamp.

"And I almost forgot." Lyra unzipped a backpack Gemma knew she must have stolen from April's grandparents' guesthouse. "Before she died, Nurse Em gave three pieces of art to her next-door neighbor. I found these hidden in the backing." She passed Lyra two printouts and one handwritten sheet of names. Gemma's stomach turned over. *Brandy-Nicole Harliss* was the third name on the list, but there were forty-seven others. That might mean that all these names, all these children, had been taken from their parents or from foster homes when Haven was in danger of running out of funding, used as bodies before new bodies could be manufactured.

"Can I keep these?" Gemma asked, and Lyra shrugged, although she saw the expression of hunger there—it was the same way Lyra had stared at the bookshelves, like a starving person confronted with a feast. "I'll give them back, I promise." There was no point in delaying anymore: she had to tell Lyra about her father. She didn't know why she felt so nervous. Lyra would probably be happy. She would be happy. She had a dad, which meant she probably had other family out there—cousins, aunts. "There's something I need to tell you, Lyra. Something about your past."

"*Now?*" Pete said. "Here?"

Gemma pivoted to look at him. "What's the point in waiting?"

"What?" Lyra said. When Gemma turned around again, she noticed that Caelum and Lyra were holding hands. Or not holding hands, exactly—they were touching palm to palm as if they *wanted* to hold hands but didn't quite know how to do it. "What is it?"

Gemma took a deep breath. The sun was bleeding red on the horizon. "You weren't actually made at Haven."

"What do you mean?" It was Caelum who spoke. There was an edge to his voice. Not anger, Gemma thought. Fear. "Where was she made?"

"Nowhere." Gemma hadn't realized how hard it would be to explain. "This list, and all the names on it? I'm pretty sure these are all kids who got taken from their families or from foster care and were brought to Haven, at a time the institute couldn't afford to keep making human models." Lyra was sitting there huge-eyed, white-faced, and Gemma had the sudden urge to apologize, to take it all back. But that was insane. Maybe she simply didn't understand? "The third name, Brandy-Nicole Harliss. That was your birth name. Your *real* name. That was the name your parents gave you."

"My . . ." Lyra inhaled whatever else she was going to say.

"You have parents," Gemma said. She thought Lyra might cry, or laugh, or at the very least, smile. But she just kept staring, looking horrified, as if Gemma had opened up a coffin to show her a dead body. "Well, you have a father. He's been looking for you all this time. He's loved you all this time."

Lyra cried out, as if she'd been hit. And Caelum, Gemma noticed, withdrew his hand from Lyra's, and turned back to the window.

SEVENTEEN

IT WAS TIME TO GO home. They had no options left. Gemma would have to confront her parents. Strangely, the idea no longer frightened her. She felt she'd aged years in the past few days. She felt only a vague pity when she thought of her father, and the secret he'd been carrying all these years, and the dead child they had refused to mourn. For her father and mother thinking they could buy their way out of tragedy.

She would go home, but on her terms: no more lies.

By eleven o'clock Pete could hardly stay awake at the wheel. They weren't far from Savannah when they passed an RV park and campground, Gemma suggested they stop for the night. She didn't mind spending one more night on the road. She knew that everything would change in the morning. She had an idea that her life would never be the same, that she'd never go back to worrying about

Chloe and Aubrey and the pack wolves, that she'd never spend another gym class sitting miserably in the bleachers, fudging her way through math homework.

She had a feeling this was her last free night.

The campground was enormous and surprisingly full. Gemma estimated there were at least four dozen tour bus–size RVs and even more smaller camper vans, plus tents peaked like angular mushrooms across the sparse grass. It was a beautiful night, and outside there was a feeling of celebration. Old couples sat side by side on lawn chairs dragged out onto the cracked asphalt, drinking wine from paper cups. Children ran between the tents, and a group of twentysomethings with long dreads and bare feet were cooking on a portable camper stove. Fireflies flared sporadically in the darkness, and people shouted to one another and shared beers and stories of where they were going and where they'd come from.

Pete left in search of food from the gas station, and Caelum moved off in the direction of the pay-per-use stalls, walking slightly ahead of Lyra. Gemma suspected he wanted to be left alone, but she followed them at a safe distance, half-believing that they might once again simply melt into the darkness. But after Lyra took money for the showers she knew she could no longer delay the inevitable. It was time to call home.

She'd missed thirty-seven calls from her parents. When

she pulled up her texts, she saw they progressed from furious to frenzied to desperate.

Please, her father had written. *Wherever you are, please call us.* He must have come back early from his business trip. That meant things had really gone nuclear.

She dialed her dad's cell phone number and he picked up on the first ring.

"Gem?" He sounded frantic, so unlike himself that her resolution faltered. "Gem, is that you? Are you there?"

"I'm here, Dad." She had to hold her phone away from her ear when Kristina started shouting in the background. *Is that her? Where is she? Is she okay? Let me talk to her. . . .*

"Look, I'm fine. I'm not hurt."

"Where are you? Jesus Christ, we've been so worried—"

"Geoff, let me talk to her." Kristina's voice, slurry from crying and maybe from pills, was audible again in the background.

"Hang on, Gem, I'm putting you on speakerphone. Your mother wants to hear your voice." Fumbling, and the echo of her parents' voices overlapping. Gemma hated speakerphone, which always made her feel as if she was speaking into a tin can. "Gemma, are you still there? Can you hear us?"

"I can hear you," she said. "There's no need to shout." She watched a mom bouncing a sleepy toddler in her arms, passing back and forth in front of the RV, the kid's dark hair curling on her shoulder. She felt a momentary grief so strong it was like falling.

"Where are you?" Kristina sounded like she was crying again. "We've been so worried. We called April and she said you'd left. Your father jumped on the first plane out of London he could find. She was so upset—"

"April was upset?" Gemma asked quickly.

"What do you think? She told us you had a fight and she'd asked you to leave. She felt awful about it. She's been worried sick. We've all been worried sick."

"I'm fine," Gemma said. "I'm with my friend Pete. We'll be home tomorrow."

"I want you home *tonight*," Gemma's father said, sounding more like himself. Now that he knew his daughter wasn't dead in a ditch, he'd apparently decided to resort to playing bad cop. "Where are you? I'm coming to get you."

It was time. She took a breath. "I went down to see Haven."

There was a long moment of silence. Gemma watched the fireflies flare and then go dark.

"You . . . what?" Gemma's dad could barely get the words out.

"I went to Haven." She closed her eyes and thought of the statue of the man kneeling in the dust, that old childhood memory unearthed, the DNA of another child coiled inside of her. "I went to see where I was made."

"Where you . . ." Geoff's voice cracked, and he cleared his throat. "What—what are you talking about?"

"There's no point in denying it. I know everything." She was suddenly and completely exhausted. She felt so old—older, even, than her parents. "I know about what you were trying to do at Haven. I know you left Fine and Ives because they wanted to invest. I know the military stepped in and the mission changed." Gemma's mom whimpered. This part would be the hardest. "I know about Emma, too," she said.

Her parents were quiet for so long she checked the phone to see whether the connection had been lost. Finally she heard a kind of gasping and knew that they were still there. She imagined the lies they'd told over the years as a physical force, something with hands, something that had reached out now to choke them.

"Gemma." Her father was crying. Her father had *never* cried, not once in her life. She was shocked and also, in a sick way, glad. The mask was falling off. The cracks were showing. Let him cry, the way she had. "We can explain. Please. You need to come home."

"Please come home, baby." Kristina sounded like her voice was being squeezed through a pipe, high and agonized, and Gemma felt terrible again. Even now, she hated for her mother to be sad. But Gemma knew she had to be strong.

"Not until you agree to help me," she said. In the distance she saw Pete returning from the direction of the gas station with a paper bag tucked under his arm. As he passed beneath the streetlamp and back into the RV park, a man smoking a cigarette nearby turned to look at him, and Gemma had a tingling sense of unease. But the man turned away again and was soon lost to Gemma's view. "You have to help my friends, too."

"Your friends?"

"We rescued two replicas out on the marshes," Gemma said. Once again she had to yank her phone away from her ear as both of her parents exploded. She nearly had to shout to be heard over them. "They would have died on their own. They *are* dying. Haven's been infecting them."

"Listen to me, Gemma. You're in danger right now." Gemma's father was calm again, and she felt a swell of nausea. He hadn't even reacted to the news about how Haven was using its clones. Which meant, of course, that he knew. She wasn't surprised, but it still made her feel sick. Had he known, too, about the children stolen from their parents, shunted into the foster care system and then conveniently lost? "I know you must be angry. I can only imagine how you feel. I swear to you that your mother and I will explain. But you need to come home now. Tonight. There are people out there, people still involved in Haven, dangerous people. . . . I can't protect you when you're hundreds of miles away."

She thought of Nurse Em, and Jake, both found swinging by their necks. "You have to swear to help us, or I'm not coming home at all," she said. It was a bluff. She had nowhere to go, and if her parents cut off her credit cards she'd be doubly screwed, but she was counting on the fact that her parents were too upset to think clearly.

"This isn't a game, Gemma." Geoff sounded as if he was going to lose it. Gemma had never heard her father so out of control. "You don't understand how big this is—"

"Swear or I hang up the phone," she said firmly.

For a second there was nothing but the sound of her father breathing hard on the other end of her line, of her mom whimpering in the background.

"I swear," he said at last. "I'll do everything I can."

Gemma exhaled. She'd unconsciously been holding her breath. "I'll be home in the morning," she said, and hung up. Immediately she powered off her phone. She didn't want them calling her back, bugging her all night. She leaned against Pete's minivan, listening to the sounds of the mothers calling their children to bed, watching lights dim one by one in the windows of parked RVs. All these people on their way to something, on their way from something. All these stories and lives, all of them orbiting temporarily around the same parking lot before spinning away from one another again. She said a little prayer for Jake Witz.

She thought of her sister—could Emma be called a sister, if she was really Gemma, if Gemma was really her?—and the shadow-life she might have lived, might still be living off in some parallel dimension.

She felt small. She was so tired.

Pete was back. He'd bought water and soda, candy and chips, burritos, and even a tray of gas station nachos. "I thought we'd do a buffet," he said, squatting to place food out right on the pavement. When he saw Gemma's face, he stopped. "What's the matter?"

"Nothing," she said. "Just tired. Just scared about what comes next."

He stood up. Backlit by the lights from a nearby camper, his face was unreadable, and his hair looked feather-light. He reached out and touched her cheek, and his hand was so warm, so instantly familiar. A strange and baffling truth: that the people we're supposed to know best can turn out to be strangers, and that near strangers can feel so much like home.

"We'll be okay," he said, and she loved that, loved hearing him say *we*, loved being a part of him. He traced a thumb lightly over her cheekbones, and where he touched her she felt beautiful. Like he was sewing up the ugly parts. He smiled, that goofy smile Gemma couldn't believe she hadn't always been in love with. "Just think about it. Clones at school. *Real* clones, not just Chloe and the rest of her drones."

"Yeah." Gemma forced a smile. It was a fantasy. Lyra and Caelum would never go to school. If they wanted to stay alive, they'd likely have to go underground, stay hidden, stay on the run. And they would only get sicker. But it was a nice idea and she didn't want to spoil it.

"Go to sleep," Pete said more quietly. He leaned forward and touched his lips to hers, but just that light pressure made her whole body shiver. "I'll keep watch for a bit."

With the backseats folded down, the minivan was more than big enough to lie down in. Pete had a blanket, too, and he insisted she use his sweatshirt as a pillow.

"Good night, Gemma." Pete leaned over to kiss her again. This time, he let his lips stay longer, and she felt his warmth on top of her, the impossible and delicious solidity of his body. The bones and blood and skin that separate but also bring us back together. The gift of them.

Even though she was tired, she didn't think she'd be able to sleep, not after everything that had happened. But she did.

Sometime later she woke up because Pete was shaking her.

"Someone's coming," he said.

She sat up. The darkness was gummy-thick, and her whole body felt sticky. The rear door was still open, letting in the noise of tree frogs and the occasional muffled sound of a door opening and closing as people went or returned from the bathroom. She didn't know what time it was, but she couldn't have been asleep very long. Pete didn't look as if he'd slept at all. He was wide awake, alert, staring.

He pointed at the beam of a flashlight moving between the parked vans. She could tell from the pattern it made that whoever was out there was making a tour of each vehicle, as if looking for something specific.

Looking for *someone* specific.

"Where's Lyra?" Gemma whispered. Her body was electric with fear. "Where's Caelum?"

"Outside," Pete said. "Sleeping."

How on earth could they have been followed? Gemma was sure they had been careful, switching highways, watching constantly for cars that seemed to be pursuing them. Maybe, she thought, someone was monitoring her phone calls. She'd seen stuff like that on the cop shows on TV, how police could triangulate phone calls to find wanted criminals. Hunted. That was what she felt like—like an animal crouching in a hole, just waiting to be torn apart.

There was no way she could wake Lyra and Caelum and get them in the car without being seen. Already the flashlight—and the person behind it—was less than twenty feet away, moving around an RV that belonged to an older couple Gemma had spoken to earlier. There was no tearing out of here, either, not in the dark, not without risking mowing down some poor dad on his way to the toilet or kids sleeping in a tent.

"Lie down," Gemma said. Their best bet was to pretend to be asleep and pray they would be passed over—that in the darkness they wouldn't be recognized. Pete had covered her with a blanket and she drew this up over their faces, so the sound of their breathing was amplified beneath it. She was too scared to process even how close they were lying, his knees pressed to her knees, his chest rising and falling with his breath and their noses practically touching.

But no sooner had they lain down than she heard a voice.

"Gemma? Gemma?"

Instantly, she sat up again, half-delirious, disbelieving. She *knew* that voice.

"*April?*" she whispered.

"Oh my God, *Gemma*. Thank God." The flashlight thudded to the ground and for a quick second, as April bent to retrieve it, revealed her familiar green Converses.

"Shit. Where *are* you?"

Gemma shook off the blanket and scooted out of the van. She felt clumsy with happiness. "I'm here," she said, and the flashlight swept over her and held her momentarily in its light. "I'm right here." She held out both arms and a second later, April was rocketing into them.

"I was so worried about you," she said, nearly taking Gemma off her feet. "I was so mad, you know—Latin temper and all that—but then a few hours after I left the house I started feeling really, really awful. Like my-stomach-is-trying-to-eat-itself awful. And I came home, and you were gone already, and then your parents called me. . . ."

"How did you find me?" Gemma was half tempted to touch April's hair and nose and shoulders, to doubly make sure she was real.

"Find My Phone app, duh," April said. Gemma almost laughed. Of course. "But then you turned your phone off, and then of course as soon as I got here *my* phone ran out of charge. So I've been walking around like a total perv, peeking in people's windows. . . . *Perv?*" she squeaked, as Pete climbed out of the van.

Gemma was glad that it was so dark she couldn't make out April's expression. "April, you know *Pete*," she said, deliberately emphasizing the name and hoping that April would take the hint. "Pete was the one who drove me down to Florida."

"Uh-huh." April seemed momentarily speechless, a first for her. Gemma could practically see her making calculations—the size of the van, the fact that both Gemma and Pete had been sleeping inside, *together.* "Where are the . . . others?" She was deliberately avoiding the word *clones,* and Gemma remembered what they'd fought about, and what she'd now have to confess to April: that she was one of them. Made. Manufactured. She would have to tell April about her parents' first child, the lost child she'd been made to replicate. She would have to tell April about Rick Harliss and Jake Witz's murder. She was hit by a wave of exhaustion again. This was the world she lived in now.

As if he knew what she was thinking, Pete put his arm around her. "They're sleeping," he said. "They're okay."

Gemma leaned into him, grateful, not even caring what April thought. "We're all okay," she said. She reached for April's hand and gave it a squeeze. There in the darkness, in the middle of nowhere, her boyfriend and her best friend: under the circumstances, she could hardly ask for more.

EIGHTEEN

APRIL SLEPT IN HER CAR. For most of the night, Pete kept his arm around Gemma's waist, breathing into her hair, and she woke surprisingly refreshed, considering the fact that she was lying with her cheek squashed against the van's scratchy carpeting and one whole arm was numb.

It was just after six o'clock. She eased out of the van and saw that Lyra and Caelum were still sleeping, their bodies tented under a blanket pulled all the way over their heads. Beneath it they appeared to be one person. She showered and brushed her teeth in the semi-slimy bathroom, next to little kids giddy with the experience of camping and their bleary-eyed moms. Afterward, she woke April, and they went in search of breakfast from the little mini-mart and gas station where Pete had bought all the junk food the night before. They bought hot coffee and muffins the texture of sponges, but were so hungry they didn't care.

They ate at a picnic bench slick with dew and watched the sun beat the mist off the ground. It was going to be another beautiful day.

Gemma told April everything. When she explained what had happened to Jake Witz, she realized she was trying not to cry. But she forced herself to keep talking. She told April about what she'd learned from Rick Harliss, about what her parents had done after their first child had died. About why and how she'd been made. By then she *was* crying, not even because she felt sorry for herself, but weirdly because she mourned the child, Emma. She even felt sorry for her parents. They must have grieved. They must have been grieving for years. What would it be like to look at your daughter and see a perfect reflection of a child you'd lost?

To her credit, April didn't freak out. She waited until Gemma was finished, and then she scooted closer on the bench to give Gemma a hug. April gave the best hugs. Even though Gemma was much larger than April was, somehow April made her feel totally enfolded, totally taken care of.

"I'm proud of you, bug," April said, using an old nickname, which made Gemma laugh and cry harder at the same time.

Gemma pulled away. "Jeez. I'm like a snot factory," she said.

"I hear there's big money in snot nowadays."

Gemma laughed again, choking a bit, wiping her face with a sleeve. "Do you think I'll ever feel normal again?"

April snorted. "Come on, Gemma. When did we ever feel normal?" She nudged Gemma's shoulder. "We're aliens, remember?"

"You're an alien," Gemma said. "I'm a clone."

"*The Adventures of Alien and Clone.* Sounds like a Marvel movie. I'm in," April said. And then, in a different voice, "Besides, normal is overrated. Normal is a word invented by boring people to make them feel better about being boring."

"Maybe you're right." Gemma did, in fact, feel a little better. A little lighter. She was still dreading going home to confront her parents, but she knew she couldn't delay it forever. The sun had risen. The sky was the color of a Creamsicle, and full of whipped-cream clouds. She stood up. "We should probably wake the others."

"No way. Uh-uh. You skipped over the most important part of the story." April grabbed Gemma's wrist and hauled her down onto the bench again. She was grinning, shark-wide, the way she did. "So," she said, leaning forward on an elbow. "'Fess up. What's the deal with you and Perv?"

They were on the road by ten. April followed the van in her car, occasionally tooting her horn or pulling up alongside the van to wave or give a thumbs-up. Pete kept up a constant stream of conversation, as usual, but this time he spoke mostly to Lyra and Caelum, trying to explain all about the world they hardly knew.

"Strip malls are like the arteries of America. They keep the whole country alive. Pizzerias, nail salons, shitty hardware stores . . . this is it, you know? The pinnacle of human achievement. If we ever get to Mars, I bet we'll build a nail salon first thing."

Mostly, Gemma listened. Mostly, she turned her face to the window and saw her double reflected there, ghostly over the passing landscape: a different Gemma from the one who'd left home less than a week ago—stronger, both more and less sure of herself. She didn't know what was coming for her, but she knew that she'd be ready. They were safe for now. They were together. She had April and Pete. Lyra had her. Caelum had a name.

And despite what she'd said to April, she felt a little less alien than she had before. A little smarter. A little more amazed, too, by all the mysteries she'd seen, by the complexity of the universe and the people inside of it.

A little more human, even.

ALSO BY LAUREN OLIVER

Before I Fall

Liesl & Po

The Spindlers

Panic

Vanishing Girls

Curiosity House: The Shrunken Head

Curiosity House: The Screaming Statue

THE DELIRIUM SERIES

Delirium

Pandemonium

Requiem

Delirium Stories: Hana, Anabel, Raven, and Alex

FOR ADULTS

Rooms

*This is a work of fiction. The characters, incidents, and dialogues
are products of the author's imagination and are not to be construed as real.
Although many of the larger geographical areas indicated in this book do,
in fact, exist, most (if not all) of the streets, landmarks,
and other place names are of the author's invention.*

Library of Congress Control Number: 2016931028

ISBN 978-0-06-239416-3 (hardcover)

ISBN 978-0-06-256193-0 (international edition)

ISBN 978-0-06-256730-7 (special edition)

Typography by Erin Fitzsimmons

16 17 18 19 20   PC/RRDH   10 9 8 7 6 5 4 3 2 1

First Edition

Photo by Charles Grantham

LAUREN OLIVER is the author of the teen novels *Before I Fall*, *Panic*, *Vanishing Girls*, and the Delirium trilogy: *Delirium*, *Pandemonium*, and *Requiem*, which have been translated into more than thirty languages and are *New York Times* and international bestselling novels. She is also the author of two standalone novels for middle grade readers, *The Spindlers* and *Liesl & Po*, which was an E. B. White Read-Aloud Award nominee, as well as the Curiosity House series and a novel for adults, *Rooms*. A graduate of the University of Chicago and NYU's MFA program, Lauren Oliver is also the cofounder of the boutique literary development company Paper Lantern Lit. You can visit her online at www.laurenoliverbooks.com.

FOLLOW LAUREN OLIVER ON